MURDER
ON THE
CHAMPS-
ÉLYSÉES

A BELLE-ÉPOQUE MYSTERY

ALEX
MANDON

AVID PRESS

For my grandmothers,
Laura Genevieve and Lucille

HISTORICAL NOTE

The term "homosexual" was not verifiably in use in the French language before 1907, though it was coined by the German Gustav Jäger near the end of the 19th century. According to *Homosexualité et Prostitution masculines à Paris*, at the turn of the century in Paris the most common term gay men used to describe themselves was *Pédéraste*, but for modern day readers, the term pederast has negative connotations. Thus, I've chosen to use other less common terms in use at the time, such as *inverti* and *Uraniste*, to describe Guillaume Devré's sexuality.

—**Alex Mandon**
September 2016

PARIS,
1900

ONE

~~~◈~~~

Monsieur Paul Bacard had been a pleasant-looking man in life, mused Inspector Guillaume Devré as he looked down at him.

Despite the thin light of dawn and the shadowy interior of the hansom cab, Guillaume could discern that the man's thick hair was blond. He could also make out the shape of a square, cleft chin and a wide jaw. Bacard's mustache was neat and stylishly full, and he had a solid build dressed in expensive clothing. His ungloved hands were the well-tended ones of a bourgeois.

But in death, as was true for most everyone, M. Bacard had been stripped of any attractiveness. His face was waxy, grimaced, and twisted. His fingers curled like talons. His lips were flat and awkward. His skin was flushed red. His fine clothing was stained with vomit and other bodily fluids.

Still. Guillaume had seen many more unpleasant corpses than the one sprawled inside the taxicab carriage. But even more curious was the fact that a wealthy young man such as Bacard was even *in* a hired fiacre. Men of his standing had their own modes of transport—carriages (often multiple ones) and, increasingly, motorcars.

Fully aware of the gathering crowd, the impatient officer who'd initially been called to the scene, and his own constabulary assistant who waited in silence, Guillaume nevertheless spared a long, unhurried moment to take in the scene as a whole before commencing with a closer examination of the body and its stage. He observed the surroundings of death, building his impressions of the body, the man it had been, the environment...and his sense of the tableau as a whole. He created in his mind the before and after of whatever had caused a young, wealthy, seemingly healthful man of thirty to die during a brief trip from the Champs-Élysées to his apartment above Spontorini boulevard. There was no blood, no signs of struggle. No obvious cause of death other than the fact that he'd been ill. *Poison.*

Guillaume took it all in, breathed the scent of mortality, identifying the layers of male cologne and that of a female's as well—floral, probably rose—a hint of whisky and tobacco, bodily fluids and waste, and closed his eyes. Absorbed.

"You say the driver opened the door and found him like this?" he asked the officer who hovered nearby, trying to keep curious bystanders from getting too close.

The *rue* was filled with early morning merchants on their way to open their shops, servants from the great houses of the ridiculously wealthy *le gratin* located in Faubourg Saint-Germain on their way to run errands before the household awoke, and newspaper boys on bicycles or on foot. Today was also *La Fête du Muguet*—Lily of the Valley Day—which meant even more traffic and activity due to labor parades and demonstrations. The attending officer was wearing a small sprig of the aromatic white flowers tucked into his belt in deference to the holiday.

Several blocks away on the Champ de Mars loomed the monstrosity known as Eiffel's Tower. The filigree wishbone, which had been completed for the second World Expo in 1889, was gilded with dawning light. Guillaume, along with the majority of the city's residents, had originally despised this steel addition to the Paris landscape. Now they merely tolerated it.

At the time of creation, it was meant to be a temporary aberration—but here they were, more than a decade later, and it was still standing over the city. Since it was wildly popular with the tourists attending the current World Expo—and had turned out to be an excellent radio tower for overseas messages—Guillaume suspected the structure would remain, along with many of the other buildings that had been erected for this year's fair.

He returned his attention to the officer *de la paix* who'd been on patrol when the body was discovered. "The driver didn't move Bacard, or try to rouse him?" He would take a full statement from the fiacre driver in a moment, but for now, the basic information would do.

"*Bien sûr que si*, he tried to, but...when they arrived at this address—which is the destination he'd been given—Bacard didn't alight from the vehicle. The driver waited for several minutes, then he drove around the block twice. Finally, he became concerned, parked, and knocked on the door. When Bacard didn't answer, the driver opened it to find him like this. He claims he didn't move him, for he knew the man was dead by the way he looked—and the smell."

Guillaume nodded. "Very well. Have him report to la Sûreté to give his statement. Also advise him we will take the fiacre into custody for a time for examination." He knew from experience how popular that decree would be, especially from a man who made his living with the cab. "Officer Houssaye here will assist." He gave Houssaye, his colleague, a nod, and the eager young man tipped his head in acknowledgment.

Then Guillaume at last entered the carriage, taking care not to crush or knock his hat or to disturb any of the scene. He knelt on the steps, privately bemoaning the ruination of another pair of trousers, and began his investigation from that vantage point. This way he would avoid stepping or slipping in the half-dried, stinking puddles slopped on the floor.

Bacard appeared to have had some sort of convulsions, sliding off his seat and slumping to the floor, curled up as if fighting off great pain. He was fully clothed, his evening white bow tie loosened but waistcoat still in place and...yes, there was most clearly a smear of rouge or lip color on his stiff shirt collar.

Guillaume made out the scent of roses mingling with the other putrid smells. According to the driver, there had been no one in the vehicle with him, so the unmarried M. Bacard had obviously acquired these feminine decorations prior to his journey.

Guillaume leaned close, sniffing around the body's mouth, lifting the dead man's ungloved fingers to examine and smell them, pulling collar and cuffs away to look for wounds or marks. There would, of course, be a complete postmortem at the morgue, along with numerous photographs of both body and scene, but any information he could gather now would be valuable.

He did a cursory search through Bacard's pockets, discovering a generous wad of francs held together by a monogrammed clip, along with a few sous and two gold louis, an un-snipped cigar, a receipt from Maxim's dated yesterday (the total amount paid was enough to make Guillaume catch his breath), Bacard's business cards in an engraved silver case, and a violet-purple rose with petals that bled into pale pink, and ended in white. The exquisite blossom was bruised and wilted but not yet dry, on a stem the length of his finger.

The benches in the fiacre were empty, and though Guillaume pulled the curtains wide to let in the early morning light, he found nothing of interest there—no smears, smudges, debris; nothing out of the ordinary. On the floor, it was a different matter: dirt and dust (did the driver never sweep?) made a putrid soup with the vomit. There was also a piece of paper he recognized as part of a ticket for the expo and a forgotten centime in the corner, but who knew how long they'd been there.

Satisfied for the time being, he backed out of the carriage to discover the morgue wagon had arrived, and the crowd was growing larger. A trio of scruffy dogs barked and chased each other through the bystanders, and traffic—that eclectic mix of horse-drawn and motorized vehicles—had ground to a complete halt, being rerouted down rue de la Pompe. The fresh smells from a nearby patisserie reminded Guillaume his dinner last night had been late and unsatisfying, and he'd had nothing but thin coffee this morning. A strong beam of the new day's sun cut over the creamy bricks of Paris, turning them a lovely rosy gold.

"Officer Houssaye, please take samples of the vomit and whatever else that is on the floor," he said to his constable. "And at least a dozen photographs of the interior of the fiacre both before and after the body is removed. Not sure how well lit it will be, but do your best. Damaris can assist."

He turned to the men waiting with the morgue wagon. "Jackson has been advised, *n'est-ce pas?*" He looked from their blank faces to Houssaye, who nodded, gesturing to the harried constable. "He's on his way?"

"I made certain of it, though the patrol officer didn't care to make a specific request."

"I want him delivered to Jackson for the postmortem—not anyone else. Do you understand?" The last was directed to the morgue wagon driver, who shrugged in compliance. Then Guillaume turned to the officer who'd called him to the scene and who clearly didn't comprehend the brilliance of a certain medico-legist. "Where was Bacard when the driver picked him up?"

The officer—a young man of no more than twenty—seemed both impressed and mortified by his necessary response. "He picked him up from Château Lisette just after three o'clock this morning."

That explained the rouge and heavy cologne.

Guillaume couldn't hold back a grimace. That meant after he delivered the sad news to Bacard's family, he would have to pay a call on the resident and owner of Château Lisette—the infamous, most celebrated woman in all of Paris...known as La Balise.

Nearly two hours later, Guillaume's carriage pulled up at the home of La Balise. The street was empty, and he considered it a blessing that it was too early in the day for any reporters to be lurking about.

Guillaume climbed out of the carriage and got his first full look at the sprawling *hôtel privé* known as Château Lisette.

La Balise's home was a far cry from the bleak, impoverished rooms or cheap hotel apartments wherein the vast majority of streetwalking prostitutes (both male and female) existed as they plied their trade, and most certainly it was an improvement over the licensed brothels known as *maisons closes*, which catered to a careful and wealthy clientele and were expertly managed by the madams who ran them.

Wielding his copper-knobbed walking stick, Guillaume made his way up the elegant walkway with his customary stride: deceptively easy but quick. He could grumble all he wanted about having to engage with one of *les cocottes*—which, unless he was inordinately lucky, would also likely mean incessant hounding by the gossipy, scandal-mongering press—but there were certainly worse cases to catch.

To wit, the scandalous death a year ago of France's president Félix Faure was still a favorite topic of discussion among his peers at la Sûreté. Faure's young mistress Meg had been discovered with him in the president's private office. The man—more than twice her age—had died while being fellated, and his grip on Meg's hair was so tight she was unable to extricate herself after he expired.

After hearing her cries of distress, the servants investigated. They had to cut her hair to free her, but nevertheless managed to whisk her away before the priest arrived to give last rites. There were headlines, cartoons, and jokes in the newspapers for weeks suggesting that if a young, vigorous woman was going to perform oral sex on a much older man with a heart problem, perhaps she might consider wearing a wig...or at least a false hairpiece.

Guillaume could only hope the case of Paul Bacard would be an opened and closed investigation, or at least unexceptional enough to keep the press uninterested. Though anything that involved La Balise was bound to be a headline lure.

And if the famous courtesan turned out to be the perpetrator... Ooh-la-la. Guillaume shook his head mentally, grumbling inside again, but the writing was already beginning to show on the proverbial wall. He'd wait for confirmation from Jackson, but he was certain Bacard had been poisoned.

And as poisoning often implied a feminine touch...well, one could easily be looking at the owner of Château Lisette herself. That meant he would certainly be in for a circus.

He'd already met with Bacard's parents, having them awakened at half past four in the morning so he could deliver the unhappy news regarding the demise of their son. Both M. and Mme Bacard were shocked and genuinely grief-stricken at the news, and though neither could offer any suggestion as to what might have happened— Guillaume hadn't yet mentioned the words *poison* or *murder*—they did give him the names of Paul Bacard's closest friends.

"He was a nice, well-mannered young man," the butler at the Bacard home had told Guillaume as he showed him out. The older man's eyes and the tip of his nose were tinged red with emotion. "And I would not say that if it weren't true, *monsieur l'inspecteur*."

"Thank you, monsieur," Guillaume had replied—having already heard similar praises from the deceased's parents. Still, when the servants said such things, one tended to believe them more than family or friends. They knew. The downstairs people—as they were so quaintly called in England—always knew what was really happening in a household.

The trick was to get them to divulge the secrets.

The Bacards resided in a large, elegant home in Faubourg Saint-Germain. As grand and expensive as it was, that residence was merely one-third the size of the Château Lisette—which now loomed before him.

An elegant four-storied creation, taking up an entire block on the fashionable Champs-Élyseés, where the *tout Paris* chose to reside, La Balise's home was both stately and ostentatious.

In the center of its broad facade was an iron gate that likely led to a private courtyard, *porte cochère*, and perhaps even a small stable. But thick ivy grew on the undulating iron spikes, making it difficult to discern for certain what lay beyond its opening.

Unlike many of its neighbors, Château Lisette's exterior was not the familiar cream brick introduced by Haussmann half a century ago during the city's renovation. In this case, the building's facade had slightly darker and grayer, biscuit-colored rows of brick. Large, tall windows, which were framed by ornate, flowing *art nouveau* designs in tiles of some indeterminate material, studded all four stories.

The walkway to an imposing front door was an abbreviated gray brick trail flanked by urns spilling with ivy and vibrant red blossoms Guillaume couldn't identify. Two patches of clipped, perfect green lawn flanked the walkway and continued around the perimeter of the monstrous building, fading into grass corridors shadowed by a tall hedge of boxwood that appeared to circumnavigate the extensive property.

La Balise had acquired her nickname—"the Beacon"—because she'd been described as a brilliant and shining example of femininity and beauty, accomplishment, and wit. She must possess at least a modicum of intelligence and cunning as well, Guillaume reflected, considering how wealthy and famous she'd become since arriving in Paris a mere three years ago—and the number of powerful men who seemed determined to enjoy her company.

Courtesans were a tradition in Paris, and had been since long before the First Republic. They sold their companionship to the highest or most convenient bidder, although a courtesan of La Balise's stature could be as particular and selective as she wished about with whom she consorted.

Unfortunately, in his business, Guillaume encountered all sorts of ladies of the night—from the lost and desperate streetwalkers, to the more celebrated *chahut* dancers at Zidler's infamous Moulin Rouge, to the licensed prostitutes...all the way up to the *cocottes* who called themselves the *Dégrafées* (the Unbuttoned), or, more graphically, *les grandes horizontales*: the upper-crust courtesans like La Balise.

And La Balise was the current grandest of the *grands*, surpassing even the celebrated Liane de Pougy and her rival La Otéro in notoriety and popularity. There was nary a day La Balise wasn't photographed or written about in *Le Petit Journal* or *L'Écho de Paris*. Her appearances in the press weren't limited to the gossip column Pall Mall, but could even grace the front page if there was big news—such as an updated mode of style, or a newsworthy *on dit* such as her being seen on the arm of a different escort.

Most often a courtesan of this stature began her career in the business of entertainment, then collected protectors and lovers and worked her way up the societal ladder, so to speak. Unlike her peers, La Balise had not appeared onstage as a singer, actress, or dancer—but as an illusionist and escape artist. In this way, she had set herself apart from her contemporaries with her own brand of entertainment—one that even the great Sarah Bernhardt had described as "unworldly and brilliant." (Apparently, and shockingly, Mlle Bernhardt was an admirer of La Balise—quite possibly because she was not a rival to the stage actress.)

The grand horizontal La Balise was often seen about the city on the arm of one of her paramours or conducting her business transactions (Guillaume couldn't avoid the knowledge that La Balise owned an enviable riding stable, a country home near Lyon, a closet the size of a small home, three hunting hawks, and reams of jewels). If she stepped over the threshold of a shop, her implicit endorsement sent the proprietor into ecstasy and became cause for a new advertisement or sign in its window, proclaiming "La Balise's favorite!" or "Seen on La Balise!"

This La Balise—whose real name was Mme Lucie-Geneviève Madeleine—had many powerful friends and lovers, which meant it would be difficult for Guillaume to gain her cooperation if she was reluctant to assist in the investigation. This was part of the reason for his dour mood. And God forbid she should become a suspect in what appeared to be the poisoning of Paul Bacard. If that happened, Guillaume would have his hands tied quicker than a nun's drawers.

Merde.

Yet Paul Bacard didn't seem old enough or powerful enough to attract the likes of La Balise. She tended to be seen with those in the highest political echelons or the oldest of the wealthy families, like the Daudets and the Hugos—although she had, for a time, been linked with M. Christophe Calmette, a wealthy shipbuilder and philanthropist of the *bourgeoisie*.

Guillaume had already learned Bacard was barely thirty, he was of the *bourgeoisie* himself (although that alone wouldn't necessarily preclude him from the company of La Balise), he had significant wealth from the family business of importing Kentucky bourbon, and he spent his leisure at the racetrack, boxing rings, and cabarets.

Not precisely the way Guillaume imagined the beacon of femininity would deign to spend her time. Although she did have her own table at the loud, raucous Maxim's...

Guillaume lifted and dropped the heavy door knocker, noting its unusual design. A fish of some sort, writhing as if in mid-enthusiastic-leap, in a style that was distinctly Oriental. Japanese, he thought. He didn't count himself an expert in art—or the Orient, for that matter. Nevertheless, a superlative homicide detective needed to know at least a little bit about everything, for one never knew when a bit of trivial knowledge would help close a case.

The door swung open, interrupting his musings, and he found himself facing a tall, slender butler who looked as if he'd just crossed the channel from England.

"*Bonjour.* I am Inspector Guillaume Devré from la Sûreté. It is necessary I speak with Mme Lucie-Geneviève Madeleine. The matter is urgent."

"*Bonjour,* inspector. Of course. Please, if you will." The butler, who wore tailored striped trousers with a sharp crease down the center, in the popular English fashion, moved back to allow Guillaume entrance.

He stepped inside, taking in the sight of the imposing three-story foyer. Directly across from the front door was a gentle rise of five stairs that created a shallow dais, which split into matching staircases angling elegantly upward while overlooking the circular entrance. On either side, beneath the twin staircases, were corridors that led off into God knew where. Even from his position, Guillaume could see an infinite number of doors studding the corridor. Why would any one person need this much space?

The foyer decor was relatively plain, considering the current fad of *fin de siècle,* or decadence. There was nary a gold leaf, an undulating flower, or a kidney-shaped mirror to be found. Instead, the floor was mosaic tile set in a circular design that appeared to match the fish door knocker. On the table between the two staircases was a tall ebony vase with a lone tree branch studded with flower buds instead of a clichéd bunch of lilies spilling from it. The faint scent of something pleasant hung in the air.

"This way, if you please, monsieur. I will inform mademoiselle of your request."

Guillaume followed the butler into a parlor decorated in feminine tones—much more of what he'd expected from a *cocotte* of her standing—and refrained from pointing out that his wasn't a request but an authoritative demand. He wondered how long La Balise would keep him waiting, and the very thought of cooling his heels in this small, decadent pearl-pink chamber for an hour or more had his irritation blossoming.

It was approaching six o'clock, and someone of La Balise's ilk would have retired for the night within the last hour or so—*night* being a loose term. Unless Guillaume had been fortunate enough to catch the woman before she got to bed. That was a hopeful thought— the first one he'd had since seeing the deceased gentleman in the carriage.

Fine white lace curtains filtered the light from an east window, and a spotless white-on-white paisley divan graced one side of the small chamber. The walls were painted a vibrant blushing rose, and the curtains echoed the color and flower with dinner-plate-sized images printed on them.

Guillaume prowled the room, examining the fine craftsmanship of the cherry Queen Anne table, the lace doilies beneath Sèvres china, and a massive white vase bursting with fresh roses. Bright violet-purple bleeding into a blushing pink, of course, to match the decor—*and* the crushed blossom he'd found in Bacard's pocket. It was not a common color for a rose. In fact, he'd never seen one that color before.

Guillaume was just about to slip out and help himself to the sleek black telephone he'd seen in the hallway—waiting be damned— when he heard a sound at the door. The knob turned.

He straightened as it swung open, and La Balise herself swept in.

TWO

Mademoiselle Lucie-Geneviève Madeleine, who was known throughout Paris as La Balise, had had an unusually eventful evening dining at Maxim's. There'd been excellent food, deliciously witty and charming companions, the brilliant headwaiter Hugo (as always), spectacular wine, a decadent dessert tray...and an unexpectedly unpleasant incident involving herself, M. Pierre Lansac, and M. Paul Bacard.

Though she had escaped harm from the shattered vodka bottle (Lansac claimed it was an accident), Lucie was still flabbergasted over his reaction to something that had been pure fun and entertainment—at least for everyone else in the restaurant. She still wasn't certain what precisely had set him off, but the worst part of it all was that one of those bloody reporters—and a female one, at that—had been there and witnessed it. There'd even been the bright flash from a camera tray, which meant there'd be photographs instead of just illustrations in tomorrow's paper.

Though she left Maxim's slightly before Lansac and the others in his party, Lucie couldn't put the incident out of her mind. Thus distracted, she'd divested herself of all her companions earlier than usual (by four o'clock instead of five), including the very handsome and amusing Vicomte Fouquier—whom she normally might have invited into the luxurious purple chamber for a cozy interlude—and sent all of her servants away, save Piquette.

"I'm finished with this," Lucie said to her maid, pulling at the tapes that connected her bodice to her petticoats. "I cannot wait to breathe normally. I swear, you and Aloysius must have laced me tighter than usual."

"No, Lucie-san, I promise you we did not. It's the same grommet as always." Her lady's maid shook her head and caught Lucie's eyes in the mirror, a regretful smile on her face over the price of fashion and beauty.

Piquette had been with Lucie since the twelve months she spent in Kyoto, which was almost five years ago now. Though she barely reached to Lucie's shoulder and had child-sized hands and feet, she was quick and strong—and was nearly as much a confidante to her mistress as Aloysius. "And I will say once more that I cannot understand why your fashion dictates such a restrictive mode of dress," she muttered in a fascinating combination of British and Japanese accents.

"I don't know either," Lucie said, dragging the bodice from her constricted torso without waiting for her maid to assist. "But it's a damned crime. Whatever man designed this contraption should be drawn and quartered. Or laced into one himself for eight hours."

The cage of boning and metal made her long for the years she'd spent with the gypsy circus: gloveless, corsetless, and shoeless. Hungry and cold, too, she'd been most of the time—not to mention un-bathed—but there were days when that discomfort almost balanced out the fact that now she couldn't draw a complete breath from the time she was fully dressed until the time she was preparing to retire. What if she ever had to run, swim, or fight for her life again?

Piquette's smile broadened and her eyes glinted with humor as she unfastened her mistress's layers of petticoats. "Perhaps you could suggest it to M. Bardot some evening when he is feeling particularly feisty. I seem to recall you telling me he enjoys the pleasures of ties and laces."

Lucie laughed in spite of herself, for the handsome M. Bardot did have a proclivity for leather restraints—and he had such broad shoulders and muscular arms that the sight of him in a corset would be quite interesting, though perhaps not very erotic when it came down to it. "Please, Piquette, get this bloody thing from me so I can at least laugh properly at your jokes. And what a titillating thought, I must say. Though Bardot would never be caught dead—or otherwise en déshabillé—in a corset, there are plenty of other men who do wear them."

"They do?" Piquette's quick fingers had already untied the laces at the base of Lucie's spine. "Why ever for?"

"Jean Lorrain is one of them, you know. He has an interesting approach to fashion, one might say."

"The man who writes about you and Liane de Pougy in *Le Journal?*" Piquette's eyes danced. "I believe he adores you even more than he does her—at least since you smacked him with the riding crop. Or was it she who did that?"

Lucie laughed. Liane de Pougy had been the reigning queen of Parisian courtesans until Lucie drew the attention of the gossip columnist Jean Lorrain a mere six months after her debut in Paris. That had been less than three years ago, and her popularity had grown steadily ever since. It was Jean Lorrain, in fact, who'd given her the nickname of La Balise.

"Alas, no, Piquette, that was Liane who used the riding crop to put M. Lorrain in his place—and to win his everlasting admiration. I wasn't nearly as dramatic; I merely introduced him to Georges-Pierre. And ever since then, I've been fortunate that any mention of La Balise in Pall Mall has made me appear nothing short of brilliant and fascinating."

The introduction of Jean Lorrain to Georges-Pierre, Lucie's personal fabric broker, had been a calculated and well-played move that had reaped more benefits than anything else she'd done in Paris since Onni died—except her liaison with Christophe Calmette.

She sobered, then ruthlessly purged the thought of him—for a *grande cocotte* was never supposed to actually *love* her lover—and chattered on more easily now that the corset boning was releasing her imprisoned flesh.

But her dear Onni was the one who'd truly launched her career and paved the way for her life today. She missed him dearly, and she was overdue for visiting his grave. This afternoon, perhaps she'd take Aloysius to the cemetery and bring flowers to brighten up the cold marble marker. And it was the first of May—he'd want to go to Mass with her too.

"Jean Lorrain looks like a pigeon," she told Piquette. "His valet laces him so tightly into the corset he actually has a bosom. Of course, since everyone knows he prefers men in his bed, perhaps that's intentional." And yet another reason she'd put him in touch with Georges. The two men had more than a passion for rare and unique fabric in common.

"Is he the one who left a smear of rouge on the neckline of the blush pink Paquin?" Piquette asked. "Mathilde tried for three hours to make the stain come free."

"Most likely. Jean's quite liberal with the rouge and eyeliner," Lucie said, her attention straying to the rosewood box on her bedside table. Inside was the small brown bottle that promised relief. Sweet, thick, soothing relief...and deep sleep. Something she still fought for, even after more than four years of liberation. Her mouth watered and a finger trembled. She didn't need the laudanum, but it would help her sleep tonight.

A knock at the door had both mistress and maid looking over in surprise.

"Miss Lucie?" Her butler, Stanton—who was perhaps more British than even Queen Victoria herself—reverted to using the titles from his homeland more often than those of his adopted country.

"Yes? What is it? Come in, then." She frowned. It was nearly six o'clock in the morning. Her staff knew never to bother her between the hours of five and noon for any reason.

Stanton opened the door and stood in the gap, keeping his eyes prudently averted and one hand on the knob, as if prepared to yank the door closed in the event he saw something inappropriate. He was so very British. "Miss Lucie, I tried to send him away, but he was quite insistent. There is an inspector here, from la Sûreté."

"From la Sûreté?" Lucie's heart tripped. La Sûreté was the investigative arm of the Paris police force...including the homicide division. "Did he say why?" Her words were very smooth and terribly careful, for even Piquette didn't know everything about her past.

"No, Miss Lucie. He gave no indication of the purpose for his visit."

Despite the fact that her corset was loose, her lungs were suddenly tighter than they had been only moments before. Damn. First the incident at Maxim's last night, and now this.

But surely it was nothing. She'd been living in the limelight for two years now. If anyone was going to recognize her, it would have happened before now.

Lucie made a quick decision, based on both the desire for comfort and the simple fact that she was well versed in distracting and disarming the male gender. But she was damned if she was getting manipulated back into that steel contraption...and so she'd greet this inspector in a less formal manner than he might expect— and use that to her benefit.

"My red retiring dress, Piquette," she said, and at last shimmied the rest of the way out of her corset. That particular gown, though fitted and informal, was hardly more than a fancy dressing robe, and did not require her to be strapped into any sort of body shaper. "And we'll leave my hair down. I could keep the inspector waiting while I re-attire myself, but that would serve no purpose other than to delay my bed, which is the last thing I'm about to do."

"What else would he expect from a *grande horizontale*," murmured Piquette with a smile.

"Precisely."

Lucie wasted no time. She wanted this interview to begin and end as quickly as possible, and so she left her chamber on fleet, slippered feet without even summoning Stanton, and made her way quickly to the Pink Parlor.

She opened the door and nearly walked into the man himself. He looked as if he'd been about to leave the room.

"Inspector—Devré, is it?"

"Yes, of course. Inspector Guillaume Devré. Mme Madeleine, I presume?" His eyes swept over her, taking in her artful *déshabillé* of the red silk gown with luxuriant black fur cuffs at the sleeves and another wide black strip around the hem. Gold and black embroidery, tiny jet beads, and gold sequins decorated the front of the frock, which clung to and shifted along her body in a sensuous yet coy sort of manner. The beauty of this lovely piece was that very little was left to the imagination, yet every bit of skin from throat to toes was prudently covered.

"You presume correctly, *monsieur l'inspecteur*. Please, make yourself comfortable." As he had done to her, Lucie ran her attention over the man in front of her. He was slightly above average height, neatly groomed and dressed for a police officer—and with a particularly well cut, possibly expensive coat. She mentally lifted a brow at that.

Devré wore his dirty blond hair shorter than fashion dictated, parted on the side and with its thick waves combed slightly up then back to reveal an excellent hairline. His mustache was neither too bushy nor too sparse, and it was neatly trimmed and brushed, and its tips subtly waxed. Overall, he was an unusually fashionable package for a working man who spent his time hunting down clues and dragging criminals off to jail. If one didn't know better, one might even mistake him for *le gratin*, the upper crust of society.

However, it took only a solid meeting of Devré's sharp golden-brown eyes with her own for Lucie to realize the inspector wasn't the least bit interested in her as a woman. Her immediate reaction was that he was what was known as an *inverti*—a man who sexually preferred men. Though he might have some appreciation for feminine beauty, that particular asset would not be helpful to her in this situation.

Bloody hell. I could have remained in my dressing robe and been a world more comfortable.

Lucie settled into her chair and toyed with the idea of ringing for Aloysius to join them. He generally had a profound effect on male and female alike—and judging from the suppressed sexuality rolling from this broad-shouldered, intense-eyed Devré, she suspected

Aloysius would prove to be an excellent distraction, if for no other reason than that he was a noteworthy specimen of the male gender.

"Mme Madeleine," began Devré as he took his seat, and her nerves shot to attention in spite of her calm demeanor. The interrogation was about to begin.

"Mlle Lucie will suffice," she told him, curling her fingers around the front of the chair's mahogany arm. She took care not to tighten them too much for fear Devré would notice the white of her knuckles, but she had to place them somewhere to keep them steady. He had no way of knowing how her insides churned.

But surely he wouldn't be sitting here comfortably if he'd come to arrest her. And of course he wouldn't be using the name Mme Madeleine, would he? No, he'd be using her real name, that stout British one with which she'd been saddled by her irresponsible reprobate of a father—a ship's captain who forgot about her (and left her behind) more often than not.

Or perhaps Inspector Devré meant to take her off guard somehow, to lure her in before springing his trap.

And perhaps none of this was true and she was being foolish. Lucie forced herself to relax. "How may I help you?" she asked, and then, widening her eyes in feigned surprise and dismay, went on, "But, oh, forgive me. I've been a terrible hostess. There has been no coffee brought for you—unless you'd prefer tea. I'm the only one in this household besides my maid who will drink tea, but if you like I can have that brought instead of coffee. And surely you'd appreciate a pastry. It's very early."

She smiled and reached for the electric bell in the wall next to her chair, sliding its lever twice with her finger. She might not get to this man via his heart—or another more intimate organ—but perhaps by his stomach.

Devré spoke, briskly and leaving no room for argument. "No thank you, mademoiselle. Now then, as I can see I've interrupted your *toilette*, allow me to proceed with my business. I am here regarding M. Paul Bacard."

"Paul Bacard? Why...of course." Lucie's taut insides shifted into a less unpleasant position. Well, this topic was unexpected, but welcomed.

She was certain she didn't reveal relief in her perplexed response, but the way Devré was watching her, she wasn't certain. He had dark amber eyes like that of a tiger—and she knew from personal experience what tiger eyes looked like at close range. Dangerous and arrogant. And they missed nothing as their owner prepared to spring.

"Of course?" he repeated, that feline gaze steady and far too interested. "So you are not surprised at the purpose for my visit."

Lucie gave him a benign smile. This man was very quick, making him very dangerous. "It was merely a figure of speech, inspector. Now, how may I be of assistance so early in the morning in regards to M. Bacard?"

"I understand Bacard left Château Lisette much earlier today—at approximately three o'clock."

"This morning? I am not certain what time M. Bacard left, and, in fact, I wasn't even aware that he was here. I saw him at Maxim's earlier in the evening..."

"You weren't aware that he was present in your home, mademoiselle?" Devré's skepticism was subtle, but present nonetheless. "I realize this is a vast residence with many hallowed halls and a number of convenient alcoves, but are you not the hostess? Is not La Balise the most—how did *L'Écho* describe it?—'brilliant and gayest chatelaine of pleasure and hospitality in all of Paris'?"

Despite her wariness, Lucie couldn't help but appreciate Devré's sense of the absurd, for surely the likes of him never gave *L'Echo* a glance. Indeed, she found it a rare pleasure to engage with a man without the necessity of managing him as a potential suitor—especially now that she knew the benign reason for his visit.

She gave him an arch look, her famous smile playing about her lips. "As you have noted, Château Lisette is *obscenely* large—and has quite a unique design, thanks to the fantastic Hector Guimard. Surely you recognized his work, even though his Métropolitain stations aren't yet open? Perhaps you also noticed we've taken the entire block, combining three older buildings into this one and renovating them so they are hardly recognizable. That's because I not only enjoy—and require—privacy and space, but also because although I own the building, I lease out parts of my home to several other ladies who share my profession.

"To wit, *monsieur l'inspecteur*, Paul Bacard does not visit Lisette for my sake, but rather to enjoy the company of my friend and tenant Hélène Brosette. So if he was here last evening, it was as her guest. Not mine."

He didn't speak, seeming to absorb her speech, and Lucie took it upon herself to explain further. "Hélène rents a generously sized suite from me, as do two other friends of mine, Rose-Marie and Camille. We share common areas and some of the same staff—including the cook, housekeeper, and some of the chambermaids—but we each require space in which to entertain privately, when we so choose. Let me be clear: this is no *maison close*, Inspector Devré, and I am not a madam, culling from the top of and managing my girls' income. We are equals here, Hélène and the others and I, and Château Lisette is merely a boarding house."

"A boarding house." Devré's voice was drier than a ship's deck in the sun. "Such an understatement."

She permitted her smile to blossom into one of appreciation. "I thought it rather droll myself."

He stood abruptly, his perfect mustache quivering with quickly squelched humor. "I shall need to speak with Mlle Brosette."

"Of course." Lucie rose, a bit startled he hadn't asked about Pierre Lansac as well. She wondered if something else had happened after the gentlemen left Maxim's. "Please follow me."

"You mean to take me to her yourself?"

Lucie gave him an amused look over one shoulder as she opened the parlor door. "But of course. I have two legs, and they seem to be working quite properly—do you not agree?"

If it had been anyone other than Devré, she might have managed to flip her dressing gown open just a bit at the split to reveal a good bit of her calves, but such a gesture would be wasted upon him... although perhaps he would enjoy it simply for the skill it would take to be so subtle and overt at the same time. He seemed like that sort of man.

"Forgive me, inspector," she said as they walked down the corridor that connected the main house to Hélène's wing, "but you've not said how this visit pertains to M. Bacard. I hope he isn't in some sort of trouble."

"I am afraid I must disappoint you, mademoiselle," said Devré gravely. "Paul Bacard is dead."

Lucie halted and spun to look at him. Devré obligingly stopped as she laid a hand on his arm. "He's *dead*? Poor Bacard is dead? But I just saw him at Maxim's—oh, Hélène will be beside herself! I beg you, inspector, please allow me to be the one to tell her."

"I would prefer to divulge that information myself, mademoiselle; therefore, I must ask you to remain silent during the interview."

"Interview?" Lucie tightened her fingers on his arm. "That sounds ominous." Her eyes narrowed. "How did Bacard die? Was it an accident—no, no, you would not be here if it were an accident..." A chill wiped away the last vestiges of her ease with him. "What happened to him?"

But the inspector was not forthcoming. "I can conduct the interview here in the privacy of Mlle Brosette's apartments, or I can insist she accompany me to meet with the judicial magistrate at la Sûreté. If you are correct and Mlle Brosette will be overset, then surely she would prefer to speak to me here. Do you understand?"

Lucie removed her hand from his fine woolen coat. She understood perfectly. Lucie was expected to remain silent; otherwise Hélène would be carted off to a grueling interview at the pleasure of the authorities. They would confine her in a small, windowless room, withholding water and food as well as the comfort of even a chair to sit upon or a pallet on which to rest...and then when they were certain she'd weakened enough, was utterly exhausted and confused, the detective would come in and fling rapid-fire questions at her, one after the other, trying to trip her up and—

"Mademoiselle?"

Lucie jolted from her memories to find Devré watching her circumspectly. Blast it all—that was the last thing she needed, this chisel-eyed man believing he'd unsettled her for any reason. That would only lead to him becoming curious about her. "I was just thinking of how terribly upset poor Hélène will be. This way, now, please, inspector, and you have my word I'll do nothing but hold her hand during your interrogation."

"I prefer the word *interview*," he murmured.

"A wolf in sheep's clothing is still a wolf, inspector," she told him, halting at the door leading to Hélène's suite.

He flashed her a smile that bordered on being wicked, and she had a twinge of regret that there wouldn't be any serious parlaying between them.

Devré would have been an interesting lover—in many senses of the word; his thick head of hair alone was delicious—there was no doubt. But instead, she would have to take great care around him... and perhaps keeping him just slightly amused was the way to do so.

She lifted her hand to press the bell.

Guillaume privately admitted he was disarmed by Mlle Lucie more than he should have been, and he began to understand why a good number of the wealthy men in Paris were throwing themselves at her feet.

She was no disappointment in any way—for the woman had an exceptionally beautiful face, with full, lush lips and high cheekbones that were nonetheless not too sharp, her cheeks not too gaunt. Her skin was a dewy, peachy hue, and her hair a remarkable combination of bronze, copper, and gold. She had thick, dark lashes and possessed startling dark green eyes that burned with intelligence and wariness.

In addition to her physical beauty and obvious good sense, she neither took herself too seriously nor underplayed her assets, and she was at the same time both attentive and witty.

It would be a bloody shame if he had to arrest her for murder. Even worse if the guillotine was to separate that lovely head from its equally lovely body.

She claimed she hadn't known Bacard was here last evening, but that unique purple-to-pink rose in his pocket implied a different tale.

And if Guillaume was surprised that Mlle Lucie so easily recognized he had no interest in finding his way into her bed—or any woman's bed, for that matter...well, why should it be a surprise that a woman who made it her business to entertain and pleasure men would immediately recognize where his preferences lie

He had other things to occupy his mind, which he commenced with doing as he followed her through one of the corridors that led from the grand foyer. It was a curious arrangement she had at Château Lisette, he mused. The women living herein had pooled their resources, shared expenses, and yet had their private apartments in which they lived as if independently. Were they truly all independent? Or was there some less innocent—possibly illegal—connection?

Mlle Brosette's suite was on the ground floor in the left wing of the house. Guillaume stood aside as Lucie pushed what appeared to be an electric bell. A pleasing three-note chime rang just beyond the imposing double doors whose height stretched several meters above his head.

"You see, inspector—we respect each other's privacy. Even I, the landlady, will wait to be invited entrance. If nothing else, this should make it clear I am not violating the law by running an unlicensed *maison close*."

"Indeed. That only leaves one wondering what laws you *are* violating." Guillaume meant his comment partly as a jest, but when her face went taut, he sharpened with interest. *Well, then.*

The door opened before Lucie could respond, and Guillaume was faced with a second woman who was clearly preparing to retire to bed at the time most Parisians were rising to go about their business. She was younger than La Balise, perhaps twenty-three to her landlady's age of thirty.

"Oh," said Mlle Brosette, utterly taken aback. Her gaze jumped between them. "Lucie?"

"This is Inspector Guillaume Devré from la Sûreté. He wishes to speak with you about...Paul." Lucie glanced at him as if to ensure she hadn't overstepped, and he gave her a brief nod.

Turning his attention to the disheveled Hélène Brosette, he said, "If we may come in, mademoiselle?"

"Paul? This is about Paul?" Mlle Brosette stared at him with weary blue eyes. They were slightly bloodshot. Had she been crying, or was it merely from exhaustion...or were they red for some other, artificial reason? "Is something wrong? Has something happened?"

"Please. May we?" Guillaume asked, and this time his request resulted in Lucie gently removing her friend from the doorway. She slipped an arm through hers in that way women did when they needed to provide support to the other—or when they wished to share a moment of whispered gossip or a giggle. Mlle Lucie didn't seem to be the type of woman who giggled.

Moments later, they were inside Hélène Brosette's elegant sitting room, which was clearly a space reserved only for intimates. Guillaume realized he hadn't come via the route through which visitors would normally be received. He understood that in a building of this size, there must be private entrances for servants and the like, as well as a public street entrance for each apartment. It was no wonder La Balise had taken over an entire city block with her home.

As they settled in and Mlle Lucie rang for her friend's maid—apparently, Guillaume was to be plied with coffee whether he wished it or not, and, he realized at this point, he definitely *wished* it—he observed the two and their interactions.

Hélène Brosette appeared much less deliberate in her *déshabillé* than her more successful friend. In fact, she wasn't in the same sort of charming disarray at all. Along with heavy-lidded red eyes and pale skin, she had masses of curly blond hair carelessly tied in a single ribbon merely to keep it out of her face. She wore a chenille dressing robe that covered her from throat to feet and looked as if it were the better part of a decade old. Its hem was rough and dark as if it dragged upon the floor.

"What is this about Paul?" Mlle Brosette asked, her hands clenched in her lap. She looked ill, and not merely due to his presence.

"I regret to inform you that M. Bacard is dead."

Guillaume never enjoyed sharing this type of news, for the vast majority of the time he was delivering a terrible blow to someone. Yet, having been a homicide detective for upward of seven years, he rarely avoided the opportunity to do so. A font of information about not only the deceased but those around him could often be gleaned in those first moments of revelation. Bacard's parents—rousted from separate bedchambers—had received the news with shock and grief, just as had Mlle Lucie.

"But *no!*" Hélène Brosette's reaction was shock, followed by horror. "It cannot be! Why, he was only here...just here... He only just left a short while ago." Her voice shook, and she was looking at Mlle Lucie as if expecting her friend to deny it. However, true to her agreement with Guillaume, Lucie merely took her friend's hand and squeezed it while leveling a cool stare at him.

She was a remarkably calm, organized, and controlled woman, was La Balise.

"And what time precisely was it that M. Bacard left Château Lisette?" Guillaume pulled out his notebook and pencil, giving a clear indication that he was getting to business.

"Lucie," whispered Mlle Brosette, still clinging to the other woman's hand. "It can't be true. He was just here. How could he... What happened?" The last was directed at Guillaume, and now there was a spark of anger in her eyes. "What happened to Paul?"

"That is precisely what I'm attempting to discover, Mlle Brosette. If you could please answer my question—what time did he leave here this morning?"

"I—I think it must have been around three o'clock. I—we—I was...I wasn't feeling well, and he was waiting for me to...well," she looked away, her cheeks pinkening. "I required some privacy, and when I returned to my private chamber shortly after, he took his leave. Please, inspector, what happened? Was it an accident?"

"Was he displeased that you were...indisposed?" asked Guillaume. "Did it cause your evening to end prematurely—and how did he feel about that? If he engaged your services for the evening, perhaps he was unhappy about an early end to the night?"

Mlle Lucie straightened up. "Inspector Devré, might I remind you that neither Hélène nor I are common prostitutes. There is no 'engagement of our services for the evening'—as if we had an hourly rate, like a bloody fiacre driver! We're entertainers and companions, and we freely socialize with whomever we choose. There are no expectations or fees set upon our time or activities. Particularly with someone like Paul Bacard, who is a dear friend."

Guillaume felt a mild sort of surprise at her diatribe. It certainly didn't work that way in any other sort of pleasure-service industry he'd encountered. Still, La Balise was clearly in a class of her own, and he had no reason to disbelieve her.

"Very well, then. My apologies for any insult, mesdemoiselles. And so when M. Bacard took his leave, all was well, then, Mlle Brosette? He didn't seem upset or ill, or—you said you were feeling indisposed, mademoiselle? Was M. Bacard taken in the same way?"

"Oh, no." Mlle Brosette shook her head and glanced away. "He could not be— Well, inspector, it was of a female nature, my indisposition."

"Ah." That was one thing with which Guillaume had not much experience—the female hysteria or megrims or whatever one wished to call those mysterious illnesses or spells that plagued the so-called lesser gender. "So M. Bacard seemed perfectly hale and hearty when he left? And what time did he arrive at Château Lisette?"

Mlle Brosette seemed to struggle with her memory, her grief apparently clouding her thoughts. "It was well before midnight, inspector. Perhaps eleven? He had come from dinner with some friends, I believe."

"At Maxim's," said Mlle Lucie. When he glanced at her sharply, she added, "We were seated at different tables, though I did interact with him and his companions."

Guillaume turned his attention back to Mlle Brosette. "And so he did not dine with you." This information corroborated what he'd already learned from the elder M. Bacard. "But surely you offered your guest some refreshment?"

"Inspector Guillaume, perhaps if you could tell us how poor Paul died, Hélène and I might be of more assistance in your investigation.

This sort of cat-and-mouse method of interrogation seems to be serving no purpose other than to upset Hélène, and to waste your time. And you do not seem to be the sort of man who abides waste." Mlle Lucie seemed to have lost any remaining warmth toward him since his comparison of her and her friend to the common *fille de joie*. "From your line of questioning, one must infer that Paul Bacard died from some sort of illness, rather than an injury or accident."

Her eyes glinted and she sat up even straighter, her mouth settling into a firm line. "And now it becomes clear to me. You believe Paul Bacard was poisoned. Else, why would you be questioning us as to his time of departure and the state of his health?"

Guillaume no longer had reason to prevaricate. "When a young, otherwise healthy man takes his leave from a social call and, hardly more than an hour later, is found dead and alone inside his taxi with no obvious sign of injury, then, yes, one would tend to look toward a fast-acting poison as the cause."

"*Poisoned? Paul?*" Mlle Brosette gave a soft, strangled cry and fairly surged into her friend's shoulder. La Balise curved an arm around the younger woman, patting her as the woman sobbed into her dressing gown.

"I can only imagine in what direction your questioning is now about to go," she said coolly. "It's well known—at least by those who read the adventures of Mr. Holmes—that poison is a so-called woman's weapon. And though your next step might be to add Hélène Brosette to your list of suspects, I can assure you most heartily that my friend would never have harmed Paul Bacard—or anyone, for that matter."

"You may believe that to be the case, Mlle Lucie," said Guillaume, "but that doesn't mean I won't be interested in everyone who knew Bacard was here early this morning—including yourself. Now, if Mlle Brosette could please answer the last questions? Did he eat anything while he was here?"

"No," said the blond woman, sobbing. "Only a glass of wine, and I had some as well."

"From the same bottle, Hélène?" asked her friend, but her eyes were fixed on Guillaume.

"Y-yes, of course."

"Mademoiselle, do you know how M. Bacard might have come to have a rose blossom in his pocket last night?"

"A rose blossom?" Hélène Brosette's eyes were wide and confused. "I–I don't know. Is that important?"

"What a strange question," Mlle Lucie interjected.

"It is a strange occurrence, mademoiselle," Guillaume said, looking at her. "Mlle Brosette, did you give him a token of your affection in the form of a rose last night?"

"No," she replied, shaking her head with a confused expression.

"Thank you, mademoiselle. That's all for now." He rose, tucking his unused notebook inside the pocket of his coat, and directed his attention to La Balise. "I'll be taking my leave for the moment so as to allow Mlle Brosette and yourself to retire. Perhaps you would be so kind as to show me out—but please, via the route M. Bacard would have taken. I am curious about the rest of this creation of M. Guimard's, you see."

Hélène Brosette dabbed at her eyes with a handkerchief that had appeared from somewhere in the depths of one of the ladies' dressing robes as Mlle Lucie rose to comply with Guillaume's request.

"Inspector," she said as soon as they left the small sitting room and were out of earshot, "once again, let me assure you that Hélène would never have hurt Paul Bacard. You see, he had just recently asked her to marry him."

The facts began to stack into Guillaume's mind like dominos. He paused just as he and Mlle Lucie reached the foyer leading to an exterior door. A glimpse through one of the sidelights told him the sun was out, and that this entrance was facing the side street of rue La Boëti. And, curiously for this time of day, a gentleman was approaching the small porch.

"I see," he said. "Proposals of marriage are not particularly unusual for the likes of the *grandes horizontales*—unlike your poorer counterparts, who are relegated to much less luxury and a dearth of selectivity in the *maisons de close*. But," he said, watching her closely, "if Mlle Brosette were to marry M. Bacard, that would mean you would lose a tenant, Madame Landlady."

"I would also lose a friend," she replied. Her eyes were as cool as her demeanor. "But neither loss would induce me to poison Paul Bacard."

"But of course not, mademoiselle." Guillaume thought of the unique rose and kept his mouth closed. For now.

The door's chime sounded above their heads. A butler—astonishingly, not the same one who'd greeted Guillaume at La Balise's street entrance—appeared immediately from a small sideroom. His step hitched when he discovered the two of them standing in the foyer, but nevertheless, he moved immediately to answer the bell.

"*Bonjour, docteur*," said the butler, stepping back immediately as he pulled the door wide.

In stepped a tall, slender man dressed in an excellent fog-gray coat. At the sight of Mlle Lucie, he swept off his hat to reveal a head of thick, curling caramel hair and gave the topper, as well as his walking stick, to the butler. When the doctor rose from his brief bow to the lady, his blue eyes slipped over to Guillaume as he moved to embrace La Balise.

"*Bonjour*, Émile." Lucie greeted him by presenting both cheeks and then her hand for a kiss. "It's rather early for a call, but we are, as always, pleased to see you."

"*Bonjour, ma chère*," he replied, "and I do apologize for the abominably early time of my visit, but I'd promised to come today, and I find my schedule has quite packed up later on." Then he added, "All is well, I hope?" His eyes lingered on Guillaume, who found it difficult to pull his own attention from the man. He had slender, elegant hands, one of which was carrying a dark medical bag of fine leather that had just begun to wear at the bottom corners.

"There has been an unexpected tragedy," Lucie told her guest. "But first—Doctor Émile Huvet, please meet Inspector Guillaume Devré. He is from la Sûreté, and as he arrived much earlier than you have and single-handedly destroyed my *toilette*, I will forgive you for your early intrusion." Though her words were charming and light, her smile was strained.

"*Bonjour*, inspector," said Huvet. "But the odd hours—they are a normal part of the job for a policeman and a physician, *non?*" They smiled at each other, then the doctor turned a concerned expression toward his hostess. "La Sûreté? But what has happened? Surely none of the girls are ill?" He glanced back toward the depths of the suite. "Shall I attend to them? Is it Hélène? She did mention she wasn't feeling well yesterday, which is why I've come."

"It's Paul Bacard," Lucie replied. "He's dead."

"Paul—Bacard?" Huvet's eyes widened. "Is *dead?* No. But...how? Was it a carriage accident?" He moved to the side table and set down his medical bag.

"He died sometime between leaving here last night and arriving at his home. It wasn't an accident—and Inspector Devré is casting his net of suspicion over all of us at Château Lisette. The inspector believes it was poison of some sort."

"*Poison?*" The doctor repeated, staring at Lucie. "But I cannot believe it. It cannot be true. Surely there is a mistake! And how terrible that anyone here should be suspected. That's absurd," he said, his voice filled with emotion as he turned to Guillaume. "Just because these are women living alone, without a man to manage their affairs, does not mean you can terrorize them."

"Does Mlle Lucie appear terrorized to you?" Guillaume asked. "Did you know Paul Bacard, M. Huvet?"

"Paul Bacard? Yes, of course I knew him. He was a frequent visitor here. And a particular favorite companion of both Mlles Lucie and Hélène. As you might have guessed, I too am a frequent visitor here—but on a professional basis, rather than a social one." A subdued smile appeared, then evaporated. "I still cannot believe it—all of it. It's simply impossible..." He turned back to Lucie, taking her hand in both of his. "Perhaps I should take my leave, then, for now? It appears there's no urgent need for my services, and you all—especially poor Hélène—have much to deal with. Although perhaps I should mix up a sleeping draught for her?"

"That is an excellent thought. And I have one I can give her," Mlle Lucie told him.

Huvet walked over to where the butler had stowed his hat and stick, and gathered them up. "If you need anything, Lucie, any assistance, please—you will call me, *non*? You know I will do anything to help you and Hélène and the others."

"Of course, Émile, and thank you." She presented her cheek to him once more, and Guillaume watched as the doctor pressed a light kiss there.

"*Au revoir*, inspector," said Huvet, gathering up his medicine bag. He held Guillaume's eyes a trifle longer than necessary as he said, "Please feel free to contact me if you require any further information about M. Bacard."

"That is quite possible," Guillaume replied smoothly. "*Au revoir*, M. Huvet."

The doctor let himself out, and Lucie closed the door behind him, giving Guillaume a moment to realign his thoughts. "So Bacard was one of your—er—companions as well, Mlle Lucie? That was not the impression you gave me earlier."

She appeared startled for a moment, then her expression smoothed. "Paul and I spent some time together, that is true. But it was Hélène he truly fell for, and Hélène whom he asked to marry, and as for me...I have plenty of other suitors and companions with whom I socialize. I certainly didn't miss Paul's attentions, if that's what you're attempting to imply."

"It was no attempt, mademoiselle." Guillaume allowed his eyes to glint with humor—and warning. "Now, I shall take my leave, but I don't expect this will be the last of our conversations, Mlle Lucie."

"No," she said regretfully, "I suspect it will not."

THREE

The moment Lucie closed the door behind Inspector Devré, she heaved a long breath.

Damn and blast. Of course he'll be back.

She'd seen the suspicion in Devré's eyes, as well as the shock in Émile's face. Did they both suspect her?

Surely not simply because she was an independent woman of means—although that was certainly a prejudice carried by many men. Nor, unless she had completely misunderstood Émile these last three years, was it because she was a woman who lived outside the restrictions and expectations set by society.

She must quickly disabuse them both of the notion that she could be involved in this, for Lucie well knew how helpless a female could be when a man meant to control a situation. And the last thing she needed was anyone digging too deeply into her past, though Onni had assured her there was nothing left to be found.

She felt an eerie little prickle over her shoulders. *If only he were still alive.*

"Mademoiselle?" Duchagne, Hélène's butler, was standing there, fairly wringing his hands. "Is there something you require?"

"No," she replied, forcing her voice to be brisk. *I must tell Aloysius. Poor Paul. And poor Hélène.*

She would go back to Hélène first—the dear thing was understandably heartbroken—and then after that, she could seek out Aloysius for her own support. Or perhaps she would find relief in her private chamber first. She thought desperately of the rosewood box and the tiny bottle therein.

Regardless, she had no time to wallow in fear or paralysis. The most important thing she could do for herself would be to find a way to divert Inspector Devré's attention from her and Château Lisette. If someone had murdered Paul Bacard, it was to Lucie's benefit to help him find out who it was—far from here.

"Hélène?" she said, knocking gently on the door to her friend's private apartment.

Hélène's full suite, though smaller than Lucie's, was similar in scope and layout. It included the intimate sitting room in which they'd conversed with the inspector, as well as a compact front parlor (similar to the Pink Parlor, in which Devré had awaited Lucie), a small dining room, a toilet for guests, a larger, more private parlor with a luxurious bedchamber attached to it, and a smaller cluster of rooms known as *la suite privée*.

This private subset of chambers was attached to the smaller parlor, and guests were never invited into this area. It was, as Lucie was fond of referring to it, the backstage, the green room, or even the sanctuary. The apartment included a full bath with running water, a dressing room, a smaller, more personal bedchamber, and another tiny sitting area.

"Lucie!" Hélène's voice was scratchy and rough.

Lucie took that as an invitation, and slipped into the chamber to find Hélène uncurling herself from the fetal position on her mattress. Her face was drawn and wet, her eyes rimmed red, and her hair even more bedraggled than before. A chamber pot peeked from under the edge of the bed. From the odor, Lucie realized her friend had been vomiting.

Concern zinged through her. Could Hélène have been poisoned as well? "How are you feeling, *ma chère*?"

"Paul's dead," Hélène said as Lucie sat on the bed next to her. "I can't believe it. We were going to be so happy together."

"I know." Lucie stroked her friend's hair. She'd first met Hélène two years ago at an after-party for the young actress's new show, and the young, doe-eyed woman reminded Lucie quite a bit of what she would have been like at the same age...had she not had her life interrupted the way it had been. Though Hélène could be prickly and unpleasant at times—she'd grown up with three sisters in abject poverty in Marseille and still had heart-wrenching memories of scrabbling for bread scraps and selling herself on the street corner—most often she was calm, with a lovely, well-modulated voice designed to soothe and delight. "Would you drink a bit of tea?" Due to growing up in England, Lucie preferred tea over coffee (as did her Japanese maid), but everyone else in the household eschewed that British predilection in favor of French, or even Italian coffee beans. "You know Aloysius makes that special blend—"

"No, thank you, Lucie. But perhaps some coffee with a big splash of brandy in it? That will help me sleep."

"Of course." Lucie rose and rang for the maid. When she returned to her seat, Lucie said, "I'm so sorry about Paul." She wanted to ask more about Hélène's illness, to determine whether they should call for the doctor to return, but Hélène had more to say.

"Who could have done it to him? Who would have wanted to kill Paul? He was so kind and charming and sweet." Helene's sobs choked off the rest of her words, and Lucie rose once more, to retrieve a dry handkerchief. "He hadn't an enemy in the world!"

Before the events of last evening, Lucie would have agreed without reservation. But now, after the unpleasantness at Maxim's, she wasn't so certain.

"You've been ill, Hélène. What if you've been poisoned as well? Are you certain you and Paul ate nothing last night or this morning? When did you start to feel ill?" Even as she asked the same questions as Devré, Lucie realized what this possibility portended: if both Hélène and Paul Bacard had been poisoned, there was indeed a murderer in Château Lisette.

But no. That was impossible. She knew everyone here personally, trusted everyone... "Hélène?" Her voice was tight and urgent.

Her friend's eyelids fluttered and she looked away. "I don't believe so. I have suspected for two weeks now that I'm pregnant, and that"—she nodded down toward the chamber pot—"is likely the proof."

"Pregnant." Of course. That would have been Lucie's first suspicion had she not been distracted by murder—and a visit from la Sûreté. "Are you certain? You've not said anything about it to me. Have you not been using the contraception sponge?" She glanced toward the shelf that held this most personal of objects in a glass-covered bowl. Next to it stood the bottle whose alcoholic contents were poured onto the sponge to saturate it before insertion. Thus it was an extremely effective means of preventing pregnancy: as a physical blockade, and with the alcohol as an antiseptic.

"I've not said anything to anyone—even my maid. But I've not had my flux for six weeks, and I've been ill in the morning. And late at night—as I was when Paul was here." Hélène's mouth twisted into a sad smile. "I told him last night—well, this morning—what I suspected, and he..."

"He what?"

"He questioned whether it was truly his child. I told him I was certain it was his." Tears began to spill faster now. "But he was very upset. He said he didn't know if he could still marry me, not knowing whether the baby was his. I-I think he was looking for an excuse not to! And then I felt even more ill, and I...I had to be sick, and when I came back he was pacing the room...we were here in the *suite privée*, you understand, because of course, he is—*was* to be my husband, and I had tried to seduce him, but I was feeling so ill...and he was sad and angry at the same time."

Lucie could only stare at Hélène as the story tumbled out. "I am so sorry," she managed—but at the same time could only be grateful Inspector Devré wasn't present to hear this. The man would likely twist this tragedy into a story of murder. A crime of passion.

"I felt certain Paul would go home and think about it, and that all would be better today, when he came back. You know how he is—was...always so lighthearted and kind."

Lucie couldn't disagree with her friend. Paul was a Mr. Bingley sort of man—pleasing to look at, steady of heart, light of mood, a bit dull when it came to solving problems...and as interesting as a slab of concrete. Nevertheless, she agreed with Hélène's optimism.

But that optimism no longer mattered, and they were still faced with the knowledge that someone had killed Paul Bacard.

Lucie's head was beginning to thud in time with her pulse, and she knew she had to take her leave.

"Shall I call Tillé now?" she asked, rising from where she'd perched on the edge of the bed. "She can help you wash up, and I'll give her a draught to help you sleep, for after you finish your coffee." Lucie felt a pang of desire for her own easy and dreamless slumber, and the trembling of her hands became a little more pronounced as she thought of the relief that awaited her in her own chamber.

"I sent her away, but you can ring for her." Hélène pulled herself up so she was sagging against a mound of pillows. "Who could have done it, Lucie? And when? Why would the inspector suspect anyone here? No one at Château Lisette would do such a thing—why would they? He only came to visit me—well, of course, after you introduced us."

Hélène gave a soft gasp and looked at Lucie with suddenly wide eyes. "I never asked...but...you didn't mind, did you, Lucie? That Paul and I were together?" The younger woman turned sheepish and concerned, as if the thought had just occurred to her now—three months after the fact.

"I did not mind," Lucie told her firmly and truthfully. "I introduced you, did I not? Paul was very kind, and a delightful companion, but I felt no particular affection for him."

And thank the Blessed Mother she had the choice at this stage in her life to make such a decision, to allow that relationship to deflate. For there had been too many times in the past when she hadn't had such a freedom.

That was why Lucie not only would never marry again, but why she exercised her right to be particular about with whom she socialized—and even more particular about who came into her bedchamber or acquired her affection. She very much enjoyed making love, and had

had many lovers in her three decades of life—some of them chosen willingly, and others not so willingly.

Nonetheless, there were far more men in Paris who claimed they'd crossed the threshold of her bedchamber than had actually done so. Whether he had nor not, no man would admit he'd not been invited into her bed, for fear of what it would do to *his* reputation, and Lucie used that fact to her advantage. Such was the reputation of La Balise, but it was a reputation she cultivated—for a variety of reasons.

She went on. "Devré only suspects someone here at Château Lisette because this was the last place Paul was seen. But he could just as easily—he *must* have—been given the poison before he came here. Can you think of anyone else who would have wanted to hurt Paul? Anyone he might have mentioned? Think hard, Hélène. You knew him better than anyone here."

Hélène shook her head wearily. "Everyone loved Paul. I loved him. There was nothing about him not to like."

"What about Pierre Lansac? They've been friends for so long, and sometimes...well, is it possible there was anything that caused strife between them?" Lucie couldn't help but think of Lansac's violent reaction last evening when she displayed her pickpocket and sleight-of-hand trickery. And the tiny blue bottle he seemed so eager to hide. A little chill rushed over her.

A tiny bottle that could contain poison.

"No, not that I know of. Paul and Pierre have been friends for years. But I'll think about it. It's the least thing I can do."

"Very well, then. You rest now." Lucie was relieved to have an excuse to take her leave, for her hands were starting to tremble more noticeably now. She needed to go, to get to her private chamber, to open the little brown bottle that awaited her. "Tillé should be here anytime now. I'll have Duchagne turn any visitors away today. Unless...shall I call for Émile? He said his schedule was tight, but I'm certain he'd return under the circumstances."

"Not yet," Hélène replied. "I just want to be alone for a while."

Lucie took her leave, eager to return to her own set of rooms. She had just opened the door connecting Hélène's suite with her own when she found herself confronted by the tall, broad figure of her half-brother. "Aloysius," she said, feeling a combination of relief and frustration. Now she would be further delayed getting to her chamber. Nevertheless, she was glad to see him. He'd seemed a little distracted lately, and they crossed paths far less than she was used to.

"What's this, Ginny? Why were the authorities here?" Aloysius spoke in a deep, velvety voice that matched the rich coffee color of his skin. He was the only person who called her Ginny, and only when they were alone. Every time he used the endearment, Lucie was reminded of the comfort and stability Aloysius had always represented ever since they'd found each other a decade ago. Though their father had often forgotten about Lucie and even left her behind, Aloysius always found her. He always came back for her.

Though they were within months of the same age—fathered by a sea captain who had women in many ports—he was nearly three times larger than Lucie: broader than a river, tall enough that he had to stoop through most interior doors, and bald as the day he was born. Which was to say, shiny and smooth.

"Paul Bacard is dead," she told him, linking her arm through his elbow, curling her fingers into the cotton of his sleeve. Immediately, she felt a rush of comfort and affection.

He was so large and muscular that his shirts and waistcoats had to be specially tailored from an excess of cloth. Another reason she patronized the excellent Georges-Pierre, for he was entree to the best tailors in the city. "And I am now juggling an inspector from la Sûreté, a grieving Hélène, and the worry that someone in Château Lisette is a murderer."

As she'd expected, Aloysius took this list of information in stride as they strolled toward her *suite privée*.

"I certainly hope there's not a murderer among us," he said with his Moroccan inflection. "That would have a detrimental effect on my slumber." His smile flashed, quick and startlingly white, yet imperfect with its crooked front tooth. But he sobered immediately and pressed her for more details.

She told him as succinctly as possible. "And now...I've been up since yesterday at noon," she told him at the end, just as she opened the door to her private parlor. "I'm about to fall over on my feet, my love. And yet...I don't know if my mind will allow me to sleep. There's just so much going on."

Aloysius's brows drew together. "Perhaps a cup of camomile tea and some lavender oil," he suggested. "I can rub it into your hand, and you'll smell it when you curl up to sleep."

"That's an excellent idea," Lucie replied, thinking instead of the small brown bottle she kept in the rosewood box next to her bed.

"Ginny," he said, his eyes sober, as if he read her mind. "I'll bring you the tea myself. It won't take but a minute." His voice was pleading.

"Good night, my love," she said, rising on her toes to press a kiss to his smooth cheek. He had to stoop so she could reach. "I'll be fast asleep before you return. And when I awaken, we'll talk—and will you take me to Onni's grave after Mary Day Mass? It's been too long." She was strangely anxious for his response, given the number of times he'd been gone over the last week. Something was different about him, and it made her uneasy.

"Of course. I would love to be seen in the company of La Balise." He flashed a smile.

She reached for the doorknob. "Oh, and by the by, I believe our inspector friend is a—as they say—gentleman of the cuff."

"Is that so?" he said with mild interest. "Well, that ought to be interesting...watching you unable to work your wiles on the likes of him. But then again, you've had great success slaying Jean Lorrain, so I've no doubt you'll manage this man too."

"Ah, but this Devré is quite a different sort of man than Jean Lorrain. I suspect fashions and face powders hold little interest for him—although he did wear an excellent coat today. Perhaps I shall amend that statement." She smiled.

"Regardless, the next time he visits—for he's fairly promised he'll do so again—I'll make certain you're there to meet him. You are quite a distracting figure." She patted his cheek fondly, then gave his boulder-like shoulder a little shove toward the door. Not that it caused him to move, but he got the message.

"Ginny," he said one more time, and she saw his attention slide to the rosewood box. "Just go to sleep."

"I have every intention of doing so."

I just need a little sip.

FOUR

There were several medico-legists who worked in the Paris morgue. Nearly all of them had been trained by the celebrated pathologist Alexandre Lacassagne, who had made great strides in forensic science over the last two decades. But when faced with a problem like Paul Bacard, Guillaume preferred to take his chances with the brusque, gruff Dr. Thomas Jackson.

Jackson was an American. Though he'd never actually verbalized this information, his accent and dearth of civilized manners—as well as his lack of appreciation for both good tailoring and excellent wine—clearly indicated his country of origin.

Whether the American pathologist had been exiled to the basement by his coworkers or had selected the most remote laboratory in the Paris Morgue for his own reasons (including that of the very large dog he'd recently acquired, which tended to slumber on the floor of the laboratory), Guillaume didn't know. He grumbled internally as he made his way through the side door used by the employees—which had the benefit of enabling him to avoid the busy public entrance—down into the dark, chill cellar in the morgue building. The lighting was dim, for there were no windows in the corridor, and the passage needed a sweep. The air smelled of damp and chemicals. But Jackson's location in a cooler subterranean room did keep the bodies from decomposing as quickly as on the main floors, and the lab itself was well lit with bright white walls and countertops. There was even an attempt at ventilation by several small windows that had been propped open, and in the summer, Jackson insisted that massive blocks of ice be brought in to keep the room even cooler while he worked. They melted slowly over a drain in the floor.

Guillaume was acutely thankful the Paris morgue was not a barge, as the one in Lyon had been for years. He could only imagine the stench that had wafted from the vessel as it floated on the Rhone.

Jackson's lab was neat and painfully organized, with tools, flasks, books, specimen jars, and trays lined up on pristine metal shelves and counters. Guillaume noticed a new rack of test tubes, and an unfamiliar device with a curved tube attached to flasks and more tubes that looked like something Dr. Jekyll would use.

He stepped over the massive gray dog who lay sprawled near the laboratory entrance, its foreleg bandaged from paw to elbow. The beast hardly stirred, opening one eye from behind a fringe of thick hair as it groaned softly, then slumped back to sleep. If the creature had been positioned there to act as a deterrent or watch dog, it failed miserably.

As was usual, Jackson was in a foul mood. Perhaps one need not limit the description by calling it a mood—it was simply the man's personality. He also needed a haircut and a shave, and Guillaume didn't want to conjecture where the man kept his shirt when he wasn't inside it—for the cotton, though whiter than its surroundings, bore more crisscross lines than a sieve. Jackson was tall and lanky with broad shoulders, strong facial features that were just shy of being homely, and boats for feet.

"Oh, it's you. Jesus, already? Body hasn't been on my slab for more than two hours, and you're here, expecting answers." Nevertheless, Jackson had already made the standard Y-incision over the torso and begun to remove organs.

Guillaume had asked once why they didn't just cut straight down from the throat through the breastbone, and had been informed with a sneer that it was because the undertakers requested it done that way. (He wasn't certain whether the sneer had been directed at him or the undertakers.) Apparently, shirt collars didn't hide an incision made in the throat. Speaking of shirt collars—Bacard's clothing was hanging neatly on hooks nearby, ready to be examined more closely.

Jackson was currently wrist-deep into Bacard's abdomen, with a small lineup of its contents on a lab table next to him. Guillaume spotted the heart and a lung, as well as a pale white purse that looked like the stomach. It was tied off at both ends with some sort of string. He avoided looking at the dead man's tongue, which swam in some sort of aromatic fluid in a large glass jar.

He sidled in. The graphic nature of Jackson's business didn't bother him so much as the smell—*merde*, the *smell!*—and the fact that someone would have to clean up the random blood spatters and God knew what else at some point. At thirty-five, he'd seen more than his share of carnage and had become relatively immune to it. But he did have to breathe through his mouth whenever he approached this room.

How the hell did Jackson survive it, day after day? The odor—it was the worst smell anyone could ever imagine. A moldering stew of death and age, raw bodily fluids, and decomposing flesh clung to Guillaume's own clothes for hours afterward, and he only visited the place.

"My arrival might be a little premature, but I'm confident you already have some of those answers, monsieur," he said, watching the doctor's large, long-fingered hands as they removed a slender intestine as if it were a strand of pearls. Despite their size, Jackson's digits moved with the dexterity of a pianist and the sensitivity of a painter. Guillaume admitted privately that at least part of the reason he sent work to him was simply so he could admire the man's hands.

"Damn right." Jackson glanced up, then yanked a towel from the pocket of his apron and wiped his hands. "No sign of trauma on the body," he said, looking at the corpse. "By all indications, man was otherwise healthy; I can find no reason so far that he would have died during a short carriage ride. But we've got dilated pupils, and the skin is deeply flushed. I haven't had the chance to test the contents of his stomach yet"—he gave Guillaume an icy glare—"but I did a brief palpation, and there appears to be no solids, only liquid, and not much of it. Last meal, then, would have been at least six hours earlier. But he probably had something to drink within a few hours of death, which would explain the remnants of liquid. As you know, he vomited during the throes of death. A cursory examination tells me there's both vomit and some other substance staining his clothing. Possibly whatever he was drinking." He glanced at the dead man's clothing. "Take a look if you want."

Jackson picked up a new scalpel and gestured at the clothing, making Guillaume appreciate that the instrument was clean and didn't have bits of skin, muscle, and heaven knew what else clinging to it.

"When the body was found, it was curled up in a fetal position. The fingers were tight and the face contorted as if he'd been in great pain," said Guillaume as he walked over to examine Bacard's clothing. "I sniffed around his mouth—no almond smell."

"No blue tinge on the skin, no red splotches," Jackson said. "No bloody foam in the mouth—though, interestingly, there seemed to be an excess of saliva. So that eliminates cyanide, and arsenic as well—the hands and face would have a bluish tinge. But the flushed skin, the dilated eyes—it could be digitalis. I'll test for it if Robert ever makes his way back here. How long does it take to catch some damned frogs?"

Guillaume looked at the clothing, refraining from pointing out it might be too early in the year to find a lot of frogs.

There were dried vomit stains and spatters on the front of the victim's coat and sleeve, as if he'd wiped his face the first time but later lost control, throwing up all down the front of himself. On the thighs of the trousers too, as if he were kneeling on the floor, gasping and gagging. But there was a yellowish stain high on the front of the white shirt. Based on the placement, Bacard wouldn't have been wearing his coat or waistcoat when this stain occurred. So that stain had been made during some intimate situation—such as while in his paramour's bedchamber, for a man like Bacard never removed his coat, and definitely not his waistcoat, unless he was at home or in private.

Guillaume sniffed at the stain. Roses. And...something that made him think "sweet." That fit with his theory—his lover's cologne, likely. But how had perfume gotten on the front of his shirt? It smelled sweetish too. Hmm. And the stain was on his undershirt as well, he noted as he checked that garment. Was that some sort of love play—dousing him with her perfume? He shook his head and spoke as he continued his examination of the clothing.

"Whatever the poison was had to have acted very quickly. According to witnesses, Bacard seemed fine when he got into the fiacre," Guillaume said.

"Where was he prior to the taxi?" asked Jackson, pulling Devré's attention from his examination of the shirt.

"Château Lisette." Guillaume walked over as the medico-legist slid his scalpel into what appeared to be a liver.

Jackson didn't pause his careful incision. "Who?"

"Château Lisette. It's the home—although perhaps castle is a more appropriate term—of La Balise. Surely you've heard of La Balise."

"No." He sounded more irritated than usual. "What is it?"

Guillaume began to explain, but his voice trailed off as Jackson began to mutter to himself, clearly more interested in his work than the finer details of *la grande horizontale* known as La Balise.

"Hmm," Jackson said, his nose uncomfortably close to the liver. Good God, was he *sniffing* at it?

The pathologist muttered something indiscernible, then, carefully lifting a small slice of the organ, he placed it in a small glass dish. "Have to check the blood levels too—grab me that syringe, and a test tube." He jerked a finger toward a table with supplies, and Guillaume moved to comply. The man really did need an assistant—although who would be willing to work with the bastard, he couldn't imagine.

"I'll also extract what remains in his stomach. If there's any poison, there may be traces left. But it's what's in the blood and possibly the organs that's going to tell us what poisoned him and how fast it was absorbed. Anything still in the stomach likely wouldn't have had time to act. But if we can determine what he last ingested, we might be able to follow the trail back to the source."

"I'd like to know what the stains are on the front of his shirt, too."

"I need more time," Jackson said with a steely look under heavy, dark brows. "Come back tomorrow."

Guillaume was thus dismissed, and though he didn't have all the answers, his suspicions were becoming stronger: based on the timing, Bacard had most likely been poisoned at Château Lisette.

Someone there had had the best opportunity. But he wasn't yet clear on a motive, and that meant a little more digging into Paul Bacard's family, friends, and associates.

As Guillaume started up the steps to the main floor of the morgue, he passed a boy with a dirt-smudged face. The urchin was tearing down the steps, carrying an oiled sack with contents that moved violently of their own accord. Jackson's frogs. Well, that would make the man happy. Perhaps.

Guillaume pulled out his watch. Nearly half past ten, and he hadn't eaten since eight o'clock last night. Time for that *café* Mlle Lucie had suggested—but he'd sit at an outside table and enjoy the spring weather before delving back into the dark, ugly world of murder.

And he would absolutely not think about how Monsieur Émile Huvet had looked at him with those intense blue eyes.

FIVE

La Sûreté Nationale had been in existence longer than the famed Scotland Yard of Conan Doyle's Sherlock Holmes tales, and was certainly more effective than the portrayal of the British agency therein. In fact, the Parisian detective bureau—which had been started by a reformed criminal named Eugène Vidocq during the Napoleonic era—was the oldest and most respected one in the world.

Its building was located on the Île de la Cité, the island in the center of the Seine that, interestingly enough, contained representation of both civil and religious governance. The criminal investigation arm of the city's law enforcement bureau sat in a building opposite the Palais de Justice and the Prefecture of Police, and at the westernmost tip of the island was the Paris Morgue—where Guillaume had accosted Jackson a short while ago.

The tall dual towers of Notre Dame rose to the southwest of la Sûreté, separated from the cluster of judicial buildings by a large square which was filled with tourists waiting for entrance to the building made both famous and tragic by the city's beloved Victor Hugo.

Adjacent to la Sûreté rose the magnificent stained-glass windows of Sainte-Chapelle, which Guillaume never failed to find breathtaking despite the fact that he passed it daily. And there was nothing like the experience of walking through the apse and into the nave of the upper chapel, where the fifteen tall, colorful windows loomed overhead. The thirteenth-century glass images were held in place by a mere lacelike framework of stone. One could be nothing but overwhelmed when surrounded by on three sides by light glittering through thousands of pieces of colored glass, creating an intricate mosaic of color spilling into the church.

As a result of these two landmarks, Île de la Cité was always thronged with tourists. But *l'Exposition* had brought even greater numbers of them to the city, and that made everything more crowded and inefficient.

Due to the fact that Guillaume was fueled only by coffee and a mere four hours of sleep, along with the disadvantage that la Sûreté didn't have a dedicated fleet of vehicles, he was feeling rather grumbly as he exited la Sûreté. It was nearly half past eleven, far later than he'd anticipated leaving the office to continue his interviews—this time of Paul Bacard's friends.

But after visiting Jackson, Guillaume had gone to his office to drop off the evidence he'd collected at the scene of Bacard's death, and he'd been wrangled into an unexpected meeting with Chief Inspector Houllier.

"Cochefert told me the Palais is about to announce the new investigative magistrate," Houllier told him. "I thought you'd want to know soonest."

"Yes. I see." Guillaume stifled a sharp pang of disappointment. He knew he lacked the scholarly legal background for the position, but he had interviewed for it regardless. He had seven years as a homicide detective, and five years before that as an *officer de la paix*, patrolling the streets for the prefecture. But he'd never finished university—though he'd had a year at Cambridge—and that apparently made the difference.

The investigative magistrate usually had a law degree, and worked with the prosecutors to prepare their cases, coordinating and organizing the data from all parts of the investigation: the findings of law enforcement and the detective on the case, as well as from the postmortem. He would interview and prepare witnesses and arrange for expert witnesses for the court case, and could even conduct searches and issue arrest warrants.

"And how did you find the great La Balise?" Houllier asked, changing the subject with a wry smile. "Audoux's been ringing my ears that you caught the case instead of him. He was grousing that you got to meet her and he didn't."

Guillaume laughed. He and the loud, outspoken Denis Audoux shared an office, and, fortunately—due to their close quarters and the volume of his voice—were also friends. "I don't believe Renée would like to hear that," he replied.

"No, I think she might box his ears if she caught wind. But I wanted to warn you because he is going to want to hear about it all—and once he starts talking, they'll *all* want to hear about it. If you're in a hurry, perhaps you should avoid him," Houllier added quickly as they both looked toward the door, for Audoux's voice boomed through as he walked by. "Though it's not Audoux you should worry about. When Cochefert finds out Mlle La Balise is your favorite person to suspect, he won't be happy."

"Thank you for the warning," Guillaume said, fully agreeing on both counts. He was thus grateful he'd already been on his way out when Houllier caught him, so he didn't have to go back and get his coat, hat, and walking stick and chance encountering either Denis or Armand Cochefert, the administrative head of La Sûreté.

As usual, Houllier glanced at Guillaume's copper-headed walking stick, lifting his brows in amusement. "You're the only one of my men who insists on such an accessory," he commented—not for the first time. "The dandy detective. Next perhaps you'll adopt a pipe and deerstalker hat."

"Please do not compare me to that English fable," Guillaume replied as he swept up the stick. "Or I'll give you no details about La Balise—and the dressing gown she wore during our interview." With an arch smile that he suspected didn't quite reach his eyes, Guillaume swept from the room.

He heard Houllier's barked laugh as the door closed, and Guillaume quickly made his escape before he could be cornered by

Denis Audoux—or any of his other nosy colleagues. As far as he was concerned, they could have La Balise and her ostentatious mansion.

Now, as he hurried down the steps of the building, he glanced at the food wagons arranged on the far side of the *quai*, but their long lines put him off. He didn't have time to wait among the tourists, most of whom couldn't speak French and would take an undue amount of time to decide on their choices, let alone correctly communicate them then count out the appropriate francs and sous.

Thus, given the state of public transportation in the city (he was cautiously optimistic about the Métropolitain, the underground railroad that was supposed to open within the next month—though it had already been delayed twice), Guillaume surrendered the possibility of a full meal and instead called over a fiacre that would take him to Sainte Honoré. He could have used a bicycle, which was often faster than a four-wheeled vehicle, but he wanted time to review his notes before arriving at his destination, and he could do that while riding—as well as perhaps having a small bite to eat. Aside from that, there was the problem of his walking stick—which came in handy far more often than Houllier realized—for it didn't work very well on a bicycle.

There was talk about la Sûreté and the prefecture investing their own fleet of vehicles, and he was eagerly awaiting that day—but not holding his breath.

He stooped to purchase a baguette from a boy selling them from a canvas bag just before he climbed into the carriage—and this one didn't seem to have been swept or even wiped down for months. He was almost afraid to open the bag of his paltry lunch for fear of it being contaminated.

But his empty stomach won out over the fear of poisoning himself from the interior of the taxi. Breaking off a piece of the crusty bread, he silently bemoaned the lack of a good napkin and a place to brush the crumbs other than the floor of the carriage—though clearly his predecessors had no such qualms—and pulled out his notebook.

There were several things of interest he'd noted, including the unique purple-pink rose in Bacard's pocket. Surely there couldn't be many roses of that color in Paris, especially since it was too early for them to be blooming outside of a hothouse.

The rose had been crushed, but it wasn't dry or wilted enough to have been in Bacard's pocket for very long—surely no more than a few hours. And Guillaume hadn't seen any more of that particular type of flower in any other location—inside or outside—at Château Lisette, except in Mlle Lucie's front parlor. So unless another violet-purple rose with petals that became pink had miraculously found its way into his pocket before Paul Bacard left at three o'clock this morning, the flower had been introduced by someone from Lisette—likely Mlle Lucie.

If so, then she had lied to him about knowing Paul Bacard was at Château Lisette. Unless she somehow had given it to him at Maxim's—which would have meant she'd brought it to the restaurant last night. He'd have to determine what she'd been wearing, and whether the purplish-pink rose would have been a likely accessory.

Or...there was another possibility. Mlle Brosette could have obtained and given the flower to her lover...although why she would bestow on him a rose that clearly represented Paul Bacard's previous lover would be another mystery.

Thus, so far, he liked Mlle Lucie the best for the crime. She had a motive—possibly more than one. First, if Bacard had tossed her over for the more delicate, ethereal, and younger Hélène Brosette, Lucie-Geneviève might very well have wanted revenge on him. A woman scorned, and all of that.

And the physician, Émile Huvet, had unintentionally given Guillaume a piece of information he'd been missing—for he mentioned that Bacard had been a companion of La Balise's as well. That was a fact Mlle Lucie had managed not to mention.

And then there was another, more obvious reason Lucie might want Paul Bacard out of the way: he would be snatching one of her golden geese from under the barn roof. As wealthy and comfortable as Lucie-Geneviève Madeleine might be, running and owning that massive, ostentatious home surely cost more in a fortnight than Guillaume made in a year—probably two or three years. Hélène Brosette must pay a princely sum to her landlady—and where else would La Balise find a suitable replacement for her if she should leave to marry Paul Bacard? Perhaps Lucie-Geneviève wasn't as rich and comfortable as one might think, and the funds from her tenants were all that kept her in the manner she was accustomed.

But the most pressing question, for which Guillaume hoped to narrow down an answer at this very moment, was when and how the poison had been administered.

According to Bacard's father, Messrs. Pierre Lansac and Robert Druot were the most likely candidates for the young man's dinner companions, and Guillaume knew quite well he'd likely be rousing the two men before they normally rose from sleep (generally sometime after noon). Ah, the life of the *tout Paris*. Sleeping till midday, leaving for the club at four, dining at eight, partying until dawn.

The cab had pulled up in front of an imposing hotel, which was where Pierre Lansac currently leased his rooms, having moved out of his parents' home two years earlier.

Brushing the last bit of crumbs from his sleeves and lap, Guillaume alighted and, with regret, was forced to leave the majority of his baguette with the driver as a tip of sorts. "Wait for me. I don't expect to be long," he said—but had little hope of compliance. As soon as another fare came along, the driver would seize upon it and disappear into the stream of traffic.

The front desk manager rang to Lansac's rooms, and, after a brief conversation on the telephone, suggested Guillaume wait in the private parlor.

Waiting. Traveling. Waiting. Traveling. Waiting some more. Sitting in a cab and crawling through traffic. Such was the life of a homicide detective, and part of the reason he missed a number of meals, many hours of sleep, and why his little house was not as tidy and kept up as he'd like. It often took more time to travel from the Right Bank to the Left than it did for him to conduct the actual interview. Perhaps he should consider using a bicycle more often. But then there was the potential grease that would get on his trousers, not to mention being at the mercy of the weather, and—

"Would monsieur like some coffee?" A neat and crisply attired waiter poked his head into the parlor. Their eyes met and then recognition flashed between them. The waiter immediately averted his gaze.

Guillaume nodded, keeping his expression impassive. "That would be excellent, thank you."

His heart was pounding even after the waiter withdrew, and now his insides were in turmoil. He didn't know the other man's name, but he remembered the single occasion on which they'd met.

It wasn't on the Champs-Élysées, the most common place for men to cruise and find other men for pleasure. Nor was it in one of the public urinals, another location often used for those known as inverts or Uranians to enjoy a moment of anonymous intimacy.

No, they'd met in one of the cabarets near Rochechouart boulevard. Just two men, enjoying their evening out, watching the performers—both men and women—on a low, close stage in a loud, dimly lit establishment where the wine was mediocre and the brandy barely passable. Guillaume had been alone at a table and the other man had been standing across the way, leaning against the wall.

As often happened, two gazes connected and a sizzle of interest sparked between them. Guillaume sent a drink over to the young, dark-haired man with a thin, neat mustache, and not long after, they left the public area to meet up in a more private setting.

The parlor door opened, and the waiter returned. He set a tray in front of Guillaume with an elegant coffee service, two small biscuits, and a slice of cheese. There was also a bud vase with a single stem of lily of the valley in celebration of the labor holiday.

"Monsieur appeared hungry," murmured the waiter as he laid the napkin over Guillaume's lap with great care and a hand that slid smoothly against his groin. "If you care for anything else, monsieur?"

"No." Guillaume's response was sharp and short out of necessity and tension. The last thing he needed was for the waiter—whose name he hadn't learned and didn't care to know—to spread the tale that a detective from la Sûreté had met up with him at a cabaret.

He was always so very careful when he gave in to his need for companionship, and now he felt physically ill at the thought of his superiors learning of his intimate activities. Though sodomy wasn't illegal and it occurred far more than most people would believe, inverts were seen as deviants and as having an inherent criminal nature. What an irony for a man who lived to enforce justice.

If his preferences became known, at the very least it would earn him a dismissal from the department—which alone would destroy his life—and at the most... Well, he'd been privy to many a situation where criminal charges had been manufactured against a man simply because he was an invert—and often ended up in long-term imprisonment or execution. Even the lauded Dr. Lacassagne spouted the abhorrent theory that those who had sexual preference for members of the same gender were more prone to criminal and violent activity.

Guillaume turned his attention firmly to the stream of coffee the waiter was pouring into his cup. The possibility of his tendencies being discovered did not bear thinking about.

"*Merci beaucoup, garçon*," he said curtly, and pulled out his notebook in a clear message that there would be no more napkin adjusting. "That is all."

The door slammed behind the waiter in a manner that would surely not be tolerated from the young man's supervisor or the hotel manager were either to witness it, and Guillaume wondered if his brusqueness would turn on him and cause the waiter to spread tales. His insides tightened and he forced himself to drink the scalding coffee, to focus on the discomfort in his burning mouth instead of anything else.

He'd barely recovered when the parlor door opened and in strode, presumably, Pierre Lansac. His eyes were heavy-lidded and the parts around his mustache and beard were unshaven, though he was fully dressed in an unwrinkled coat, tie, and trousers. His hair, beard, and mustache were damp, clearly having just been washed and combed into place. There were dark sprinkles of water along the top of his shoulders. The faint waft of lemon emanated from his rosy skin.

Guillaume rose politely, catching his napkin before it slid to the floor. "*Bonjour.* M. Pierre Lansac? I am Inspector Guillaume Devré from la Sûreté. I apologize for interrupting your morning, but I am in need of your assistance." He offered one of his cards.

As often happened, the announcement that he was from the department of security caused no little consternation and wariness in the young man's face. "La Sûreté? That's what they said, but I don't know what you think I can help you with." Clearly, Lansac didn't care for being shaken out of his bed unexpectedly. Not that Guillaume could blame him, though it was nearly noon.

"Yes, please, monsieur, I assure you, it won't take much of your time." He gestured to the chair across from his and waited until the man was seated. Since the waiter had thoughtfully provided two cups for the coffee, he poured one for Lansac and eased it across the tray toward him. "I understand you were at dinner last evening with Paul Bacard, as well as Robert Druot and some other companions."

Lansac took the coffee with enthusiasm, but wasn't as eager to drink as Guillaume, and therefore spared himself a scalded tongue. He slurped—a sound that, unfortunately, reminded Guillaume of Étienne, and that random thought made his day grow even more miserable.

"Yes, we had dinner, but what has that got to do with anything? We paid our bills, and yes, we might have knocked over one of those vases and broke a bottle of Bordeaux, but I told the waiter to put it on my tab. I don't know what else they want me to do." The coffee cup clinked alarmingly against its saucer as Lansac set it on the table.

"I'm not here at the behest of the establishment," Guillaume informed him. "I'm here regarding Paul Bacard."

"Paul didn't do anything," Lansac said, then nervously lifted his cup to slurp again. Guillaume winced, for it was no longer charming. Had his nursemaid not taught him any manners? "It was Druot and me—the vodka was too good to pass up, and we'd had a good day at the track, and—"

"M. Lansac, Paul Bacard is dead."

"He's—what?" The young man's coffee sloshed everywhere as he fairly dropped the cup onto the table, the cup tipping to one side as it caught on the edge of its saucer. "Did you say *dead?* Paul is dead? But—no. That cannot be." His shock appeared both sincere and strong.

"Yes, and I am very sorry to have to deliver such news to you, monsieur. He was found in his cab early this morning, just before four thirty. He had died between the time he left Château Lisette and arrived at his residence."

"What happened? Was it an accident?"

"We aren't certain, but if you would please answer some questions for me, it might help to determine how he died. You all ate dinner together at Maxim's, I believe?"

"Of course. We always eat at Maxim's."

"And did you taste any of Bacard's food or drink?"

"Yes, we always eat together. From the same plates. To sample everything, you understand. Is he really dead? But he was just— We were going to go to the hippodrome tonight!"

"And you haven't been feeling ill at all? Was there anything on his plate that you did not sample? What about wine? Did you share the same bottle?"

"Why are you— Wait." For the first time, Lansac's expression lost its vagueness, and he became startled. "Do you think he ate something that was *poisoned*? That someone deliberately poisoned him—or tried to poison all of us?" Now there was an edge of hysteria in his tone. "We all ate from each other's plates, and we had two or three bottles of wine among us. The same—all of us had the same. And now Paul is *dead*?"

Guillaume nodded. "If you could please tell me, monsieur— when did your meal begin, and when did it end?"

"We...um..." Lansac frowned. "Robert and I were at Maxim's when Paul arrived—it must have been just after seven o'clock. We started a little early last night. And we didn't settle up the bill until after ten."

"And is that the time Monsieur Bacard took his leave from your company?"

Lansac shook his head, running a hand through his damp hair and thoroughly messing it up. "I don't really remember... We sat and talked for a while at a cabaret. Maybe after eleven?"

"Did he say where he was going?"

"I know where he was going—we dropped him off at Château Lisette." His expression soured slightly.

"On Champs-Élysées?" asked Guillaume innocently.

"No, not there...it was on rue La Boëti."

Interesting. So Bacard had not gone through Lucie-Geneviève's parlor? And therefore could not have acquired the unique rose that way. "What time did you drop him off?"

"What time? Hell, I don't— I'm not certain. We left the cabaret some time after eleven...I don't remember. I was... I'd been drinking."

Guillaume waited patiently as the man worked through the schedule in his mind, and was rewarded when he continued, "Probably it was after half past eleven when we dropped him off. Maybe close to midnight. I'm afraid I don't remember."

"And you saw him go inside?" Guillaume asked to be certain.

"Yes—no—I don't remember, to be honest. I was arguing with Druot when he got out. He—Paul—had an appointment with Hélène Brosette—you've probably heard of her," Lansac said, and then, realizing that the likes of a Sûreté detective would hardly be mingling with the upper echelon of *cocottes*, he added, "She is very lovely...and very accommodating." He leered nervously. "That was the last we saw of him." His smile faded. "And the last we'll ever see of him. Are you certain he's dead?"

Guillaume nodded. "Yes, I am sorry to say that he is quite dead." He declined to mention the dismantled condition in which Paul Bacard's body was currently arranged. "Did Bacard seem ill or out of sorts at any time during the night?"

"Not at all. He was in a jovial mood. We discussed some business..." Lansac's brow furrowed. "Do you think someone poisoned him purposely? That it was murder?"

"I think that's quite likely. The question is—who would do such a thing? And that brings me to my reason for disturbing your sleep, M. Lansac. Do you have any idea who might have wanted to kill Paul Bacard? Anyone who hated him, or with whom he had a serious conflict? A gambling debt that he couldn't pay, perhaps? Someone he'd cuckolded? Some other sort of rival?"

"Paul? No! Everyone loved Paul! No one would want to hurt him—he was much too fun and entertaining and easy to get on with. No one would kill Paul Bacard!"

Guillaume sighed inwardly. Bacard's parents had said the same thing, as had his supposed fiancée, and Lucie-Geneviève seemed to have the same opinion. No one had it in for the man, everyone loved him, he was the kindest, most considerate of gentlemen...but *someone* had poisoned him.

All too often, such was the case. No one liked to speak ill of the dead—especially the murdered—and so it was incredibly difficult to get accurate information from the deceased's family and friends.

"Very well then, monsieur. I thank you for your time, and once again, I apologize for disturbing your rest." He gestured to the card Lansac still gripped. "If you think of anyone who might have wanted revenge on Bacard, or who didn't like the man, please contact me at la Sûreté. If you think of any details at all, no matter how small, please let me know." Guillaume stood, and when Lansac extended his hand, he accepted it for a brief, firm handshake.

"Believe me when I tell you, inspector, you won't find any skeletons in Paul's closet. He was as genuine and jovial as a man can be. Sometimes he was even too easygoing, and that's why his father kept a rein on his funds, and promised to do so until he got married." Lansac shook his head, a small, sad smile curving his mustache and beard. "That was Paul...just too easy."

"Married?" Guillaume decided to play dumb. "Ah. Was there a special lady in his life? Had he spoken of marriage to you?"

"Not recently...but there was a time not very long ago when Paul was certain he'd found the woman he wanted to marry. We tried to talk him out of it—his parents would have been mortified—but he was adamant."

"And who was this woman who had captured the heart and soul of such a wonderful young man?"

Lansac shook his head, and the fond smile slipped into something ugly. "It was that damned bitch they call La Balise."

Thomas Jackson wiped his hands, which he'd just washed in the small, cracked sink in the corner of his laboratory. That extra sink, with running water courtesy of a floor pedal, was one of the reasons he'd picked this particular room for his work.

That, and the fact that it was far away from the rest of the morgue staff so he didn't have to listen to chatter, field personal questions, or—God forbid—be invited to sit with people for lunch or tea. Not to mention it allowed him to avoid the streams of curiosity seekers flowing in through one of the main front doors, and exiting through a second one. Thus, for the most part, everyone left him alone, no one cared that Madame slept on the floor...*and* he had an extra sink.

A sink just for washing was imperative, because it was nearly impossible to remove the stink of death from his hands without the use of his personal recipe of bicarbonate of soda and apple cider vinegar, followed by the oils from cinnamon and clove. Even then, the stench could linger unless he scrubbed vigorously under his fingernails and palms with a stiff brush, using a slightly softer one for the rest of his skin.

Nevertheless, this treatment often left his hands sore and red—requiring a balm before he went to bed—but at least he didn't smell too bad. Not that he'd ever even realized it, for his nose had long become immune. It was Amanda who'd complained about the stench and the amount of time he spent in his laboratory with corpses, and now that she was tucked away with her new husband in Boston—a blessed ocean away—Thomas could spend as much time as he wanted with the dead.

That was all he ever wanted to do—study death and help to tell its story. Which was why the minute his divorce was final, he'd booked passage on the next steamship for England and got himself to Paris less than two days after arriving in Southampton. A month later, he was employed by the morgue.

If a man wanted to immerse himself in the burgeoning field of forensic pathology, the place to be was Paris with Alexandre Lacassagne and his program at the University of Lyon. The celebrated Gouffe case, and then just over a year ago the incident with the serial killer known as the French Ripper, had clinched Lacassagne's reputation as the world's most celebrated medico-legist.

Now that Jackson's hands were tight and stinging, but clean, he could attend to the next step in the postmortem. Paul Bacard's insides were laid out neatly on the long table, and the contents of his stomach and blood, liver, and pancreatic samples had been collected in vials and tubes. He'd likely be returning to those samples, but for now, he was going to attend to the stains on the clothing.

Thomas paused to scratch Madame on the head, and she looked up at him with her tongue lolling out of the corner of her mouth, her bandaged front leg lifted languidly. Then he went over to check on the frogs. He refused to use any other four-legged animal besides rats for his work, despite the fact that other medical examiners had no problem injecting dogs or stray cats with various potential poisons. Frogs didn't look you in the eye and want to be petted or fed. And rats...well, no one protected a scuttling rat.

The six frogs he was using were still hopping around, climbing over each other...no...that wasn't true.

The one in the corner, marked with a dot of blue paint on his back, wasn't moving. The others were struggling up and over the creature, climbing heedlessly on top of their companion, for he was dead.

And as Thomas poked gently through the mass of frogs, he realized a second one wasn't hopping—it was twitching and convulsing. It too had a blue paint mark.

He felt a surge of complacence as he removed the deceased amphibian from the bottom of the box—not because the poor beast was dead, but because it was one marked with blue paint on its back. Thomas had a pang of remorse when he saw the way the poor thing's tiny toes had curled and its limbs were contorted. If there were another way to do this, he'd sure as hell be using it.

But it was a necessity, and here he was, with one—no, two—dead frogs, both of which had been injected with a solution from the contents of Bacard's stomach. And...he looked at the clock. It had happened in a matter of forty minutes.

Definitely poison. And a fast-acting one. It wouldn't kill a person that quickly, for the frog had had what appeared to be the raw poison injected directly into its blood, and a human would have to ingest and digest it—but still, it was quick and powerful.

He'd injected two red-marked frogs with a solution derived from Bacard's organs, and there were two unmarked frogs as a control. Those two seemed particularly vigorous, while the red-marked ones appeared less enthusiastic about life.

If the red-marked frogs died as well, that would seem to indicate that whatever Paul Bacard had ingested last had caused his unpleasant death.

Thomas worked carefully and methodically, scraping the dried vomit from Bacard's coat for testing, and then turned his attention to the yellowish stain on the front of his white shirt. It smelled of flowers—roses, perhaps; his sense of smell was fairly destroyed from years of working in a morgue. He clipped the stained piece of fabric from the rest of the shirt and set it to soak in order to extract what he could of the stain.

It was only after that he noticed another very small discoloration on the back of the shirt. He bent close to smell it and pulled away, his brows lifting when he was fairly certain he recognized the origin of the stain.

"Looks like I've got more work to do," he said to the corpse, relish in his voice.

SIX

Guillaume tipped the driver a few sous, then stepped down from the omnibus. The horse-drawn double-decker vehicle was generally his least favorite form of transportation, but on a sunny day like today, sitting on the top, open level of the bus was a welcome pleasure in the face of the violence and murder that otherwise filled his thoughts. He waited on the sidewalk until the majestic Percherons clip-clopped off before he crossed the street to M. Druot's townhouse.

Though he'd pressed Pierre Lansac further about "that bitch they call La Balise," Guillaume didn't get any more details. But clearly, Mlle Lucie-Geneviève was not well liked by the man. Guillaume wondered if that opinion extended to the second member of Paul Bacard's duo of friends, Eugene Druot—and, more importantly, why.

Like his counterpart had been, Druot was still abed—but it was after one o'clock!—and Guillaume was once again forced to cool his heels while waiting for his quarry to be roused and put to rights. He used the time to make more notes on the case, and was just about to take matters into his own hands and seek out the slugabed himself when the parlor door opened. A servant entered, bearing a tray with coffee service, followed by the master himself.

Druot's valet had done his job, and well, for the young man was shiny-faced and combed, and every button was fastened. His aubergine and rose waistcoat—the colors that reminded Guillaume of the mysterious rose blossom—was neat, and his shoes were buffed.

"What's this? You're from la Sûreté?" Druot was a stocky individual, and the chair gave a protesting creak as he chose his seat. "Is this about last night?"

"As a matter of fact, yes it is," Guillaume replied as the servant poured two cups of coffee. At this rate, he'd be swimming in the fluid and his stomach would still be empty. "You were at Maxim's, I believe? With Paul Bacard and Pierre Lansac?"

"We had a bloody rowdy time, but we paid for everything," Druot said quickly. His bloodshot eyes were the only evidence of the evening's debauchery—whatever it had been. "They're used to us, you know. And even so, Paul and Pierre and I—we aren't anywhere near as bad as Maurice Bertrand, and they never throw him out. Do you know, the other night he jumped up on the platform with M. Boldi's quartet and began to conduct them—using two pieces of asparagus! Hollandaise was flying everywhere." Druot's eyes gleamed with appreciation, and Guillaume was hard-pressed to keep his own face straight. "It left a big stain on my paisley coat."

"I'm sorry to hear that," Guillaume said truthfully. Anything with butter and eggs was fairly impossible to wash out, and a ruined paisley coat, while not his particular style, sounded as if it would be worth grieving over. "Now, please, monsieur—about last night. Who was with you? Surely you were accompanied by some female companions, *non*? Did anything unusual happen?" He decided to keep the news about Bacard to himself for a moment and see what he could learn about La Balise.

"It was really just us boys. What do they call us in the papers? *Flâneurs?*" Druot laughed in delight. He seemed the sunny sort who was bothered by very little. "Fancy walking gentlemen, *non*, with not a care in the world but pleasure? Well, last night it was just us *flâneurs* for dinner. We had some business to discuss, and the ladies only serve to distract."

"Business? Were you in business with M. Bacard? I was under the impression his family is quite successful in the bourbon trade, and that was where he spent his professional time."

"Not me." Druot paused to sip his coffee. "It was Bacard—Paul—and Lansac who had business. I wasn't involved except as an advisor. They were investing in a racing stud—I don't care much about horses except when they're actually racing, so I stayed out—and Paul had to cut the line."

"Cut the line? Do you mean he backed out?"

"Well, that's how Pierre saw it—but there was no possibility Paul could go on. His father was cutting back his allowance, and things were tight. He had no choice, as I see it."

"And did M. Lansac accept this cutting of the line gracefully? Or was he displeased?"

"Well, it was going to cost him three thousand francs to lose his bid on the stud, so Pierre wasn't exactly popping a magnum in delight. His father's cut him off completely until he gets married—but I told him he could find another partner. It wouldn't be hard."

Guillaume barely managed to contain his astonishment that the half-ownership of a racing stud cost more than he made in two years of work. He lived in such a vastly different world than these *flâneurs*. "Do you know why M. Bacard's allowance was being cut?"

Druot opened his mouth to speak, then set down his cup and looked at Guillaume as if really seeing him for the first time. "What's this all about, inspector? Why exactly are you here?"

"I regret to inform you that Paul Bacard is dead."

His cup rattled alarmingly as Druot withdrew his hand. "*Dead? How? What happened?*" He looked as if he were about to bolt from his chair, then as if he were to look around the room, he'd see his friend standing there to prove Guillaume wrong.

"He was found by the driver in a fiacre he'd hired to take him home from Château Lisette, early this morning. It's very likely he was poisoned, M. Druot."

"Poisoned? Purposely? Do you mean *murdered*? Is that why you were asking about Pierre— Wait, no, no, you don't believe he could have done it? He would never— No, no, no." A thick lock of damp hair fell onto Druot's face as he shook his head. "Certainly not." His plump lips firmed.

"We are attempting to determine when the poison was administered to M. Bacard. Could you tell me whether he ate or drank anything that no one else consumed?"

"We drank from the same bottles of wine and vodka. And our meals—we all shared and passed dishes around. Even when we joined the ladies, there was nothing new. I don't see how anyone could have—or even *wanted* to—put anything in his food. No one at Maxim's would *ever* do such a thing." Druot still looked shocked, but he'd found a coherent voice.

"The ladies? Didn't you say it was merely the three of you because you were discussing business?"

"Oh, that was later." He flapped his hand. "La Balise and two of her companions—and that big Moor of hers and some of her gentlemen friends—invited us to taste a new cava. I generally dislike Spanish wines, but this one was bubbly—well, that's neither here nor there." He sobered. "It turned out to be a disaster, anyway."

"The broken bottle of vodka?" asked Guillaume.

"No, no, it was Pierre. He became quite irritated with La Balise—but she was just doing what she normally does. He should be used to it by now."

Having never been to Maxim's, and never in the presence of high-end courtesans of the likes of Liane de Pougy or La Otéro, Guillaume could only imagine what Mlle Lucie "normally" did. If it was the same as the less sought-after *cocottes*, that likely meant standing on a stage or table and singing or dancing erotically while removing a good portion of her clothing. Perhaps the only difference between the *grandes horizontales* and their more affordable counterparts was the amount of jewels and furs that decorated the soon-to-be-discarded clothing.

"And what is it she did that irritated M. Lansac?" *Cut him in the face with a bejeweled, flung garment?* Guillaume kept that suggestion to himself, partly because, in spite of himself, he couldn't quite imagine Mlle Lucie behaving in such a manner.

And yet she made her living by selling her companionship to those who could pay the price.

"But of course you must know—she is an illusionist. A magician of sorts. And an escape artist." A wicked smile twitched at the corner of Druot's lips. "It's a great jest among her companions that even if one got lucky enough to tie her to the bedposts, she'd be able to free herself in a trice. There's a three-page wager in the book at the Jockey on whether anyone could keep the woman thus restrained for more than five minutes."

"I see." Guillaume almost could. "And so...she was shackled up last night and freed herself, and that somehow angered M. Lansac?"

"No, no, no." Druot sloshed coffee into his cup once more. "La Balise's favorite party trick is to relieve her companions or whoever is around of the contents of their pockets. She could give those damned pickpockets on Champs de Mars a lesson or two, I'll say. I don't know how she does it—without even seeming to come near enough to you, she slips your money clip or cigar cutter right from your pocket. Once she even removed Hugo's favorite handkerchief from his jacket pocket."

What a unique, useful, and curious skill. Guillaume wondered how she'd come to be so versed in what surely must have had an illegal genesis. Mlle Lucie was becoming more and more fascinating by the minute. "Hugo?"

"The headwaiter." Druot's tone indicated that Guillaume should have been aware of this. "He's been there forever."

"As I'm not altogether certain I'd want the contents of my pockets displayed for all to see, I suppose such a trick could result in some hard feelings. Is that what happened last night with M. Lansac?"

"Yes, it did." The other man appeared surprised Guillaume had made such a leap so readily. "He was quite rude and ugly about it—I almost felt sorry for La Balise, for surely she hadn't expected him to shout at her in that way. He shoved the table back—that was how the bottle of vodka got broken too. He must have still been angry over the broken deal with Paul." Druot appeared more than a little abashed. "Ugly scene, to be honest. Surprised Cornuché didn't throw us out. The manager."

Most enlightening. "What was it she'd removed from his pockets that caused such a public clash?"

Druot shook his head. "I haven't the faintest idea. All of the items were jumbled in a basket, and he retrieved whatever it was that made him angry immediately—quite forcefully. I didn't really care, for I had finally had the opportunity to sit next to Mlle Rose-Marie—surely you know her, one of La Balise's friends. Less expensive, too, when it comes to baubles, but quite beautiful and even witty in her own right. I'm thinking of sending her a pearl choker with a sapphire centerpiece." He smiled with affection, then seemed to shake himself from his thoughts. "But I digress—surely none of this has to do with poor Paul's death. *Murder.* How can that be?"

"Can you think of anyone who might have wanted to kill M. Bacard? Anyone with whom he didn't get along—perhaps any other business partners he left in the lurch for more than a mere three thousand francs?" Guillaume's wry tone seemed to be lost on the other man.

"No, not at all. He has no enemies. Hardly had a cross word for anyone. Everyone loved Paul Bacard."

Everyone, perhaps, except the man whom he'd caused to lose three thousand francs...or the woman who'd lose much more than that if Bacard whisked away her tenant in order to marry her.

A woman who clearly had the ability to use her sleight-of-hand skills to sneakily obtain objects...or to pass unseen over a glass and slip poison into its contents.

The first time Lucie-Geneviève visited the Paris Morgue, she'd only been living in the city for a few months. But one of Onni's acquaintances had insisted that Lucie and Lord Mellifleur—the name Onni had been using at the time—join a small party on a visit to the morgue.

Apparently, there were two young children, both females, whose bodies had been pulled out of the Seine within two days of each other, and the police were trying to identify them. Word spread through the city, and simply everyone made a visit to Île de la Cité, where the morgue was situated directly behind Notre Dame.

"It's like going to the wax museum," Lucie's acquaintance had trilled. "But the people at the morgue are *real*."

Real, and most definitely, at times, grisly. But, as Lucie learned, very nearly everyone in Paris did visit the morgue: to gossip, to stare, to conjecture, to feed their curiosity, and to simply look.

Yes, the French could be a gruesome lot—though Lucie could hardly point too sharp of a finger, as her British countrymen still lined up to watch public executions.

Less than a decade earlier during the celebrated Gouffe case, it hadn't been a body that had attracted hordes of curiosity seekers to the morgue, but a re-created wooden trunk. The investigators working on the case of a murdered bailiff had built a copy of a trunk in hopes of tracing its origins in order to identify the persons who'd placed the dead body of M. Gouffe inside the same vessel. Hand-sized copies of the infamous trunk were fashioned and sold as souvenirs during the several weeks the trunk was on display. Tens of thousands of people had passed through the morgue, ogling the trunk during the sensational case. This was, fortunately, before Lucie was living in Paris—though she had been gifted with one of the souvenir trunks.

Today, as on most days, there was a line going into the morgue on the far left of the three front doors, and a regular stream of people exiting on the right. The middle door was kept locked so as to keep the heavy flow of traffic moving in one direction as the tourists passed into the *salle d'exposition*.

The bodies on display each day were laid out on black marble tables, covered modestly with a sheet. The victims' clothing and other belongings hung behind each body, the hope being they would be of assistance in identifying the corpses. Water dripped constantly from taps in the ceiling in an effort to keep the bodies chilled and to slow decomposition as much as possible. Though most of the women and many of the men held handkerchiefs or smelling salts to their noses, that didn't stop them from chatting with each other as they made their way through the exposition room, and back out onto the *quai*.

Lifting her robin's-egg-blue skirt and the underlying layers of petticoats, Lucie climbed the front steps and entered with the crowd.

But she passed by the display behind the floor-to-ceiling glass wall and instead sailed up to the security guard who stood at the tall double doors leading to the interior of the morgue. His eyes widened in recognition, and he didn't even attempt to stop her when she reached for the knob; instead, he returned her dazzling smile and tipped his hat. She slipped a small roll of francs into his pocket as she brushed by, having long ago realized that sleight of hand worked equally well for weighing pockets down as well as lightening them.

"*Merci beaucoup*, La Balise," he murmured in her wake. His smile had become very nearly giddy when he realized who she was.

She made her way down the dull white corridor studded with wooden doors that appeared to lead to offices and laboratories. Though she'd never been in this area before, Lucie nodded regally at the several passersby she encountered in the hall, as if she had every right to be in the inner workings of the building.

At last she saw a young, shy-looking man and she paused, gently blocking his passage. "Excuse me, monsieur...could you please help me?"

He halted, his eyes going wide with immediate recognition. "Madem–Mademoiselle–uh–Balise," he stammered, his face during bright red. His feet moved as if he were trying to regain his balance—both literally and figuratively.

"I am terribly lost, and I'm attempting to find the room where my poor, dear friend M. Paul Bacard is being..." She allowed her voice to trail off delicately. "If you could simply show me the way there, I would be most grateful, monsieur—or perhaps it is *docteur?*"

Now his face went so scarlet beneath his wispy mustache and sideburns that Lucie felt certain it would burn her hand should she touch his cheek. "Oh, no, mademoiselle, no, I'm not a doctor, I'm just an aide. I... Who did you say?" Even the tips of his ears were red, and so Lucie decided it would be a charitable act *not* to pat his arm.

Instead, she said sweetly, "Monsieur Paul Bacard. I believe they brought him in early this morning. You see, Inspector Devré told me I should come to ensure the body was properly identified. Do you know where he is being held?"

"Oh, er, yes, mademoiselle, but you don't want to go there. Down there. Dr. Jackson—he—and the body—and—"

"*Merci beaucoup*, monsieur," she said, cutting him off firmly now that she had the required information. His eyes had even darted toward a dark, battered door at the end of the hallway, which obviously led to "down there"—wherever that might be. "Of course."

She walked past the young man, leaving him wide-eyed and gasping like a trout that had flopped onto the ground.

"Down there" turned out to be the cellar of the morgue—and as Lucie descended the dirty, dim stairs, she had occasion to wonder whether she'd misinterpreted the man's communication. This certainly didn't seem like any place that was regularly used, and definitely not for an official autopsy. It was silent and dusty and seemed abandoned.

She was halfway down the steps and considering turning around when the first sign of life came in the form of a young boy of about ten, bounding up toward her.

"Excuse me, young sir," she said, noticing the empty burlap sack he carried. "Could you tell me where Dr. Jackson's room is? I believe I might be lost."

"No, madame, you aren't lost at all. He's down that-a-way." The boy, whose face could have used a wet cloth (but at least he didn't smell as if he hadn't bathed in a while), jerked a thumb down and behind him. "But I don't think he wants to be bothered, madame. He just wants more frogs. Or rats. He's not picky, you know, not really, but he when he wants them, he wants them right straight away. And it's easier to get rats this time of year than frogs because it's so early."

"Is that so?" Lucie asked with amusement. She had a flash of memory—so quick and unexpected that it startled her—of her ten-year-old self, standing in squishy mud up to her ankles as she tried to close her hands around a frog without losing her balance. The thought brought the scent of swamp and summer to her nose, and a shocking sense of happiness and ease. It had been a long time since she'd felt so carefree.

"It is, madame, it is. Now I have to go find some more frogs, and the other boys have been taking my spot down by the bridge—though Doc Jackson, he'll take rats too, but never dogs or cats, he says. Never, *never*. Don't even suggest it." He shook his head, yet Lucie could tell that in the back of his mind, his thoughts were scurrying just as fast as his words, as he wondered where he was going to find some elusive frogs.

"Very well then, Master Young Man," she said, suddenly and oddly overwhelmed by affection for the boy. She dug into her small pocketbook and withdrew a handkerchief. "Take this and go out across Quai de l'Archevêché, where you will see a very shiny bright blue landau parked. It's the color of robin's eggs—like my frock—and it's very smart. There are gold scrolls on it, and the coachman and tiger are in blue and white livery with red epaulets."

"And the horses, madame?" he asked, his eyes sparkling with interest. "Are they perfectly matched and are they white?"

Lucie laughed. "Why, yes indeed, they are white as snow. My groom washes them every day to keep them so. And perfectly matched—except that one has a black left foreleg and the other has a black right foreleg."

"Gahr," he exclaimed, which seemed to be an expression of approval and delight. He took her handkerchief and looked at it. "What you do want me to do with this, madame?"

"Give it to the tiger—the boy who rides on the back of the landau—and tell him Mlle Lucie wants him to help you catch a whole bag of frogs for Dr. Jackson. And," she said, pulling out twenty centimes, "when you've finished, you can buy a coconut slice for each of you from the vendors on the *quai*." She fixed him with a very stern look. "I'll be asking young Claude whether you shared the coconut slices with him, so don't be tempted to keep them for yourself."

"No, madame, no, I would never do that, or Maman would flay me alive. She says I got to keep my job with M. Jackson, and so I better do it good. And I *know* what a tiger is." He had the audacity to roll his eyes at her, sending another bubble of delight through Lucie.

"Very well. Off with you. And now I'm off to see M. Jackson."

"Don't say I didn't warn you about him, madame," said the urchin as he thudded up the steps, handkerchief and coins clutched in his hand.

Still amused, and now even more curious regarding this Dr. Jackson about whom two people had been so reticent, Lucie finished her descent to the cellar and followed the direction the boy had indicated. Not far down the corridor, she came upon a door with a large glass window that gave a clear view of the pathologist's workspace.

In contrast to the rest of the cellar, the laboratory was clean, spacious, and well lit. The walls, ceiling, and floor were blindingly white, and there were several high, shallow windows propped open. She could even see grass growing just beyond the openings and hear the sounds of people passing by. Paul Bacard's body lay on a table in the middle of the room, covered by a white sheet with a large Y-shaped bloodstain. Only his head was visible. There were counters, shelves, and cabinets that ran all around the perimeter of the space.

From her limited vantage point, the room appeared empty, so Lucie tried the door. It opened, and she pushed until it came to an abrupt halt only about a half-meter in. There was an odd noise that sounded like a groan, followed by a scrambling, skittering sound, and the door swung open wider as the blockade apparently moved.

"Back alread— Who are you?" A masculine voice with a strong American accent came from a corner of the room, and its owner came into view.

He was younger than she'd expected—though she hardly knew why she had any expectations whatsoever; perhaps it was all the warnings about him that made her expect someone much older. Lucie guessed he was in his mid-thirties, perhaps almost forty. The doctor was tall and lanky with a head of too-long, very messy dark brown hair and a prominent nose, and, against current style dictates, he was clean-shaven—so to speak. He obviously hadn't applied a razor within the last day. His features were much too strong to be considered handsome, and this dour countenance was exacerbated by the fact that he looked at her as if she were an unwanted insect.

"Dr. Jackson?" Lucie asked as she noticed the large, dark gray dog that had likely been the cause of the door blockage.

"That's me. What do you want? The public viewing room is upstairs." His voice bordered on unpleasant, tinted with sarcasm. "That's why my lab is down here, so I don't have to contend with the masses." Now it was very nearly a snarl. "Ladies in skirts they can hardly move around in, and their damned smelling salts," he muttered, glancing at her with a sneer. "Ridiculous hats. Feathers and fruit and insects bobbing about."

No wonder she'd been warned about him.

"Inspector Devré suggested that I should identify the body of Paul Bacard," she lied blithely.

She eyed the dog—really, dog was an understatement. The beast was the size of a wolf. The only thing that kept it from looking utterly ferocious was the too-long mop of hair that hung down over its eyes and the way it was panting happily up at her...and drooling onto the hem of her skirt. "Move, dog," she suggested, a little wary about whether the creature would let her pass.

"That's Madame," Dr. Jackson told her. He returned to his work on the counter tucked into the corner. "She's just recovering from a broken leg, and you nearly mowed her over when you burst through the door."

"Madame? That's her name?" Lucie edged past, and wasn't ashamed that her heart skipped a beat when the dog moved along with her. Those were some very big teeth.

"Yes. Why are you here?" He was doing something with a curved test tube and a metal tool tipped with a small blue flame. "I'm busy."

"I'm here to identify the body," she replied. *And to see what I can find out about his death.*

"Devré didn't send you." Jackson was matter of fact, and he hardly glanced up as he continued his work.

"Ah, well, then monsieur, you've caught me out," Lucie said with a charming smile that bordered on seductive. "My name is Lucie-Geneviève Madeleine, and—"

"Madame, I don't give a damn what your name is. I'm trying to work here and I don't need anyone bothering me. So...leave." He turned around, his back to her once more, muttering a curse as he lifted the test tube to eye level.

Lucie blinked at his rudeness—wasn't that just like an American—yet ignored his order. Blustering men didn't put her off in the least. She was only wary of the ones with violence in their eyes.

By now, she'd circumvented Madame and wandered over to the clothing hanging on the wall. She recognized Paul Bacard's waistcoat and jacket from last night at Maxim's, and noticed there were several pieces cut away.

"What poison did he die from?" She realized the pieces cut from the clothing were likely stains Dr. Jackson was analyzing.

He grunted. "Digitalis. Some form of—" Then he spun around. "Are you still here?"

"Digitalis? Isn't that from belladonna? And foxglove?"

"And other flowering plants. What do you want, Mlle Madeleine? What do I have to do to get you to leave—short of throwing you out?"

She curled her lips in a provocative smile, surprised that he'd actually heard her when she introduced herself. "Would you truly do that, monsieur? Throw me out?"

He said something under his breath that sounded like a curse—probably something uncivilized and American—and glared. "Don't tempt me, mademoiselle. The last woman who annoyed me, I—" He straightened, an expression of faint shock crossing his features, as if he hadn't intended to speak. "If I tell you what you want to know, will you leave me the hell alone?"

"Most certainly, monsieur. And you won't even have to dirty your hands removing me from the premises."

"Praise God," he muttered, looking at his hands—which still held the test tube and the small flame torch.

"So he's dead from digitalis. Can you tell when he ate it or drank it?"

"Not very long before he died. Perhaps three hours at the outside, for there are traces in his stomach and in his blood. It was very strong and the carrier was thin and easily absorbed. Probably a liquid."

Three hours. That meant after he arrived at Château Lisette. Lucie's shoulders tightened. Who could have poisoned Paul?

"You can't tell what the carrier was?" she asked, an edge of desperation settling over her. "Food or drink? Wine? Coffee?"

"There is a stain on the front of his shirt and it is not repeated elsewhere. There are traces of digitalis in it, and also the scent of roses. And honey, I believe." Dr. Jackson's demeanor had changed from irritable to perplexed. "A cologne, perhaps? But he would not be drinking a cologne."

"Roses and honey? There is such a thing as lavender- or rosemary-infused honey. Perhaps it was something of that sort."

"But it wasn't honey precisely. There was fermentation in it as well." A vertical line appeared between his thick brows. "I have more tests to finish—if I am not interrupted."

"And what was the stain on the back of the shirt?" Lucie asked, gesturing to the hanging clothes. "You cut a hole in the cloth—there must have been a stain there. It's a very strange location to have spilled something, for the shirt would have been untucked...and it's near the base of the spine."

Dr. Jackson bared his teeth in a triumphant smile. "That stain, madame, is semen. I will leave you to draw your own conclusions about that. Now, mademoiselle, leave me in peace."

SEVEN

Shortly after leaving M. Druot's apartment, Guillaume found himself approaching the Champs-Élysées entrance of Château Lisette once again.

This time, however, he was accompanied by the eager Officer Bernard Houssaye, who had more than once expressed the desire to be promoted to homicide detective.

Houssaye was slender and tall, with a prominent Adam's apple and a decided hump in the bridge of his nose. His fingers were freakishly long and slim, and his soft black hair had no more substance than the down of a chick. Having just attained the age of twenty-one and with two years at the prefecture under his belt, the young man was still somewhat naive when it came to the ways of criminals. Though inexperienced in dealing with perpetrators, he was attentive to detail and interested in learning. Just as important, he strongly believed in the law and justice.

He was also Guillaume's favorite nephew, the son of his sister Henriette.

"Are those reporters?" Houssaye asked. "Just standing there?"

Guillaume had already noticed the cluster of three newspapermen, standing just down the boulevard from Château Lisette. He grimaced. The circus was about to begin. "Unfortunately, yes. Say nothing to them. Don't even give them eye contact or you'll never get away."

"Yes, sir."

As soon as they stepped down from the carriage, the reporters swarmed, notebooks in hand, greatcoats flapping.

"Are you from la Sûreté? Are you here to arrest La Balise?"

"Inspector! Inspector! Do you have a suspect? Is this about the Bacard case?"

"Give us a statement! Do you know how Paul Bacard died? Is it true it's murder?"

"How do they know we're from la Sûreté?" Houssaye asked—a trifle too loudly, which put the reporters into more of a frenzy.

"Are you the inspector on the case? What's your name? Can you give us a statement?"

"Get out of my way," Guillaume growled, raising his walking stick. He took his nephew by the sleeve and propelled him up the walkway, using his cane to clear the path of reporters. By God, Houllier would be proud of his "dandy detective."

By the time they got to the front door, Guillaume had "accidentally" tripped one of the shouters and knocked the notebook from the hands of another.

When the butler, Stanton, opened the front door, he didn't appear pleased to see the two authority figures on the porch—but he seemed even less pleased at the proximity of the press. "We've nothing to say to you," he said, stepping back to allow Guillaume and Houssaye into the house. "Get off madame's property, or I'll have you arrested!

"I am sorry to inform you, *monsieur l'inspecteur*, that madame is not at home at the moment," Stanton said as soon as he closed the door. Though every hair was in place and every crease in his clothing as sharp as a paper's edge, the butler had a harried look in his eyes.

"She is not at home—or not receiving visitors?" asked Guillaume.

"She is not at home, inspector."

"I'm in the middle of a murder investigation, monsieur, and it is necessary for me to speak with her promptly. Where might I find your mistress?"

"She has gone to the cemetery and to Ste-Berthilde's." The butler seemed delighted to provide them with this information. "Surely you would not interrupt mademoiselle during Mass, inspector. Even the reporters won't do that."

"Mass?" Guillaume felt Houssaye gawk in surprise next to him, but kept his own countenance blank. A courtesan who attended Mass. Did she go to confession as well? And curious that she should choose today to darken the threshold of a church. Perhaps she had something to confess.

"Very well. Do you know when she will return?"

"Likely not until after five o'clock, inspector. And she has an evening engagement for which she will need to prepare."

"I see." Guillaume consulted his timepiece. It was almost half past two, and he sure as hell didn't care that La Balise would have to prepare for an evening engagement. "Well, then, I suppose Officer Houssaye and I will simply have to wait to speak with her. *But*," he said when Stanton made a move to open the door, "I do have other business here at Château Lisette. I seem to have lost a button when I was here this morning. Perhaps it fell under the sofa."

The butler couldn't refuse, though reluctance tinged his expression as he directed them to the parlor.

Once admitted to the pink and pearl chamber, Guillaume did a quick "search" for the missing button. He also took the opportunity to examine the vase of purple-blushing-to-pink roses, and found it enlightening that there was an even dozen bursting from the vase, and none of the stems had been denuded of its blossom. It didn't appear that a flower was missing, which led him to believe Bacard's rose had not been taken from this parlor—unless the missing stem had already been replaced.

He reflected on the matter as he finished his extensive search of the room (Houssaye followed his lead and poked around beneath the hems of the floor-to-ceiling curtains). The stem in Bacard's pocket would have been the perfect length for inserting the rose in a lady's coiffure.

Perhaps Mlle Lucie had either removed a flower from her hair to give to Bacard, or someone had taken one from her private greenhouse. He'd caught a glimpse of its glass wall through one of the windows overlooking the courtyard, and conjectured that must be the source of the chateau's many fresh flowers. But why? It seemed an odd thing to do—make a trip to a private greenhouse merely to obtain a rare rose to tuck into his or her pocket.

Unless Bacard had somehow had access to the greenhouse and had taken the flower himself...but again, what was the purpose? Was it some sort of signal? A code—similar to the way an "invert" man might wear a red rose in his lapel, as a silent invitation?

"You didn't find the missing button, inspector?" asked Stanton with cold, knowing gray eyes when Guillaume returned to the foyer.

"Unfortunately, I did not. But we have some further questions for you and some of the other household staff," Guillaume replied. "And I'd like to see Mlle Lucie's greenhouse."

"Monsieur, I don't believe the mistress—"

Guillaume smiled and shook his head. "The questions I have must be answered for certain—unless you'd like me to have you escorted to la Sûreté, where we could talk in much less luxurious environs. And the greenhouse as well. I'd like to see the special rose created for mademoiselle. That is all. What harm is that, and surely your mistress wouldn't mind in the least?"

Whether it was his appeal to logic, or the fact that the butler realized he was fighting a losing battle, Guillaume didn't know—but the man nodded.

"You and I can speak right here, M. Stanton," Guillaume said, gesturing to the foyer. "I have only a simple question—and that is, did Paul Bacard visit Mlle Lucie yesterday? Did he wait for her in the parlor?"

"No, monsieur. He visited Mlle Hélène, but he didn't come to this side of the house. He no longer calls on Miss Lucie."

"And you're certain this is the case? Could he have visited when you weren't present? Perhaps you were attending to something else and had stepped away for a moment? This is very important, for I'm certain you know by now the man was poisoned."

"Monsieur, I assure you, I do not take my duty lightly. I know every person who crosses the threshold of Miss Lucie's house. There was only one brief time in the late afternoon when I was not on duty, and in that case it was Michel, the first footman, who was to answer the door. He reported to me everyone who called during that time, and M. Bacard was not one of them."

"Perhaps it was a secret meeting, and Michel was ordered not to tell you."

"There are no secrets in this house that I do not know. It's my job to know all that occurs herewith." The nose lifted higher and the eyes became a frostier gray.

"Indeed. Well, then, if I am to take you at your word—that you know all secrets in this house—perhaps you might be able to tell me the biggest secret of all—who it was who poisoned Paul Bacard? For it becomes increasingly clear that he ingested the poison at Château Lisette."

To Guillaume's surprise, Stanton's expression thawed into sorrow. "That I cannot tell you, Inspector Devré, for I cannot imagine anyone would have wanted to harm M. Bacard. He was kind and pleasant and always took the time to say hello and to ask how I was faring that day. That's how I know for certain he was not on this side of the house yesterday. We—all the servants—know him, and we all like him, and believe me when I tell you that we are all aggrieved by his death."

Such a popular man, Bacard had been. Not one enemy in the world. Even the servants liked him.

So who would have wanted to kill him? Unless Bacard had some well-hidden secrets yet to be exposed, Guillaume kept circling back to the same suspect: the woman scorned.

But there was also the would-be business partner, Pierre Lansac.

For some people, three thousand francs would be more than enough incentive for murder. But for the likes of Lansac, who lived in the expensive Hôtel Briö and lived a life of wealthy idleness, it was laughable.

"Perhaps it was an accident," ventured the butler. "The poisoning."

Guillaume inclined his head. "Possible. Now, then. Perhaps you will be so kind as to take me to mademoiselle's greenhouse—she does have one, non? Oh, and I must also ask—how often are the flowers changed? The fresh flowers in the vases?"

"Just before they begin to droop, monsieur. Mme Frousand—the housekeeper—would know precisely what the schedule is. She is particular that the housemaids change them as soon as they no longer appear fresh. I believe it depends upon the type of flower, too, monsieur, when they are changed and whose responsibility it is. And, yes, Mlle Lucie has a lovely greenhouse."

"*Bien sûr*. And would Mme Frousand know whether a floral arrangement has been disturbed?"

"Her attention to detail is second only to mine," replied Stanton with frost in his voice. "I assure you, if anything were amiss, she would know."

"Very well. Officer Houssaye, would you please speak with Madame Frousand and Michel the first footman and confirm these details?"

"Yes, inspector."

"Find out when the roses had been placed and how many of them there were. And whether anyone noticed any of them missing or otherwise disturbed. I'll meet you back at the office later."

"Yes, inspector."

"Sir, if you don't mind my asking—why are you so concerned with the roses?" asked Stanton.

"I'm quite certain one of those roses figures in the mystery of M. Bacard's death. Forgive me, but that's all I can say at the moment."

"Very well, then, monsieur. I see you are like Mr. Holmes in that regard—keeping information to yourself until the very end."

Guillaume continued to keep his thoughts to himself at being compared to the fictional detective. If he was to be likened to anyone in a book, he preferred it to be Monsieur Lecoq, a criminal-turned-detective, who, like Guillaume, worked for la Sûreté. Lecoq, who starred in the immensely popular crime and adventure stories, had a much more interesting background and exciting exploits than Arthur Conan Doyle's creation. But most importantly, he was *French*.

The butler took Guillaume through the servants' corridor, past the butler's pantry and the housekeeper's office. As they passed a large window, Guillaume caught a glimpse of the generous rectangular courtyard he'd seen through the ivy-covered gate during his initial approach to Château Lisette. One wall of the courtyard was glassed off into the semicircular domed greenhouse that was his destination.

It took Guillaume only a few moments to examine the rosebush in the greenhouse and see that it had been neatly trimmed, each stem at an angle. Conversely, the rose in Bacard's pocket had been torn or cut straight across.

"When was the last time the gardener was here?" If someone had broken off a stem—which was the case with the one Bacard had—the gardener might have noticed the degradation and trimmed the offending stem back into place. Based on the perfect condition of every other plant in the conservatory, that was a definite possibility.

"This morning, of course. He—Lelo—isn't here now, however, monsieur. I believe he went to look at some equipment."

Guillaume frowned. Now he would have to return to Château Lisette once more. No, no...perhaps he would assign Houssaye to follow up on this little detail as well. His mood lifted a bit. It was a mixed blessing having the young man dogging his footsteps.

"Very well. I'm grateful for your assistance, M. Stanton," Guillaume said. "Now if you would show me how to get back onto the street; there is no need for me to return to the house."

There was a small side gate, its wrought iron design again in Guimard's curving, undulating style. The butler's ring of keys had a selection that opened the ornate door, and Guillaume found himself in a small, grassy alleyway when he stepped through.

Fortunately, there was not a reporter in sight.

It took him only a moment to orient himself: the main entrance on Champs-Élysées was to his left, and just around the corner to the right was the rue La Boëti, where Bacard had come to visit Mlle Brosette. Tall trees and thick bushes provided a thick barrier of privacy between Château Lisette and her neighbor along the entire length of the mansion.

"Thank you," he said, tipping his hat to the butler.

He strode along the neat flowerbeds bright with tulips and other spring flowers, following the secluded path of lawn around to the right as he considered his next step. Beneath a long row of curtained windows, boxwoods and lavender topiaries were trimmed into tall, slender pyramids. Low-lying ground cover with minuscule white blossoms filled in between clumps of bulb flowers. Fat bumblebees bounced from blossom to blossom, their soft buzzing barely reaching his ears over the noise of traffic. The only discord in the landscaping was a section of wilted, browning leftovers from the lilies of the valley that had been cut for the holiday.

Somewhere, someone was baking bread, for the scent wafted along the late afternoon air. Guillaume sighed, for that pitiful piece of baguette had been so long ago. When he got home—whatever time it would be; surely later this afternoon or more likely into the evening—there would be no one waiting to cook a meal or preparing to serve one. He'd be settling for week-old bread and leftover sausage at the very best.

As he approached the entrance on rue La Boëti, Guillaume turned his thoughts from his empty belly to Paul Bacard.

Messrs. Lansac and Druot would have dropped him off somewhere along here around midnight. Neither Lansac nor Druot remembered the exact time, but Hélène Brosette said that Bacard had arrived a little after midnight.

Lansac estimated the men had left the cabaret around half past eleven. If that was true, depending whether they'd been in Montmartre or Montparnasse, it would have taken between ten and twenty minutes at that time of night, barring anything unusual. Which would have put their arrival—Bacard's arrival—here well before midnight. Possibly a span of fifteen to twenty minutes unaccounted for.

It was enough time for a brief assignation, Guillaume mused. *Lansac's carriage leaves, Bacard hails a different vehicle or, more likely, walks a short way down les Champs-Élysées and meets someone there at a café or even in a carriage.*

Or he comes around to that entrance of Château Lisette and is admitted there.

It was possible. At least a quarter of an hour...perhaps longer, if Lansac was off on his time estimate.

And that also explained why, later, Bacard ordered a cab to go home instead of using his own carriage—he hadn't had it with him.

Guillaume was just about to approach the front door when he noticed something bright pink and out of place on the small patch of emerald grass near the corner of the house. Something about it compelled him, and he left the stone walkway to investigate.

When he crouched to see what had dared to upset the clipped, pristine lawn, Guillaume was very glad he'd done so...for the object, he discovered, was a petal from a brilliant purple-pink rose. It had been torn from its bud, and from the shape and size of it, he could tell it had come from the outermost part of the flower. A single crease in the velvety petal was just beginning to turn brown.

It was fairly fresh, and he had a feeling he knew from what particular bloom it had come. Carefully, he tucked the delicate object into a folded piece of paper from his notebook and slipped the resulting packet inside his coat pocket.

A rose petal that could easily have found its way onto this expanse of lawn during Bacard's unaccounted twenty minutes.

Guillaume gave the area a minute examination, but found nothing else of interest: no more rose petals, no footprints, no other apparent disturbance. Still, his fingers were prickling.

He was getting closer.

As Guillaume approached the front door to Mlle Brosette's wing, he was gratified to note the absence of any reporters, at least on this side of the block.

The door opened to reveal the butler, who was so similar to Stanton that Guillaume had to look twice to make certain it wasn't the same gentleman. He'd only met Duchagne briefly when M. Huvet arrived this morning as Guillaume was leaving. But this butler was a trifle shorter and a trifle wider than Stanton, and he wore blue pinstriped trousers instead of gray ones.

"Good afternoon, monsieur. I am Inspector Guillaume Devré from la Sûreté and I would like to speak with Mlle Brosette." He offered his badge.

"Yes, monsieur, I remember you. I am afraid the mademoiselle is indisposed at the moment." His tone was so nasally that Guillaume almost winced. It sounded as if it actually hurt the man to speak. "She is understandably upset over the death of M. Bacard."

"Indeed. Most understandable." Guillaume smiled pleasantly. "Let's not trouble her, then, for it's really the staff with whom I wish to speak. I've already interviewed Mlle Lucie-Genevieve's personnel, and they have been very helpful. If I may?" He lifted his toe to step onto the threshold and noticed his shoes were in need of a polish. The butler stepped back after only a breath of hesitation, though he didn't appear terribly pleased about the invasion.

"I only have a few questions, monsieur. For you and then for the housekeeper," Guillaume said as they stood in the foyer. "Perhaps we might sit in the parlor? I'm certain Mlle Brosette won't mind, under the circumstances."

Moments later, Guillaume was sitting in the parlor—a room that was decorated in yellow, gold, and spring green, with no sign of the unique pink-purple roses. Duchagne did not deign to take a seat, nor did he seem inclined to call for any refreshment. Guillaume was disappointed, for this time, he would not have declined any offering.

"When did M. Bacard arrive, and did you see what mode of transportation he used? Was it a taxi?"

"It was six minutes past midnight that he arrived. I don't believe I recognized the vehicle—it was dark, and I didn't see it very well. It wasn't M. Bacard's carriage, for it's well known here."

"That's a very precise time," commented Guillaume.

"I am a very precise man."

"Indeed. Very well, then, when he arrived was he immediately announced to Mlle Brosette, and did he wait in the parlor or was he brought to some other location? Being a regular visitor, one must assume he was treated differently."

"He is a regular visitor—pardon me, he *was* a regular visitor. We are all quite shocked and saddened that he is gone." The nasal tone became more pronounced, and the man blinked rapidly. "Being as it is, M. Bacard generally had the run of the house, so to speak, and made his own way to mademoiselle's suite once I answered the door to him."

"Did you get the impression he went immediately to her suite last night? Or did he...wander about?"

"He might have stopped in the kitchen." His lips spread into an affectionate smile, but then it disappeared immediately. "And though, yes, he did have one of La Marquite's—that's the cook—one of her special basil-lemon biscuits, that was the only thing he had to eat here. We have been talking about this since last night," the butler said firmly. "La Marquite is beside herself that something she served might have been the cause of his demise—but it's simply impossible."

"And to drink? Did La Marquite serve M. Bacard some *café* when he came to the kitchen? It was late at night and surely he was sleepy by then, after a large meal."

"Yes, of course, but it was from the same pot we all use. No one else has been ill, monsieur inspecteur."

"I should like to speak with the cook as well when we are finished. Just to ensure I have all of the information. Now, at what time did M. Bacard take his leave? And was there any food or drink provided to him while he was visiting with Mlle Brosette?"

"They weren't together for very long, monsieur. No more than three hours. Mlle Hélène was not feeling well, and she was indisposed in her lavatory for much of the time during his visit."

"Is that so? And was she feeling better this morning?"

"Dr. Huvet was here last evening for Mlle Camille—she had some sort of complaint"—Duchagne's expression seemed to indicate that was an all-too-common occurrence—"and he was kind enough to see to Mlle Hélène as well. From what Tillé—Mlle Hélène's maid—has said, the doctor believed she was merely suffering from female megrims." The butler appeared slightly uncomfortable with the topic, though why he should be, living in a house like this, Guillaume wasn't certain.

"And is she still feeling ill today?" he asked.

"She's better."

"And M. Bacard—what time did he leave? Did he ask you to call for a cab?"

"It was nearly three o'clock when he left—and there was a cab waiting outside. They often do," added the butler. Guillaume noticed his nasal tendencies had relaxed a bit as their conversation went on. "Along with the reporters." His mouth flattened with disgust. "They cannot seem to leave the mistresses alone, even when they are at home and private."

"Very well, monsieur. You've been very helpful. Perhaps I could speak with the housekeeper and La Marquite as well."

His interviews with the housekeeper and the cook went in a similar fashion. They both confirmed what Duchagne had told him. This left Guillaume with no further sense as to when and how Paul Bacard had taken the poison, although there were many indications when he had *not*.

Guillaume considered whether he should speak with Mlle Lucie's two other tenants, Mlles Rose-Marie and Camille and their staff. But of course he should—particularly to confirm that M. Bacard hadn't visited any other wing of the mansion—including the greenhouse.

When he made this request, Duchagne seemed relieved, as if ready to pass Guillaume off to yet a different butler and set of household servants.

"Perhaps I could wait here for the ladies here," Guillaume said from his seat in Hélène Brosette's parlor.

"Of course, monsieur." Duchagne's disapproval was barely hidden. "I shall send word to Mlle Rose-Marie's wing."

Moments later, the door opened, prompting Guillaume to stand. A diminutive, dark-haired woman entered, dressed in a supremely casual gown of some material that was light in both hue and weight. He saw that it was adorned with pink velvet ribbons and tiny imprints of roses.

"Good morning, Mlle Rose-Marie."

"Good morning, *monsieur l'inspecteur*," she said. She looked slightly wary at the moment, but he suspected that when she was not about to be interrogated by an officer of the law, her eyes would dance and little dimples would appear in her pretty, round face.

Her small hands were ungloved, and he saw that they were soft and dimpled, with short fingers and well-tended nails. Her mouth was in the shape of a bow, and her lips were a natural rose. She had a generous bosom, generous hips, and a small waist that would surely be formed into an even smaller diameter when dressed in evening wear. His first impression of Mlle Rose-Marie was that of a lovely, seemingly good-natured, feminine personification of a cream puff. A strawberry cream puff.

"Please, sit, mademoiselle," he said. "I am Inspector Guillaume Devré, and as you certainly are aware, I've come from la Sûreté. I'm investigating the murder of Paul Bacard."

"Yes, monsieur, of course. There's been little talk of anything else." Her dark brown eyes scored over him as she took a seat on the settee, arranging her simple skirt over her lap. "I cannot believe it's true."

He nodded. "You are not alone in that sentiment, mademoiselle. Now, I have some questions for you. Did you see M. Bacard here last night?"

"No, I didn't see him—at least here. I was at dinner at Maxim's—surely you've heard about that fracas by now, monsieur?"

He inclined his head, lifting his brows in an invitation to continue. She was delighted to do so.

"Lucie has her own reserved table, of course—they've even put a plaque for her—and so do I, but last night we were sitting together at her table with some gentlemen friends. Paul and his friends Pierre Lansac and Eugene Druot came in, and they were at their own table. Vicomte Fouquier, Joseph Oller, Alphonse Daudet, and François Bertrand were with us."

Guillaume kept his expression blank, though he was startled by the variety, wealth, and notoriety of Lucie-Geneviève's four companions—though why that still surprised him, he didn't know.

"Fouquier is quite taken with Lucie, and he was flirting outrageously with her, threatening to pour champagne into the hollow of her throat—do you see, here"—she indicated—"and also here, above the collarbone, and sip on it until he became drunk or she took him home to her bed." Two dozen dimples danced in her cheeks as her eyes glinted mischievously.

"Señor Oller was becoming jealous—did you know he built an indoor swimming pool that is *heated*?—and he ordered three bottles of Spanish champagne...cava, I think it's called. He ordered it for everyone, and we were all drinking it, and he made a bet with Lucie that she couldn't pickpocket from one of the men at Bacard's table without them noticing. Of course, Lucie replied that she could not only pick the pocket of one, but empty the pockets of all three of them…and that if she didn't succeed, she would pay for all of the dinner for everyone at both tables."

"And who paid for dinner, then, mademoiselle?" Guillaume asked with a smile.

"It wasn't Lucie, monsieur." Rose-Marie laughed. She seemed to have a true fondness and admiration for her landlady, if the continued sparkle in her eyes was any indication.

"But you said it was a fracas," he reminded her.

"Oh, yes, of course. Pierre Lansac was furious when he realized that when Lucie came over to offer them some of the Spanish champagne she'd picked their pockets—and had even taken Druot's timepiece right off the front of his lapel! It was quite a scene."

"Why do you think Lansac was so angry with Mlle Lucie? Is he not the type of man to take a joke, or does he not like her for some reason?"

"I don't know. It was all so loud and angry, and they broke a bottle of vodka—it nearly hit one of the reporters in the head when Lansac threw it across the room. I wasn't paying much attention by that point, for François had just given me a four-foot rope of pearls. The clasp is crusted with diamonds."

"A valuable gift, to be sure," he replied. "Now, can you tell me when Bacard left and with whom, and when Mlle Lucie left and with whom?"

"Lucie left early with Fouquier—by half past ten, I think. François and I settled our bill shortly after and went to Galliard's to watch the dancing. Paul and his friends were still at Maxim's when we left."

"And did you see M. Bacard when he visited Château Lisette last night?"

"No. I wasn't home until very late—or should I say early?" She smiled briefly. "François and I were together until after four o'clock, and then I went to bed. I knew nothing of what occurred until Lucie sent word this morning."

"How well did you know M. Bacard? What was your impression of him?"

"Yes, of course I knew him. He is—was—a very nice man. Charming, handsome, *wealthy*"—she gave a short laugh—"and he was always kind." Her dimples disappeared. "I cannot imagine why anyone would want to murder him."

"Indeed. There was no one with whom he might have had a conflict—a jealous lover, perhaps? Someone he fancied for a while and then dropped when Mlle Brosette came onto the scene?"

"No. No one at all."

"And he and Mlle Brosette...they were together for how long?"

"Oh...let me see...it's been three months? Perhaps four? It was just after the first of the year, if I remember correctly."

"And they were happy together?" Guillaume asked.

"Hélène was very happy. She talked about him all the time. I didn't know M. Bacard well enough to engage in such a conversation with him, but he was around quite often. I do believe," she said, leaning forward to whisper, "that Hélène meant to convince him to marry her."

"Indeed. And would that have been difficult for him to be convinced thus?"

"He *was* quite besotted with her—at least, he was after Lucie gave him the shoehorn." Rose-Marie giggled, the dimples flashing again. "I shouldn't have said that—about the shoehorn, but it was rather like that. He was horribly infatuated with Lucie, and he wanted her to marry him, but she would have none of that. He wasn't her type, and she is not the sort to want to marry."

Well, at least Guillaume and Lucie-Geneviève had something in common.

"And M. Bacard, he did not take it well when Mlle Lucie declined his advances? Was he upset about it?"

"Oh, for perhaps a week or two, but then Hélène charmed the trousers off him— Oh!" Her eyes flew open and a charming rosy blush made her appear even more sweet and cream-puff-like.

Guillaume couldn't hold back another smile, but he sobered quickly. "And so after Mlle Lucie, M. Bacard easily transferred his attentions to Mlle Brosette. And all was well. There were no arguments or jealous rages? And Mlle Brosette...she wasn't bothered that M. Bacard had been in love with Mlle Lucie-Geneviève first?"

"No, not at all. Not that I knew." But Rose-Marie's expression changed into one of thoughtfulness, and Guillaume waited. "No, Hélène wouldn't be jealous," she said after a moment. "Not of Lucie, anyway."

"But of some other woman, perhaps? Does Mlle Hélène have that sort of temperament, then?" He watched her closely.

She fidgeted with the fringe on the pillow next to her. "She wouldn't be jealous of Lucie, no. But perhaps...she is a...well, she isn't always the *nicest* person." Her voice had dropped to a low tone, and she glanced around. "She's not exactly been mean to me or Camille, but she can be cutting and sharp. And I *could* imagine her being jealous of another woman. She— Once I sat next to M. Bacard when we were all at dinner—this was after they became attached—and I could see that she didn't like it at all."

Guillaume nodded, waiting to see if she had more to add. When Rose-Marie said nothing else, he stood. "Thank you very much, mademoiselle. I appreciate your time."

"That's all? We're finished?"

She was rather adorable, if one liked feminine confections. "Well, if you insist...perhaps I shall ask one more question, then, mademoiselle. What do you think would have happened if Mlle Brosette had married Paul Bacard, and moved out of her apartment here? How would Mlle Lucie-Geneviève have reacted?"

"Lucie? I think she would have been sad to see her go, but also very happy for her. We all know Hélène wants to marry."

"She wouldn't have been upset to lose a tenant?"

"Oh...no, I don't think so. I don't believe so. Not Lucie."

"I see. Thank you, mademoiselle."

Rose-Marie stood, and to Guillaume's surprise, she hesitated from leaving and gave him a smile. "This wasn't nearly as unpleasant as I thought it would be, considering what Hélène and Lucie have told me."

He inclined his head and decided not to mention that murder was the height of unpleasantness. "*Bonne journée*, mademoiselle," he said as she excused herself from the parlor.

Guillaume was thoughtful after she left. Lucie-Geneviève. She seemed to be as much a paragon as Paul Bacard—if one didn't consider the fact that she made her livelihood by offering her companionship—and body—for compensation. He wondered whether a four-foot rope of pearls with a diamond-crusted clasp would have bought an entire night with La Balise, or merely an hour or two of flirtation.

His thoughts were cut short when the parlor door opened once more.

Mlle Camille was a stark contrast to Rose-Marie—at least in a visual way. Where Rose-Marie was curvaceous, warm, and pink, Camille was tall, slender, and elegant to the point of being icy. Her hair was white-blond, falling loosely over her shoulders to past her breasts, and she wore a silk robe of cream trimmed with Chantilly lace. To his mild surprise, the robe was closed up almost to her throat. On her feet were matching slippers. Someone had not finished removing her makeup, for there was a small black smudge beneath one eye.

"Mlle Camille, I am Inspector Guillaume Devré from la Sûreté, as you no doubt have been informed. Please, sit."

"Y-yes, of course," she replied, and took the exact position on the settee that Rose-Marie had just taken. As she bent forward to move a vase on the table between them, from his standing position, he caught a glimpse down the opening of her robe. The skin at the top of her chest was an angry red with irritation. Presumably the "complaint" to which Duchagne had referred.

Guillaume resumed his seat and began his interview. "*Bien sûr*, you are aware of the reason for my presence, mademoiselle, so permit me to begin immediately. Paul Bacard was here last evening before he died of what appears to be poisoning. Did you see him?"

"Yes, I-I did." Now she was moving one of the pillows on the settee, smoothing the damask design as she settled it in her lap.

He waited.

"I-I wasn't feeling well. I canceled my engagements and didn't go out last evening, and so I was here, and I wanted to have some dinner. And La Marquite...she allows me to come to the kitchen."

Guillaume nodded. "And did you see M. Bacard in the kitchen then? Or somewhere else? Did you come over to this side of the house, perhaps, when Mlle Brosette was here?"

Camille gave him a small smile. "It was in the kitchen. He was there, asking for one of La Marquite's lemon-basil biscuits."

"And? Did he get any of these famed biscuits? And some coffee, perhaps? Or a glass of wine?"

"He was only there for a moment, then he left. I stayed. I didn't see him eat anything other than some of the biscuits. La Marquite— the cook—especially liked M. Bacard, and she wasn't stingy when he was around. And we all drank from the same coffee pot."

"What time was this, that you saw him in the kitchen, Mlle Camille?"

"Oh." She released the pillow fringe she'd been worrying, and frowned. "A short time after midnight, I think. Yes, that would be right, because Émile—Dr. Huvet—was here to see to my—my— I have a— Well, someone must have put strawberries in the tart, and I break out in hives when I eat them." She gestured to her front, while keeping her robe closed up tightly once more.

"And you know it was after midnight when you saw Bacard because you went to the kitchen at that time?" Guillaume asked.

"Yes. I had to wait until Dr. Huvet arrived so he could give me the salve I use for the hives. By then I was very hungry, and it was after eleven when he finally left, and so I wanted to go to the kitchen to see La Marquite."

"And you were in the kitchen from some time after eleven until after midnight when Bacard appeared?"

Camilla's face pinkened a little. "I—I like to sit and talk with La Marquite. She reminds me of my nanny." She lifted her chin as if to challenge him to laugh.

Guillaume saw no reason to even crack a smile. "And so Bacard came to the kitchen as well, but you left shortly after he arrived? I understand Mlle Brosette was feeling ill as well."

"Yes, he said that's why he was there, in the kitchen. She was ill, and he—he wanted to give her some privacy. Why is this so important?"

"I am trying to ascertain when M. Bacard would have ingested the poison."

"Oh. Yes. Of course." Her eyes lifted to focus on him. "Lucie says you think someone here poisoned him."

He shrugged. "It's very possible. But perhaps not. Thus my very specific questions about times."

"Oh. Yes." She nodded, looking nervous again. "I was back in my suite at half past twelve.

"And did you see M. Bacard again?"

"No. I went to sleep. Early." She was still fidgeting. "The hives... they are uncomfortable, you see, and I hadn't slept all day before."

"Very well, Mlle Camille, that was very helpful. Can you tell me—just your opinion, please—who might have wanted to murder Paul Bacard?"

"Oh." She bit her lip, shifted, forced her hands to relax into her lap. "Well, I can't think of anyone. He's always quite nice, and very handsome. And he is jovial and makes witty jests. He doesn't seem to be the sort to make someone angry enough to kill him. He's—he was—a wonderful man."

"And Mlle Brosette...she was in a liaison with him. They were happy together? Or was it—ah, volatile?"

"Oh. Yes. I think they were happy together. But he still—well, I think he always had un petit faible for Lucie. It was she who introduced Paul to Hélène—and to Rose-Marie and me as well. We all met him at the same time. But it was Hélène who got to know him the best."

"But perhaps he was still infatuated with Mlle Lucie at that time. Do you think— Yes, I know this is a delicate question, mademoiselle, but murder is a business that knows no boundaries. Do you think Mlle Brosette is the jealous sort of woman?"

Camille tilted her head, then lifted her sharp, pointed nose, looking at him fully for the first time. "I think, monsieur, that if anyone stood in the way of something she wanted, Hélène would do whatever she thought necessary to remove them from her path."

"Including murder?"

She didn't respond, other than to look back down at the pillow she still nestled against her abdomen.

After a moment, he continued. "And is it possible that Mlle Brosette would have been jealous of Mlle Lucie-Geneviève, since she was the woman with whom M. Bacard had fallen in love first?"

"I think it is very possible, monsieur."

"But she and Mlle Lucie seem very close."

Camilla's lips tightened. "They are good friends, that is true. But that doesn't mean there isn't jealousy between them."

Guillaume couldn't argue with that. "Was it true that she and M. Bacard had been engaged to be married?"

Camilla's eyes narrowed. "That was what Hélène claimed. But I never heard Paul say anything to that matter."

"And, mademoiselle, one last question. What do you think would have happened if Mlle Brosette and M. Bacard had married and she left Château Lisette? How do you think Mlle Lucie would have reacted?"

"I think Lucie would have been secretly relieved for Hélène to move away," Camille said flatly. "She isn't a nice person. Hélène, I mean."

Guillaume stood, and smoothed his trousers so they fell properly in their British-style crease. "Thank you very much, mademoiselle. You've been extremely helpful. If you think of anything else I should know, I beg of you to contact me at la Sûreté."

"I will do that, monsieur." She swept out of the room, cool and elegant and lovely in her paleness.

He sat quietly and thought about the difference between the two interviews, the two perspectives on Hélène Brosette, Paul Bacard, and Lucie-Geneviève. There was one bit of information that seemed consistent between the two very different discussions: neither Rose-Marie nor Camille particularly cared for Hélène Brosette. It was far more obvious with Camille, of course, but he'd read the same sort of wariness from the cream puff.

And he found it quite interesting that all three women had been introduced to Paul Bacard on the same night—but Hélène Brosette, the woman who wanted to marry, had been the triumphant one when it came to getting—and keeping—his attention.

He checked his timepiece and saw that it was after four. He wanted to speak with Lucie-Geneviève again, but she wasn't expected until five. Houssaye could finish confirming with the housemaids, footmen, and the other two butlers the timeline that had already been established. While he was waiting for Mlle Lucie to return home, Guillaume had other people with whom he could speak. Including the blue-eyed Dr. Huvet.

Being a physician, Huvet might be able to shed some light on the subject of poisoning...as well as any other impressions about the four women in this household.

It wasn't difficult to obtain Dr. Émile Huvet's office address, but it was with uncharacteristic hesitation that Guillaume alighted from his horse-drawn taxi two blocks from the destination.

Interviewing witnesses, suspects, and persons of interest in murder cases was what he did every day. It was what he loved to do, despite the many drawbacks of such a profession. Yet he felt a lingering doubt as he paid the driver and glanced down the street.

Was he wasting his time by tracking down the physician? Perhaps he was merely manufacturing an excuse to see him again. Perhaps he'd imagined the lingering of Huvet's gaze when they said goodbye this morning. Had it been an invitation, that connected pause, or merely politeness?

Guillaume frowned, irritated with himself for wasting his brain cells with such thoughts. He had work to do, a case to solve, a murderer to capture. He didn't have time to wonder—and even if there *had* been something more in their silent exchange, he certainly dared not risk the chance of his private life being exposed. That was why, since Étienne, he'd confined himself to anonymous encounters with the likes of hotel waiters he met in cabarets...

Disgruntled, he brushed past a particularly determined boy who was selling bunches of lilies of the valley in honor of the laborers. It was the only day of the year the flowers—any flowers—were sold without tax, and the duty-free sale of the small, fragrant white blossoms had become a symbol over the last few years, representing the general workers and laborers of the city.

Further along the narrow sidewalk beyond the boy selling flowers was another youth, this one in front of a knife shop sandwiched between a milliner and an empty, dingy storefront. The boy was offering copies of the afternoon edition of *Le Petit Journal*. Grateful for an excuse to delay his visit, Guillaume stopped to buy a copy.

On the front page, halfway down, was the headline he'd expected, but hoped not, to see: *Who Killed the Bourbon Golden Boy?*

He sighed grimly. The headline was just above the fold, and the lede to the article announced that the wealthy young Paul Bacard had been found dead under mysterious circumstances in his taxi carriage this morning.

The ink smeared as his fingers curled into the paper, and Guillaume scanned the article to see what the press had gotten right, wrong, and—more importantly—what it had sensationalized. Though the story was brief and mostly true, its last lines left little hope for the story to fade.

Who administered the fatal dose? Could the femme La Balise have ushered her former flame into the afterlife? Or did M. Bacard have a secret worth killing for?

Two photographs accompanied the article, one of Bacard and one of La Balise, wearing a broad feathered hat and a seductive smile. Hers was the larger picture, of course, and the caption beneath the images read: *A former companion of La Balise, Paul Bacard had lately been seen on the arm of the younger, lovely Hélène Brosette. Could La Balise be the woman scorned?*

"Inspector?"

The surprised sound of his name jolted him from the newspaper, and Guillaume looked up to find himself face to face with Émile Huvet.

His eyes were as crystal blue as Guillaume remembered.

"M. Huvet." He succeeded in masking his own surprise. "What a happy coincidence. I was on my way to your address, and here you are. It appears you're returning to your office—perhaps you have a few moments between house calls?" He noticed the doctor was carrying the same sturdy medical bag and still wore the fine gray wool coat. It fit his shoulders perfectly.

"Of course I have a few moments for the good inspector. It's a bit of good luck that we met up here, otherwise you would've arrived at my office to find me absent—for I was on my way to a table at the café for a tardy luncheon—or perhaps I should call it a premature dinner. I admit, I have been racking my brain all day to see if there is anything I could tell you that might help in the investigation—being the regular visitor to Lisette that I am." He gestured for Guillaume to turn and walk with him. "I don't suppose you'd mind if we conduct our business over a glass of Bordeaux? Or coffee, if you prefer."

"A glass of something would be most welcome, and a bite to eat even more so," Guillaume replied with a smile that immediately felt too warm and eager for the business at hand. Guillaume sobered. He was merely relieved because he'd at last be able to have a decent meal.

"It's been a difficult day," said Huvet a few moments later, when they'd taken a seat at one of the cloth-covered tables at a small café three blocks from his office.

Their table was only a meter away from the broad, busy boulevard. Yet it was tucked next to a large potted boxwood that was as tall as Guillaume, offering a bit of privacy while still allowing them to watch the comings and goings on the boulevard.

"I still can hardly believe Paul Bacard is dead. And now it's in the press everywhere." The doctor shook his head and snapped his fingers at a white-aproned waiter who'd been hovering. He bolted over to their table like a gangly colt.

"Armagnac. A double, if you please." Huvet smiled wanly. "I hope you don't mind, monsieur, but I've decided the circumstances require something a bit stronger than a mere fermented grape."

"Make it two," Guillaume said. He'd sip slowly and make it last. He didn't like to drink when he was working a case, but, he told himself, it would make the interview feel more informal. And it had been a very long day, starting before dawn. Nevertheless, before the waiter went off, he pointed to an option on the dinner menu and asked for that to be brought as well. At least the bread and *charcuterie* would soak up the brandy.

"Thank you," said Huvet. He sounded weary. "I'm not feeling terribly hungry at the moment, but I'm sure when it arrives I'll remember I've missed breakfast and lunch." He fixed Guillaume with his gaze. "What can I do to help with the investigation? And please, monsieur, accept my apology for my accusations earlier today. I was shocked to hear about M. Bacard, and Mlle Lucie seemed so overset. It was obvious you hadn't been terrifying her in the least."

"But of course." Guillaume waved him off. "I have the sense Mlle Lucie is rather difficult to terrify anyway." The physician's sharp words had been nothing compared to the sort of fear and rudeness Guillaume often encountered when going about his job. No one liked homicide detectives. Hell, no one liked or trusted law enforcement of any kind. That mistrust dated back to the time of Napoleon Bonaparte, when the core responsibility of the police force was to spy on the French citizens.

Guillaume continued, "Right now I'm simply trying to build a timeline of where Bacard was all day and evening yesterday. I'm hopeful the pathologist will be able to determine what poison the victim ingested, and with that, along with the details of where he was and what he ate and drank, we can determine how it happened."

"Is there any chance it wasn't deliberate? That it was an accident?" asked Huvet. "I know everyone at Château Lisette, monsieur, and you must believe me when I tell you none of them, simply *none* of them, would have wanted to hurt M. Bacard. I know them as well as anyone, for they come to me with their most intimate and worrisome problems."

"It's always a possibility that it wasn't deliberate, that somehow Bacard took the poison accidentally. But even so, it's my job to determine how—if for no other reason so no one else is hurt or sickened."

The brandy arrived, and Guillaume tasted his. It was all he could do to keep from humming at the warm, smooth essence. Émile Huvet had excellent taste. Guillaume felt a little prickle of awareness, and looked up to find those blue eyes watching him.

"I trust you approve, monsieur?" Huvet lifted his own glass. "To the pleasures of distillation." When Huvet lowered his drink, he was smiling. "Mm. And I approve as well. Now, again, to business—I'm certain you have plenty to do, and the last thing I want to do is keep you from your work. Though I suppose you will need to wait for your meal, so at least I shall have your company for that long."

Guillaume had to sip again in order to hide his shock of awareness at the man's words. *Don't be an imbécile.* He set down his glass. "I understand you were at Château Lisette around the time Bacard arrived last night. Permit me to ask what you were doing there at such a late hour?"

"It was a late hour, indeed. But, you understand, I am a physician, and like yourself, *monsieur l'inspecteur,* every time I attempt to place myself on a regular schedule, I am circumvented by urgent summons. The ill—just like the dead—do not follow bankers' hours, do they?" Huvet lifted his glass again and drained it, then flicked his forefinger at the waiter.

He returned his attention to Guillaume. "As it happens, I make a visit to Lisette nearly every day. I... Ah." He stroked his mustache. "I hope you'll permit me to explain that many of my peers aren't willing to provide services to the ladies of...that sort of lifestyle. Regardless of their ability to pay. You comprehend what I am saying, *non?*" When Guillaume nodded, Huvet continued. "And so I have a great number of patients who would otherwise be left to their own devices—or at the hands of quacks."

"That's quite admirable of you, monsieur."

"How kind of you to say. The truth is, I've come to learn over the years that what many of my colleagues call female hysteria can be remedied not by a vibrating apparatus applied in the physician's office, but by other, more natural means. Therefore, I have made it a practice—while building my practice," he said, his smile quirking at the witticism, "to avoid judgment when it comes to the choices people make in their intimate lives. Thus, I have no argument with the choices made by the *Dégrafées.*"

Guillaume was taken far more off guard by the bluntness of this statement than he should have been as a man who'd worked in law enforcement for more than a dozen years, and who'd grown up in near poverty. It wasn't only the frankness of the man sitting across from him, but the fact that Guillaume found him incredibly attractive, both physically as well as intellectually. All from this brief conversation.

"However," Huvet went on with a more sober expression, "far more of my patients than those at Château Lisette not only have an inability to pay my fees, but also subsist in a more hand-to-mouth manner. And they often cannot get treatment even from the charitable hospitals. They live on the streets and are subjected to the most vulgar of lifestyles." His eyes flashed. "And so it's important for me to keep my wealthy patients happy, so that I can afford to treat the ones who cannot pay."

The waiter approached with their second round of drinks, and Huvet looked back at Guillaume after the young man left. He wore an abashed expression. "I apologize, monsieur, for my long speech. You're certainly not interested in my business practices, and I fear I've bored you with my diatribe. Please, let me return to answering your questions. You wished to know what time I was at Château Lisette last night."

Guillaume nodded.

"I did arrive rather later than I liked yesterday—perhaps it was just after ten o'clock—for Mlle Camille had contracted a rash on her neck and décolleté. You understand, inspector, that to a woman such as she, that is very nearly the death knell, a life-or-death situation—even if it was merely the result of a brush with fresh strawberries...which she'd forgotten were in the rhubarb tarts." His smile was warm and lingering, and Guillaume was once again struck by the pleasant shape of his lower lip.

"After I finished my business with Camille, I went on to the main wing and spoke with Lucie, who had just returned from dinner at Maxim's. She happened to be in no need of my services, but it was a courtesy, of course."

"Mlle Lucie was in residence? And what time was that, that you spoke to her? I confess, it surprises me that she would be home so early—considering what one reads in the papers."

"It was, perhaps, quarter past eleven that I spoke to her. Lucie spends more time at home than one might imagine. I often wonder if she purposely feeds the press information so she appears busier than she truly is. I found her playing chess with Aloysius."

"Aloysius?"

The *charcuterie* had arrived, and it looked delicious, accompanied as it was by small tomatoes, stemmed capers the size of blueberries, and radishes. Guillaume selected a piece of prosciutto and slathered spicy mustard over it and a hunk of baguette.

"Ah, of course," replied Huvet, plucking a caper from the plate and slipping it into his mouth. "Aloysius is Lucie's— Please excuse the informality, monsieur; sometimes the constant use of titles can be so inefficient. He's Lucie's brother. Half-brother, actually. They shared a father, who was a ship's captain—but don't tell Lucie I told you that. She prefers to maintain a sense of mystery about her background." He grinned. "Aloysius is Moroccan, and is as big as a house, with skin dark as black coffee." The doctor said this with a subtle relish that made Guillaume look up to see whether he'd read him properly.

He was beginning to think he had.

He was also grateful for the doctor's continued loquaciousness, for it gave him the opportunity to have a few bites and take away the gnawing edge in his belly.

"After I spoke with Lucie and Aloysius, I went to Hélène's wing to make certain she wasn't in need of me. That must have been nearly half past eleven. Bacard wasn't there yet. Hélène was bathing, and so I went to visit La Marquite in the kitchen." Huvet grinned broadly. "If you have any reason to return to Château Lisette, Inspector Guillaume, I encourage you to create an excuse to try one of her basil biscuits drizzled with lavender honey. You'll believe you had *la petite mort* right there in the kitchen!"

Guillaume had been reaching for a tomato, but when he looked up, Huvet was involved with selecting a piece of cheese to go with the baguette in his hand.

"Did you see M. Bacard when you were in the kitchen? I understand he had a fondness for La Marquite's cooking as well," Guillaume said.

"No, I didn't see Bacard at all. Camille was sitting with La Marquite when I came in to beg a basil biscuit for myself, and then I took my leave." Huvet sobered, spreading mustard on his bread. "It's a tragedy about Bacard. The man was a remarkably pleasant and charming individual."

"So I'm told." Over and over. It really did make one wonder.

"I—" Huvet stopped sharply. He made a dismissive gesture and reapplied himself to the mustard. But he wore a faint frown that intrigued Guillaume.

"Were you about to say something, monsieur?"

Huvet sighed and rested his elegant wrists on the edge of the table. "I don't know. I just... Well, you understand, it's just an impression. I don't wish to cause problems for Hélène."

Guillaume narrowed his gaze, all thoughts of flirtation evaporating. "Mlle Brosette? What is it, this impression of yours?"

The other man hesitated, looking off into the distance. "As I said, I don't wish to cause problems, and it's only an impression, but I suppose it's your job, monsieur, to make a picture of all these puzzle pieces, *nest-ce pas*? Even if they seem random to one like me."

"Go on. You're correct—something seemingly unimportant to you might be very important to the investigation. Please."

"Very well. You have been warned." Huvet's smile was laced with chagrin. "I got the impression—and I can't quite tell you how or why, though I'm racking my brain to figure it out—that it was Hélène's desire that she and Bacard should marry. She seemed rather desperate to make it happen."

Guillaume nodded for his companion to go on, declining to mention that Hélène seemed to have gotten her wish—at least, until Bacard had died.

"As I said, it's an impression. And I don't see how it plays into the situation anyway—why would Hélène have a reason to poison the man she hoped to marry?" Huvet paused, another caper halfway to his mouth. "Unless... No, no...there's been no gossip from the servants that their liaison was in question. No arguments overheard, no tears." He shook his head, smiling. "Now I see the attraction for the profession of detective. One can create theories and scenarios all day long."

So Huvet was suggesting—in his polite, very subtle way—that perhaps Hélène Brosette could be the woman scorned? The man certainly knew the players in this situation better than he did. And Mlle Brosette would have ample opportunity to poison her lover.

Both Rose-Marie and Camille had implied that Bacard never stopped loving Lucie-Geneviève. Even Pierre Lansac had given off that impression, as much as he seemed to despise La Balise.

And then there was the fact that neither of Bacard's two closest friends seemed to know about the man's purported engagement to Mlle Brosette.

Could the engagement have been a lie, made up by Hélène Brosette? But to what purpose, now that Bacard was dead?

Still. Something didn't feel quite right. The young woman had seemed genuinely grief-stricken this morning upon learning the news about Bacard. Yet Guillaume knew better than to discount any possibility at this early stage. He checked his pocket watch and was dismayed to see the lateness of the hour. After six already. He wanted to go back to the morgue and bully Jackson a bit before the man left for the night, but he might have already gone. Pathologists did not keep the hours of a *flâneur*.

And he must hurry if he was going to catch Lucie-Geneviève before she left for her evening's engagement.

He folded his napkin and placed it on the table. "Thank you very much for your time. I appreciate your candor, M. Huvet. And you can be assured I'll be extremely circumspect with my investigation going forward."

"Monsieur? Is it still monsieur even after we've shared a meal, then, Inspector Devré?"

Once again, he felt a little jolt of awareness, a little spark of possibility. But he quickly suffocated it, despite the warmth in Huvet's eyes and the slight smile curving his lips.

Investigating that possibility was a risk Guillaume dared not take.

EIGHT

L a Balise! Look here!"
    "Mlle Lucie! Mlle Lucie!"
  "Lucie-Geneviève! Over here!"
  "Here! Over here! Give us a smile, *ma chérie!*"

Small explosions popped from the camera trays, blinding Lucie as she approached the moving sidewalk—one of the most popular features at l'Exposition Universelle. She was already smiling, looking toward the sea of reporters with eyes that watered, but could discern nothing but vague shadows and flashes of light.

"Mlle Lucie," murmured a porter near her ear as a steadying arm directed her onto the softly rumbling platform. "If you would, please step to the right, and now a bit down... Yes, here we are."

She had a moment of irritation laced with worry that Aloysius wasn't the one guiding her into place, as he most often was when she went out without one of her gentlemen friends. After she returned from her visit to the morgue and the curmudgeonly Dr. Jackson, her half-brother had taken her to visit Onni's grave and then to afternoon Mass at Ste-Berthilde's. Immediately after they returned to Château Lisette, Aloysius had gone out again. He hadn't returned by the time she was ready to leave for the evening.

The visit to the morgue had been enlightening, to say the least. The worst information she'd gleaned was that Paul Bacard had

105

most likely been poisoned at Château Lisette. The most confusing information was the semen stain on the side of his shirt—whether it meant what she thought it meant, or whether he'd merely been clumsy while he and Hélène had been intimate. But had they even been intimate? Hélène said she'd been ill and indisposed.

Was there any chance Hélène could have accidentally poisoned Paul? Lucie couldn't imagine that her friend would have purposely done so. That these very thoughts were racing through her mind made Lucie alternately ill at heart and ashamed that she should even contemplate them.

Her foot touched the ground and she felt the slow slide of the remarkable moving sidewalk as she lowered her other foot onto the wooden platform. Still partially blinded, still bathed in the incessant photographic flashes, she lifted her face as if to look out toward the towers, arches, minarets, and facades of the World Expo, though she could see little of their detail. Fortunately, this wasn't her first visit to the two-week-old exposition, and so at least she knew what it was she was supposed to be looking at.

Additionally, Lucie was fully aware of the image she herself made, with her bronze-honey-copper hair in its ornate figure eights and small whorls at the back of her head, spiked with a spray of delicate emerald, black, and gold feathers. The feathers were held in place by two large combs created by Lalique, studded with glittering emeralds and topazes (a recent gift from the Comte de Chambrun, to the dismay of the attentive Vicomte Fouquier), with a large matching brooch that closed the cape of gold-spun fabric whispering over her shoulders. Lucie knew that her regal pose, with the wasplike shape of her corseted silhouette and its prominent bustle at the base of her spine, made her appear like an untouchable goddess, a "beacon" of femininity. The epitome of Parisian fashion, culture, and beauty.

"La Balise! Is that Lalique in your hair?"

"I don't believe M. Lalique would deign to sit among feathers and curls, but his work looks quite fine there indeed, *n'êtes-vous pas d'accord?*" she teased the unseen reporter. Had that been Franco? She rather enjoyed his pieces in the papers. Her eyes were beginning to recover, partly because the rhythm of flashes had slowed as the sidewalk carried her along slowly.

She allowed the press these moments—even cultivated them, carefully arranging opportunities for photographs without appearing to do so—because such was her position in society. Her role, her life, was one of a public figure: a magnet for scandal-mongering and gossip, an expression of culture, a fascination to the news-hungry Parisian—and a fantasy for men (to have) and women (to copy) alike.

Lucie-Geneviève had made a deliberate choice to embrace this notoriety, for such notoriety (however short-lived it might be) led to wealth, and wealth created power, and power meant she would never be owned or managed or controlled by a man—or by anyone—ever again.

No matter the cost—and the price was much higher and more desperate than she'd ever imagined when she and Onni had dreamt about such a life—she would protect herself and that which belonged to her.

Thus, though today the papers had trumpeted *La Balise Dodges Vodka Bottle in Fight at Maxim's*, tomorrow they would read *La Balise Enjoys Moving Sidewalk* or *La Balise Graces the Expo!* or other such headlines—and she would be grateful for them.

Yet even as she smiled and waved to the crowd who'd gathered to ogle La Balise, the woman who was merely Ginny in her own mind was acutely aware of how quickly the fame could turn on her. The press had only become more ravenous and scandal-driven in the last twenty years since the abolishment of the French government's censorship laws, and the more horrifying and graphic the story, or the more scandalous the topic, the more the papers became like vultures...or bulldogs with bones, like Inspector Devré was turning out to be.

She desperately hoped the front pages wouldn't soon bray something more along the lines of *La Balise Arrested for Murder!*

But considering her second, recent encounter with Inspector Devré—whose personality she no longer found quite so amusing or delightful—Lucie feared it was all too likely such a headline would become reality. She feared he was nearly ready to arrest her for a murder she didn't commit, simply so he could close the case.

And she could not tolerate the authorities sniffing around her for any reason, for surely it would lead to a look into her background and history.

On top of everything else, Inspector Devré's unexpected arrival at half past six had nearly made her late for tonight's engagement, for he'd presented himself at Château Lisette in the midst of her preparations. Then he'd refused to leave until she agreed to see him.

Fearing he *would* arrest her, or take her down to la Sûreté as he'd threatened to do to Hélène, Lucie sent word via her footman that she would not leave her dressing chamber. Devré must come to her if he wanted to speak with her.

He did, seemingly without hesitation, despite finding her barely finished having her corset laced (the most excruciating moment of a lady's *toilette*), and wearing little else. He didn't flicker an eyelash at her *déshabillé* and instead took a seat directly next to all the clothing—lacy, silky, frivolous undergarments and a gown by the Worth brothers with trimmings that cost more than he made in a month—that was laid out on the valet stand.

And even in the midst of her dressing room, with its vast array of feminine accoutrements, and shelves, drawers, and cubicles, plus a wardrobe the size of a small cottage, Devré appeared fully at ease. He was wholly uninterested in the process of dressing the most celebrated woman in the city.

He had more questions about Paul Bacard...no, that wasn't precisely true. Many of them weren't questions at all, but statements and accusations clearly meant to upset her. His tone was pointed and cool, and his assumptions were unsettling.

"I understand you and Bacard were close enough only some months ago," he said smoothly, "that you wanted to marry him. But now suddenly, he has asked Mlle Brosette to be his wife. How difficult that must have been for you, Mlle Lucie, to have lost the man you loved to a younger, more vibrant woman."

"Who told you I wanted to marry Paul Bacard?" Lucie paused in applying a light touch of blackening to her eyelashes. She was grateful Piquette had momentarily left the chamber to iron her gloves. And *where* was Aloysius? She'd sent for him as soon as Devré had been announced, counting on her half-brother to help buffer the situation.

"His friends, Messrs Lansac and Druot," Devré replied, his tigerish eyes watching hers in the mirror. They looked at her not in an appreciative manner, but in a predatory way—and not as one who wished to win her, but one who wished to entrap her.

"Ah, I see. Well, allow me to disabuse you of that notion, Inspector Devré. Although Paul Bacard and I socialized—"

"And surely were intimate," he said, casting his eyes deliberately toward her "public" bedchamber door. It gapped open enough to reveal the lush, fussy midnight-blue and aubergine curtains and wallpaper. Her private bedroom, the *suite privée* that one no one entered but herself and the servants, was stunningly different in decor.

"Whether I was intimate with him or not has no bearing on the fact that I never had any desire to marry Paul Bacard—and to be clear, I have no desire to ever marry ag—*ever*." Lucie caught herself in the nick of time and hoped Devré hadn't noticed her slip. "I will never marry."

"Again?" His gaze narrowed on her. "You'll never marry again... is that what you were about to say?" His voice was smooth, yet it sent prickles over her bare shoulders.

She kept her face bland. That might have been a costly mistake, but he didn't need to know it.

"*I will never marry.*" Lucie turned from the mirror and held his stare with hers, knowing how cold and glasslike her green eyes could become when angry. "And I did not kill Paul Bacard. You are rooting around the wrong tree, Devré, and I will thank you to leave me to finish my *toilette*."

"And what venue is the great Balise going to illuminate this evening?" he said, standing politely.

She considered ignoring him, but in the end decided it was best to remain civil. "L'Exposition."

"Indeed? But is it not rather tardy of you to just be making an appearance—the front gates have been open for two weeks already. *Tsk, tsk,* mademoiselle."

She gave him an arch smile. "But of course it's not my first visit, inspector. I was invited to the private grand opening by President Loubet. And I also attended as the guest of the Comte de Chambrun."

"Ah, of course. How foolish of me." He started for the door, then paused and removed a hand from his pocket. "I wanted to comment on the uniqueness of this particular rose—I've never seen one of this shade before. Such an unusual shade of violet turning to pink, and with delicate white tips. You had a vase of them in your parlor. But even I know it's too early for roses—where do you get them?"

Lucie glanced at the crumpled flower he held, and the back of her shoulders prickled unpleasantly. "They grow here, in the small greenhouse in the courtyard. You've not seen it before because it's a special variety, created for me by M. Gravereaux. He and I are the only ones with that bush—and his is at his gardens in L'Haÿ. I can only imagine how you obtained that blossom."

"Never fear that I disrupted the arrangement in your parlor due to my curiosity, mademoiselle. This particular flower I discovered elsewhere. In the pocket of M. Bacard." He tucked it back into his own pocket with an air of nonchalance that was belied by his last words. "One can only imagine how it came to be in his coat. Especially when this specimen of flower is only found in the possession of a woman who claims she didn't know he was present at her home last night."

Lucie wondered whether the rice powder she'd applied would hide the fact that her face paled. How on earth had that flower gotten into Bacard's coat?

"Inspector Devré, I did not kill Paul Bacard. I don't know how many times or ways I must tell you, but it's true. If you truly want justice, and to find the real murderer, I suggest you stop trying to build up a fantastical case against me and look for someone who had a *reason* to kill him—and the opportunity to do so. I had neither."

"So you've stated, mademoiselle. But the case against you is compelling, and continues to become even more so." He actually sounded regretful, which irritated Lucie even more.

"That may be the case, but I suggest you take a closer look at M. Lansac and find out what was in the tiny blue bottle he had in his possession last night at Maxim's."

That, she saw with satisfaction, made the inspector's eyes flicker with interest. "So that's what your clever fingers lifted from his pocket. Yes, yes, I heard about the incident. Are you suggesting there was poison in this little blue bottle?"

"I'm suggesting you find out why M. Lansac was so furious when he saw that I'd...discovered it."

"Discovered. Is that how you describe it?" His lips stretched into a smile beneath his luxurious mustache, and his eyes glinted. "One wonders how long, and in what capacity, you've been 'discovering' objects in pockets."

"And that is something that must remain untold, monsieur. A woman must have her secrets." Lucie stood and gestured to the door. She considered telling him what she'd learned at the morgue, but suspected he wouldn't be pleased she'd been snooping around. And he'd learn soon enough anyway. "And now I bid you good evening, inspector. I have a *toilette* to complete."

It was more than thirty minutes after Devré left before Lucie was finally able to put the conversation from her mind—and she realized with an unpleasant shock that Aloysius still had not responded to her summons.

That was very strange—unless he'd gone out, but surely someone would have told her he wasn't around to be found.

What if Aloysius had been poisoned?

What if whoever—or however—Paul had been poisoned did it again?

Terror rushed through her, and Lucie surged to her feet, knocking away Piquette's hands. "Miss Lucie?"

"It's all right, Piquette. But I must find Aloysius." She rang for Stanton and Madame Frousand and, unwilling to wait, started out of her dressing room into the middle parlor.

"Where's Aloysius?" she demanded of her butler when he came into view wearing a startled expression. He must have just returned from seeing Inspector Devré to the door, for Stanton was looking in askance at her half-dressed person. "Have you seen him? Do you know where he is?" Without waiting for a reply, she rang the bells for the footman and the groom as well.

"I believe he went out, mademoiselle," replied Stanton. "Just before the inspector arrived."

So he was definitely gone. Not lying in agony somewhere. Lucie frowned, then immediately smoothed out her features; wrinkles, and besides, she didn't want the servants to recognize her consternation. She trusted all of them...but there was a poisoner in her home. She was becoming more and more certain of that ugly reality—especially with Devré's latest announcement about the rose still ringing in her ears.

"Thank you, Stanton. I don't know why I didn't ask you first."

"It's my fault, Miss Lucie. I was attending to the inventory in the wine cellar, and left Michel in charge. I neglected to mention that Mr. Aloysius had left."

She turned to make her way back to the dressing room, her mind a riot of thoughts.

Had Aloysius left because of the inspector's arrival, or had he simply been on his way out? But why would he leave her at the man's mercy if he knew the detective was here? And where would he have been going at five o'clock in the afternoon?

Those thoughts—and others—sat like heavy, sticky mud in her mind a short time later as she rode in her landau from Château Lisette to the expo's entrance.

"Lucie! La Balise!" A particularly urgent voice drew her attention from her anxious thoughts, bringing her sharply back to the sea of reporters.

She looked over and saw a slender figure holding a notepad and brandishing a pencil. The reporter was dressed in baggy trousers and a simple white shirt striped with suspenders. A single lock of light brown hair—too long to be that of a man—had fallen from the cap she wore. It was the same reporter who'd been at Maxim's last night, blast it. She'd narrowly missed being hit by the wild vodka bottle. But hers was a new face—one Lucie hadn't encountered before last night.

"La Balise," shouted the reporter. "What happened to Paul Bacard?"

Lucie barely managed to control her reaction as a rumble of interest and surprise rippled through the crowd. Already? Already the press was sniffing around?

"Is it true he was at Château Lisette when he died?" demanded the female reporter over a rush of other questions as her peers took the bait.

"M. Bacard is a dear friend, and I will miss his company," Lucie replied.

"Is it true he was poisoned?"

"That you will have to ask Inspector Guillaume Devré of la Sûreté," Lucie informed them with heartfelt relish. "I'm certain he will be most pleased to answer your questions." She gave one last wave, and turned to go into the gallery.

"And what about Pierre Lansac?" cried the reporter. "You were in an altercation with him last night."

Lucie paused. Something in the reporter's tone bothered her. "What about Pierre Lansac?" she asked, turning back slowly.

"But you haven't heard? You do not know? Pierre Lansac is dead! They have just found him in his rooms at the hotel."

NINE

Pierre Lansac's body had been found hanging in the boudoir of his hotel suite. It had taken more than an hour for Guillaume to be located and called to the scene, but to his surprise and relief, when he arrived, Jackson was already there.

Ah, bien. The constables were learning: if it was a case for Guillaume Devré, M. Thomas Jackson—and no one else—was to be called in as medico-legist. Excellent.

Now if Guillaume could just impress upon his junior colleagues to provide him with a cup of coffee and a croissant when they summoned him to a crime scene before dawn...

Nevertheless, it wasn't dawn now, but it was after nine o'clock in the evening. Less than twenty-four hours since Paul Bacard's body had been found, and now one of his closest friends and former business associates was dead.

By all appearances, the man had hung himself with a drapery cord. Yet as Guillaume pushed his way past the two constables stationed at the door to the hotel rooms, he cleared his mind of any assumptions. Three times during his career he had been called to a scene of apparent suicide only to realize that in two instances the death had, in fact, been murder...and nothing but an unfortunate accident in another.

114

The reminder of the Guilles accidental death case also brought with it the memory of Étienne, and Guillaume thrust both thoughts away so he could focus on the matter at hand.

The body was still hanging from the chandelier fixture overhead (Guillaume took a moment to admire the quality and stability of the hotel's lighting), but Jackson had just commanded in his flat, imperfect French for Lansac to be lowered to the floor.

"No reason to keep him dangling," said the doctor, moving forward to assist Houssaye with the delicate task. The familiar underscore of cinnamon and clove followed Jackson, and as usual, his hair and clothing—sans both tie and hat—looked as if he'd just rolled out of bed. That was an image Guillaume also nudged away as he commenced exploring the chamber and its contents, confident his colleague would complete a thorough examination of the body whilst he attended to the rest.

His first impression was that these were the private rooms of a well-off young man with barely passable taste, and furnished with heavy furniture draped in cotton, linen, and even silk. Fine clothing from Poiret hung in a wardrobe whose doors gaped wide, and several discarded neck and bow ties were slung over the back of a chair. A pile of evening clothing that stank of cigar smoke and spirits lay nearby. The wooden valet stand stood naked but for a dressing robe carelessly slung over one arm.

There was no art on the walls to speak of—unless one considered the half-dozen playbills pinned to the wall, from places such as the Moulin Rouge and the now defunct Le Chat Noir, to be art.

There was, however, a note on the escritoire. Its writing implement, a pencil nub, lay to the left of it. Scrawled on a torn scrap of the hotel's stationary it said merely: *Forgive me.* –PL

As suicide notes went, it wasn't wholly convincing in its authenticity, but nor was Guillaume about to dismiss it. Once the photographs of the scene were taken, he'd slide the paper into one of his ever-present cream evidence envelopes and take it back for closer examination.

He withdrew a long pair of tweezers and used the metal implement to poke around the rest of the desktop without disturbing the way the papers were arranged. Inside the drawers, he discovered a few more scrawled notes—at first glance, the handwriting appeared similar to the "Forgive me" note—along with a calling card for one Mlle Batiste that had been liberally doused with expensive perfume, and several invitations to dinner parties and soirees from names familiar to Guillaume from business and high-society articles in the newspapers.

And a lot of bills. Some were third, fourth, even fifth notices, dated within the last six months. It wasn't, Guillaume had come to understand, unusual for le gratin to receive dunning notices and demands for payment—the class as a whole, though readily able to afford the luxuries they purchased, was nevertheless reluctant to actually part with the funds when required to do so—but even so, the number of bills was excessive. And the amounts...

Guillaume shook his head at the hedonism of the rich, and continued his investigation. He searched the pockets of the crumpled evening coat that reeked of last night's pleasures, suspecting the jacket was from last night, for it was the only one not hung up. Apparently, Lansac's valet had either not been in the room recently, or he'd still been wearing the coat when he last was. The large stain on the front—from the bottle of vodka that had been broken at the restaurant?—bore out Devré's supposition.

Yet there was little of immediate interest in the pockets—an outrageous receipt from Maxim's dated yesterday (yet not as high a sum as Bacard's had been), a small wad of francs, another calling card, and, the most interesting item of all: what appeared to be the cap to a tiny bottle...but the vessel, whatever it might be, was absent.

The blue bottle Lucie-Geneviève had removed from the dead man's pocket?

Guillaume sniffed lightly, then moistened the tip of his finger and dipped it into the underside of the cap to sample any hint of the bottle's contents still clinging to it. There was nothing but a faint astringency.

He turned from the rumpled clothing, moving next to make a close examination of Lansac's dressing table as he asked, "Docteur, do you have an estimate of the time of death?" He looked over at the pathologist, who was crouched on long, awkward legs next to the victim. One of his cathedral-sized feet was angled out like a pigeon's. Its well-worn shoe didn't seem to be acquainted with shoe polish. "And the cause?"

"Asphyxiation, obviously," Jackson replied impatiently as he eased the cord from around Lansac's neck.

"But obvious is not always the right of it," Guillaume said, and earned a quick glance and acknowledging nod from the pathologist.

"Yes, yes, but today the obvious assumption wins. See the finger marks at his throat? He changed his mind...but it was too late." His voice was grim. "He's been dead five hours, perhaps six." With that, Jackson rose to his feet, neglecting to smooth his rumpled coat. Guillaume had to resist the urge to do it for him, for the way it gapped in front offended his sense of order. Of course, with it being Jackson, it was admirable that he'd even remembered to put on his coat. "Time of death—this afternoon. Four o'clock, five o'clock."

"I interviewed him shortly after noon, and he had just been rousted from bed," Guillaume commented as he looking at the clutter of items on the dressing table. There was no sign of the bottle that fit the small cap, and though it wasn't necessarily important, it niggled at him. Why keep the cap but not the bottle?

"But—mademoiselle, *please*—you cannot—"

A frantic voice in the chamber beyond drew Devré's attention just as Mme Lucie-Geneviève Madeleine appeared in the doorway. One of the constables hovered behind her, literally wringing his hands, as if loath to put them on her esteemed person, yet fully cognizant of the breach of security he'd just allowed. In the distance, from below, were the sounds of more voices and other mild disturbance.

Mlle Lucie's gaze flitted from the body on the floor up to the crooked chandelier, then flashed to Jackson, and finally to Guillaume himself—where her attention remained.

"Ah, Mlle Lucie," he said in a gallant voice that was nevertheless lined with the steel of admonishment. "What is it that brings you here? I was under the impression you and M. Lansac— Well, there was no love lost between the two of you."

He could have been strict and autocratic, banning her from the scene immediately, esteemed personage or no. It was his right, and was probably what most detectives would have done...but Guillaume was much more interested in her actions and purpose for being there than to use his authority to bully her out of the way.

Had it been the founder of la Sûreté, the famous criminal-turned-detective M. Vidocq, who first claimed the culprit always returned to the scene of the crime? *Précisément*...and perhaps here she was, making that suggestive appearance.

And what the devil was going on downstairs? It sounded as if an army was arriving.

"I heard the tragic news," Mlle Lucie said, stepping uninvited into the chamber. The tips of the black feathers that arched high over her elegant hat brushed the top of the doorway.

If she was surprised to see that Guillaume was present, the *cocotte* gave no indication. "Under the circumstances, I thought it wouldn't be inappropriate to pay a visit." Her jade eyes met and held his without a hint of artifice or abashment.

If he had thought La Balise stunning in her artful *déshabillé* at dawn today, or during her *toilette*, which he'd grandly interrupted earlier this evening, he had sadly underestimated her capacity for powerful beauty. For this woman, fully cloaked in all manner of feminine armor, was womanly perfection. Even Guillaume, who had never felt even the slightest stir of lust at a woman's form, was very nearly entranced by her.

It wasn't merely that her figure and clothing were exquisite—yet he must acknowledge that they were works of art: the sea-foam-green evening gown fitted to those magnificent curves dripped with lace, ribbons, and beads; the elegance of her hat, with its graceful feathers and fronds; the whisper-thin golden cape she'd thrown back to reveal creamy white shoulders and a generous swath of bosom. But more than that, her power and potency was in the way she carried herself. She burned with a glow that seemed to emanate from deep inside, mingling with the essence of her exotic scent, and the command and confidence inherent in her every movement and word.

It was no wonder the constables hadn't had the wherewithal or the desire to stop her entering. They'd likely been stunned into paralysis by the woman. But though appreciative of the sight, Guillaume was neither struck dumb nor paralyzed.

"And precisely which circumstances are those, mademoiselle?" he asked.

She gave him a modest smile, but that didn't cease her continued observation of the chamber as she stepped further inside. He followed her gaze. Was she looking for something?

Mlle Lucie continued in her throaty voice, "Surely it hasn't escaped your notice that two of the three young men with whom I dined last night are now dead, *monsieur l'inspecteur.* I assumed you'd wish to speak with me about *those* circumstances."

Guillaume nearly grinned at her cheekiness, then became sober. She might try and distract him with her wit, but this was, after all, death—and quite possibly murder. He found little to jest about when standing over the form of a corpse. The timing was simply too coincidental. "How kind of you to oblige, mademoiselle."

"Think nothing of it." She'd angled closer to Lansac's body under the guise of conversing with Guillaume. "I was about to enter l'Exposition when a reporter arrived with the terrible news. Somehow I was certain I'd find you here. At least if I came to you, you wouldn't feel the need to find your way to my dressing room again, interrupt my *toilette*, and upset my entire household."

Ah. A bit of steel had crept into her voice.

Jackson, who'd continued his examination unabated, seemed to notice Mlle Lucie for the first time as her beaded and ruffled hem came into view next to him. He squinted up at her. "If you would keep back, *madame*," he snarled, then proceeded to finish unfastening Lansac's shirt cuffs to check the man's wrists.

"As grateful as I might be for your efforts, Mlle Lucie," said Guillaume, "I must decline the chance to interview you just now. As you can see, I'm rather preoccupied at the moment—and you... Well, it appears this tragedy has interrupted your evening's social engagement."

"A tragedy, *bien sûr*. Even more so that he seems to have taken his own life." Might there be a hint of relief in her voice? Had she, like Guillaume, expected something more sinister?

Still looking down at the body, she made the sign of the cross and murmured something, then looked up at Guillaume.

"No final conclusions have been drawn," he heard himself say—then was exasperated that he'd even responded to her implicit question.

"But how else could it have happened? There is the cord still hanging from the chandelier where he has now been cut down, and there are marks on his neck from his fingers, trying to pull it away at the last moment..." She gave a little shudder that struck him with its sincerity. "And even there—on the bureau. His footprints, made with perspiring feet, from where he stood before he jumped off."

Mlle Lucie looked up at him, but there was no sign of triumph in her eyes as she ticked off all of the information he'd already collected—including the fact that the dresser had been moved slightly away from the wall on one side so as to be in the best position.

"Aside from all of that, how very difficult it would have been to fake such a death—lifting him either alive or dead to such a height. Such a pity that he should have done it to himself," she continued.

Guillaume had no choice but to acknowledge her conclusions. "But the question is, why should he have done so? Since you are here nosing about my investigation, perhaps you have a theory, mademoiselle?"

"He was an unhappy man, I think, and seemed particularly tense last night. But I don't know what specifically would drive him to this irreversible action." Now she was searching the room without appearing to do so—her eyes wandering over the escritoire, the bureau, the bed and bedside table—until they stopped, focusing on a corner of the chamber Guillaume hadn't yet reached during his close examination. She made a satisfied sound and pursed her lips.

To his mild surprise, Lucie made no attempt to hide her discovery, but immediately made her way to whatever had caught her interest. Using the wall as a support, she lowered herself gingerly into a crouch, reminding Guillaume how restricted she must be, strapped into the wasp-shaped corset that gave her such a fashionable figure. It was a wonder the woman could draw in a breath, let alone move—and bending at the waist or twisting her torso seemed very nearly impossible.

He spared her vanity a moment of sympathy, moving to her side to assist. "You've found something?"

"Yes." The single syllable was breathless, and she gratefully took the hand he offered. "I cannot— Blast this damned body cage," she muttered, the words belabored, as he helped her to her feet. "I swear, I shall murder the man who invented it."

"Are you so certain it was a man?" inquired Guillaume dryly, choosing to ignore the fact that his favorite suspect had just announced a murderous intention in favor of repartee.

"No woman would have created such an atrocity." She held a hand in the vicinity of her diaphragm as she attempted to catch her breath. "If I had known I'd be at a crime scene, I wouldn't have had Piquette lace me so damned tightly," she added from between gritted teeth. "As it was, I expected to be upright and on display all of the evening," she admitted ruefully. "Inspector, if you please—you might find those shards of blue glass of interest."

But Guillaume had already noticed what appeared to be a small blue bottle—one that could very possibly be the mate of the tiny cap he'd discovered—now shattered on the floor. There was a small dent in the wall above it, and he felt certain that when he employed his magnifying glass, he'd discover slivers of blue glass embedded in the plaster wall.

"Ah. The mysterious blue bottle." Taking care of its sharp edge, he picked up the largest piece, which, fortunately, was the bottom third of the tiny bottle, and sniffed.

He got more of the sharp, pungent scent he'd noticed on the cap, but much stronger now. Still, he couldn't identify it, and once more he gingerly used a finger to swipe the dregs collected therein. Its taste was sharp and bitter. The contents weren't heroin, cocaine, or opium—none of which any more illegal than spirits—or pornography, for that matter—but nor did it appear to be any sort of grooming or beauty aid. Not obviously cologne or hair balm, especially not in such a small vial.

He found all of this both curious and suspicious. Why would a man have such an item in his evening coat pocket?

And why would he have thrown it against the wall and then hung himself...if indeed that was what had happened. Though Guillaume tended to agree that was precisely what had occurred.

"Can you tell what was in it?" Lucie asked, blatantly avoiding his question.

"Though you expected to find it here, you don't know what it is?"

She shook her head. "As I told you, it was in Lansac's pocket last night, and he was quite furious when I—er, discovered it. I thought... Well, I'm certain under the circumstances of Paul Bacard's death, you know what I was thinking, inspector."

Guillaume nodded thoughtfully. Either she was more clever and manipulative than he'd believed and meant to send him off on a tangent, or she was telling the truth and genuinely wanted to know about the bottle.

"What do you think of this, Thomas?" He offered the chunk of glass to Jackson.

The pathologist, who'd just risen to his feet, sniffed, tasted, and rubbed a bit of the essence between his fingers just as Guillaume had done. "Nothing yet. Nothing obvious." His thick, dark brows drew together, and he held the bottle up to the light, squinting at it as he turned it in his fingers. "I'll take it to the lab."

He didn't make it a request, or even wait for permission. Manners and finesse were entirely lost on Americans.

Mlle Lucie held out her gloved hand. "May I?"

Jackson looked at her as if startled to find someone else in the chamber, then relinquished the piece of bottle. She sniffed but declined to taste, then handed it back to the doctor.

"I thought perhaps it might be a gentleman's cologne, but it's certainly not pleasant smelling enough to—"

"Do you have any idea what you're doing to your organs?" he growled, appearing to actually see her for the first time. His attention was focused on her unnaturally tiny waist. "Bound up in that contraption? It's a wonder you can even take a damned breath, let alone move. Damned fool females."

Mlle Lucie blinked in astonishment. "I assure you, I'm—"

"Inspector Devré."

Guillaume turned at the sound of the urgent voice, and saw one of the uniformed officers in the doorway looking harassed. "What is it, constable?"

"The press, monsieur. Reporters, a dozen of them—they are demanding to come up. We're only two of us at the top of the stairs and having a difficult time holding them off. They're in the lobby and trying to take over the elevator, and the manager is about to tear out his hair." Even as he said this, Guillaume heard the sound of pounding footsteps approaching down the hotel corridor.

"The press? How did they come to know about this so quickly? And why so many of them?"

"I'm afraid the blame—for that, at least—lies with me."

Guillaume turned back to Lucie, whose expression had settled into one of resignation. "Ah. Of course. Your band of admirers." He'd predicted this, hadn't he? A damned circus, with La Balise the ringmaster. *God help me.*

"I'll give them a statement," he said to the constable, and prepared to have words with the reporters.

But Mlle Lucie stopped him with a hand on the arm. "They're here for me, monsieur. If I go, they'll follow. Well, most of them, anyway."

He hesitated, then nodded. "Very well."

"Then I do have your permission to leave, inspector?" she asked, a little smile flickering at the corners of her lips.

"Go on with your evening of being upright and on display," he said, suddenly feeling surprisingly agreeable. "And I am grateful, mademoiselle, for your information about the blue bottle."

"And *I* would be grateful," she said, looking over her shoulder as she swept toward the door, "if you would refrain from invading my dressing room in the future. And preferably my household."

"That, mademoiselle, is something to which I'm afraid I cannot commit—at least as long as Paul Bacard's murder remains unsolved."

Her expression turned hard. "Then, *monsieur l'inspecteur,* you might just as well get used to my band of admirers," Lucie said, and he noticed for the first time how her fingers curled around a small piece of the blue glass. "For I expect you shall see them—as well as myself—more often than you might wish. *Bonne soirée,* messieurs."

TEN

Guillaume watched as Mlle Lucie took two steps toward the chamber door, but was forced to halt when the wild-eyed hotel manager—whom he had met earlier today on his visit to interview Pierre Lansac—burst in.

"*Monsieur l'inspecteur*, I must insist—it is a madhouse down there, and— Oh! Pardon, mademoiselle—*La Balise!*" He stumbled to a halt both literally and verbally, and immediately bowed at the ringmaster's feet. "Mademoiselle, please forgive me. I did not realize—but may I bring you something to drink? Some wine, some *café*? An aperitif? Perhaps a bit of cheese, a place to sit and rest your—"

Guillaume cleared his throat loudly and stepped over to the manager. "M. Rochard, if you please. This is not a restaurant, this is a crime scene."

"Not at all, monsieur," Mlle Lucie said to the manager, angling in front of Guillaume in both words and deed. "I was just leaving. But perhaps you will be kind enough to show me out through a private entrance? I wouldn't wish the press to be tempted to follow me before they've finished the story."

Guillaume took her arm firmly before she could slip away with the ecstatic manager. "Mademoiselle," he said in an undertone, "do not think that simply because you came here voluntarily and appeared to offer your assistance regarding the mysterious blue vial that I've forgotten about your connection to Paul Bacard. While Lansac's death is a tragedy, it has in no way distracted me from my real purpose in capturing his friend's murderer."

Her bottle-green eyes were cool and steady, and close enough that he could see the black flecks in them. Her exotic perfume filled his nostrils, and her skirts with their ice-crisp crinolines rustled against his trousers. "Like a dog with a bone, you are, Inspector Guillaume. I suppose that must be considered commendable, given your occupation. Nevertheless, you will soon learn I had nothing to do with Bacard's death." She turned to go, drawing her silken-gloved arm from his grip...then paused and pivoted back toward him. "But as you do seem to have the propensity for barking up the wrong tree, *monsieur le cabot*, one cannot be surprised at your mistaken determination."

"The wrong tree, mademoiselle? And which tree is that?"

"You will never get what you want from the attractive doctor," she replied softly.

At first, Guillaume thought she referred to Émile Huvet—which was a shameful indicator of the state of his mind—but in the next instant he realized she was looking at Jackson, who was packing up his medical bag to leave.

By the time he made the correct correlation, Lucie had exited the chamber in a swish of skirts and feathers, leaving him gritting his teeth.

Good riddance. They would both be happy if he never needed to set eyes on La Balise again.

"Jackson," he said quickly, knowing it was necessary to catch the man before he took his leave. The pathologist had been known to disappear from a crime scene without a word to anyone, oblivious to good manners or information that might be needed by the detective. "Have you any other news from earlier today? I meant to stop in your lab, but the time escaped me—"

"Digitalis," Jackson said, scrawling a note in the tiny book he always managed to have even when forgetting his hat or tie. "Bacard was poisoned with some form of digitalis."

"Any idea how long before he died?"

Jackson jammed the book into his breast pocket without looking. "Not long. You know how quickly digitalis works. Couple of hours, maybe three. All indications that it was in something he drank."

"So not at dinner. But at Château Lisette," Guillaume muttered to himself. "Ah, Mlle Lucie, you shall not shake this dog from the bone so easily."

When he looked up to ask about the stains on Bacard's clothing, Jackson had disappeared.

Guillaume sighed. Damn the man. It was too late to catch him now. He had no choice but to corner him in the lab first thing in the morning.

As if to underscore that thought, somewhere a clock struck ten. The press was still making insistent noises below, and he wasn't prepared to give them a statement tonight. Houssaye was hovering in the doorway with the bulky camera equipment, and the maid who'd found Lansac's body was waiting for Guillaume in the next room. Her occasional wails had punctuated the mood during the entire course of his visit.

Merde. He'd been up since before dawn and had eaten little but half a baguette and the small repast he'd enjoyed—far too much—with Huvet. He needed to forget about those damned blue eyes and focus on the investigation.

Yet his inclination was to turn the interviews as well as the photography over to his eager younger colleague, for it was hardly debatable that Pierre Lansac had hung himself—though Guillaume would wait for Jackson's confirmation on that. Delegating those tasks would allow him to go home for something resembling a meal and a much-needed glass of Burgundy while he reviewed his notes and collected his thoughts. Then he could be up and ready to work in the morning, where he'd catch the elusive Jackson first thing.

With that decision made, Guillaume gave the orders to Houssaye and slipped out to avoid the mob of reporters who seemed to have no idea their quarry had left. But, alas, it wasn't quite as simple as he'd anticipated.

For just as he descended the last step from a side hall staircase—having eschewed the elevator and main stairs in favor of a more unobtrusive exit—he found himself confronted by a young woman.

Though tucked up inside a newsboy cap, her hair had lost its moorings, and a big hank of it hung like a soft brown tail over her shoulder. Her large eyes seemed much too soft and long-lashed to be that of a boy, and despite her gabardine trousers and man's shirt, Guillaume could see the curve of breast and hip. Though she barely reached his chin and her figure was reed-thin without the help of a corset, he estimated her age to be in the early twenties.

The fact that she held a notebook and pencil like weapons told him he'd not managed to avoid the press after all.

"*Monsieur l'inspecteur*, are you the detective for the Bacard murder?" she asked, stepping in front of him with the confidence that a gentleman would not physically move her out of his way. She was fortunate that she'd accosted Guillaume and not Jackson, and was therefore correct in her implicit assumption—though the last thing he wanted to do was answer questions from a reporter.

"I am working on it under the direction of Chief Inspector Houllier of la Sûreté, yes."

"I understand the woman known as La Balise is the prime suspect. Is she also a suspect in the death of Pierre Lansac?" Her French, though adequate, was heavily accented in a British manner.

"The investigation is quite immature at this point, mademoiselle...?"

"Anna Smith."

"And for whom do you write, Mlle Smith?"

"*The London Times*," she replied after a hitch of breath. "And—and other publications."

"And you are not confined to society pages and women's interests when it comes to your stories?" he asked, unaccountably curious. He'd never heard of a female reporter who wasn't doomed to writing about those feminine topics.

She pursed her lips and gave him a mutinous look from under her low-brimmed cap. "I write about real news, not women's fripperies," she scoffed. "I'm a real journalist like Nellie Bly, and I would like to get some answers from you, inspector. Pierre Lansac was found dead in his rooms today. Is there evidence of foul play?"

"No, mademoiselle, there is not," he replied.

She seemed disappointed. "But La Balise? She *is* a suspect in the death of Paul Bacard, is she not?"

"There are a number of persons I find of interest in that investigation. Now, if you excuse me, mademoiselle, I have no further comment." He made to move past her.

But Anna Smith was not about to be dissuaded from her cause. "She killed Paul Bacard, inspector. I know she did. The woman who calls herself La Balise."

There was something in her voice that gave Guillaume pause, and he stilled, looking closely at her. "You sound very certain of that, mademoiselle."

The small, pointed chin lifted again as she fixed him with her steady gaze. "This isn't the first time the woman known as Mme Madeleine has killed, monsieur. Once a murderer, always a murderer."

"And you have proof of this?" he asked very softly. "Mademoiselle?"

Now her gaze dropped away and her mouth twisted. "Not yet. But I'll prove it. Someday, I'll prove it. She's like a black widow spider, that woman. I know for certain: La Balise is a murderer."

Lucie was still furious when she entered the magnificent home of the Comtesse de Loynes, located at 152 Avenue des Champs-Elysées—only a few blocks from her own Château Lisette.

She was arriving at the society matron's post-dinner reception far later than she'd planned, and this was the second time today that Inspector Devré had had a hand in disrupting her schedule. Although, to be fair, it had been her choice to cut short her visit to l'Exposition and go to the hotel where Pierre Lansac had died. Both apprehension and curiosity had brought her there, for she could hardly believe two men she had dined with on the same night had perished within twenty-four hours.

Still, between the fact that Devré had invaded her dressing room and then told her quite plainly that he believed she was Paul Bacard's murderer, Lucie had no qualms about depositing the blame for her foul mood at his proverbial feet. Thus, she'd purposely avoided the press when she left Lansac's hotel so the insolent detective would have to wade through the crowd of reporters and their camera-toting companions in order to go on his way.

At least she'd pointed out all the reasons Lansac's death was nothing more than it seemed: a suicide. So Devré couldn't threaten her with that crime as well. She didn't believe he hadn't already come to the same conclusion, but her purpose was to make him understand *she* had come to the same conclusion.

"Lucie-Geneviève! How gracious of you to join us." The Comtesse de Loynes, who had been the reigning queen of Parisian society for more than three decades, greeted her with a genuine smile.

Surely past sixty (for no one knew her precise age), but still boasting a fine figure and luminous dark eyes, Mme Loynes was a delightful combination of confidence, charm, and excellent taste. A too-heavy coating of rice powder over her papery skin and the imperfectly blended spots of rouge dimmed some of her aging beauty, but her mauve evening gown and signature sprig of fresh Parma violets was perfection, and her voice was delightfully melodious.

Having been raised from meager roots, Jeanne de Loynes had nevertheless married well (her beloved, deceased first husband's cousin), and, despite her wealth and status, never completely ignored her past—which had been nearly as checkered as Lucie's. Perhaps that was why though most *cocottes* like La Balise would never be welcome in the salons or homes of le *gratin*, Lucie-Geneviève was an exception—partly because both Mme Loynes and La Bernhardt found her charming and entertaining, and partly because she was not the garish sort, like the wildly vulgar and uncouth La Belle Otèro.

Lucie smiled warmly at her hostess as she entered the salon, where the budding playwright Maurice Donnay was playing gentle guitar music, and stowed her private thoughts in favor of the public persona. She leaned forward to exchange a kiss on each cheek with the violet-scented comtesse. "I intended to be here an hour ago, darling madame, but I was unavoidably detained. I know it's nearly half-ten and you'll be retiring soon, but I couldn't resist visiting."

"But you must have something bracing, Mlle Lucie," said Jules Lemaître, the comtesse's devoted lover. "For I do believe any unavoidable delay by definition requires sustenance."

Lemaître was closer in age to Lucie than he was to Jeanne—being in his forties—but unlike many of his peers, his attention never flickered beyond the love of his life, his adored comtesse. As a playwright, he was a literary artist of his own accord, and was also a brilliant critic who had recently been inducted into the Académie Française.

Lucie accepted the gold-rimmed goblet that was fancier than any chalice she'd seen in a church. Made from cut crystal, the vessel had a slender, fluted stem with a tulip-shaped cup, and was engraved with a delicate rose and vine design just below the fourteen-karat rim. Its contents were just as exquisite: a light Burgundy with a hint of floral and strawberry essence. She sipped with pleasure, relieved to be able to relax in these informal, untaxing surroundings.

Acknowledging and offering her own greetings to the others, Lucie wandered further into the room. Besides M. Donnay, who sat to the side fingering classical pieces on his guitar, the space was filled with perhaps a dozen more men sitting, standing, or otherwise lounging—many of them poets, playwrights, or other literati. Only a smattering of the attendees were women, most of whom were their wives. As Mme Loynes was a great patron of the literary arts, the conversation at her post-dinner parties, which were held every Friday night, was often filled with literary and political discussions, as well as poetry readings and, occasionally, singing.

"There will be no bawdy songs, *mon cher*," warned the comtesse every time Donnay pulled out his guitar to sing.

Lucie was just about to take a seat on the rose velvet divan opposite Duval's famous painting of Jeanne de Loynes when someone came up behind her. He slid his hand beneath her bent elbow, then curled gentle, familiar fingers around the arm above her gloved wrist.

"Good evening, *ma lumière*," he murmured into her ear. "I had heard the rumors, but by now had nearly given up hope that you would grace us with your presence tonight."

Lucie subdued a shiver of surprised pleasure and pivoted to look back and up at him, sliding her bare arm from his touch. "M. Calmette," she said with a warm—but not too warm—smile, very aware of several pairs of interested gazes sliding their way. "What an unexpected delight to discover you've returned."

"Unexpected" and "delight" were two words that were rather far removed from the truth. Of course she knew he had returned from Marseille—it had been in the press. And whether it was more a delight to see him than not? That was yet to be determined.

For a short time, Lucie-Geneviève Madeleine and Christophe Calmette had been the talk of Paris, the darlings of gossip, the center of society: *The Sun and Moon Casting Their Exquisite Brightness Over the City of Light*, as Pall Mall columnist Jean Lorrain had dubbed them. But Lucie had ended the liaison more than eight months ago, and she had invited no one into her *suite privée* since then. She had taken lovers, of course—for she was a woman who fully enjoyed sexual relations when they were of her choosing—but none of her partners had been allowed into that most private of chambers.

No one before, and no one since, Christophe Calmette.

He looked, if possible, handsomer than he had the last time she saw him. His fair skin had tanned into a soft golden hue, thanks to the sea near Marseille. The contrast made his blue-gray eyes appear luminous beneath dark brows and even darker lashes. He had high cheekbones and a long, Gallic face that was topped by a head of soft sable hair, now combed neatly into place. His mustache was full and trim, revealing a sensual lower lip and a hint of the finely shaped upper one.

He wore an expensive evening coat of cocoa over a pristine shirt and white bow tie, and highly polished shoes. Mme Loynes' butler would have taken his brushed topper, but that accessory, too, would be of the highest quality and fashion. His only nod to *fin de siècle* vanity was a brocade waistcoat of plum and amethyst, along with jade studs down the front of his shirt.

Lucie's palms had gone a trifle damp beneath her gloves, and her knees weren't quite as steady as they'd been, but she'd die before she admitted it. He smelled so damnably familiar, so terribly delicious.

"You are breathtaking as usual, *ma Lucie*," said Christophe, still standing far too close and speaking far too softly for his words to be anything but a seduction. The heat in his eyes indicated this was no exaggeration. "I could not be happier to have returned to Paris. I've missed you." His voice was rough and filled with emotion despite the prying eyes and ears around them.

"You are indeed a sight for sore eyes, monsieur," she replied, projecting just enough that the nosy gossips nearby would hear, but not loudly enough that it was obvious she'd meant for them to do so. "And I'm certain Yvette is pleased to be returned to Paris as well."

His smile tightened a bit and she noticed his pupils dilate in a flare of shock, but otherwise he gave no indication that her seemingly innocent statement had really been the point of a dagger.

Of course everyone in Paris knew that Christophe Calmette, the gracious, witty, philanthropic heir to the Calmette shipping enterprise, was married. Yet it had been no terrible scandal that the *bourgeoisie*'s favorite son had fallen in love with La Balise, the most celebrated of the *demi-mondaine*, the beacon of the city. There were few men in Paris who wouldn't have changed places with Calmette— or women who wouldn't have changed places with La Balise.

At any rate, at the upper levels of society, one hardly batted an eyelash over such things as marital infidelities. Husbands and wives, who were often married for pragmatic reasons, commonly took lovers. And as long as those indiscretions were either discreet or mutually agreed upon, it was considered no great sin. That was not to say there weren't domestic altercations, tears, and threats when infidelities were discovered...but they were as commonplace as an empty wine bottle in Moulin Rouge, and even the priests prescribed barely taxing penances over such confessions. It was only the scandal of divorce that caused heads to turn and reputations to be ruined.

But things were far more complex than they appeared between Lucie and Christophe, and to him, the very mention of his wife

Yvette was tantamount to not just a bucket of cold water to the ardor, but an entire ice bath.

"She is barely tolerant of the change of weather here in the north," Christophe replied, a bit warier now. "For the sea agrees with her health far more than the Seine." His gray-blue eyes had not left her face, as if he needed to soak in the sight of her after a long drought.

"I should expect that will change now," Lucie added smoothly. "I hear she recently delivered a healthy son for you. You have my sincere felicitations, Christophe, on the arrival of your long-desired heir."

He stared at her, hurt and shock in his eyes.

Lucie ignored a pang of guilt for this second, and more painful, dagger thrust, and forced herself to put distance between them. She had a convenient excuse to do so, stepping away as the diminutive comtesse passed by toward her preferred chair beneath the Duval portrait. Lemaître followed, handing his lady into the seat as she adjusted her skirts and crinolines, then setting next to her a tiny tulip flute filled with pink champagne. He patted her hand, a simple touch that nevertheless exhibited the volumes of devotion in their summer-autumn love affair, then settled onto a chair immediately next to hers.

Lucie looked away from that sweet, automatic gesture. All at once, she was so overwhelmed by regret that she caught her breath painfully beneath the iron cage compressing her torso. Her eyes stung, and she blinked rapidly, turning away on the pretext of admiring a table-sized Rodin.

To have a partner, a man, like Jules Lemaître—one who would love her for who she was, what she thought and knew and believed, even as her beauty faded...one with whom she could share her deepest desires and most frightening of secrets...someone to whom she could completely and utterly open her heart. Someone to share her bed every night and awaken with every morning.

Someone who expected nothing from her but her heart...

But that was not her course.

It was by choice, true. But it was the only way for her.

"Shall I read one last verse?" Lemaître asked the room at large, sitting on a chair close to his beloved. He'd picked up a book of poetry that had been resting open side down on a hassock. "Maurice will provide the background music, I am certain. A private performance for our lovely *dame aux Violettes?*"

"Lucie." Christophe had recovered at least somewhat from her barbs, for he returned to her side as soon as the poetry reading began. The soft plucking of the guitar strings accompanying the sure, modulated voice of Lemaître covered their conversation. "Will you at least speak with me in private for a moment? Madame will be taking down her hair at any moment."

Indeed, it was true: at precisely eleven o'clock, the comtesse's companion Mlle Beer would enter the salon and unpin her mistress's long, hennaed hair, combing it out in preparation for the night. That was the signal for the guests to leave.

"I will," Lucie agreed reluctantly, even as her heart pounded with anticipation. He would surely ask to return to Château Lisette with her, and she wanted—oh, indeed, she wanted—to allow herself to acquiesce. Even though she should not.

Lucie led the way from the salon back to the main foyer of the house, through which the guests would be passing on their way home. It was part self-preservation that she chose that location, for neither of them would want anyone to witness whatever scene might follow: whether it be a sensual encounter, or a heated one. This public location would prevent either intimacy from happening.

"Lucie, I heard about Paul Bacard," Christophe said, surprising her. His patrician face was a mask of concern. "Is it true that la Sûreté has named you a suspect? Who is the inspector that is harassing you? First thing tomorrow, I'll have words with Cochefert—"

She blinked rapidly, for her eyes had begun to sting once more. "It's true. Bacard is dead, and there is suspicion that he was poisoned while visiting Hélène at Lisette last night. I'm not being harassed by anyone," she added firmly. "And if I were, my love, you know I would be capable of dealing with it myself."

His eyes widened a trifle, and she gritted her teeth. It had been a telling slip, using the familiar endearment.

Before he could press his advantage, Lucie continued, "And now Pierre Lansac is dead. Did you hear that too?"

"Surely this inspector doesn't suspect you there as well?" His expression had grown hard. "A second murder in two days?"

"No, not at all. Pierre hung himself. I saw the body."

"*You* didn't find him. Tell me you didn't," Christophe exclaimed, then, when she shook her head, he swore under his breath with relief. "But two? Surely it's a coincidence." He stepped closer. "Lucie, I–"

She read the look in his eyes, and reacted quickly, pulling the shard of cerulean glass from her handbag. It was most of the top half of the bottle. "Do you recognize this?" she asked, determined to divert him from more dangerous topics. "I've never seen glass this color before, and the bottle was small and ornate..." She knew it was a long chance that anyone would recognize the contents of a bottle from a piece of it, but the glass and its design were very distinctive. And Lansac had been so very protective of it. Surely there was something there.

To her surprise, Christophe took the piece and screwed a monocle into his left eye in order to look at it closely. "I've seen something like this before," he said, holding it up to the light. He sniffed it, and, as Devré and Jackson had done, slipped his fingertip along the curved inside.

"Pierre had the bottle in his pocket last night, and when I played the pickpocket game, I lifted it from him. He became infuriated when he realized I'd emptied his pockets, and I believe it was because I had the bottle. I'm afraid...I'm afraid there might have been poison in it."

"But why would Lansac poison Bacard?" Christophe asked, easily following her train of thought. "How did you get this piece?" He removed his monocle and tucked it back in his breast pocket, but still turned the glass shard over in his fingers.

"It was in his rooms. At Hôtel Briö."

"May I keep it? I think I might know how to find out about it. If you give me some time, I'll make certain."

"Where are you going to look? I'll go. You needn't become involved." The last thing she wanted was to become entwined with him again. Her heart hurt.

He shook his head, a bemused smile curving his mustache as his eyes lit with affection. "The Jockey. Even the bold and beautiful La Balise cannot cross the threshold of that men's club."

Lucie succumbed to logic, though she wasn't happy about it. "Very well. Thank you, Christophe. I appreciate it."

"And your interest in all this is what, precisely?"

"To clear my name, of course—and that of Hélène as well, for Inspector Devré seems to think one or both of us fed Paul the poison. If I can prove that Lansac was involved, then surely Devré will leave us be and sniff up some other tree."

He nodded and slipped the glass into his coat pocket, and then, looking down at her, took her face gently into his fine, ungloved hands. "Lucie," he murmured, and stepped close to cover her lips with his.

She closed her eyes when he touched her mouth with his, when the warmth of his lips fitted to hers in that sweet, familiar way as he cupped her face. His mustache was soft, and his lips firm and skillful, and the interlude lasted far too long before she had the presence of mind to pull away.

But by then, her body was flushed and damp, her hand had curled over his muscular shoulder, and his eyes burned with avidity.

"Lucie," he murmured, his breath warm against the cheek she'd turned toward him. "Ah, Lucie...I—"

He must have felt her stiffen, for at that moment, a dark, massive figure appeared in her sight, standing directly behind Christophe. He wore a thunderous expression.

Aloysius, at last. Thank God.

But, *damn* it all...could he not have arrived five minutes earlier?

ELEVEN

Guillaume couldn't put Anna Smith's accusation from his mind. The certainty in her eyes and voice rang in his head. *La Balise is a murderer.*

Though he didn't necessarily disagree with the reporter's assessment, he didn't yet have proof of any wrongdoing. Still, there was no doubt Lucie-Geneviève Madeleine—if that was her real name—was wholly capable of taking such steps, should she feel it necessary.

But clearly she had not strangled and hung Pierre Lansac—at least by herself. It would simply have been impossible for her to manipulate a deadweight body into such a position without help, even though Lansac wasn't a particularly large man.

And, true, there were sex games that included asphyxiation, and certainly the likes of La Balise would have some familiarity with such erotic tendencies. There was, then, an outside possibility that somehow Lansac had expired during a sort of intimate horseplay, and that she'd somehow arranged it to look like a suicide...

And she had been mysteriously absent from Château Lisette earlier today, during the appropriate time period. One was to believe the likes of her was at Mass—midday on a weekday? One of the *Dégrafées*, at church? Hardly likely.

Guillaume had paused in the pouring of his second glass of wine, and now he set down the bottle without finishing the task.

It *was* possible. She was clever enough to do all of it—and had she not almost immediately pointed out the bare footprints on the dresser, from where Lansac had presumably launched himself with a noose prepared around his neck? As if to make certain he saw that very obvious clue? And had she not turned up at the rooms so very conveniently, and immediately "discovered" the broken bottle, and...

Sitting in his napkin-sized kitchen, he sipped slowly from the dregs of the glass, but no longer tasted the wine.

It was possible.

But something was missing.

In the ranks of the homicide division at la Sûreté, Guillaume was second only to Chief Inspector Houllier—and that only because his superior had been in the position for eight years, unmoving as a boulder. Guillaume hadn't ascended through the ranks as quickly and efficiently as he had by accident or due to political maneuvering. Despite being passed over for the investigative magistrate position, he and those above him knew he possessed an uncanny ability to place himself in the time and location of a crime, to imagine every last detail as if he were there, watching it as if from an omniscient viewpoint.

And more often than not, it was these instincts, this ability to play out the scene in his imagination—traveling through the labyrinth of the perpetrator's mind, comprehending motivation and emotion, watching the action unfold—that made him the superlative investigator he was. The fourteen silver medals in the velvet-lined box in his desk drawer were a testament to that ability.

No, he knew in the deepest part of his bones that Lucie-Geneviève had nothing to do with Pierre Lansac's death. And though he liked her very much for Bacard's, he was not yet certain of that either.

And so tomorrow, he must corner Jackson in his blinding white lab, with its smell of antiseptic death and neatly arranged slivers of liver, kidney, and brain. He must return to Château Lisette and once again question the staff, now that the time of the poison ingestion had been fixed to a general time frame. He must speak to both Bacard's and Lansac's friends and family. He might even construct a valid reason to meet with Émile Huvet.

At that titillating thought, Guillaume rose abruptly from the tiny dining table, moving so quickly he startled Mimi, his cat. She yowled in protest—after all, he'd awakened her from a nap—and, to apologize, he dropped a slice of sausage next to her bowl of milk.

In exchange for companionship and mouse patrol, the sleek cocoa-brown feline ate like royalty, whereas Devré's meal, by his standards, had been meager and unsatisfying. The bread had been a week old, for he'd returned home too late the last few nights for the *pâtisserie* to be open. The final third of a pepper-cured sausage, along with some *cornichons*, had completed the repast. He'd scrounged for the last bit of pâté out of an empty jar and ended up with hardly any more substance than what he'd swiped out of the fairy-like blue bottle—

Guillaume froze.

Imbécile.

He was a damned fool.

How could he have missed it? How could he not have realized it immediately? He of all people—

Guillaume knew from whence the bottle had come, and what it was for. He knew it.

But he had to be certain.

It took him only a moment to adjust his attire to look less like an officer of la Sûreté and more like a *flâneur*. He combed his thick hair flat to the sides, slicking it with far more pomade than he ever used, then brushed out his mustache so the tips were no longer neatly waxed and instead the whole thing fluffed out like a messy bristle brush. He abhorred the look, but it was crucial he not be recognized.

Not for the first time, he reviled the current trend wherein *every* man in Paris—excepting the conscienceless Dr. Jackson—wore at least a mustache, and oftentimes a beard or sideburns. It would be much easier to obscure one's identity if he were able to *add* facial hair, rather than attempt to alter it.

His hat was a slightly out of date but expensive topper he rarely had occasion to wear, and he settled it on his head at a lower angle than fashion dictated. He left his badge on the bureau—God forbid something happen to him, and it was found on his person. The waistcoat and evening coat he wore were both unremarkable brown serge wool, but of excellent cut. He tucked a pistol into his pocket and the requisite monocle into a different one, then retrieved his walking stick.

And then, grimly but with acceptance, he pulled a wad of francs, which he kept for last-minute adventures such as this, from a box beneath the floorboard. Tonight would be an expensive proposition, and one for which he'd receive no recompense from la Sûreté. But he knew no other way to confirm his suspicions.

Secreting the bills deep throughout the hem of his coat, he pulled on gloves and bade Mimi goodnight. Just as the clock on his mantel struck midnight, he closed the front door behind him.

Though only a short while ago he'd been past ready for his bed, Guillaume found himself surprisingly energized as he walked along the street. He lived on a small, narrow street at the bottom of the Second Arrondissement, near the Opéra and rue de las Pépinières. This meant it was little more than a brisk fifteen-minute walk to rue des Moulins.

Neither the roadway nor the sidewalk were empty by any means, for late-night diners were transferring via fiacre or on foot from café and restaurant to cabaret or nightclub. Places like the Grand-Guignol, currently popular for its short, grotesque shows, and the Moulin Rouge, renowned for the racy *chahut* dance that had originated there, were only a couple of the destinations to which the *bourgeoisie* and *gratin*, and even the anarchists, gathered, all mixing together in a single *ragoût*.

Now that he was back on the street, Guillaume found himself stimulated by the beauty of his city in the center of the night. Electric lights had replaced nearly all of the gaslights, but they glowed with a different kind of charm in the clear, warm evening. He smelled a waft of flowers as a laughing couple strolled by in the opposite direction, and then walked through a cloud of cigar smoke as he passed a trio of men chatting on a street corner. A dog pissed on the cornerstone of a print shop, then, tail wagging, bounded off at his owner's call, leaving the strong scent of urine on the night air.

A stab of loneliness caught Guillaume by surprise as he passed yet another couple—this one paused on a street corner waiting for the traffic to clear. The road was currently empty of carriages and fiacres, but neither man nor woman seemed to notice as they stood, looking tenderly at the other as if no one and nothing else existed.

Guillaume's mouth twisted bitterly as he turned sharply down a narrow, empty side street. A wife, children, a family, home...none of that would come to pass for him. He would live out his life alone, buried in work—possibly stuck in the same position of mere detective inspector for the rest of his working days. And he'd be limited to the basest, most superficial of clandestine activities in order to find companionship and affection.

Why must I be this way?

He'd asked himself the question a thousand times. He'd locked it away deep inside, along with the need for love and partnership.

A normal life was not possible. Not for him.

And he'd never have the answer to why, until perhaps when he faced God at the end of his days. Perhaps then he would have the answer. Perhaps then he would understand *why* he'd been destined to an unfulfilled, solitary life.

Étienne's face, of course, flashed in his mind, along with the memory of their brief time together. Their brief, blissful time—living, loving, laughing where no one cared who they were or what they were about.

And then it ended—the way it always must. For it was the way of the world.

Guillaume tightened his jaw and thwacked his walking stick angrily against a jut of crumbling stone steps as he strode past them. *Damn me.*

He nearly missed it, he was so caught up in the sudden tangle of his misery—but at the last moment he saw the shadow sliding into another from the corner of his eye. The little angled street was empty and silent, only a block from the busier thoroughfares...but nevertheless far enough away for danger to lurk.

With an unobtrusive movement, he eased the pistol from his pocket and allowed it to hang alongside him, obscured by the flapping of his greatcoat. At the same moment, the grip of his other hand on the dragon-headed knob of his walking stick changed. He pressed a release with his thumb, and there was the soft *snick* of a blade ejecting from the bottom of the cane. Its smooth metal gleamed in the streetlight just as one shadow became two ominous ones, facing him on the deserted side street.

One of the shadows was holding a pistol.

TWELVE

T he pistol was pointed at Guillaume, and he stopped but did not
raise his hands.

"It would be in your collective best interest," he said to the thugs,
"to walk away now, *messieurs*. This is your only warning."

The second of the shadows had metamorphosed into the shape
of a man, edging up from behind and to the left. He was holding a
knife, and a derisive laugh escaped him.

"We'll be happy to walk away," said the pistol bearer, "once we've
relieved you of the weight in your pockets. Now raise your hands
slowly."

This sort of event was precisely the reason Guillaume hadn't
put the francs in his pockets. Pickpockets were hardly more than
a nuisance, and he knew how to spot them, but armed thugs were
another thing altogether.

He smiled congenially, all at once feeling as if the impending
altercation might just be what he needed to top off the day.
"Unfortunately, my pockets are already relieved," he said, lifting his
gun hand slowly, then bringing the pistol wide to aim it at the knife-
wielding man who'd crept up behind him and stood close by—all
without turning his head.

He heard the softest hiss of indrawn breath from his target and
saw how the two sets of eyes settled on the glint of his firearm. His

pulse was up, and the blood pumped strongly through his veins. It had been years since he'd been in such a dangerous situation, and he'd missed the energy and excitement of it.

Guillaume smiled beneath the ridiculous bristle of his mustache and cocked the gun, then adjusted it threateningly to make certain to draw their attention to that hand. Just as the man across from him tensed, shifting slightly as if preparing to move, Guillaume swung up his walking stick, slamming it into the assailant's pistol with great force.

The thug cried out as the gun discharged, the bullet whizzing harmlessly above Guillaume's head and down the street. By the time the attacker recovered, Guillaume had transferred the attention of his own pistol to him.

"Drop it," he said softly.

The man hesitated, and from the corner of his eye, Guillaume saw the assailant on his left move slightly. "I would not advise it, monsieur," he said, lifting and gesturing with his walking stick. "Now, you—drop the pistol or I will use mine."

The gun fell to the stones with a dull rattle. Guillaume turned his weapon onto the knife holder and used his walking stick to drag the dropped pistol closer to him.

"And here we are," he said, still very polite, still very prepared. "I could call for the *officer de la paix*. But," he continued quietly, "I will not, tonight. Just this once, for I have business to attend to and I want no further delay. Step into the light—*you*. And now you." He took a moment to memorize their faces (who knew when he might choose to call in a favor), and saw both anger and dismay therein...but a curious, and welcome, lack of violence and evil. They were young, too—hardly more than twenty. He spared a moment of pity, remembering what he was doing at the age of twenty. Hardly anything more admirable than they.

"I'll remember your faces, and you'd best pray you don't accost me again. Now, be off." He purposely allowed the one to retain his knife, but kept the blade of his cane poised over the abandoned pistol. "And pray I don't hear of any other similar exploits in this area tonight."

He waited until they'd melted into the darkness before bending to pick up the gun. He checked the chamber and was astonished, and then amused, to discover there were no other bullets inside.

Shaking his head, he slipped it into his other pocket. Feeling strangely exhilarated—though compared to his younger years growing up near the butte of Montmartre shortly after the Siege of Paris, tonight's incident had been hardly more than a polite conversation—he continued down the narrow street, took a small dogleg turn onto a slightly broader one, then at last ended at rue des Moulins, where he paused for a moment.

Directly to his right was an imposing home, well lit and filled with activity. It boasted an unusually large house number: 6, and a small light shone on the numeral to amplify it even more. The buildings on either side had much more discreet markings, but number 6, like most high-end brothels, took no chances that potential clients would pass by without noticing its address. The overly large house numbers were a not-so-subtle code for the type of sensual entertainment offered by *maisons de close*.

However, 6 rue des Moulins was not Devré's destination. It was number 13, a short distance away, that catered to a different clientele. And because of that, in the interest of discretion and obscurity, this particular establishment did not hang a large number on its facade. Additionally, entrance was not gained via the front door, as at 6, but via an obscure entrance accessed through a thick boxwood passage between numbers 15 and 17, which wound around to the rear of the business. A tongue-in-cheek, sly wink to its particular customers, no doubt.

Guillaume had visited once Maison de Bleue, but he did not possess the funds to make it a regular habit, even if he desired to do so. Still standing on the corner, he fluffed his mustache, drawing it as broadly and full as possible, lowered the hat nearly to his brows, and turned up the collar of his coat, then strode briskly down the street.

There was a discreet sign at the entrance to the boxwood alley—hardly noticeable unless one was looking for it. It read *Maison de*

Bleue in an overbearing script, and Guillaume turned into the dark, narrow passage.

Moments later, he'd made his way to the door, which opened onto a small courtyard filled with the blooming white and pale hued flowers of a moon garden. Since most of the *maison*'s visitors came at night, that was a fitting choice for landscaping.

Guillaume rang the bell, which gave a melodious tinkle from within, and the door opened. He was grateful for the single light that burned just outside the door, for it kept himself as well as any other visitors in the shadows.

Not many men would want to be identified as visitors to the Blue House.

He stepped inside, moving past a butler who exuded discretion. As soon as the door was closed, Guillaume turned to the man, who was holding a small salver. On it was a menu of services on a thick crème paper.

Guillaume took the menu and did not gasp at the prices, but just barely. To simply walk through the door, he owed one hundred francs.

He discreetly withdrew the requisite fee from inside his coat and placed it on the silver tray, hoping he wouldn't be required to pay anything else in order to prove what he thought he already knew.

The butler did not count the bills, but instead gave a brief bow of acknowledgment. "Excellent, monsieur, *merci beaucoup*."

During this entire time, the butler, who was surely used to men bundled up behind scarves and beneath hats to obscure their identity, had hardly looked at Guillaume. "Would you prefer the doctor or the chemist, or perhaps some other sort of entertainment?"

"The chemist, if you please."

"Of course, monsieur. If you would." He gestured to a hallway, and led Guillaume to a door. "Please, monsieur. I will advise him you are waiting."

Guillaume stepped into the chamber and looked around as the door closed behind the butler. The space was paneled with glossy walnut, and a fine indigo and maroon Oriental rug decorated the floor. The furnishings were heavy, solid, and gleaming.

On one wall was a serving table laden with bottles of wine, liquor, and other spirits. Heavy cut-crystal glasses were arranged, waiting to be filled.

Guillaume considered a glass of brandy—based on the prices paid for the discretion and services of Maison de Bleue, he suspected the vintage would be stellar—but decided he'd best keep his head clear for several reasons.

He'd barely finished contemplating the liquor tray when the door opened and in walked a short, slight man with flyaway gray hair. He wore round spectacles and was dressed in a dark blue jacket and trousers, with a forest-plaid waistcoat.

"How may I help you, monsieur?" he asked.

Guillaume, in deference to his intention to keep himself as obscured as possible, had not removed his hat—normally a breach of etiquette, but not in this case. For the same reason, no introductions were made between either of them.

"Do you recognize this?" he asked, withdrawing the section of the cerulean-blue bottle he'd retrieved from Lansac's room. He placed it on the small side table and waited.

The man, who was presumably the chemist Guillaume had requested, approached and nodded. He picked up the piece, still nodding. "Yes, monsieur. Why do you ask?"

"It's what is called 'the blue dragon,' is it not?"

"Yes, monsieur. Are you in need of the assistance of this mighty blue dragon? I would be happy to prepare a bottle for your use."

Guillaume kept his features impassive. If only it were that simple.

He'd heard of the blue dragon, but had never considered the option of partaking of it. And until now, he wasn't certain the bottle had been one of the dragons. "Thank you, monsieur, but no. I would like to know, if you please, whether you can tell how long ago the bottle that you have in your hand was...er...filled. And I should like to review your customer list."

The chemist's face turned blank. "But of course our clients are quite confidential, monsieur. Surely you would require the same discretion should you become a client. Even if I should want to divulge the names of those who come here, alas, I cannot—for we keep no records, no names, no identifying information. Surely you understand. As to when it was filled—no, monsieur, I cannot tell you even that."

Guillaume was not surprised at this information, and he was also strangely relieved. So all identities were protected, and all visitors were anonymous. "Can you at least tell me whether there is any other place besides Maison de Bleue that a gentleman might obtain the blue dragon?"

"There are, of course, unauthorized, untested copies being mixed and sold in Paris. We cannot stop that. However, the glass itself, as you have likely noted, is specific to our establishment. I cannot tell you who bought it or when, but I can tell you with great certainty that it was from me, and only me, that the transaction was made."

"Thank you, monsieur, for that at least. Now, if I were to tell you that it was a matter of life and death, could you perhaps assist me further? If I were to inform you that a man now lies dead in his chamber, and that it's suspected he was in possession of the blue dragon, and that it is of vital importance that I know whether he was, in fact, in possession of the dragon, could you be of assistance?"

The man blanched, and his face turned dull pink. "I assure you, monsieur, that my tonic was in no way responsible for this man's—or any man's—death. And for that reason—"

"No, no, monsieur," Guillaume said. "It is not believed to have caused his death...only to possibly be a factor in the investigation."

Pursing his thin lips, the chemist shook his head. "I cannot help you, monsieur. The only thing I can tell you with any certainty is that, yes, that bottle at one time held the tonic known as the blue dragon, and yes, it came from my establishment. And no, it could not in any way have caused this man's death."

"Very well." Guillaume knew he could push no further, and he was also acutely, painfully aware that he could not identify himself as from la Sûreté, let alone use that as an excuse to demand further information. Not only to protect his identity herein, but also to protect himself from his colleagues—for there would be questions as to how he would even know to come here in search of the special tonic. "Thank you for your time, monsieur." He gave a brief bow.

"Are you quite certain you have no need of my blue dragon?" asked the man, his eyes narrowing.

"Quite certain," Guillaume replied, though his mouth was dry as he spoke. If only it were that easy, he thought again. If only it could change things, to take a potion that would enable him to act like a normal man in the presence of a woman.

He understood why a man who visited Maison de Bleue would subscribe to the use of the medication. But more importantly, he understood why Pierre Lansac was so infuriated when La Balise exposed the distinctive blue bottle at Maxim's.

And even more interesting, he now realized that he and Lansac shared a most dangerous secret. Whether that secret was the reason he took his own life, Guillaume could only surmise...but he could see it.

He could see it.

The half-moon was shining valiantly through a cloak of stars, and the streetlights continued to cast their bright electric pools along the street.

It was balmy with a slight breeze, and as Guillaume left Maison de Bleue via a different doorway than he entered, he unbuttoned his coat and turned down its collar. The weight of his hat combined with the thoughts and realizations plaguing him made Guillaume feel restless and unsettled. The emotions that concerned him weren't only related to the case he was investigating, but also to the way of life—the way of *his* life.

His was a life of subterfuge and dishonesty juxtaposed with a vocation spent uncovering truth and promoting justice. He worked and lived and socialized with the same men who, if they knew who he really was, what he truly thought and felt and desired, would lock him up more quickly than they'd done to Alfred Dreyfus: an innocent man who'd been accused—and convicted—of treason because he was a Jew.

Frustrated, Guillaume swept off his hat and coat while standing on the street corner, desperate to relieve the sense of the overbearing weight and stifling heat that suddenly smothered him. None of the many people still making their way along the street at two o'clock in the morning seemed to notice the sudden, frenetic movements as he slung the overcoat over his walking-stick arm and continued on at a brisk pace—not back home, not to his empty bed and lonely flat, but north toward Montmartre, the highest spot in the city—in more ways than one. There, at least, he would find a place in which to lose himself: both physically and mentally.

Guillaume's fellow nightwalkers were in groups of drunken glee, pairs of intimate companionship, or single striders with a clear destination in mind—all of which made him feel even more isolated.

He'd walked only two blocks from Maison de Bleue, and was waiting to cross the street after a sudden influx of fiacres, bicycles, and an automobile, when a single figure approached the pedestrians waiting at the corner and stopped next to him.

Guillaume wasn't certain what compelled him to even take note of the other man, but something did, and he was shocked when he recognized him.

"M. Huvet?" he said, doing his best not to sound as wildly delighted as he was. *Imbécile*, he reminded himself.

But when the other man looked over at the sound of his name, and the same surprise and delight widened his eyes, Guillaume was unable to completely subdue a spark of something he hadn't felt in a long time. He shifted his hat into the grip holding his walking stick and extended a hand toward the doctor.

"Inspector Devré," said Huvet, giving him a firm handshake. "I cannot even believe it is you! Surely you haven't been following me all night simply in order to interrogate me further about the happenings at Château Lisette," he continued, his mouth curving into a smile that underscored his witticism.

The doctor was looking at Guillaume with those blue eyes. And their handshake had lasted a trifle longer than necessary.

"Alas, no," Guillaume replied, resisting the urge to pat his mustache back into its normal orderly style. *Imbécile*, he told himself again. *Your mind is influenced by your activities tonight.* "I had other business that brought me to this part of town."

"I see. Well, if you are doing the business of la Sûreté, I suppose I shall be required to go on my way, and allow you to continue your work." Huvet gave a brief nod, but it was accompanied by a warm smile.

Guillaume felt a prickle of disappointment at the prompt brush-off. "Yes, of course. And the hour is late—"

"Though the night is still young," Huvet replied, glancing up at the moon. Then he looked at Guillaume. "I'm sorry; I've kept you talking when you were waiting to cross, and now look—here comes another line of traffic. We shall be waiting another several minutes now."

Guillaume hadn't even noticed the ebb and flow of trundling vehicles, but he shrugged. "I'm in no great hurry."

"Ah, *bien*. Oh, then perhaps you might be able to assist me. I confess I'm a bit lost, M. Devré, and I've been walking along this and the other street for several minutes now. I cannot seem to find the establishment I seek."

"I know all the streets of Paris," Guillaume replied matter-of-factly. "Even the most obscure alleys in Montparnasse. From my days as an *officer de la paix*, you see. What address are you attempting to locate?"

"I'm afraid that's the problem, monsieur," Huvet responded. "I don't have the street address. I know it only as the Blue House." He lifted his eyes to Guillaume's and held his gaze for a long moment, then tore it away. "But perhaps you haven't heard of it."

Guillaume realized he'd stopped breathing. "On the contrary," he managed. "I have heard of that establishment. It's not far from here."

"Perhaps," Huvet responded, "you could show me the way? Or perhaps instead, we— But no. You're very busy, are you not, *monsieur l'inspecteur*? And it's late. I was about to suggest that perhaps we find a quiet place for a drink first, and—"

"A quiet table for a drink would be quite welcome," Guillaume said. "Do you have a place in mind?"

"Ah, but I think the police detective who knows all of the streets of Paris should be the one to select the establishment," Huvet replied with a smile.

Moments later, they were seated at an outdoor table on a narrow side street. The doors and windows of the nightclub had been thrown wide, and music, laughter, whistles, and other sounds of gaiety spilled onto the patio, along with a rolling cloud of cigar smoke. Most of the seats both inside and outside were filled, but Guillaume spotted a small table at the edge of the block of light coming from the establishment that would offer some anonymity.

Not that he had anything to hide. There was nothing remarkable about sitting at a table with a male acquaintance at a club at two o'clock in the morning.

As long as no one noticed the way the doctor was looking at him.

Guillaume ordered for both of them, since Huvet had done the honors earlier in the day. "I hope you appreciate a well-aged single-malt whisky," he told his companion. "The one I ordered is excellent."

"I trust your judgment...Guillaume."

Their eyes met over the table, and this time, the heavy feeling he'd been fighting all evening felt far more interesting than suffocating. He smiled, wished briefly that he hadn't used quite so much pomade to flatten his hair, then settled back into his seat as the waiter arrived with their drinks.

Guillaume regarded the view with pleasure as Huvet lifted the glass, sniffed its contents with his fine, aquiline nose, and sipped. Guillaume studied him openly as Huvet's brows rose with surprise and delight, enjoying the sight as his companion tasted the smooth, fiery, buttery drink, swishing it delicately around in his mouth, leaving his lower lip glistening after he finally swallowed it.

"Exquisite," he said, catching Guillaume watching him.

Guillaume lifted his own glass and drank. The whisky burned satisfactorily, suffusing him with heat, stoking what was already smoldering. He nodded to the waiter, silently ordering another round. He was, as he'd said earlier, in no hurry. Not now.

"Have you seen much of l'Exposition?" asked Huvet idly. His ungloved hand still curled around his empty glass, and he was absently turning it in circles as he spoke. "What do you think of all the lights? I wonder if it might not be a bit garish—even for our *fin de siècle* city."

"The tourists are calling Paris the City of Lights now," Guillaume replied. "More than five thousand bulbs lighting the pavilions, they say—but I haven't seen it at night...well, except from a distance." He smiled, giving a gesture in the general direction of Champ de Mars, where the bulk of the exposition sprawled in the shadow of La Tour Eiffel. "It's impossible to miss their blaze."

"But the Ferris wheel," Huvet said with a grin. "And at night... that would be a splendid way to see the fair. What a view it would be, to behold the all the pavilions with their thousands and thousands of lights."

"It would."

"Guillaume..." Huvet said slowly. He glanced up briefly, wearing a completely different sort of expression now. Almost hesitant. "I don't wish to be impertinent, but...how much trouble is Lucie-Geneviève in?"

A mild sense of disappointment stuttered through Guillaume. Was that it? The only reason Huvet wanted to sit with him? No. He *had* mentioned Maison de Bleue...and there would have been no other reason to do so if there hadn't been...something else. The very mention of Maison de Bleue was almost as much a code as a red rose in the lapel or a crimson necktie. Nevertheless, he was warier now.

But before he could respond, Huvet shook his head. "I only ask because she is a dear friend. I've known her for three years—almost since the day she came to Paris. I know her. Lucie would never have poisoned Paul Bacard." Huvet pursed his lips, causing his mustache to thrust outward, then looked up at Guillaume, a light of humor in his eyes as he grinned. "I cannot say she wouldn't be *capable* of murder, you understand—for you've met the woman, have you not?"

His forthright and very true statement caught Guillaume by surprise, and he gave a short laugh. "I cannot disagree with you about her being capable," he replied. "And I can see why you would find

her fascinating enough to be a dear friend. She is quite magnificent."
He thought he was successful in keeping all trace of bitterness from
his voice.

"Devré? I thought that was you there. Beautiful night, *n'est-ce
pas?*"

Guillaume looked over at the familiar voice. As luck would have
it, one of the policemen from Houssaye's former *commissaire* was
walking by, along with his partner. They both stopped and removed
their uniform hats, revealing damp hair plastered to their foreheads.
Apparently Guillaume wasn't the only one feeling the heat tonight.

"Officers Marceau and—Tulane, is it? This is Émile Huvet." He
utilized his empty glass, using it to gesture the trio of introductions.
"I'd invite you both to join us, but, alas, you're on duty." Guillaume
smiled, but felt unsettled nonetheless. "And you're missing out on
an exquisite single-malt scotch."

Marceau leaned against a hitching post, crossing his arms over
the middle. "I might be missing the whisky, but I heard you caught
the Bacard case—and La Balise is involved. It's all over the papers."

"It's a damned circus," Guillaume said, just as the waiter
approached with their second round of drinks—which he suddenly
found far less interesting than he'd anticipated. The sweet tension
between him and Huvet had poofed. "Speaking of excitement—if
you're looking for some, I had a bit of an altercation with a pair of
would-be pickpockets a few blocks away."

"Damned thugs are getting bolder all the time," Tulane said,
his fingers closing over his billy club. "You don't look too worse for
wear."

Guillaume shrugged. "I'm not as easy picking as one might
think." He went on to give them a detailed description of where
they'd accosted him, and what they looked like.

"Better be off, then. We'll take a walk over there. Tell Houssaye
we miss him at the station," Marceau said.

"*Bonne soirée,*" Guillaume said, and they melted into the night.

"A circus?" Huvet was grinning. "Lucie will be complimented."

"Perhaps even bigger than a mere circus. Perhaps it's a damned
world exposition with two hundred and ten damned pavilions."

Guillaume's jaw felt tight, and he took a large gulp of his whisky. Why did he feel as if he'd just barely avoided something even worse than a circus?

"Guillaume."

He looked up, and this time found himself the object of the other man's regard. The unpleasantness of seeing his colleagues evaporated. "Monsieur?"

"I hope you'll take what I am about to say in the spirit in which it's meant." Huvet tossed back his drink with a serious lack of respect for its perfection. He lifted his empty glass. "What do they call this? Liquid courage?" His gaze was still fastened on Guillaume. "Now that I've downed my dose of courage, I must confess all to you...particularly how disappointed I am that you weren't, after all, intending to accost me tonight. I believe I would have stood up to your methods of interrogation quite well, monsieur."

Guillaume went hot. Instead of responding, he made an urgent gesture to the waiter, who approached immediately to settle the bill.

"Where?" he said to Huvet as they left the café.

The other man gave him a deliberate look, then stepped boldly into the street and whistled, heedless of an oncoming carriage. The driver in the fiacre waiting across the way gave a responding whistle and jostled his horses to life.

Guillaume didn't hear what his companion told the driver. He simply climbed into the fiacre, tossed his hat, coat, gloves, and walking stick onto one of the seats, and sat.

Huvet followed moments later, flung his topper onto the seat, and latched the door behind him. "We won't be disturbed," he said, dragging off his coat.

"Praise God."

Huvet tasted like the fine scotch, and his mustache was just as soft and smooth. Beneath the layers of cotton shirt and brocade waistcoat were sleek muscles and salty, vetiver-scented skin.

Guillaume sighed, "Émile," when Huvet touched him for the first time, and his companion gave a soft laugh that whisked against his jaw.

"I thought you'd never say my name," Huvet murmured. "So bloody proper, you damned copper." And he squeezed his fingers tighter, drawing another groan from Guillaume.

After that, neither of them spared a breath for mere talk. Though the confines of the fiacre and its unsteady bumping over the cobbles weren't the best of conditions, those inconveniences lost ground to hot mouths, greedy, knowing hands, and the pleasure they both sought.

When it was over and they were gasping for breath, hands braced next to the other on the seat, thigh to flank, Guillaume pressed one last kiss at the nape of Émile's neck and eased away. His shirt was disordered, the buttons at the back half undone. His trousers were past his knees, his body hot and damp from exertion and pleasure. His tie was lost in the chaos of clothing, and God knew where his gloves had gone.

As he settled back onto the opposite side of the carriage, still hot and vibrating with gratification, the enormity of what had just happened struck him.

He, an officer of the law, had just engaged in carnal activity in a carriage—in public—with another man. Anyone might have seen him climb in with Émile. The driver might have heard them. For all he knew, the driver might *know* Émile.

He could be found out. Though it wasn't strictly illegal, they could take him away. They'd done it to Étienne—

Guillaume viciously reined in his careening thoughts and blocked his wild emotions. He focused on the mundane actions of tucking his shirt back into the trousers, fumbling with the buttons at the back of his neck, fastening his waistcoat. All without looking at his companion.

He was slightly nauseated now, and that reminded him he'd been up nearly twenty-four hours, he hadn't had a full meal in longer than that, and he'd been fueling himself with brandy, wine, and scotch since afternoon.

"I need to get out," he said, rapping hard on the roof of the fiacre. "I need to go."

"Guillaume," Émile said, watching him from across the way. "I thought— Did I misunderstand?"

"No," Guillaume said as the fiacre jerked to a halt. "No, it's not that. I just— I must go." He snatched up his coat, hat, gloves, and walking stick, and flung open the door.

The fresh night air was a cool contrast to the close, musky smell of the carriage. He fumbled for some bills in his suit pocket and thrust them up at the driver.

Then, with weak knees and a pounding, spinning head, he looked back into the dark interior of the carriage. "Good night, monsieur."

THIRTEEN

I thought you were finished with Christophe, Ginny," Aloysius said at breakfast the next morning. His dark brows drew together as he settled penetrating black eyes onto Lucie.

She sighed, settling back in the chair in her small outdoor dining nook. She'd managed to avoid this topic of conversation last night after they left Mme Loynes' home only because she'd distracted her half-brother by telling him about Inspector Devré's invasion of her dressing room, as well as the news about Pierre Lansac.

It had been a godsend, Aloysius showing up at Mme Loynes' that moment, for otherwise she greatly feared Christophe would have insisted on seeing her back to Château Lisette. And she feared even more that she knew how that would have ended.

But now, bleary-eyed from too few hours of restless sleep, and strangely hungry despite the unsettling disruptions in her life, Lucie was at a disadvantage as she and Aloysius sat alone in a sunny alcove near the greenhouse. It was her favorite place to eat breakfast on a pleasant morning—though by the time she rose, on most days, one could not call the meal breakfast but more like *déjeuner*.

Today, however, she could fairly use the term breakfast to describe the event, for it was the ungodly hour of half past eight.

"I am finished with him," she replied, brutally forcing back the tension headache that threatened to break through her skull.

"I didn't know he would be there last night, and thank God you arrived when you did. You saved me from having to extricate myself from a delicate situation."

"Extricate is an exacting word to use," he said, "considering you were quite engaged in his embrace. Ginny, you were so determined never to see him again, and I saw how much he hurt you and how you began to—"

"Nonsense," she said sharply. "It was nothing more than my pride bruised, when I learned he'd lied to me. We were together for a length of time—"

"Far, far longer than you'd been with any man—"

"Since Onni," she said with a wry smile. Ah, Onni. If only he were here, he'd surely have plenty to say about the entire situation.

"Aye. Since Onni. And even that..." Aloysius shrugged, smiling softly. But his eyes, oh, they were so sharp and delving, and Lucie knew she could hide very little from the man who loved her more than any other person in the world.

Suddenly overwhelmed by affection, and also regretting her moment of weak, self-indulgent emotions last night, she reached between the delicate cups and plates and covered his large hand with one of hers. It barely did half the job.

"Loy-loy," she said, "I know you're only worried for me. But you needn't be. My heart is fully intact. You know it belongs only to you, and always will." She squeezed, then deftly changed the subject to one that would surely distract him from the lies she was speaking. "But perhaps I need be worried about you. Where were you all day yesterday? You were here, and then you were gone—and then you returned and were gone again."

He withdrew his hand, ostensibly to pour coffee for himself. But she'd seen the way his eyes skittered away, and felt his slight stiffening. "I had some things to attend to. Nothing important."

"But you were supposed to escort me to l'Expo last night," she said, feeling a strange pressure in her chest. He was definitely hiding something. But how could he? What would he hide from her? They had been through so much together—

"I'm ashamed, Ginny. I did forget. But even I'm not perfect," he added with his infectious grin, so very white in his clean-shaven face. "And I've never done so before, now have I? We went to Mass, and the cemetery, and then after I brought you home. When you took a nap, I thought you had no more need of me. I had some business to attend to, and it took longer than I thought. When I returned, you'd already left for the expo. I couldn't arrive dressed as I had been, so I had to clean up. And then when I got to the expo, I learned you were gone, and it took me quite some time to track you down."

It was a lovely explanation. A very practiced one, in fact. And the pressure in her chest increased when Lucie acknowledged that she didn't quite believe it. She might have pressed the subject further, but Aloysius flipped the subject yet again—and this time to something even more disturbing.

"And what about that reporter?" he asked. "The woman? Have you seen her again?"

Lucie had the sudden urge to slip into her room and open the rosewood box she'd placed in the drawer of her bedside table. She needed something to ease her tension. Her fingers trembled a bit as she imagined the laudanum's sweet, cloying taste. It would bring her much-needed ease.

"Yes. She was there last night. At the expo. It was she who told me Pierre was dead. And the way she looks at me—Aloysius, I believe she wishes me ill. It's the way she watches me. She was hovering about the entire evening at Maxim's when—the night Paul Bacard died."

His full lips firmed into a tight line. "I'll find out what I can about her. What paper she writes for, where she comes from, everything."

"She's from England," Lucie told him softly. Her chest was very tight. "And, oh, God, but I think...I think I might know her. She seems familiar, somehow."

His expression was grave. "I'll find out what I can. Don't worry, Ginny. There's nothing she can do to you."

Lucie wanted to believe him—to believe that her past was dead, buried, and there was no way to connect her to what happened—but neither of them could possibly know that for certain. "You won't—you won't hurt her."

He looked at her, lines crinkling between his brows, his eyes filled with surprise. "Have you ever known me to touch—let alone hurt—a woman, for any reason?" His voice was very quiet and very flat.

"No, of course not," she said quickly. "Oh, Loy, of course you wouldn't hurt her. I didn't really mean it that way—I just meant— No. I'm sorry. I shouldn't have said that, let alone thought it. I have no excuse. Please forgive me." What was wrong with her? Of course she knew him better than that. She felt ill for having hurt him so.

"Yes, I forgive you," he replied. Then to prove it, he offered her the plate with the last buttercup-yellow muffin on it. "You should have this, love. You're looking a bit peaked." Hardly larger than her thumb, the butter muffin was moist and sweet, and topped with sugared violets. It was his favorite, and Lucie always saved them for him, for the chef could only make them when violets were in season.

"Thank you, Loy-loy." She wasn't hungry anymore, but she ate the sweet anyway, and washed it down her too-dry throat with a few sips of coffee.

"Miss Lucie."

She looked over to see Stanton standing in the arched glass doorway that led from the greenhouse to the main house. "Yes?"

"It's that man from la Sûreté," he said. "The inspector. He's insisting upon speaking with Miss Hélène, and Duchagne was certain you'd wish to know."

Damn and blast. Lucie rose abruptly, sloshing Aloysius's sweetened black coffee from its overfilled cup into the saucer below.

"I'll come too," he said.

"Thank you," she replied, grateful that he and his bulky and male beauty would be there as both distraction and security. "I don't know what he could want from her again."

Moments later, Lucie swished into Hélène's salon, still wearing her simple blue kimono. The loose robe was a style she'd come to appreciate from her days in Kyoto, for it allowed her to move much more quickly and smoothly than any other attire forced upon her by Parisian or London style. They'd never heard of corsets in Japan.

"Inspector Devré," she said, gracelessly interrupting his interrogation. "What brings you back to Château Lisette? And so early?"

He rose from the chair next to Hélène's divan. Lucie could see that, like herself, he appeared to be suffering from a severe lack of sleep. There were dark, puffed circles under his eyes, and his cheeks were gaunt above his mustache. Even his hair seemed more listless than yesterday's buoyant waves.

She saw his attention move to Aloysius, and stay for a moment—but that wasn't unusual, for nearly everyone stared at the massive Moroccan man the first time they met him. He was impressive not only in height, but in the muscles that defined even his lower arms and neck. It took yards and yards of material to make his clothing, a fact that Jean Lorrain waxed on about nearly every time he mentioned him in his Pall Mall column.

"*Bonjour*, Mme Madeleine," said Devré, swinging his eyes back to her. "I didn't intend to disrupt your morning, at least, but alas, it appears the best-laid plans are not always executed as intended. Please accept my apologies, but I find it necessary to speak with Mlle Brosette once again."

"That's been made quite obvious by your presence," Lucie replied coolly. "I find it necessary to be present while you do so."

"And your...companion?"

"Yes, of course. Inspector Guillaume Devré, this is Aloysius de Marchande. Aloysius, *monsieur l'inspecteur*. From la Sûreté."

"Inspector. I cannot say it is a pleasure to meet you, but one cannot fault a man for doing his job to carry out justice." Aloysius offered his hand in a gentleman's greeting, and Lucie noted the quickly banked surprise in Devré's eyes. Clearly he—as most others—had not expected the mountain of a man to have such civilized manners, such excellent French—or such a sense of egalitarianism.

Lucie, for her part, was slightly annoyed at the cordial greeting her beloved brother had given the fly in her ointment. He didn't need to be *quite* so pleasant.

"As I was saying, Mlle Brosette," Devré continued, "I should like to see the rooms—all of them, whichever they might be, including those most private ones—where M. Bacard was on the night he died." He glanced at Lucie. "Mademoiselle has already assured me once again, and so has the staff, that M. Bacard had nothing to eat or drink while he was here other than a small glass of wine from the same bottle as Mlle Brosette, and perhaps a cup of coffee. Yet the postmortem tells us the poison was introduced during the time Bacard was here at Château Lisette.

"Therefore, unless someone is lying," he said, looking meaningfully at Hélène, and then Duchagne (who'd lingered just outside the door, clearly hoping not to be noticed), and then back to Lucie, "one can only surmise that M. Bacard ingested something unbeknownst to mademoiselle. Perhaps while you were attending to your...er...personal matters? When you were ill and indisposed?" He turned back to Mlle Brosette.

Lucie moved to stand next to her friend. Hélène's fingers trembled as Lucie curled hers around them.

"I— He was in my private bedchamber," Hélène said. "As I told you before, inspector. And there is never anything in there that he might have had to drink, other than the bottle of sherry I often sip before I go to bed. But I just finished it last week, and have not yet replaced it—and so there is nothing there. Nothing at all."

"May I, mademoiselle?" Devré stood, gesturing toward the door that clearly led to the chamber in question.

Lucie felt her friend's intense reluctance, but there was no way around it. "Would you like me to show the inspector, Hélène?" she asked. "You can sit here."

"Yes, please, Lucie. I just... I feel faint. I am not... It's the morning. And I've been ill."

"Yes, of course, darling. Inspector? If you wish to follow me, and to destroy every last bit of my friend's privacy by invading her personal chamber, let us go and do it now."

Devré didn't seem shamed by her dramatic comment at all, and that caused Lucie to fume even more. Blast and damn the man.

While she understood his predicament, surely he didn't expect to find anything in Hélène's chamber.

Her mouth flat and hard, Lucie led Devré from Hélène's salon, where they'd all been sitting, through to the small alcove that led to another set of rooms—the rooms she used for entertaining. But to the left in the alcove was a door leading to another short hallway, which led to the main house kitchen, and also Hélène's private bathing room, bedchamber, and dressing room.

Devré stopped at the lavatory first, looking around with those feral eyes, making short, angular notes in his notebook. He drew back the curtain that surrounded the bathtub and minutely inspected the tile as well as the cake of fragrant soap and floral bath oils. He sniffed the pair of candles, then looked through the two glass-fronted cabinets in the room, flipping through a pile of towels and washcloths.

"And this is where Mlle Brosette was when she was ill? The night Bacard was here? There is, of course, the chance that she was poisoned as well, Mlle Lucie," he said, pausing to give her a serious look. "And that's what caused her illness. Perhaps they drank from the same bottle of wine, but perhaps he had more—much more to drink, and—"

"Hélène's illness is not due to anything she ate or drank," Lucie told him. She hated breaking a confidence, but the more information Devré had, the more certain he must become that neither she nor Hélène had had anything to do with Bacard's death.

As she'd expected, the detective turned those all-seeing eyes onto her. "And you are quite certain of this?"

"As I believe Hélène previously told you, her illness was of a female nature. One that will be resolved in approximately seven months."

His eyes widened with comprehension, then narrowed, and she imagined how that bit of information was filtering down inside his quick mind, settling in among all of the other facts and bits of interest he'd collected so far. "I see. Thank you for that, mademoiselle," he added sincerely. "Do not think I don't realize what that cost you."

Lucie gritted her teeth. He had no idea what all of this was costing her—betraying the confidence of a friend, having the police breathing down her neck, invading her home and her thoughts and mind, keeping her from sleep—and the reporter. That woman reporter.

"And now for the bedchamber. This is *la suite privée?*"

"Yes," Lucie said as they entered the small room. She stood at the door, feeling surprisingly awkward as Devré prowled about in this most intimate of all rooms. Poor Hélène. No wonder she didn't want to be here to witness this. Lucie couldn't blame her.

"And what is this?" Devré had lifted the bed skirt, and now he emerged with a small glass. There was a glint of satisfaction in his eyes as he held it up for Lucie to see, as well as so the light streaming from the lace-draped window shone through it as he gave it a close inspection.

"So Hélène had a glass of water before bed," Lucie said with a shrug. "That means nothing."

"Perhaps." He sniffed inside the glass, then, as he'd done last night, swiped a finger inside. "There was something other than water in here recently—and not very long ago, for there isn't any dust. The residual liquid has a heavy, sweet scent."

"She keeps a bottle of sherry in here, monsieur."

"But she said she hasn't replaced her bottle of sherry in a week. The glass would be dusty if it were more than a day or two old. And the contents...it smells of roses and heavy sweetness, mademoiselle. That in itself is not suspicious, of course, but what I do find interesting is...if Mlle Brosette were to have a drink, why would the glass be under the bed? Wouldn't it be on the table there? And surely her maid would remove it for cleaning, no? Unless it were knocked off the table, of course, but wouldn't mademoiselle retrieve it if she did so?"

Standing in the doorway, arms crossed over the luscious silk of her kimono, Lucie watched him. He made some small points, yes, but in and of itself, the glass wasn't suspicious. She could think of a hundred ways how it came to be under the bed. One thing was certain: Hélène's maid hadn't swept beneath it in at least two days, and that meant she needed a good talking-to.

Devré set the glass down on the bureau and continued his investigation in the room. He looked through Hélène's wardrobe, skimming through the silks and satins inside. He peered between her rows of shoes, shuffled through the scarves, hats, gloves, and capes. He opened the small cabinet next to the wardrobe, revealing a teapot, a pair of scissors, a trio of journals, shoe polish and a shoe-button hook, and a box of handkerchiefs. He moved then to the small set of shelves near the bed on which Hélène's meager book collection—mostly dime novels and erotic picture books—and some figurines rested.

"And what is this?" His voice was sharp as he reached for the unlabeled glass bottle that stood, with its ornate glass stopper, next to the dish that held one of Hélène's most intimate articles.

Before he'd even removed the stopper to sniff inside, Lucie realized it. *Roses and honey.*

"*Sacre bleu*," he murmured as he inhaled the essence of the bottle. "Mademoiselle, what is this? Mlle Brosette's evening drink, perhaps? It smells of roses—"

"And honey. Yes. No. Not her evening drink." All at once, a terrible, strange thought occurred to her as several facts fell into place. She looked from the bottle to the glass and then to the small crystal dish on the shelf. "I think...I believe I know what happened, monsieur."

"I'm beginning to see myself," he replied quietly. "But perhaps you will explain your thoughts, mademoiselle."

"That bottle is not Hélène's evening drink, inspector, but it *is* mead—so you smell the fermented honey, and it's scented with rosewater. It's not used for drink, but...uhm...well, monsieur. You see, there, in that small dish next to it?"

Devré lifted the lid of the crystal dish and exposed a small sea sponge. "She uses it to bathe, perhaps?" he asked, glancing toward the door. "But why is it not with the bath tub?"

"No, monsieur. It is a contraceptive sponge. It's used to prevent pregnancy." She forced herself to speak matter-of-factly, despite the extreme intimacy of the situation. "And before the sponge is inserted, it is soaked in a solution of the mead and rosewater. Honey alone was traditionally used by Egyptian women for contraceptive purposes, and alcohol, of course, has a disinfecting property. Together with the sponge, it's an effective method of sterilization and contraception."

"I see." His voice was very soft. "And so there is no reason there should be traces of rose-scented mead in this glass, for its purpose is not refreshment."

"Yes, monsieur. You are correct. Hélène would surely not drink from it, but...but someone else, who wouldn't know any better, might have done so."

"Someone like Paul Bacard. Someone who was left alone in Mlle Brosette's private chamber whilst she was ill, someone who was desperate for something to drink, perhaps...and who found this and poured it into a glass and drank from it...and less than five hours later was dead."

"Yes," Lucie said quietly. "I am quite afraid you might be right."

"Afraid? Yes, mademoiselle, you should certainly be afraid. For if we are correct, then you are far too intelligent not to know what this means."

"Yes," she repeated, a bit fainter this time. "It means that Paul Bacard wasn't meant to be poisoned, but Hélène was."

"Indeed." His eyes had never left hers, and they were sharper than ever. Cutting and intense and knowing. He looked at her in a way he hadn't before: as if he saw all of her secrets. "And thus the question would become: who would want Hélène Brosette dead?"

FOURTEEN

D amn it. You again? Don't tell me you've got another one."
Jackson used his forearm to push a lock of hair from his face.

"And *bonjour* to you too, *docteur*," Guillaume said.

The pathologist sounded testier than usual, and Guillaume was glad he hadn't barged into the lab earlier this morning, before either of them had had coffee.

He couldn't say whether the other man had had his caffeine, but Guillaume had managed a quick cup himself and forced himself to down a large hunk of cheese with a piece of bread. After last night, he knew he couldn't begin another day without a decent meal.

Last night.

A volley of emotions and thoughts threatened to distract him. There was no time to think about it now—no time for regrets, for shame, for sadness...

"How quickly can you test this?" Guillaume set both the glass and the bottle of rose-scented mead on the table next to an array of tubes and dishes where the doctor was working.

"I'm in the middle of som— It smells like roses." Jackson looked at Guillaume, a glint of interest replacing irritation.

"Indeed it does, monsieur. And I'm quite certain within that bottle you'll find not only the sweet, honeylike substance that has stained Bacard's shirt, but also some significant dosage of digitalis."

Muttering something unflattering about possibly either Guillaume or the world in general, Jackson finished with the dropper he was using to place some chemical on some other substance in a petri dish and set it aside. "I need two hours. Minimum. Go away and don't come back until then. Maybe get some sleep—you look like hell."

"It would be my pleasure, monsieur," Guillaume replied, "but first, you must express your gratitude by telling me what you know of Lansac thus far, and if there is anything else you've found of Bacard."

"Gratitude? What the hell for?" Jackson paused, fixing Guillaume with suspicious eyes. Madame, who lay in her usual place in the center of the lab, lifted her head to listen, watching them from beneath the heavy fringe of black hair. Then, determining nothing of interest was being said, she dropped back to the floor with a groan and stretched out one of her unbandaged legs.

"For not coming here as early as I intended," Guillaume replied smoothly. "I meant to be here at half past seven, because I know you arrive at seven o'clock."

"Good God, I would have thrown you out," Jackson said, already taking a sample from the mead bottle in spite of his grumbling.

"You would not, but I can appreciate your position. Which is why you should express your gratitude by telling me what else you've got on Bacard—because you left Hôtel Briö last night before I was finished talking to you."

That really was the only complaint Guillaume had about working with Jackson. The man's disgruntled mood was of no matter, but the fact that half the time he was so involved in his work and thinking of his next steps that he forgot to tell Guillaume what his examinations had uncovered was both inconsiderate and frustrating.

Most medico-legists couldn't wait to crow about what they'd learned or concluded, eagerly sharing their genius. Not Jackson. He somehow expected Guillaume to know simply by reading his mind.

"I had another corpse, dammit. Had no time to stand around conversing. You want me to rush through this, but you want to stand around talking—like now." Jackson's words were fast and irritated, but his movements as he measured and sampled and sniffed and droppered were careful and efficient.

Guillaume ignored this tirade. "On Bacard: anything else? The stains on his clothing? What did you find?"

"Didn't I tell you? Christ's crutch, I thought I did. Honey on his shirt—could be this stuff right here, and if it is, will it get you out of my damned lab?"

"Yes, indeed. But the other stains? Vomit? Yes? Anything else?"

"Vomit, and— Oh, perhaps there is something I didn't tell you." He looked up from the microscope. "Bacard had semen on the side of his shirt. Near the *back* of his shirt. And I confirmed—he'd recently been sodomized."

Guillaume stilled. Well, now. That was rather unexpected. But... perhaps not completely surprising, given what he'd discovered about Lansac. "Was it violent?"

"It didn't appear to be. No tears in the skin. There was some blood, but he was very ill from the poison, and that could be from the forceful expulsion of his bowels. There was blood in the vomit too."

If it had been anyone other than Thomas Jackson speaking about this discovery and its implications, there would be an undercurrent of disgust, distaste, and cold judgment. Guillaume had experienced it from his colleagues—from officers, detectives, magistrates, pathologists—with every previous situation he'd encountered. The famous pathologist Alexandre Lacassagne—Jackson's mentor and the head of the forensic science department at University of Lyon—had written extensively on this sort of behavior, along with his own opinion about the morals and criminality of those who practiced these so-called "Greek tendencies."

Thus, Uranians, inverts, mollies: whatever one called those men who preferred sexual encounters with other men, they were seen as inherently criminal, hardly more respectable than dogs, and even less tolerable than gypsies or Jews.

And Guillaume was one of them, walking carefully on a line balancing the light and dark sides of his life. Climbing heedlessly into carriages with handsome men, flirting with them in public—

"Anything else?" he said, swinging his thoughts from those unpleasant ones.

"Isn't that enough?"

"Not yet." Guillaume forced himself to press on. "Have you heard of the tonic known as the blue dragon?"

"The blue dragon? It's a drink that makes a man crazy. Hallucinating crazy."

"No, no, monsieur—that's the green fairy, better known as absinthe." He understood the correlation, though, because that was precisely how he'd made the connection last night: the thought of a blue fairy's bottle had made him think of the infamous green fairy, and then that made him remember the blue dragon.

"The blue dragon is another sort of drink?"

"It's a potion for a man who is—who has those sort of Greek tendencies," Guillaume said, suddenly wishing he hadn't brought it up. What if Jackson figured it out? What if he read between the lines, wondering how Guillaume would know so much about this topic?

"Greek tendenc— Ah. I see." Jackson nodded brusquely and, in doing so, poked his eye with the narrow microscope eyepiece. He swore and blinked rapidly, but didn't pull away. "Is the potion supposed to cure him of it?"

"After a fashion." Guillaume still felt as if he were walking on one of the tightropes he'd seen at the circus, where a lithe young Chinese man in very tight clothing that left nothing to his imagination had minced and flipped and run along its length. Afterward, Guillaume had found himself unable to resist a stroll along the Champs-Élysées for a quick, impersonal meetup in one of the public urinals.

His insides squirmed with distaste and shame, and he put away the sordid memory.

"After a fashion? What the hell does that mean? Are they selling it to the poor sots as a damned cure?"

"My understanding is," Guillaume continued carefully, not sure how he felt about the "poor sots" part, but supposed it was better than "cocksucking dogs," "there are times when that type of man needs to be able to...consummate his marriage, for example. Or to get an heir."

"Why the hell would one bother getting married if that was the case?" Jackson muttered something and sniffed inside the glass, which had a sticky residue inside. "Smells the same to me."

"Right. About Lansac. I know you haven't had the body for long—"

"Damn right." Jackson looked up as if just remembering his solitude was being interrupted. "Why are you here? Lansac? Just got him delivered here last night at half-ten, and here you are at the crack of dawn. I've not even made the Y-cut yet, Guillaume."

Though ten o'clock was not the crack of dawn, Guillaume declined to argue. The man did have a point, and Guillaume had dismembered the doctor's schedule by bringing in the bottle and glass. Since he didn't expect Jackson to find anything that didn't support his thesis of suicide, he supposed he could be a little patient.

And as this recent information that implied Bacard's sexual activity was not confined to females, it gave Guillaume much to think about—as well as the beginning of a new theory.

However, the biggest and most concerning factor now was the reasonable suspicion that Bacard was not the poisoner's intended target. This changed everything he'd been looking at, turning his theories upside down.

Someone had wanted to kill Hélène Brosette, and that someone had access to her bedchamber. There were very few people with opportunity, and only one, thus far, with an obvious motive. He had more work to do, looking more closely at Hélène Brosette's lifestyle and history to see what enemies might lurk there, but...

La Balise is a murderer.

Anna Smith's words had been ringing in his mind since last night. And Guillaume was beginning to believe them.

Lucie paced the room. The kimono, which she had so far declined to remove in lieu of something more French though it was nearly noon, slid against her skin like a lover's hand. But eroticism and sensuality were far from a mind that was now focused on the reality that a murderer must be within Château Lisette.

There was no other way to look at it.

But *who* would want to kill Hélène?

She wasn't certain it was even possible to kill a woman in that manner, by poisoning the sterilizing solution soaked up by a contraceptive sponge—though someone clearly thought it was. The intent was all that mattered.

Lucie paced faster, her heart thudding hard, her knees weak. A murderer among them. And Hélène could still be in danger.

After she confessed Devré's suspicions to Hélène, Lucie had ordered Piquette—the only person she completely trusted besides Aloysius—to assist Tillé, Hélène's personal maid, in caring for her. Understandably, Hélène was beyond overset at the new revelations, and had had to be given another sleeping draught. Lucie decided to send for Émile in case something stronger was needed. And she'd already insisted that Aloysius remain in the private salon, and to allow no one access to Hélène or her suite for the time being.

Her brother had attempted to argue, but Lucie would not be gainsaid. Hélène's life was not to be risked, even if Lucie had to make do without Aloysius as her escort today. She hadn't yet told him the details about how the poisoner had gone about the process—even with Aloysius, it was too intimate a topic.

Nothing else was said to the staff yet either. Lucie needed to determine how to handle the problem—from who would have reason, to who would have access, to who was untrustworthy.

But they were *all* trustworthy. Surely her entire staff was trustworthy. She couldn't imagine any of them doing anything like this.

Was it possible it had been an accident? A terrible accident?

Lucie agreed with Inspector Devré that chemical analysis would determine that someone had put poison in the bottle of alcohol used to soak Hélène's personal sponge. Someone who knew about the process, someone who knew only Hélène would use it and that the mead was only used for that purpose, and not for ingestion.

Unless...what if Hélène was not the only target?

Lucie's heart stopped when she thought of her own bottle of mead, and she spun in her insubstantial Japanese slippers and fairly ran to the place where she kept the contraceptive device in a demure silver box. Next to it was her own bottle of sterilizing solution. She'd had no cause to use it recently—not in more than two months, to the dismay of Vicomte Fouquier and Señor Oller. As she opened the cabinet door and looked at the slender, innocent-looking bottle, she swallowed hard.

It would have to be thrown out—no, it would be *tested* first. She would have it tested to make certain. And oh *damn*—she'd have to take the bottles from Rose-Marie and Camille as well. But they'd been using them, hadn't they? And neither of them had—

"M. Calmette is here to see you, mademoiselle."

Lucie's heart gave an extra sharp knock due both to being startled by the voice of Estelle, one of the upper maids, and the news that Christophe was here. So early. So soon.

It was better than Inspector Devré, she told herself. But only slightly.

"Tell him I— *Christophe*. I don't believe you were invited into this chamber." Her voice was sharp, and she turned to look at Estelle, whose complexion had gone tight and white with mortification and fear. Lucie sighed internally. What could she expect from a chambermaid, who'd been reassigned to help Lucie while Piquette was with Hélène? "You're dismissed for now, Estelle. Finish with the ironing. I'll ring when I need you again." Her voice was still cold, and the maid fled, bobbing a mobile curtsy, with a face that was now flaming.

"*Bonjour, ma lumière.* You look lovely as usual, despite the early hour. But Lucie—don't you think you were a bit hard on the poor thing? She didn't have any choice—I followed her back here. You know I know the way. And what has happened to the formidable Piquette?"

"Yes, Piquette would never have made the mistake of turning her back on you." Lucie retained her cool demeanor. She was furious with him for taking the liberty of coming to her most private of rooms uninvited. No one did so. Not even Aloysius.

"And you aren't welcome in here, Christophe. No bit of charming deprecation will gain you entrance to this room again. Now, let's repair to the parlor, where we can sit and you can tell me if you've learned anything about the blue bottle."

For a moment, he looked as if he wanted to argue—or to take her by the hand and pull her up against him and kiss her senseless as he tumbled her onto the large white bed where they'd tangled and loved and laughed so many times.

The back of her throat burned, and she forced herself to focus on the present, on the slender bottle she still gripped, and on the facts that now there were at least two people in Paris who were out to destroy her—and possibly three.

"Of course." Christophe's tone had become a trifle cooler, a bit more distant. "I was... I thought..." He sighed, rubbing his forehead. "Never mind."

She led the way to her parlor—the private one, not her public sitting room where she had first encountered Devré... Damn, had it been only yesterday? Only thirty hours ago? How could so much have happened—and so much have gone wrong—in such a short time?

"Did you learn anything about the blue bottle?" she asked, after ringing for a maid to bring two cups of chocolate and a light meal.

Christophe had settled himself quite properly in the chair farthest from her perch on the small blue velvet sofa, and he set his hat—which he'd neglected to hand off to the butler or the maid since he'd sneakily followed Estelle back to the innermost rooms of the house—on the small piecrust table next to him. "I did. It was surprisingly easy, but that was because I knew just whom to speak to at the Jockey."

"And?" she asked.

"My source—who shall remain anonymous, so please don't ask, *ma chère*," he admonished before she even thought to open her mouth, "tells me it is an unusual color glass with a particular design, as you see. But it has a reputation. It's only used to contain a tonic known as the blue dragon. Have you heard of it?"

"The blue dragon." Lucie had heard the term mentioned in sly tones, perhaps once or twice, but she wasn't certain what it meant.

Though she had an idea. "Is it a liqueur? Like absinthe?" That would make sense—perhaps it was even more potent than the green fairy.

"No, it's not a drink. I'm rather surprised you haven't heard of it, all things considered. It's something that only certain men—men of certain preferences, shall we say—might be in need of. On their wedding night, perhaps...or if the man becomes too old and infirm."

Lucie's brows rose as she began to understand. "Do you mean... it's a blue potion that helps them to *perform?*"

"Supposedly." He grinned, his eyes lighting up and appearing rather blue themselves. "I suspect more than a few men would like to have help with a *blue dragon* raging from behind his fly buttons. Not that I would know of that, *non, ma lumière?*" His gaze had become very warm, and to her astonishment, Lucie felt her cheeks heat.

"To be quite honest, *I* should have called it a purple dragon," she said to prove that she was unmoved by his flirtations. "Not a blue one. Still, I take the point."

"I am quite certain you do, *ma chère.*"

"So Lansac was an invert. Or had some other problem, but I would say not. He was young, and...there was always something about him that I could not quite finger."

"Do you mean he never looked your way? He must be the only man in Paris who has not. Even Jean Lorrain or Montesquiou would be able to get it up if you but gave him the chance."

She rolled her eyes. "We aren't speaking of Jean right now— and anyway, I don't believe half of his posturing. He's not nearly as flamboyant and effeminate as he would have one believe, Christophe. I can...I can usually sense when that's the case. When it's...when a man has no interest in a woman, and when a woman has only interest in other women."

Just as she said those words, she realized she should not have done so. Christophe stilled, and that look—a taut, blanched expression— froze his features.

"If that's the case, you must know that I never lied to you about Yvette being a Sapphic." His mouth tightened. "If that's the only reason—"

Lucie looked away. "It's so much more than that, Christophe. You're aware of that. And now—you have a wife who is clearly prepared to act as one, and now a child, and—"

"Very well, then." His voice was as precisely clipped as the mustache above it. "I believe you at last. We are finished, Lucie. It's over. You can move on to your next flower, my dazzling honeybee."

"And what makes you think I have not already done so?" she said calmly. "It's been eight months."

"You haven't," he told her softly. "The way you kissed me last night tells me so."

Lucie's attention snapped to him in spite of herself. "You're a fool if you believe that, Christophe."

He merely looked at her, and the stillness was broken only when the kitchen maid tapped at the door. Lucie was vitally glad for the momentary distraction while a tray was set up and the hot chocolate was poured.

"You do know you could be in danger, Lucie," he said after the girl had left them. "After all, there is a murderer about."

She marveled for a moment at his ability to so cleanly change mood and topic, despite the emotionally charged moment earlier. And she appreciated it. "I don't think so, but..." She gestured to the slender bottle that she'd brought from the bedchamber. "I will need to have that analyzed to determine whether someone put digitalis in it."

Christophe put down his cup with a rattle. "What do you mean? Please explain."

"Paul Bacard is dead, but it seems that he wasn't the target after all. Someone appears to have poisoned the alcohol Hélène uses for her—for her sponge." She had no reason to stumble over this topic with him, at least. He was fully aware of the purpose of the sponge, and they'd had more than one argument about her eschewing it during their *affaire*. He'd desperately wanted a child, and there'd been no chance of him getting one on his wife—at least, that was what he'd told her.

Lucie gritted her teeth and continued. "The theory is that Paul accidentally drank from the bottle, not knowing its purpose, and not knowing it was poisoned, of course."

"Someone got into Hélène's private chamber and poisoned the alcohol she uses with it?" Christophe's attention went swiftly back to the bottle Lucie held. "By God, what if the maniac has gone through and done the same to yours—and the others?"

"Precisely why I must have it analyzed. At first, we were trying to determine who would want to kill Paul Bacard. But now that we know more, the question is: who would want to kill Hélène?"

"And possibly you. Lucie, you must have guards placed around the house immediately. Who knows what sort of danger you're in?" He looked as if he were about to stand and call for the police right at that moment.

"I don't believe a guard would be of any help in this instance. My fear has always been—and is now even more certain—that it's someone in the household. Who else would have access to Hélène's room? Or even know where it was?"

He stared at her for a moment. "Anyone, Lucie. It's not that difficult for someone to slip into a different room in this massive hotel of yours. A delivery boy, a maid or her beau, a footman—even one of your guests." The last was said with a taste of bitterness. "There are so many hallways and rooms, it would be far too easy for someone to find their way into places they have no business being. It's easier than you think."

"A point you have already made quite well today," she reminded him, suddenly feeling both relieved—perhaps it wasn't someone she trusted and lived with after all—and more apprehensive. If he were right, and someone *had* sneaked their way into the depths of the house, how would they ever find out who?

Christophe seemed chagrined over her pointed comment, but he moved on—far more interested in discussing the elements of the situation than his own trespassing, despite that it made his point quite handily.

"I don't mean to suggest it was a random person who just happened to walk in and decide to put digitalis—is that what you said it was?—in a bottle of liqueur. But if someone wanted Hélène—or anyone else in this house dead—they could plan a way to sneak inside and do it that way—even by hiring someone else to do it. There are so many people coming and going here, Lucie—it's like a small village. Gardeners, delivery boys, seamstresses, couriers, guests... So the question is, assuming that it is only Hélène's bottle that is poisoned, something I am fervently hoping is the case or I shall have to whisk you away to safety whether you like it or not—who would want her dead?"

Lucie was shaking her head. "I don't know. I simply can't think who would. I've been racking my brain for hours—since Devré discovered the glass under the bed, and—"

"The glass under the bed?"

Lucie explained how she and Devré had put the pieces together to come up with the newest, most reasonable story for what had happened. "Until then, we all thought Paul Bacard was the target—that someone had poisoned him, and that someone here had done it."

"But you aren't certain yet that your theory is correct," Christophe reminded her. "You and your Inspector Devré could be wrong about the bottle in Hélène's room."

She ignored his slight emphasis on "your" Devré. "That is true. I don't know when the results from Dr. Jackson's review will be finished, so until then..." She gave a shrug and eyed the plate of figs and cheese. The fruits, colored a soft purple and green, had been cut into quarters to reveal their mellow insides. There was a soft white cheese next to them, along with a dark, sweet vinegar to drizzle with a spoon, but Lucie preferred them without condiment.

"Yes, it's intelligent to be aware that the poisoned mead is the likeliest scenario. But for now, let us talk about Paul Bacard first. Because it is still possible he was the intended victim."

"Very well, Christophe, but I do think Devré is right. Paul was an accident. After all, I can think of no one who would want to kill him."

"He was quite fond of you for a while, wasn't he? You counted him among your companions...I believe it was shortly after I left for Marseille."

Lucie was about to bite into a piece of fig, and she did not allow his pointed comment to stop her, sliding the piece of fruit into her mouth. The fig should have been delicious: it was perfectly ripe, sensual, and smooth, a treat she often delighted in serving to her guests. But today, it tasted mealy, tainted by the discomfort that seemed to grow inside her as more and more information came to light.

"Paul Bacard was a nice young man. Attractive, attentive, and good-natured. We did not have a long-lasting liaison, if that is what you're suggesting. I found him rather boring and not very stimulating when it came to conversation, and Hélène was quite enchanted with him. I was more than happy to redirect his attentions toward her."

"But surely that's why this Devré is looking so closely at you. Whether it was Bacard's death or Hélène's that was intended, he can place a motive at your feet—either you were jealous of Hélène, because she was taking Bacard from you, or you were angry with Bacard, because he had chosen her over you." Christophe's expression was grave, and he'd taken little more than a sip of his drink. "Women—and men—have killed for less."

"But you know either scenario is ridiculous," Lucie replied, snatching up another piece of fig.

"I do agree Paul Bacard is not at all your style. He is—was—an eager, pan-footed puppy to your sleek, practiced feline self. But let us just take one moment to look at the situation. Who would want him dead? By all accounts—and I did take the liberty of asking around at the Jockey—he was well liked. The only word I got was that his parents were pressuring him to marry, and he had a few small gambling debts, but nothing else. No one seemed to have a problem with him."

"I agree. There seems to be no reason that anyone would want him dead. But...there is one interesting thing I learned." Lucie had almost forgotten what Dr. Jackson had told her just before he shooed her out of his lab yesterday. Yet, in light of the information Christophe had brought her just now, it could be important.

"Yes?" he asked when she didn't immediately continue, for she'd paused in thought.

At his prompting, she looked up. "There was semen on his shirt. On Paul's shirt. From the night he died."

It was to his credit that Christophe waited for her to continue, rather than to interrupt with his own thoughts and conjectures.

"Most remarkably, it was near the back of his shirt, low to the hem," Lucie said.

His eyes widened. "And in light of the blue dragon factor...I find that very interesting. The fact that Lansac was in possession of the blue dragon—and got angry about you revealing it—implies that he was in need of it."

"*Exactement.*"

"And as for Bacard...was he the same way? Would he—er—have been in need of it to stoke his own dragon?" Christophe held Lucie's gaze.

One of the reasons she'd ended things with Christophe—though not the most pressing—had been his inability to accept her choice of lifestyle. He hadn't—couldn't—understand her desire for freedom and independence.

Every man with whom she came in contact, whether she had been intimate with him or not, had been a cause for snide remarks, tense conversations, and sidelong, angry looks. Violent or even overt jealousy was not Christophe's problem, but the lack of trust and the bitter comments were an underlying grief she could do without.

Yes, she had had relationships with other men. But when she was with Christophe, she slept with no one else. He could not accept that she attracted attention from others, and he could not believe her when she told him otherwise.

And thus she knew he was now waiting for her answer about Paul Bacard for more than one reason.

"Hélène recently learned she is pregnant with his child," she replied—refusing on principle to inform Christophe that she and Bacard had never been lovers. "And they had decided to marry."

His reaction was shock and disbelief. "That cannot be true. Paul Bacard was going to *marry* her? Impossible."

"Why do you say that?" Lucie's ire rose—not for herself, not because of his implied slur on her as a *Dégrafée*, but for Hélène—who was as lovely and charming and warm as a woman could be. Certainly worthy of being a man's wife.

"Because his parents wanted him to marry Felicité Vertaine. It was all over the Jockey—the gossip at a men's club is just as fervent as it is among the ladies on the boulevard or in the salons. His family would have disowned him if he'd said he meant to marry Hélène Brosette. They probably would have disowned him even if he wanted to marry *you*."

Lucie quelled the sudden flush in her cheeks. That had, actually, been a topic of conversation between herself and Paul—he had been insistent; she had been just as insistent. And that had been the largest reason she had cut the line with him and gently redirected him to Hélène.

"That may be the case, but he and Hélène were most certainly engaged. Perhaps he changed his mind, or thought he would be able to convince his parents—after all, Hélène is quite comfortable financially. She would bring some significant assets to the family. And aside from that, she has just learned she is carrying his child. Surely his parents would have agreed."

Christophe was shaking his head. "I doubt that. But you said she is *enceinte*?"

Just as Lucie nodded, she realized the implications. Her eyes widened, and her attention darted to the bottle of mead. "If she realized she was pregnant, she would not have needed to use the sponge. So we can have no idea how long ago it was poisoned—at least, since the last time she used it. Which will make it that much more difficult to determine who had the opportunity to poison it."

"And clearly either yours is not poisoned, or you have not been employing your own as well," Christophe said, holding her eyes with his. "I wasn't wrong, was I, Lucie?"

She'd stood, and begun to pace the room, silk swishing sleekly against her skin. She would ignore his comments, ignore the way his eyes followed her, ignore the need to be held and comforted during this most tenuous of times. "Let me think on this. Paul Bacard seems to have been...flexible, shall we say...in his sexual encounters. Hélène surely never complained, and if she was pregnant by him—"

"Unless she's lying about it being his child, and was trying to coerce him into marrying him. Perhaps it was someone else's baby, and she intended to pass it off as his in order to marry a respectable man. A *wealthy*, respectable man."

Lucie spun around to look at him. The thought was both absurd, and yet not so far out of the realm of possibility. Hélène had expressed her desire for a husband more than once. And a man like Paul Bacard—handsome, kind, wealthy, from the upper echelon of the *tout-Paris*—would have been an excellent catch.

"It might not even be his child," Christophe continued. "And if that was the case, *he* could have wanted to get rid of *her*."

"But *he* is the one who died," she replied. "He wouldn't poison himself when he was trying to poison her. Besides, who would know to put digitalis in that particular bottle?" Even as she said it, though, Lucie realized that she was wrong. Nearly *anyone* would think to put poison in a bottle of liqueur that was in the private bedchamber of a person they wished to murder. Hardly anyone would realize the contents of the bottle had another use.

To wit—Bacard had most likely drunk from the bottle himself, completely innocently. Which meant that he had not put the poison there.

"The question comes back around to who would want to harm or kill Hélène. And whether there's anyone else in the house who is in danger." Lucie looked at her own bottle. It was past time for conjecture and pacing, and time to take action. At least she needed to know who was at risk. And then maybe she could get some answers.

"Thank you for coming, Christophe. And thank you for what you were able to learn about the blue dragon. I'm not sure if it factors in to what's happening here at Château Lisette, but it was kind of you to put yourself out to help me."

He stood and reached for her hand, tugging her toward him. Lucie planted her feet after one step and refused to move closer as he looked at her. "I will always be here to help you, Lucie-Geneviève. If you need anything, you only need to send for me."

"*Merci*," she murmured.

"Take care, Lucie. Take care of *ma lumière*."

"Now you—back to your beautiful new son, and your wife. I'll be fine. I have Aloysius."

"You will be fine. I have no doubt of that," he said, turning to retrieve his hat. "It's I who may not be."

FIFTEEN

⟡

This time when Guillaume, along with Houssaye, alighted from the carriage in front of Château Lisette, he saw the cluster of reporters had evolved into a small crowd.

Guillaume set his jaw. He was in no fine mood today, and if any of the press got in his way, he'd be using his walking stick for more than merely walking.

He growled at them to back off as he and his companion shouldered their way past, ignoring the shouts and demands for a statement.

Stanton gave the reporters a black look, and one almost as dark to Guillaume and Houssaye. But he stepped back and allowed the two men to enter.

"Mademoiselle is not here. She just left." Stanton appeared very tense.

"That is of no concern to me, for it's not necessary that I speak with Mlle Lucie at this time. In fact, we're here once again to interview the other members of the household, beginning with Mlles Camille and Rose-Marie, as well as the kitchen staff, the footmen, the maids... everyone we have already spoken to we must interview once more."

"Everyone—again?" Stanton's eyes grew wide and round. "Monsieur, that is upwards of twenty people."

"I am aware of that, as my colleague and I have already spoken to most of them yesterday," Guillaume replied wearily, wondering not for the first time how anyone could contemplate living in a household with so many other people. "That's why Officer Houssaye has come to assist me. Perhaps he could remain in this parlor and interview the maids and footmen who serve the other mesdemoiselles, and you could arrange a different location for me? I would not be averse to sitting in the lovely courtyard on this fine day." His smile was genuine, but his words left no room for disagreement.

"Of course, monsieur." Stanton bowed. "And which of you, pray tell, would like to interview me this time?"

A bit of cheekiness in a butler, Guillaume supposed, would keep things slightly less boring. "I think you and Officer Houssaye should become acquainted. After you escort me to a place—out in the sun, perhaps? Near the greenhouse. It's a central location, is it not?"

Stanton did as requested, seating Guillaume at an ornate iron café table with matching chairs. The trio was painted leaf green and was arranged beneath an arbor laden with some fragrant white flower.

"I shall have the maid bring you some coffee," Stanton said. "And perhaps some pastries?" The butler must have noted Devré's surprise, for he unbent enough to add, "It is a terrible thing, monsieur, what they are saying about Mlle Hélène being poisoned—or meant to be poisoned. But I can assure you, there is no one in this household who would do anything like that. I realize I am out of place in talking of this, but I do speak for everyone on the staff with the hope that you come to that conclusion as soon as possible—and so you can look elsewhere for the culprit."

"In that case, M. Stanton, I would be very grateful for some coffee—and a pastry would not hurt as well." It might even help the empty scraping in Guillaume's belly to subside—an emptiness not related to hunger, but to far different sensations. "If you could send for Mlles Camille and Rose-Marie, I will start with them."

"Very good, monsieur."

While he waited for the promised coffee and repast, along with the young women, Guillaume couldn't help but admire the lovely courtyard. Previously, he'd only caught glimpses of it from the interior. The semicircular greenhouse jutted into the garden on the opposite side of the enclosed rectangular space. He could see the condensation on the glass wall and its half-dome roof from his chair, along with green leaves pressed damply against the windows.

In the courtyard itself, there were two sets of stone benches, both set in shady areas for intimate tête-à-têtes or small group conversation, and were connected by graceful pea gravel paths. In one corner was the herb garden, having just come back from the winter. The thyme, lavender, and rosemary had been trimmed into neat bushes and had already sprouted new leaves. Sage, oregano, and mint were coming up from the ground.

But the thing that intrigued him the most was the small collection of tiny potted trees placed in the near corner to his chair and table. They ranged from miniature firs and spruces to small, elegant flowering dogwoods and others he couldn't identify. Each was pruned into a unique, balanced shape that echoed its full-sized version.

A small fountain rumbled behind this unusual forest, and even beyond that Guillaume could see a plat of sand bordered by dark-painted wood. Someone was obviously about to plant something there, for it had been raked into furrows around the trio of smooth black stones that seemed to have no place therein.

If I were rich, I would have a place just like this—to take my morning coffee, and to smoke my evening cigar.

But who would sit there in the chair opposite him? Certainly not a wife. Even if he were wealthy, he would never marry.

Don't understand why they bother to marry at all. Jackson's blunt words from this morning came back to him.

A soft skitter of stones had him looking up to see a maid with the tray of coffee and pastries. Just as she finished setting up the service, Guillaume saw Rose-Marie approaching. He waited until she was close enough, then gestured to the table.

"*Bonjour*, mademoiselle."

She took her seat, appearing just as rosy and sweet as she had done on the occasion of their previous meeting, though this time there were dark circles under her eyes.

"Is it true, M. Devré? That it wasn't Paul Bacard who was intended to be murdered? That it was Hélène's sterilizing-solution bottle that was poisoned?" Her voice was tight and her pudgy fingers clutched the edge of the filigree table.

"Regretfully, that appears to be the case. We are having the bottle tested to be certain, however. So I must ask whether you can think of any reason someone would want to poison Mlle Hélène."

Rose-Marie's eyes were wide. "No, monsieur. Not at all. I have been thinking about it ever since this morning, when Lucie came to retrieve the bottle from my suite. I cannot think of anyone who would want to hurt Hélène."

"Mlle Lucie took your bottle? You have the same sort of sterilizing solution?" *Sacre bleu.* Why had he not thought to ask that this morning? He ground his teeth, furious at his failure. He was allowing his personal life to interfere in a way he could not afford.

"Yes. Lucie took my bottle, as well as Camille's, away—in case ours was poisoned as well. Do you think that's possible? That someone is trying to kill all of us?"

"It is possible." Guillaume was not surprised to hear Lucie had already acted, but he should have been the one to take the bottles to be tested.

Now he'd have to obtain the results from Lucie—assuming she'd give the information to him. And how accurate would they be? And was it possible that she might contaminate the bottles herself, in order to throw suspicion away from her? Damn. He had made a serious mistake, allowing one of his main suspects to take possible evidence away.

Rose-Marie was looking at him. "Did you have any further questions, monsieur?"

Guillaume collected his thoughts. "Can you think of anyone who might want to poison you, or Mlles Camille and Lucie, along with Mlle Brosette?"

"No. No, I can't." The worry in her eyes was reflected in her voice. "Who would want to do such a thing?"

"That's what I intend to find out. It could possibly be someone who disagrees with your—with the way you make your living," he said. "Do you know of anyone who might have made such threats?"

"No. No, not at all. None of us are common *filles de joie*, monsieur." A fire glinted in her eyes, not unlike the one Lucie-Geneviève wore when Guillaume had made a similar suggestion.

"Of course not, mademoiselle." He hesitated. "But if it's true that the other bottles were also poisoned, it would be helpful to know when the culprit did so. Therefore—this is a most indelicate question, and I apologize for it, but—"

"Oh, yes, I understand." Rose-Marie held up her little white hands to forestall the actual words, and Guillaume was grateful he hadn't had to actually select which ones to use. "The answer is: I have been regularly using my sterilizing solution in the last weeks." She blushed a little now, looking quite demure.

"*Merci*," he told her. "And you have not felt ill? Or out of sorts at all?"

"No, monsieur. Not at all."

"Very well. Now, in regards to Hélène Brosette and Paul Bacard... they were intimate? The two of them?"

"Oh, yes, I would surely think so. I hadn't heard anything to the contrary. She would have been using the bottle as well, if that's why you ask." She shrugged. "After all, why would she keep it a secret if they weren't sleeping together? If he wasn't entertaining her, there would be no reason to keep him, would there?"

"Indeed." Guillaume could think of several reasons, but he declined to mention them. "Mademoiselle, who do you think could have put the poison into Mlle Hélène's bottle?"

"I really don't know."

"What I mean to say is—who might have had the opportunity to do so? To enter her private chamber, and to do such a thing?"

"Oh." Rose-Marie's eyes narrowed shrewdly, belying her cherubic demeanor. "Well, it could be any of her staff, of course—Tillé or her upstairs maid, her footman, or even Duchagne."

"What about anyone from the kitchen or the common areas? Or, perhaps, M. Stanton or Mlle Piquette, or any of the staff belonging to the household?"

Rose-Marie chewed on her lower lip, causing it to appear even fuller and puffier. "It's possible, monsieur. The staff crosses over quite often, despite the fact that all of the wings are separate. They all eat together and share many of the same common areas."

"No one would look strangely at, say, Mlle Piquette if she were in Hélène Brosette's suite?"

"N-no, monsieur. No, I don't think so." She crossed her arms over her middle and gave him a serious look. "But, *monsieur l'inspecteur*, I am certain no one in this household would do any such thing."

"But, mademoiselle," he said gravely, "someone has done such a thing."

He lifted his coffee to sip and nearly moaned at the richness of the taste. It was like nothing he'd ever had before. "Allow me to ask you this, Mlle Rose-Marie...how possible would it be for someone *not* in the household to gain access to her room? Perhaps someone like Paul Bacard himself—someone whom Hélène Brosette might have entertained at a different time? Or perhaps even a delivery boy, or a courier?"

He appreciated that she gave it a good few moments' thought before she shook her head. "Hélène would entertain no one in that private chamber. No one except M. Bacard, and perhaps not even him. And I don't believe she was entertaining anyone else in that fashion for more than two months—since she and M. Bacard became attached and he was a regular visitor to her. As to a stranger having access...I would think it is possible, but not probable. Someone would surely notice."

"But perhaps someone might notice, and the delivery boy or the courier or the errand girl from the seamstress might have simply gotten lost in the vast and varied corridors of this grand *maison*, and then that is how it is explained—and no one thinks anything of it."

Rose-Marie's eyes widened and she sat back in her chair. "That is possible, monsieur. And now that you say so, I think it might be very probable that that is what occurred. It must have been a stranger who did it."

Guillaume nodded as if he agreed, and eyed the pastry. He could probably sample a bit of it between interviews. "Very well, mademoiselle. I thank you again for your time." He stood, and she followed suit.

"*Bonne journée*, Inspector Guillaume," she said, and went off.

While he was waiting for Mlle Camille, Guillaume tore off a generous piece of the croissant—it was flaky and golden—and slathered it with butter. He walked over to the garden with the miniature trees arranged in their pots on tree stumps, rocks, and other natural formations. He'd never seen anything like it before, and found it not only charming, but serene and relaxing. Particularly with the small fountain running.

"*Bonjour*, monsieur."

A voice from the corner caught his attention, and Guillaume discovered a man crouched behind a particularly large boulder. He was working in the shade of a normal-sized tree that had been trimmed up to create a gentle canopy over the area. Standing, he gave a little bow, and tucked the small shovel he'd been using into a pocket.

"*Bonjour*, monsieur. Are you Mlle Lucie-Geneviève's gardener?"

"Yes," he replied, giving another bow. The Asian man reached only to Devré's shoulder, and his shiny black hair was combed neatly in a Western style. He was dressed in what appeared to be native Japanese or Chinese clothing; Guillaume wasn't certain of the difference between the two—or that of Siam, for that matter.

"You are admiring the *bonsai* trees?" asked the gardener.

"Yes. I've never seen anything like them before."

"That one is over fifty years old," said the man, whose name Guillaume was trying to remember. He'd written it down, but his notebook was on the table. "I brought it as a gift for Miss Lucie when I came from Japan to live with her. We are the same age—the *bonsai* and I."

"That's quite amazing," Guillaume replied, pausing to admire the stately fir tree. It stood on a small stonework column and its trunk was the diameter of his wrist. While he was admiring it, the gardener made a soft *tsk* noise and used a tiny pair of scissors to clip off an errant sprig of growth.

"M. Lelo"—ah, he'd remembered the name—"you tend to all of Mlle Lucie-Geneviève's gardens, and the greenhouse, no?"

"Yes, monsieur. I have two staff members, but it's I who guides—no, supervises them is the word. I make all of the decisions." The man's French was good, but careful.

"And so perhaps you can tell me about the exquisite rosebush that's such a bright violet and blushing pink. It's the only one of its kind, I'm told."

Lelo bowed his head. "Almost, monsieur. The only other one is in the conservatory of M. Gravereaux, at his home in L'Haÿ. He bred the rose specifically for Mlle Lucie, and there is no other one like it."

"So I've been told. And you tend to the bush, but who cuts the flowers? I saw them in the vase in the parlor."

"I am the only one who touches madame's roses. I cut one dozen of them at a time, just so"—he demonstrated a cut at an angle with his scissors—"and Mme Frousand arranges them in the vase." His face grew dark. "The roses are touched by no one but me—except that someone came and broke one off the bush two days ago. I noticed immediately that someone had stolen one of madame's roses."

Guillaume nodded. "Do you know when that might have happened? What day or about what time the rose was stolen?"

"Yes, of course I know when it happened. I know everything that occurs in my greenhouse and gardens—even when someone cut all the lilies of the valley too early, leaving us with none at all for *La Fête du Muguet*. It was sometime after five o'clock, two days ago." His lips firmed.

"It was two days ago when the thirteenth rose was cut?" Guillaume was not surprised—for that was the day Paul Bacard died.

"It was not cut. It was broken. The stem was jagged and cut straight across, at the wrong height. And I had to cut it back too short, and now the madame's rosebush will not grow evenly." He sounded slightly hysterical at the notion.

"Monsieur?"

Guillaume turned at the sound of a feminine voice. "Ah, *bonjour*, Mlle Camille." He turned back to the gardener, who'd apparently found another stray sprig that needed to be trimmed on a tiny dogwood. "Thank you, monsieur, for the information. Your gardens are beautiful."

The old man bowed once again. "Inspector, I hope you will soon discover what evil is going on here. I don't want anything to happen to Mlle Hélène."

"Neither do I, monsieur."

Mlle Camille was dressed very informally in a light frock that looked like hardly more than a floor-length flour sack—though it would have been a flour sack made from very expensive material. It was trimmed with intricate embroidery along the cuffs, hem, and neckline.

"I've heard the terrible news," she said, swiftly taking her seat on the chair opposite his. "It's quite frightening that someone here at Château Lisette could be trying to murder one of us." The cool elegance from their previous encounter was missing today. Now, she looked more like a wide-eyed waif than an ice princess.

Guillaume sat as well. "Yes, it is terrible, and therefore it is imperative that I ask you some more questions, mademoiselle."

"Yes. You're going to ask me who I think would want to kill us— or, at least, Hélène."

"And?"

"I don't know of anyone who would want to kill me. Or Rose-Marie."

"But what about Hélène? We're quite certain her bottle was poisoned; it's not yet ascertained whether the other bottles were. Who would want to murder her?"

"If he weren't dead, I would wonder if it weren't Paul Bacard."

"Indeed?" Guillaume hid his surprise.

Camille shrugged, seeming to realize how strange her pronouncement had been. "Surely he wouldn't poison himself, so it couldn't have been him."

"But they were in a liaison, and they were supposed to be married—according to Mlle Hélène. Why would he want to kill her?"

"What if they weren't really going to be married, but she was threatening him somehow or blackmailing him? Perhaps he'd want to rid himself of her so he could—so he could find someone else to have a liaison with who *didn't* want to get married."

"Like Mlle Lucie?"

"Perhaps. But she wouldn't be interested. She introduced him to us because she—she didn't care for him that much."

"Or perhaps yourself, Mlle Camille? Perhaps you would have been a less demanding lover for him, and wouldn't have cared if he'd needed to take a wife, no? Isn't that how it's often done?"

"It's true. I have no desire to marry, and I cannot understand why Hélène would want to put herself under the control of a man. Any man."

Guillaume nodded and jotted a few notes. "But, alas, M. Bacard is dead—and as you noted, he wouldn't have poisoned himself—so who would want to kill Mlle Brosette? A former lover, perhaps? A jealous wife?"

She shook her head. "I don't know. I can't think of anyone who'd do something like that—at least, anyone here at Château Lisette. Hélène is very popular with the gentlemen, and she never lacks for invitations. I suppose one of them could possibly have been jealous of Paul, but why poison her?"

"Indeed. Why poison her? Perhaps we should look at the question from a different angle. Who would have the opportunity to put the poison in the bottle in her *suite privée*? Besides the obvious—her maid Tillé. Who would go into that private chamber?"

"The chambermaid is the only other person who would regularly go into the room."

"And someone who might not regularly go into that room? Duchagne, for example? Or your own maid?"

"My maid?" Camilla's eyes flashed and she sat upright. "What are you insinuating, monsieur? That I would set my maid to poison Hélène Brosette?" She rose swiftly, and Guillaume, with years of manners ingrained in him, followed suit.

"No, no, mademoiselle, I am not accusing you at all. Please, sit. What I am attempting to ascertain is whether someone who *normally* doesn't have access to the chamber might have the opportunity to do so. Someone from another wing of the house, perhaps—your maid was simply an example—or perhaps someone who doesn't live in the household. A courier or a delivery boy? How easy would it be for one of them to get lost in the vast reaches of this grand mansion?"

She sat back down, but still gave him a wary look. "Lucie warned me you weren't as nice as you seemed."

"I'm merely trying to get the answers. And for all we know, your bottle of sterilizing solution—and that of Mlles Rose-Marie and Lucie—might be tainted as well."

"Well, since you ask...I do think it would be very unlikely that someone could find their way that far into the private rooms without being noticed. Someone who wasn't meant to be there—someone like a delivery person."

"I fear you might be correct about that. But one must always look at all possibilities."

"Oh. Yes. Of course." Camille seemed calmer now.

"And now here is another rather delicate question for you. Did Mlle Brosette ever give you an indication as to how—excuse me—satisfying her relationship with M. Bacard was?"

Her eyes widened, but she didn't blush. "Well, I...well, we never talked about it quite so plainly. But she did boast a little of how kind and sweet and loving he was with her."

"And did you know that Mlle Brosette is *enceinte?*"

"She *is?*" Camille's mouth dropped open. "Is it Paul Bacard's child?"

"So she has indicated. They were going to wed. But what that means, of course, is that we cannot be certain when the bottle in her chamber was poisoned—for she had not been utilizing it for perhaps a week or so—or even longer."

She went very still, and he watched while she worked through all of the implications.

"But I have been using my bottle, monsieur," she said slowly. "So that means either the poison is not in my bottle as well, or that I am already poisoned." A bit of panic crept into her tones.

"Do you feel ill, mademoiselle?"

"No. Other than from the results of eating strawberries," she added with a faint smile. "And my hives are nearly gone." Her body seemed to relax a trifle. "So it is unlikely the rest of us have been poisoned as well."

"We still have many conclusions to be drawn, but it seems likely that's the case." He made a note, then looked up. "I thank you once again for your time, mademoiselle," he said, standing.

"Yes, of course, monsieur." She started to go, then turned back. "I do hope you find him. The thought that someone living in this house has tried to kill at least one of us is very disturbing."

"I agree, mademoiselle. I agree."

SIXTEEN

Once again, Lucie found Dr. Jackson in the cellar of the morgue. As she looked through the window of the door, she got the impression he was in no better mood than he'd been last night, or the first time she'd bearded the so-called lion in his den. Was it only yesterday? It seemed as if days had passed, when really it was less than thirty-six hours since Paul Bacard had died.

And now Lucie had a problem growing bigger by the moment.

She didn't bother to knock and simply opened the door a wide crack. But she recoiled as soon as the strong scents of formaldehyde, blood, and decay assaulted her, blinking rapidly as her eyes watered and her nose stung. If possible, they seemed stronger than even yesterday.

"Dr. Jackson?"

"Who the hell are you?"

She didn't even bother to try and refresh his memory, though the idea of reminding him that he'd so rudely criticized (but rightly so) her too-tight corset last night did occur to her. Instead, she kept it simple. "I'm Lucie. Inspector Devré wanted me to bring these bottles to you for testing."

She figured in this case Devré wouldn't mind the lie. Surely he'd be as interested as she in determining whether the other three sterilizing solutions had been poisoned, or whether it was just Hélène's.

"Bottles? More testing?" Jackson's eyes fairly popped from their sockets. His hair looked as if he'd recently run both hands through it, and clearly he avoided the use of pomade. "I've got two bodies in here—*two*—and a bottle he brought me this morning, sliced organs lying around, and he wants me to test more things? Does he think I'm God?"

"I wouldn't know," Lucie said, venturing further into the laboratory. She carried the three bottles in a satchel, and they clinked alarmingly as she finessed her way around the huge, dark dog. The way the beast eyed her made the hair along her arms prickle. "Devré brought you a bottle this morning? We need to find out whether the same poison in that bottle is also in these three." Lucie felt no remorse at the use of a misleading pronoun.

Jackson had turned away and was doing something that involved some vigorous arm movements, accompanied by soft rattling at the long worktable behind him. While he was otherwise occupied, she looked around the space without allowing her gaze to linger on the aforementioned sliced organs, or the two sheet-covered bodies lined up on the far side of the workshop. The Y-shaped bloodstains on one were still bright red, and she deduced that that shrouded corpse was Pierre Lansac's.

She noticed Hélène's solution bottle sitting on the edge of one of the long tables, and was dismayed to see that it appeared untouched. There were dishes everywhere containing parts of bodies, test tubes, flasks, and funnels, and a large wooden box that held a frog with an X painted on its back. Despite the array and variety of items, they all appeared to be organized, arranged in neat rows and clusters. Perhaps one set of dishes was Paul's innards, and the other was Lansac's?

Lucie's stomach turned at the thought, sloshing the vast amount of coffee she'd consumed that morning in an unpleasant manner.

Happy to put space between herself and the glistening slices of human organs in a range of color from pink to red to purple, she wandered over to look at the second set of clothing that was suspended near Paul Bacard's belongings. Lansac's, no doubt. She was just beginning to flip through the hanging coat, trousers, shirt, and waistcoat when Jackson seemed to remember she was present.

"You." He looked up from where he was using a small glass dropper to take a sample from a flask. "What are you doing here?"

The man could use a haircut, she thought, and wondered why he didn't just grow a mustache like everyone else in Paris, instead of letting the bottom half of his face fill in with ungoverned black stubble. He was squinting a little, and she thought he should also consider spectacles, but decided it wasn't the best time to mention it.

"Devré brought this to you earlier today," she said, picking up the bottle from Hélène's bedroom. "He's quite certain this is what poisoned Paul Bacard."

"What the hell is it?" Jackson snatched the bottle away and sniffed it. "Honey. Flowers—probably roses. Why the hell would he drink this? It's hardly more than perfumed mead."

"It was an accident."

"How?"

Lucie pursed her lips, then plunged in. After all, the man was a doctor. "This is a mead solution scented with flowers, as you've noticed. It's used to sterilize a sea sponge used for pregnancy contraception. Bacard must not have known of its purpose—or didn't care—and drank from it. Someone appears to have poisoned it, and might possibly have poisoned these other three bottles. All of which are used for the same purpose."

She withdrew each of the three bottles from her satchel and set them, one by one and none too gently, on the worktable next to Hélène's.

Jackson, who appeared completely nonplussed by the topic of her speech, looked at the row of mismatched bottles on his table for a moment.

Then he said, "Clever. What a clever way to murder someone."

Lucie blinked, but once again he didn't even seem to notice her presence. Instead, he was muttering to himself as he picked up each bottle in turn, uncorked it, sniffed, then recorked it.

Then, as she watched, he went about taking samples from each of the bottles—including the original one Devré had brought earlier.

She glanced over at the sheet-covered bodies. "So it was suicide, then? With Pierre Lansac?"

"Don't be so certain of that," he snapped, surprising her not because of his tone, but because he seemed to actually have heard what she said. "He asphyxiated due to strangulation, but he might have had assistance."

Lucie stared at him. "Assistance? What sort of assistance?"

Jackson was making a sort of humming sound under his breath, and she had to repeat the question before he deigned to hear her. "High alcohol content in his blood," he muttered, adding a few drops of something from a dark glass jar into each of the four samples of the solution. As she watched, he made notes on small pieces of paper, sticking one beneath each bottle. Then he took a small brush and painted numbers one through four on the vessels.

"So Lansac was drunk. That doesn't mean anything."

"No. Not necessarily." The pathologist swirled the small beaker that held the first solution, then brought it to his nose to sniff. Then he went on and did the same with the other three.

"I'd probably want to be completely drunk if I were going to hang myself," she muttered.

Jackson moved the bottles to a side table, and as he turned back to his other work, he looked up. "You again? What are you still doing here?"

"I was waiting for the results of the—"

"*Waiting?*" His bushy brows vaulted up. "No one *waits* in my lab. Get out. Tell Devré he'll get the results when I get them." His voice was strident enough that it roused the dog. The horse-sized beast made as if to bolt to its feet, then apparently decided it was too much work and collapsed back into a heap of fur and bones.

Lucie gritted her teeth. The man was just short of the rudest, most arrogant man she'd ever met. Blasted Americans. Her jaw still tight, she gritted her teeth and smiled. "Of course. I didn't realize it would take some time."

"I've got a postmortem to finish—Devré will be in here demanding answers on that anytime now—you can tell him not to even show his face until four o'clock today. And then he brought me the other one—the strangulation." He made a sharp, irritated noise and walked over to Lansac's table.

The sheet made a sharp whipping sound as he yanked it away, then hung it over a nearby stool.

"You think he might not have actually killed himself?" she asked.

"I didn't say that," Jackson snapped. "I said he *might* have had assistance—I didn't say that he *had* assistance. That remains to be determ— Why the hell am I answering your questions? Who are you, anyway?"

This time, the dog lumbered to her feet and gave a short warning bark.

"Agreed," Jackson told the canine. "You're the only female I allow in my lab—and that's because you're a far sight easier to have around than any woman I've ever met."

"Perhaps you haven't been around the right women," Lucie replied—without a hint of flirtation or double entendre. She recognized it would have been wasted on the man, and unlike Devré, he wouldn't even have appreciated the wit. Jackson was clearly someone who needed to be managed steadily and firmly—like the barges that cruised along the Thames. Large, overbearing, and filled with hot steam.

"Probably right about that," he muttered, once again surprising her that he'd heard and registered her comment. "That's why I'm not married anymore."

She nodded, more than a little taken aback by the glimpse into the personal life of this bear of a man. He did have elegant, amazingly dextrous fingers, however.

"Very well," she said. "I'll be back at four o'clock."

Her words obviously didn't settle in until she was out the door, for just as she closed it, she heard his outraged bellow.

Lucie grinned and lifted her skirts to start the climb to the main floor. Just like a barge.

Leaning up against his desk, arms folded at his waist, Guillaume stared at what he called his crime wall as he tried to block out the sounds of his colleagues. There were shouts, laughter, and a few thuds as the rest of them went about their business on the other side of his door.

He shared an office with another homicide detective who didn't have the same propensity for neatness as Guillaume, though the two of them got along quite well otherwise. Inspector Denis Audoux was far more boisterous and loud, along with being a few years older than he, but Guillaume had been a detective at la Sûreté for two years longer than his office mate. He considered him a friend rather than a rival, and they often consulted with each other on their cases.

On his side of the office, Guillaume had taken over the longest interior space for his crime wall. It was decorated by a large wooden framework covered by stretched canvas—he'd gotten the idea from a friend who was a painter, and had created three huge canvases that, when lined up, covered most of an entire wall. Using tacks, he attached photographs and newspaper articles related to whatever he was currently investigating—in this case, the murder of Paul Bacard and the possibly related death of Pierre Lansac.

Organized by subject, the canvases held images of the bodies, both at the scenes of death and on the table in Jackson's laboratory, and images of the interior of the carriage and the hotel room where Lansac had been found.

Guillaume also had some pictures of what he considered key pieces of evidence: the rose blossom and the other contents of Bacard's pockets, Château Lisette and both of the entrances Bacard had been known to use. Additionally, he'd had one of the office secretaries find a few newspaper clippings that included photographs of Lucie-Geneviève Madeleine, Hélène Brosette, and Rose-Marie and Camille, along with Bacard's friends Lansac and Druot.

Large blackboards, made of four sections of slate, flanked the canvases. Devré used that area to make chalk notes or list questions that could easily be erased or edited. That included a list of suspects and persons of interest, a timeline (insofar as he knew it), and other interesting facts—such as the problem with the rosebush, and where the poison had come from. So far, Houssaye and Damaris had had no luck in finding evidence that anyone in Château Lisette had purchased digitalis from a local chemist, or it was otherwise in use. It had to come from somewhere, the poison, and he hoped that determining its genesis would help to narrow the list of suspects.

Guillaume jotted a note to remind himself to place a telephone call, or if that wasn't possible, to send a telegram to M. Gravereaux to determine whether there were any other purplish-pink roses of the same kind on any other bushes.

He knew better than to bother Jackson so soon after dropping off Hélène Brosette's bottle, and he wanted to give the man time to do at least an initial examination of Pierre Lansac's body to see if there was anything that would change their initial supposition of suicide.

He had a lot to think about, and he still wasn't certain how important Lansac's death was to the case, and whether the timing was related.

But even as he was reviewing the facts of the case and mulling over theories, in the back of his mind was the memory of his encounter with Émile Huvet. It continued to push its way to the front of his thoughts, insidious and tempting.

"Inspector Devré?"

Guillaume blinked, returning immediately to his office and the crime wall he was supposed to be looking at.

"Yes, come in, Houssaye." He turned from his survey of the crime wall, arms still crossed over his middle, coat hung neatly over the back of his scarred wooden desk chair.

"I have all my notes from speaking with the rest of the staff at Château Lisette. Have you tasted the cook's lemon-basil biscuits? I don't believe I've ever eaten anything so delicious."

"Not even your mother's strawberry crème tarts?"

"*Sacre bleu*, Uncle Guillaume—I mean, Inspector Devré! I was supposed to invite you to come to supper tonight." Bernard's eyes had gone wide, and his freckles suddenly stood out like caramel raindrops on his cheeks and nose. "Maman insisted I ask you yesterday for the holiday, and with all of the excitement, I'd forgotten about it. She wasn't very happy when I came home late, and without you."

"Henriette? Not happy?" Guillaume grinned in spite of his exhausted, divided mind. His sister had red hair, and the requisite temper to go with it. Bernard had missed both the red hair and the short fuse—the absence of the latter was beneficial to his role as policeman. And not having red hair helped as well, for it made him more easily able to blend into a crowd.

Eating dinner at his widowed sister Henriette's house was a treat Guillaume hated to refuse. She was an excellent cook—for she had an uncanny ability to select the perfect cuts of meat and to harangue the butcher into selling them to her for a nominal price—and the two siblings were as close as their divergent lives allowed.

"Unless something new develops, I can spare the time this evening. Shall I send word, or will you have time to stop by while on your beat?"

"I can send word. Thank you, uncle—er, inspector." Houssaye smiled sheepishly, for he'd only been working as an officer of la Sûreté for three months.

"I'm looking forward to it. Now, perhaps I could review your notes from the interviews?"

"Yes." Houssaye proudly handed him a sheaf of papers, which Guillaume perused quickly, nodding to himself all the while. Hmm. So the deliciously large and dark Moor had been gone much of the afternoon, after he and Mlle Lucie had gone to Mass. Supposedly.

Other than that, there was no new information therein, which was good, because that meant he could continue to work with the same data he'd been collecting. He was beginning to formulate a theory he liked. There were others, but there was one that seemed to make the most sense.

"What do you think, inspector?" Houssaye asked when he put the papers aside.

"*C'est bien*," Guillaume told him first. Then, stroking his mustache carefully, so as not to muss it or loosen the small bit of wax he used, he looked at his nephew. "What do you think about this case?"

The young man looked from him to the crime wall and back again. "Until we know whether someone poisoned all of the bottles"—his cheeks became slightly pink beneath the freckles—"we don't know whether Mlle Brosette was the only target."

"Correct. I hope to have that information today. But shall we assume she is the only target—just for the sake of your theories?"

"Yes. I-I think it's about jealousy. The motive is jealousy."

"That is very possible. In general, one is motivated to murder for purposes of jealousy, greed—for power or money, you understand—revenge, or love. You see, it always comes back to oneself."

A knock at the door interrupted them, and Guillaume turned as one of the clerks walked in. He was carrying a large package.

"This arrived for you, Inspector Devré."

Guillaume took it to his desk. It was addressed to Guillaume Devré, la Sûreté, and bore no other markings—including a return address.

"How did it come?" he asked as the clerk lingered.

"By courier. A young boy on a bicycle."

He examined it closely, noting the string tying the butcher's paper of the packaging. It was a malleable package, not a box, and it wasn't particularly heavy. It felt almost like clothing or fabric of some sort.

"Thank you," he said absently, gesturing for the clerk to go. Aware of his nephew watching curiously, Guillaume used a small pocketknife to cut the string.

He'd just begun to unfold the packaging when a shock of recognition, followed by instant comprehension, made him freeze.

It was his coat. The coat he'd worn last night.

The coat he'd shucked into a dark corner as he climbed into a shadowy carriage, impetuous and eager...

"Is everything all right, uncle?"

Bernard's innocent question startled Guillaume back to the present, and his hands tightened over the package. "Oh, yes, of course. I'd forgotten I'd sent out my coat to be hemmed. Had the tailor deliver it here because I'm not home during the day." He realized he was giving far more information than necessary—the sign of a lie—and he clamped his mouth shut.

"Perhaps you should send word to your mother that I'll be at dinner tonight at six," he said. "I've got a bit more work to do here."

Bernard, bless him, left without further questions. He didn't seem to notice anything amiss, and for that Guillaume was grateful—although he privately acknowledged that might not be the best tendency in a future detective.

But he thrust the thought of his nephew, and even the murder of Paul Bacard, out of his mind as he looked down at the partly unwrapped package.

If he had left his coat in the carriage, that meant the one he'd gathered up as he made his exit belonged to Émile Huvet.

A little shiver caught him by surprise, running from hot to cold.

He must return the doctor's coat.

The question was: would he send it back anonymously, so he didn't have to face the man again—or would he choose to do it in person?

"Inspector Devré."

He stifled a sigh and looked over, and his unsteady mood became even worse. It was M. Muniot, the secretary to Armand Cochefert. He didn't need the man to speak in order to know that his superior's superior had heard about the connection of La Balise to the Bacard investigation.

"M. Cochefert would like to speak with you immediately," said the short, bespectacled man. He put Guillaume in mind of a wren, with his darting, shiny black eyes and fluttery mannerisms. "Are you free at the moment?"

"Of course." Guillaume rose to comply, giving the brown paper-wrapped package a grudging look. The meeting with Cochefert would be an excellent way to put Émile Huvet and the imminent coat exchange out of his mind.

At least for a while.

SEVENTEEN

—◇—

The meeting with Cochefert hadn't been as contentious as
Guillaume had feared—for he hadn't actually been told to leave
La Balise alone—but it hadn't been altogether pleasant.

"Christophe Calmette has already rung here twice today,"
Cochefert told him sternly from behind a cloud of cigar smoke.
"He claims you've been bothering La Balise, visiting her house and
disrupting everything."

Guillaume had a feeling Mlle Lucie either didn't know or didn't
approve of her former paramour calling on her behalf, but of course
he refrained from commenting about this to the director. "I've been
unfailingly polite, monsieur, but yes, I have found several reasons to
visit her residence more than once." He went on to enumerate all of
them in his calm, even way.

It was evidence of Cochefert's confidence in Guillaume that the
man merely nodded, pursed his lips so his facial hair bristled and
shivered, and raised his brows as the facts were laid out for him.

"You will notify me *immediately* if you intend to arrest La
Balise," was all he said, after sucking hard on his cigar at the end
of Guillaume's synoptic explanation, and expelling another gust of
smoke. "*Before* you do so."

"*Bien sûr, monsieur le directeur,*" replied Guillaume.

Shortly after his interview with Cochefert, Guillaume escaped from the tourist-infested Île de la Cité and took himself back to Pierre Lansac's hotel room. He wasn't certain what compelled him to visit the scene of what clearly seemed to be a suicide, but the timing of the death along with the man's connection to Paul Bacard felt too coincidental to be completely dismissed.

The chamber was still closed off, for he'd left instructions for the room to be undisturbed, which appeared to have been obeyed. The hotel manager had been less than pleased with the directive, but, as Guillaume reminded him, this was a matter of a man's death.

M. Rochard let him into the suite, clearly hopeful that this second visit marked the beginning of the end of the investigation. "Take all the time you require, monsieur," he said with an ingratiating smile. "As soon as you are finished, with your permission I shall have the contents removed and the chambermaids clean."

The chambermaids. Ah, yes, that was a good idea. "I would like to speak with the maid and any other personnel who was on this floor yesterday afternoon, between the times of noon and four o'clock. And also the chambermaid who normally tended to this room."

"Of course, monsieur. But didn't the good constable speak with her yesterday? The chambermaid?"

"He did indeed. But I wish also to speak with her. As well as anyone else who was on the floor yesterday between noon and four. Merci."

The manager was looking unhappy again, and his bow was abbreviated. "Marie and Jeannette, and I will see who else. I shall send them to you."

M. Rochard disappeared, leaving the door open just a crack, as Guillaume stood and surveyed the space. Yesterday, he had been taking in the scene for details that his sharp memory would reserve and recall as necessary. Like painting a mental picture, or arranging for a photograph to be printed in his mind.

But today he looked at the scene from the eyes of the man who lived there: a man whose friend and colleague had been poisoned, who by all appearances was deeply in debt and who had suddenly lost the opportunity for a profitable investment in the way of a stud horse...a man who was desperate enough to obtain and presumably use a concoction designed to help him have sexual relations with a woman when he did not wish to...a well-heeled man—or at least one who appeared to all to be wealthy—of the bourgeoisie...a man who clearly was frustrated, if the shattered blue bottle was any indication...

A man who apologized in writing, leaving a conveniently ambiguous note on his escritoire.

I'm sorry.

"Ah, but for what are you sorry, monsieur?" Guillaume said, brushing his fingertips lightly over the top of the desk. He'd removed the scrap of paper yesterday and sent it with one of the policemen to show Lansac's solicitor in order to determine whether the short, scrawled note matched the dead man's writing.

"Are you sorry for taking your own life, and leaving an ugly scene for someone to find? Or are you sorry for poisoning your friend and colleague after he reneged on a business deal that would have possibly saved you from the bill collectors?"

It was a simple, neat solution presented in this room: Pierre Lansac had murdered his friend, then the next day was so filled with remorse that he hung himself.

He climbed up on the bureau here. Guillaume looked at the blemishes in the polished surface of the dresser, the footprints near the edge, and imagined the man standing there, lowering a noose around his neck. He would already have had to have thrown the rope over the light fixture—again, Guillaume was filled with admiration for the strength of its mooring—and secured it before climbing onto the bureau to launch himself off.

The noose was made from the curtain cords and, horribly, was decorated with olive-green tassels. Lansac would have tightened it around his neck, then jumped off the dresser...and swung.

And when the shock of what he'd done set in, he clawed at the silk rope, trying to loosen it, to pull it away and to save himself...but it was too late.

Guillaume pulled himself from a deep reverie as someone knocked at the door.

"Monsieur?" A shy, barely audible voice greeted him.

He turned to see a young woman, hardly more than skin and bones, with eyes sunken in their sockets and her thin brown hair coming free of its chignon. He recognized her as the maid who'd discovered Lansac's body and who'd been crying on the other side of the wall last night. Houssaye had interviewed her, but Guillaume had some different questions in mind today. The note bothered him, as well as something else he couldn't put his finger on.

"I am Inspector Devré," he said in his kindest voice. "Please, come in—Mlle Edith, is it? Or Mlle Jeannette? Please, sit down."

She came in, bobbing a quick, graceless curtsy on coltish legs. "Oh, no, monsieur, I should not. M. Rochard would not approve."

Guillaume suspected that the bold *garçon* who'd adjusted his napkin so particularly yesterday in this very hotel would have quickly taken the opportunity to sit, with no hesitation at all. "Please. You are not working right now, for this is official police business. I will speak to M. Rochard and make certain he does not give you a problem."

Marie sank down so quickly in a tufted chair that he was certain her knees had given out a trifle too early. She licked her cracked lips and folded bony white hands in her lap.

"Mlle Edith?" he asked, and she nodded vigorously. "You were the unfortunate person who came upon M. Lansac yesterday, in this very room."

She nodded, swallowing hard. "Yes, monsieur."

"I'm very sorry you had to see that, mademoiselle," he said. "You told Officer Houssaye the door was not locked when you came to it, but it was slightly ajar."

"Yes, monsieur. The door, it doesn't always close properly if one doesn't attend to it. The wood is splintered. There were many times I came to clean M. Lansac's room and the door was like this."

"The door was often in that condition—not closed tightly? Was that when M. Lansac was in residence, or when he was not in the rooms?"

"Yes, monsieur. But when M. Lansac was gone, the door, he pulled it closed tightly and locked it. But he did not bother to lock it often when he was here, and then it would come open a little."

"M. Rochard was supposed to have it fixed, but whenever he wanted to schedule the workmen, the monsieur told him it was a bad time. M. Rochard was not happy about that, for the door was not broken when M. Lansac moved into the room, and he blamed him for breaking it. He was going to make him pay for the repair. It would have to be an entire new door, and I don't think..." Edith's sallow cheeks pinkened, and she looked down at her hands curled in her lap.

"You don't think what, mademoiselle? Please, don't be shy—this is very important—all of your impressions are very important. M. Lansac is dead, and he cannot be angry at you with anything you say about him, even if it isn't nice."

"That's not true," she said, her eyes wide as she shook her head. "He could haunt me! Everyone knows to hang oneself is a mortal sin! If he won't be allowed into heaven, he could be lost here on earth still, as a ghost, and he could haunt me."

Guillaume struggled to keep his reaction to this earnest speech to nothing more than a blink. A very slow, deliberate blink—which gave him the opportunity to hold back the scoff of surprise he might otherwise have displayed, and also gave him a moment to decide how to properly react. "Mademoiselle, may I tell you a secret?"

She drew in her breath softly and nodded. He noticed she sat up slightly straighter in her chair.

"What if I told you, mademoiselle, that it is *possible* that M. Lansac did not commit a mortal sin? That someone *else* committed the sin?"

It took her a moment to comprehend, and she snatched in a gasp of air. "Do you really think so, monsieur?"

"I don't know," he replied. "But the only way for me to determine whether that's possible is for you to answer every question I ask you with the greatest of honesty...and for you to tell me absolutely everything you think about the situation. The impressions you have, the opinions you have, and anything that you have seen or noticed about M. Lansac that struck you as odd. You have obviously been working here for long enough to notice when something isn't right, or a guest behaves unusually, or whether something else is out of place. I urge you to please be free with me in answering my questions."

She was fairly quivering with importance by now.

"Now, about this problem with the door being fixed...do you think it's possible M. Lansac did not *want* the door to be fixed?"

Edith nodded. "I think, monsieur, that perhaps he could not pay for it, and he was afraid M. Rochard would throw him out. I–I've seen the bills on his desk," she added, a bit more shyly. "He owed a *lot* of money."

Guillaume nodded gravely. "Indeed. Now, if you would, could you tell me once again everything you remember about when you came into the room? You knocked, no one answered, and the door was slightly ajar, and so you came inside to do your work."

"Yes, monsieur. I came at the same time every day—at six o'clock, which is after his afternoon nap and when he is returning from his club, but before he dresses for dinner."

"And his manservant? Did he live here, or did he have adjoining rooms?"

Edith's neck and face turned bright red so quickly that Guillaume was stunned.

"What is it, mademoiselle?" he said, leaning forward with concern.

"Oh." The flush had spread to her forearms, half bare from the short sleeves of her maid's dress. "M. Lansac did not have a manservant...not that I ever saw."

"And how did he get himself dressed, then, and his clothing taken care of?" Guillaume replied, utterly intrigued. What self-respecting *flâneur* would not have a valet to tend to his wardrobe, shave him, and see to his hair?

"I-I helped him," Edith whispered. Her face was the color of a beet, and Guillaume discerned a bit of perspiration collecting at her temples. "Please don't tell M. Rochard," she added swiftly. "It was our little secret, mine and M. Lansac's, and that is why I always knew to come at precisely six o'clock, for that was dressing for dinnertime. He...he paid me extra money, and if M. Rochard knew about it, he would have been furious. *Please* don't tell him."

"No, mademoiselle, I can see no reason why I should tell him this information. It has little bearing on the investigation—that you assisted M. Lansac in his dressing." Guillaume had never heard of such a thing, but the fact that the dead man appeared not to even have the funds to pay for a valet—the most basic and important of servants for a wealthy man—spoke volumes. "I must ask you another very sensitive question, Edith. It's very important that you be honest with me—and I assure you, I will have no reason at all to tell anyone about your answer—whatever it is."

Her wide eyes were fixed on him with dread, and the suffusion of color drained from her face. "Yes, monsieur," she whispered.

"Did you provide any other services to M. Lansac—of, say, a more intimate nature? Either willingly or unwillingly? Please, mademoiselle, it could be very important to the investigation."

"Oh, no, no, no," Edith said, straightening her bony shoulders with indignation. "I am *not* that sort of girl. No, monsieur, I have had more than one resident of this hotel—and the other one I worked at, the Hôtel du Chante, which was far lower class than this one, and the residents there were even less gentlemanly than the ones here— attempt such a thing, but never M. Lansac."

Guillaume held back a satisfied smile. "Never? Not even once? He never even made a ribald comment in jest, perhaps to feel you out, so to speak?"

"No, monsieur. Definitely not. He was always the most proper of gentlemen."

"M. Lansac must have had a mistress then, no?"

"I don't know about that."

"Perhaps you might have seen receipts for jewelry he bought for her," he said. "Such items would have been difficult to avoid noticing, scattered over the escritoire as they would have been. Or perhaps there were love letters, or papers from his solicitor, or even articles of women's clothing she might have left behind, or he might have kept as a favor."

"No, monsieur. I never noticed anything that would have suggested he had a woman, or went to a *maison close*." She drew in a breath as if to continue speaking, then closed her mouth. Then she began again. "I have been a chambermaid for four years, monsieur. I can tell when a man likes women."

Guillaume heard this statement with two different sections of his mind: the part that was homicide detective, and the part that was, simply, Guillaume Devré, invert.

I can tell when a man likes women...implying that she could also tell when a man didn't like women. His gut tightened. Did his own housekeeper know the same? Had she recognized his personal proclivities?

"I understand," he said, forcing himself back to the moment and the investigation. "Did you ever notice an unusual, pretty blue glass bottle here among M. Lansac's things?"

"Was it very ornate? And only this big? And the color of a blue cornflower?"

Guillaume smiled. "When did you see this bottle? How long ago did he have it?"

"It was only yesterday. That was the day—or the night, I think—before monsieur's friend died."

"I see. How did you know his friend died?"

"He was very upset. He saw me in the corridor yesterday morning—it was several hours before I was due to tend to this chamber. He said a police officer had spoken to him." She looked questioningly at him.

"It was indeed I who delivered the sad news to M. Lansac, yes. In what way was he upset, mademoiselle? Was he sad or angry or frustrated or surprised, or something else?"

Edith thought for a moment. "He was most certainly sad. But there was something about him that was almost frightening. As if he wanted to shout and throw things about. I think he was angry as well."

Guillaume nodded. "And do you know what sort of medicine or tonic was in the blue bottle?"

"Not at all. And, of course, I would never ask him. But he did—" She hesitated, but then continued. "He did say, on the day I first noticed it, that it might be his last resort." Her eyes were wide once more, but her fingers were no longer curled into tight knots. "When

I learned that his friend had died by poisoning, I began to worry that he might have meant there was poison in the blue bottle, and that he might want to drink it." Her attention skittered to the remarkably strong light fixture, and she swallowed hard. "But he had another idea."

"He told you the blue bottle might be his last resort?"

"He wasn't really speaking to me, but it was as if he were speaking to himself."

"I see." Guillaume changed topics. "Did M. Lansac ever receive visitors to his rooms?"

"Yes, monsieur."

"Presumably they were men and not women," he said, probing gently.

"Yes, monsieur."

"Were there regular visitors—the same people that you would see all the time? Or were they always different?"

Edith smoothed her skirt. "I wouldn't know for certain, monsieur, but I don't remember seeing the same people all the time. Perhaps once or twice."

"Thank you very much, Mlle Edith," he told her, standing. "You've been very helpful and very forthright."

"I liked M. Lansac," she said, looking around the chamber with a woebegone expression. "He was very nice. And he...he fed me. He gave me food quite often as payment for my assistance."

Mon Dieu, if Lansac had given her food and she was still skin and bones, what would she do now that he was gone? Guillaume felt a stab of concern for the young woman, and before he realized what he was doing, he was dragging a few francs from his suit pocket. Never mind that he'd spent far more than he should have done last night at Maison de Bleue, but at least he had food on his table and wine in his pantry.

"Again, mademoiselle, thank you for your time. Here is something for your trouble." He handed her the wad of bills and turned away so she wouldn't see his expression.

"Thank you, monsieur," she whispered. There was a soft rustling sound as she stuffed the bills into a pocket or stocking.

"You were very attentive to this chamber, *non?* And you polished the furniture, how often?" he asked as he walked to the door to open it for her.

"Every day, monsieur. I took everything off the top and placed it on the bed or the chair, and I used lemon oil and scrubbed until it was dry and smooth as glass." She paused as she walked through the door. "Monsieur, if you would like to know more about M. Lansac's visitors, you could perhaps speak with Jean-Georges. He's one of the waiters here at the hotel, and he often brought M. Lansac his luncheon or tea tray when he chose to dine in."

"Very well. Perhaps you could ask M. Rochard if he would send Jean-Georges to me in this room

. And also Mlle Jeannette."

Guillaume left the door slightly ajar after examining the lock and determining that Edith had been correct. The door could be locked, but only if a bit of muscle and attention were applied.

The little maid had given him much to think about, as well as confirming several of his suppositions. Suicide was, he supposed, a viable—if not irrevocable—choice when a man knew he was out of funds and had no further prospects. Either suicide or taking a wife. And for some men with his propensity, the latter was a despised option.

But the blue dragon was supposed to have aided Lansac in achieving the commitment to his decision—most likely to marry. And a shattered blue bottle could very well imply frustration and anger. Perhaps it hadn't worked as he'd anticipated.

Or perhaps it had worked, and he was simply furious and angry that he had to resort to using it.

And there was, also, the possibility that Pierre Lansac had been in love with Paul Bacard. That could explain his vitriol toward La Balise—the woman Bacard seemingly never got over—as well as Lansac's sincere grief at his friend's death.

It could also explain the attempted poisoning of Hélène Brosette, Bacard's supposed fiancée. Could Lansac have managed that? Or paid someone to do so?

Yes, Guillaume could see how those different events could cause a weak, dejected man at the end of his rope to take the final, fatal leap.

And if he could prove that Lansac had had access to Mlle Brosette's sterilizing solution, that could tidy up the case and close it up very neatly.

Guillaume stood in the center of the chamber and turned in a slow circle, looking around the room. If he could determine how Lansac had acquired the digitalis, or find some evidence of it here...

This time when he approached the bureau, he looked more closely at each of the bottles there. He opened them, sniffed the contents of pomade, aftershave tonic, and even cologne. He opened every drawer and looked deep among the man's belongings...and at last he found it.

A small bottle, tucked in the back of one drawer, beneath a muddle of braces, stockings, and boxers. Small, brown, with its cork conveniently in place to contain any last dregs of its contents.

Guillaume pulled the stopper free and sniffed. A hint of astringency. Jackson was going to be thrilled with yet another vessel to test. Guillaume grimaced and slipped the bottle into his pocket just as a soft knock came at the door.

"Yes. Come in."

"Edith said you wished to speak with me," said the young man as he stepped into the room, but when he got a look at Guillaume, he stuttered to a halt.

Guillaume barely managed to control his own reaction when he recognized the impertinent *garçon* who'd served him coffee and adjusted his napkin yesterday morning.

Keeping his features impassive and giving the man a cold look, he said, "Jean-Georges, I presume? You often served the man who resided in this chamber?"

"Yes, monsieur." The waiter's gaze shifted down, then boldly back up to meet Guillaume's eyes. "I preferred to serve him whenever possible. He tipped very well."

Guillaume felt an unpleasant rush of warmth up and over his torso, and resisted the urge to tug at his shirt collar. There were so many nuances that could be read in that last statement, and the audacity of the man made him distinctly uncomfortable. And as an officer of la Sûreté, Guillaume had much more to lose than the other man should their previous encounter become known. "Thank you. That's all I need to know."

"You're certain there's nothing else, monsieur?" The waiter stepped backward into the door and gave it the required hard shove into place so that the lock could be turned. He bolted it with a sharp clunk, all the while keeping his attention on Guillaume. "I've nowhere else to be for at least a quarter of an hour." He reached up and loosened the button at the back of his shirt, then yanked down the front along with his tie, exposing a strong throat.

Guillaume battled a variety of reactions—rage, mortification, and, shamefully, a bolt of lust.

"Get out," he forced himself to say. He fisted his hands against his sides, because otherwise, he was afraid what he would do with them. Jean-Georges looked at him knowingly, then without another word turned and snapped the bolt open on the door. Then he paused, giving Guillaume a languishing look. "He had a woman visitor yesterday."

With an arch expression that defied Guillaume to ask for more information, he whisked through the opening. The door bounced loosely in its frame without latching.

Guillaume stared after him for a moment, his hands still curled into fists. *Connard.* Then he moved—out the door and down the corridor.

Jean-Georges had sashayed only a short distance away when Guillaume reached him. In one swift move, he caught the other man by the back of his coat, spun him around, and grabbed him by the lapels. Heaving him up, he slammed him against the wall, holding him with two powerful hands while the waiter's feet dangled off the floor. His eyes goggled with surprise and appreciation, which infuriated Guillaume even more.

"When did you see the woman?" he snarled, giving the cretin an emphatic shove.

"It was the—middle of the—day." The man was out of breath, but Guillaume didn't care.

"When? One o'clock? Five o'clock?"

"Maybe...two o'clock. Or—half past."

"What did she look like?"

His eyelids swooped down a little. "I don't know. I never look at women."

Guillaume thrust him away hard enough that the man stumbled and had to catch himself against the wall. "Get out of here."

"I'm here if you need anything else, monsieur." Jean-Georges smoothed the front of his coat, then reached around to button up the back of his shirt, a small smile under his mustache.

Guillaume didn't lower himself to actually flee, but he wasted no time in returning to Lansac's hotel room. He wanted to distance himself from the repellent *jésus* and his *déshabillé* before anyone came to investigate the altercation.

With iron determination, he redirected his thoughts to the matter at hand: the case, the dead man's chamber, the information he'd learned from Edith, the small brown bottle he'd slipped into his pocket, and the broken blue bottle—a sign of anger or frustration.

A female visitor, yesterday, of all days.

There was a strong case for suicide. Everything seemed to fit. Guillaume yanked his wayward thoughts from the detour they tried to take and brought them sharply back to the room, focusing on the process. What Lansac had done: taking down the curtain cords, tying them together, tossing them over the light fixture, creating the noose, climbing up onto the top of the hip-high dresser...then simply stepping off.

Yes, it worked. Yes, it made sense.

However, the biggest question Guillaume had was whether Lansac had been the one to poison Bacard, or whether he was merely grieving the man's loss.

Guillaume looked down at the smudges on the bureau where Lansac had stood before jumping to his fate. Two footprints, poised at the edge, right at the corner, like a diver.

Two *perfect* footprints. And the rest of the bureau was smooth as untouched glass.

He stilled, staring. No. *Impossible.*

He'd been wrong. Pierre Lansac hadn't taken his own life.

He'd been murdered.

EIGHTEEN

A t precisely fifteen minutes before four o'clock, Lucie alighted from her robin's-egg-blue landau in front of the Paris Morgue. Her insides were in knots. If Dr. Jackson had finished his testing of the bottles, she'd learn whether someone was trying to poison her as well as Hélène, and her other friends and tenants as well.

Knowing for certain there was a murderer in her household almost made her want to run back to England and the gypsies.

She'd just finished giving instructions to her driver—to take Piquette to pick up her new dining jacket from Paquin's and two hats from Malitte's, and then return for her in one hour—and was lifting her graceful tulip-shaped skirt to cross the *quai* when someone shouted, "Virginia! Virginia Stoddard!"

Lucie automatically glanced over, then realized with a horrible lurch of her belly that her name was no longer Virginia Stoddard. But it was too late. She'd been taken off guard and, without thinking, turned at the sound of her name...and there stood the female reporter who'd been following her. The woman had obviously been watching Lucie as she climbed out of her carriage; she'd been the one to call out—and now she smiled knowingly, her eyes appearing dark and hard even from a distance.

For a moment, Lucie wanted nothing more than to confront the reporter and demand to know why she was stalking her. But far better to pretend nothing was amiss. For to confront the woman, to let her recognize how she'd begun to creep under her skin, could also be considered tacit admission of the name Virginia Stoddard—and all Lucie had done, after all, was look over when someone shouted. People did that all the time. It wasn't proof of anything.

Yet, inside her gloves, her hands were clammy and her hat suddenly felt hot and weighty. As she continued on her way, crossing the street near where the reporter stood, Lucie realized her knees were shamefully unsteady. *Onni took care of everything. I know he did.*

She managed to give the newshound a cool, mildly interested glance as she passed by—neither fully acknowledging her nor ignoring her. And once she was inside the morgue, Lucie would lose herself within the crowd of spectators and slip down to the cellar where, hopefully, she would get the answers she needed.

Perhaps not the ones she *wanted*, but the ones she needed.

Moving quickly toward the glass doors, Lucie watched in the reflection to see whether the reporter was following her. When she saw the woman start up the steps in her wake, Lucie began to walk faster, slipping her way along the edge of the line.

"Pardon me. I have an appointment inside," she told the people in queue so they would know she wasn't cutting the line and there would be no altercation that would attract the attention of the newswoman or slow her progress.

She made it inside while the parasitic reporter was still climbing the steps, and Lucie found the same doorman who'd allowed her to slip past him yesterday. The portly man remembered her, of course, due either to the large tip she'd given him or her famous face—but regardless, he had nothing but a grin and a hospitable gesture for her as he allowed her to pass by into the restricted area of the morgue.

"You didn't see me, monsieur," she told him with a smile from beneath her broad hat as she slipped her hand into his pocket once again. "Should anyone ask."

"Louis sees no one, Mlle La Balise," was his reply as he clicked his heels together in a military manner and gave her a little bow.

Nevertheless, Lucie walked briskly to the door marked Cellar, grateful for a corset that was looser than the one she wore for evening. In fact, in her simple day skirt, tight-sleeved bodice, and low-heeled boots, she could move fairly easily. Not for the first time, she was glad the leg-o-mutton sleeve fashion craze was passé. The huge, puffed sleeves had been unwieldy—not to mention ridiculous looking.

Lucie reached the door to Dr. Jackson's laboratory and checked the timepiece pinned to the front of her shirtwaist. Three minutes until four. That was good enough.

She was considering whether to simply open the door or to give warning and knock this time when she heard voices from inside.

Easing to the side so no one would see her through the frosted glass window, she listened unabashedly. If it were Devré, she might be able to learn whether he still suspected her.

Fortunately, the door was not very thick, and there was a generous distance between the bottom and the floor. The two men inside were taking no care to modulate the volume of their voices, so she could hear much of what they were saying quite clearly.

"...murder," Jackson said. Then his voice dropped, and she lost the next part of his speech.

"...same conclusion, then." The second voice was Inspector Devré.

Lucie pressed her ear closer to the door, taking care not to rattle it in its position, and slowly turned the knob. The door eased open slightly, and now she could hear as if she were in the same room.

"I found cotton fibers in his mouth," Jackson said. "As if he'd been gagged. Extremely high alcohol content in his blood and organs."

"Someone wanted him malleable," Devré said.

"Strung up the bastard while he was gagged and drunk. He wouldn't have had a chance. Especially if it was an erotic asphyxiation game. But you didn't know this—what changed your mind?" Jackson said in a surprisingly congenial voice. Had the man had a shot of brandy or something?

"Footprints on the bureau. You saw them too—but they were too perfect. And there were only the two prints. Nothing else—no fingerprints or other smudges."

"Yes." Jackson sounded enthusiastic. "In order for him to climb up there and get into the proper position to jump, he'd have made other marks."

"Or would have had to use a stool or chair to climb up. But there wasn't one. So Pierre Lansac was murdered. This is the third time I've been called to a suicide that turned out to be murder," Devré said, satisfaction in his voice.

"Same person who did Bacard, then."

"One would think."

"You know who, then."

"I'm fairly certain I—" The voice stopped abruptly, and Lucie fairly leapt away from the door.

But she was too late, for suddenly it was yanked open and she found herself face to face with the detective.

"Ah. Inspector Devré," she said, boldly walking into the room. "Thank you. I wasn't certain whether to knock and interrupt, or wait for you to finish."

Despite the fact that he was far better dressed than most of his peers, and certainly as well groomed, the detective didn't look any more rested or relaxed than he had this morning. He fixed her with a jaundiced eye. "Mlle Lucie. What an unexpected delight."

She bit back a sudden laugh at his tone, which was in complete opposition to his words. "I suspect you're here for the same reason I am—therefore it cannot be that unexpected."

Devré muttered something, then said, "Jackson was just about to give me the results of his testing of the bottles. The four bottles, each of them unique so as to be easily identifiable." His mustache bristled outward. "I suppose I have you to thank for bringing them to him."

"I cannot say it was my pleasure," Lucie told him honestly. There was something in the way he was looking at her now. Something that made her very uncomfortable. "But sometimes the unpleasant must be done. And we must have answers. Dr. Jackson?"

"Oh, are you talking to me now? In my own lab, I'm now suddenly and inexplicably to be included in the conversation?" His attention skimmed over her. "Congratulations, madame."

Lucie lifted her brows in question.

"You aren't smothering your organs today," he replied. "As much."

"How kind of you to have noticed, monsieur," she said demurely.

"Not a kindness, madame. Simply a relief that I won't have a third body in my lab."

Devré stifled a choking sound. "Well, Jackson, I suppose now that she's here, you might as well tell us both what you've learned... assuming you've finished examining the bottles."

"Two are contaminated with digitalis. The same type as found in Bacard's body," said the pathologist. "This one," he said, gesturing to Hélène's bottle, "had a strong content of the poison. This second vessel was also contaminated, but it wasn't as strong. Perhaps because it had more liquid in it than the other, and the concentrate was diluted."

Lucie was having trouble breathing, loose corset or no. "The other two were clean?" she managed.

"No trace of digitalis," Jackson said. "Sit down, madame. There will be no fainting in my laboratory." He fairly flung a chair in her direction, setting it down hard next to her.

"The second bottle—it's yours, then, mademoiselle?" Devré asked, watching her keenly.

"Yes." She refused to sit. She wasn't going to faint; by God, she'd been through far worse moments than this and hadn't swooned. However, she held on to the back of the chair, grateful that her gloves covered what must be stark white knuckles.

"So the intended victims are you and Mlle Brosette," Devré said. "Or, at least, that is what we are intended to believe."

"Intended to believe?" she repeated. "Are you implying I poisoned myself? And Hélène too?"

"And perhaps even assisted a man to hang in his bedchamber," Devré said, still watching her with cool golden-brown eyes.

"You're mad," Lucie said. "If I were trying to cover my tracks as a poisoner, why would I not put digitalis in all four of the bottles? For that matter, why would I even bring them here to be tested?"

"Because, mademoiselle, you are a very, very clever woman." His soft voice sent a horrible shiver down her spine. "And I believe you are not only capable of killing someone, but that you have in fact done so...at least once in your lifetime."

All of the air whooshed from her lungs and she felt dangerously light of head. She gripped the chair back tighter. "You will have an impossible time proving it, M. Devré," she replied as calmly as she could, holding his gaze with hers. "Because I did not poison the bottles belonging to either Hélène or myself. I did not kill Paul Bacard, and I certainly did not kill Pierre Lansac."

"Not without help you didn't kill Lansac, no," Devré replied. "You were gone yesterday, mademoiselle, with your companion, during the time Lansac died. A woman meeting your description was seen entering his hotel room. You could easily have seduced the man—with the aid of the blue dragon, *non*? And a very large bottle of whisky—which was found in the room. Empty." His voice was cold and hard now, and Lucie realized just how powerful a man he was—used to getting his way, used to dealing with suspects, used to extracting the answers he needed from them, whether they were guilty or not.

"And then your very loyal and very strong Moor would have been there to help you drag the poor man up from the bed, where you'd promised him such delightful pleasures that he agreed to allow you to affix the noose around his neck—erotic play, you would have told him as you fed him from the blue bottle. 'This will help,' you would have said. After all, we only have your word that he had possession of that blue bottle in his pocket at Maxim's. No one else saw him with it. And then you would have watched as he clawed at his neck and strangled in front of your eyes."

"I was at Mass yesterday afternoon," she replied. "At St. Berthilde's. And at the cemetery. I was nowhere near Hôtel Briö."

Devré smiled slowly. "That might be the case, mademoiselle— and I will ascertain that, to be sure—but I understand after you returned to Château Lisette, Aloysius d'Marchande left once more. Did he go to visit your friend Pierre Lansac to take care of that loose end for you while you were otherwise accounted for? To set the stage for a suicide—to make it appear as if Lansac were feeling guilty for the death of his friend Paul Bacard, when he had intended to murder Bacard's fiancée?"

"You're talking nonsense."

"Did you suspect they were lovers—Paul Bacard and Pierre Lansac? Or is that merely a fiction of your own creation, to hide your tracks, mademoiselle? Or perhaps your half-brother did it on his own—to rid his lovely sister of the problem of being suspected as a murderer by framing Lansac?"

"No," Lucie replied harshly. "Aloysius is loyal to me to a fault, but he would never harm anyone." Still, even as she spoke, she was acutely, horribly aware she didn't know where Aloysius had been yesterday afternoon.

And he hadn't told her when she asked.

"Ah. I see you begin to wonder yourself, mademoiselle," Devré said. He was no longer the handsome, gallant detective she'd almost come to like. He reminded her once more of a tiger, claws extended as he crouched and prepared to spring. "And this," he said, swiping up a small brown bottle from Jackson's counter. "It too has traces of the digitalis in it, I suspect."

"You brought me another bottle?" complained Jackson, who'd merely watched as Devré delivered his biting accusations.

"Conveniently found in a drawer of Pierre Lansac's bureau," said the detective. "I'm certain you'll find it contaminated as well. It would all be very neat and tidy: making Lansac the culprit who murdered his friend, who then kills himself in remorse over the accident."

"As I told you last night," Lucie said in an icy tone, "you are barking up the wrong tree, M. Devré. And as long as you continue to try and sniff out stories that aren't true, the real murderer—someone who is trying to kill me as well as Hélène Brosette—will be going freely about his business." She managed, barely, to keep her voice from turning thready with desperation. How could the man be so doggedly *blind*?

He could arrest her at any moment. Lock her away, torture a confession from her. That was what the police did. They spied, they lied, they connived. Once they got a story worked out, they would do anything to make it true.

She knew.

"Someone is trying to kill me," she said, "and I, at least, intend to find out who it is. I suggest you do so as well, Inspector Devré. Otherwise, *monsieur le docteur* here will indeed have a third body in his laboratory."

With that, Lucie turned and swept from the room with trembling knees and shaking hands.

"I've been telling Bernard to bring you here to supper for weeks," Henriette said, splashing more red wine into Guillaume's glass.

He winced at the haphazard spray but bit his tongue. The few pink specks on the front of his gray striped shirt were a small price to pay for the enjoyment of Henriette's cooking. And he was, if nothing else, completely replete from the excellent, relaxed meal—as well as in possession of some leftovers to take home. "I've been busy."

"And not eating enough, from what I can tell," she said, looking at him from head to as much of him as she could see behind the table. Bernard was sitting at a desk, painstakingly writing a report he had to turn in, and Henriette's other two children were doing schoolwork in the next room.

"I get home too late to cook most nights, and the shops are closed. I'm too tired to eat at a café every night." He'd justified taking the time for a relatively leisurely dinner tonight in order to clear his head and allow everything to settle into place. Sometimes, he knew, one's brain needed a rest—and God knew he hadn't given himself much of it since the discovery of Paul Bacard's body.

"You need a wife," Henriette said, in a familiar refrain.

"I'm not home enough to keep a wife happy," he said, as he did every time.

But this time, Henriette wasn't letting it go. His older sister—who had somehow moved into the role of mother now that theirs was gone—plopped onto the chair across from him. Her movement sent the wine sloshing inside its glass and the coffee cup rattling against its saucer. "Guillaume, you need to get married. You'd be so much happier with a wife."

"Ah, but that's not what Denis Audoux tells me," he said with a smile. "And speaking of getting married—are you and Joseph ever going to? Don't tell me you aren't interested," he said, speaking over her protestations. "He loses his shirt every time you bargain with him over a lamb chop or a beef roast. He wouldn't let you take advantage of him like that if he didn't want you for a wife."

She laughed, her cheeks turning pink with pleasure, and the sight of her unfettered delight eased some of his own poor spirits—which was saying something.

Despite his confident speech to Lucie-Geneviève today in Jackson's lab—and he was still furious that she'd trespassed there—he wasn't fully convinced of the theory he'd espoused.

After Lucie-Geneviève had left the lab, Jackson said, "That's a fine yarn you spun there, Devré. How much of it is true?"

"I'm not certain yet, but I believe most of it is true. It's the only thing that makes sense. We have a saying here: *cherchez la feMme*"

"Look at the woman?"

"Yes. More often than not, one finds a woman at the center of any crime—whether it be from jealousy or revenge or love. She either knows something, or is in it up to her shoulders."

Jackson made an ambiguous sound. Then, seeming to remember he was in the middle of taking samples from a limp-looking brain, proceeded to chase Guillaume from the lab. "I have more work tonight, and Madame and I want to leave by seven. Goodbye."

It wasn't that Guillaume didn't believe it possible Lucie-Geneviève had done exactly as he'd described, with or without the help of Aloysius d'Marchande, but he didn't yet have any proof. That was the only reason he hadn't arrested her. His accusatory speech was mainly conjecture, with even a few lies thrown in there in the hopes of rattling her enough to send him in one direction or the other.

But he needed at least something to bring to Georges Beleau, the magistrate, before he could arrest her if he didn't want all hell to break loose.

Guillaume frowned bitterly as he lifted his glass to sip. If it were anyone other than the famous La Balise, he would have done so by now—let her sit in a jail cell in the depot for a few days or a week and then see what she had to say. If she hadn't done it, he highly suspected she knew who did.

After all, it was her house. Bacard had been her lover. It was her rose found in his pocket. Perhaps *she'd* seduced him and now wanted Hélène Brosette out of the way.

And then he realized with a cold, harsh start what he was doing. Was it possible he was just as bent, just as bound and determined to prove Lucie-Geneviève Madeleine a criminal—because of who she was? Just as another detective might be when faced with an invert like Guillaume himself?

How often had he witnessed biased opinions, manufactured and exaggerated criminal charges against a man or woman merely because they had sexual relations with a person of the same gender?

Was he guilty of the same sort of intolerance?

The thought didn't sit well with him at all, and the meal in his belly soured slightly.

He glanced up at Henriette, remembering to make an encouraging noise as she continued to list all of the reasons she and Joseph Bonneret would never get married, and slipped back into his thoughts. But someone had tried to poison Hélène Brosette...*and* Lucie-Geneviève. And someone had murdered Pierre Lansac and tried to make it look like he'd killed himself over guilt and grief after murdering Paul Bacard.

Something was missing. Some piece was missing, or *he* was missing something...and he couldn't quite put his finger on it.

And then there was the problem he'd tried to avoid thinking of: Émile Huvet and his coat.

Guillaume hadn't been home to retrieve the coat since he'd learned he had taken the wrong one, but once he left Henriette's house, he would to go home. He'd have to decide how to return the overcoat to the good doctor, and, to his irritation, he felt as if he'd spent far more time mulling over that small problem today than the larger, more violent ones at hand—the concerns of life and death.

Imbécile.

Lucie-Geneviève had called him mad, and Guillaume was beginning to believe she might be right.

"Don't let the cat drink that!" Henriette bolted up from the table so fast it lifted, then crashed down. "It will poison him!"

"But Maman," cried little Mathilde, "he didn't know!"

Guillaume looked over at his ten-year-old niece, who was holding her striped black and gray cat in a death grip. Its back legs were straining vainly for purchase, and its green eyes were wild. The poor thing was more likely to die from her love and protection than whatever he'd been lapping up.

He was just about to taste his wine once more when he saw to what Henriette had been referring. And suddenly, with a shock of recognition, another piece of the Paul Bacard puzzle fell into place.

Poison.

He knew digitalis was a poison derived from flowers like foxglove and belladonna. But he hadn't remembered until this very moment that it also came from another beautiful flower: lily of the valley. The cat jumped up onto a small table and had been drinking from the vase containing several sprigs of the flower and its leaves from yesterday's holiday.

Even more pertinent to his sudden realization was the fact that the patch of those flowers had been cut at Château Lisette...not for *Le Fête du Muguet*, but too early for the holiday, as evidenced by their browning leaves. Lelo had complained about not having any flowers for Lily of the Valley Day yesterday.

But someone from Château Lisette had taken them. And that someone had made a poisonous extract from the innocent-looking flowers and their leaves.

Guillaume took his leave from Henriette rather abruptly and amid a flurry of protestations, but in the end, she understood.

"Try and get more sleep," she said, pulling him into an embrace. She smacked a kiss on his cheek that was too close to his ear and left it ringing. "And eat better."

As he hugged her back, Guillaume felt a pang of sadness. He couldn't remember the last time he'd touched, or been touched by, another person that wasn't related to a brief, furtive sexual encounter. And even those, unsatisfying as they were, were few and far between.

As a result of this unnatural melancholy, he held on to his sister a bit longer than usual, and bestowed kisses on both Mathilde (with an additional buss on its furry head for the cat) and her older sister Marie. He was blinking rapidly when he left their small apartment that was, conveniently, on the same block as Joseph Bonneret's butcher shop.

Lack of sleep, lack of food, and a turmoil of emotion, he reminded himself as he started back to his own empty house. That was why he was feeling particularly lost and empty today, and why he didn't seem able to piece together the mystery of Hélène Brosette's attempted murder, and the killing of Pierre Lansac.

Even the mercenary La Balise had someone to come home to—if not her fascinating brother Aloysius, then at least her three friends and tenants. Not to mention a mansion filled with servants.

Despite that, however, he thought as he strode southeast along a *rue* filled with busy cafés, Lucie-Geneviève had an air of loneliness about her. A lack of fulfillment. Perhaps even a sense of being lost.

How a woman with her life could be unfulfilled was yet another mystery to Guillaume, but he'd proven himself to have an uncanny ability to sense the truth of a person. That was in part why he'd risen so quickly through his local prefecture and been asked to join la Sûreté after only five years as a policeman.

Which was why he still wasn't fully convinced Lucie was the murderer. She was capable of it, to be sure, and she was most definitely hiding something. And Anna Smith seemed convinced that was the case.

But jealousy did not seem to be a weakness of Lucie-Geneviève. Nor did she seem sly and vengeful. He had the sense if Lucie were to plan a murder, it would be much more...artistic. Perhaps even elegant.

More like Lansac's death, in fact.

By the time Guillaume reached his little house off rue de las Pépinières, he'd managed to avoid thinking about the looming problem of Émile Huvet's coat for nearly a half-hour—but had neglected to piece together who had cut down the lilies of the valley at Château Lisette with murderous intent. It could have been anyone who lived there, or anyone who visited—for the patch of the deadly flowers was located on a shadowy side of the house.

Someone could have crept out there in the middle of the night and remained unseen.

But someone must have seen something, and now Guillaume had a different line of questioning for his next visit to Château Lisette...which he would make as soon as he attended to one other task.

He'd determined earlier that Huvet's coat should be returned as soon as possible. After all, a man simply didn't have more than one overcoat—unless he were as wealthy as Christophe Calmette or Vicomte Fouquier.

For all Guillaume knew, Huvet's house key could have been in the pocket of his coat—and if that was the case, the man would have had a difficult time of it, gaining access to his house last night.

How had he not realized the mistake? Guillaume hadn't worn the coat, but he had thrust his gloves into the pocket as he was rushing off down the street. When he got home, he hung it on the coat rack with hardly a glance in the low light.

It was an honest mistake, but one he must rectify. Yet he was clearly fighting an unusual reluctance about making a decision.

Thus, he gave himself no opportunity to change his mind. He greeted Mimi—who gave him a disdainful look when she realized his infidelity with Mathilde's cat—then dragged Huvet's coat from the rack and left immediately.

Armed with the man's home address, thanks to his position at la Sûreté, Guillaume hailed a taxi and rode in silent tension as he debated the possibilities of what might occur when he arrived—instead of thinking about who cut a patch of lilies of the valley in order to make poison.

A housekeeper would most likely answer the door, for, as Huvet had indicated, doctors' hours were as unpredictable as those of a detective. It was hardly past eight o'clock, still quite early. Huvet could even be on a house call.

Or...no one could be there.

Or...Huvet could answer the door.

Of all the possibilities, that was the one Guillaume both feared and desired.

By the time the fiacre turned onto the correct street, he was furious with himself. He should have just sent the coat in a package as Huvet had done and been finished with it, and been on his way to Château Lisette instead.

He paid the driver and sent the taxi away when he got out, for there was a busy street half a block away if he needed another one. And Guillaume couldn't help but feel it necessary that no one see his destination.

The coat draped over his arm, he knocked on the door. It opened—and there was Émile. He was dressed only in a shirt and trousers. Even his necktie was gone, and the top button had been loosened in the back so the stiff collar sagged away from his throat.

"You got my message," he said. "I was afraid you wouldn't come." He stepped back from the doorway invitingly.

"I apologize for the mishap," Guillaume said, offering him the coat. "I was...reckless."

Yes, that was the best word to describe his behavior last night. Reckless. Wild, reckless, and dissolute.

Then he comprehended what Émile had said and repeated, "Your message?"

"In the pocket of your coat, when I sent it back. Did you not see it?" Émile gestured inside. "Please. No need to stand on the stoop."

Filled with both dread and anticipation, Guillaume stepped over the threshold into a small foyer, still holding the bloody coat that had brought him here. The door closed behind him and they were alone.

Alone.

Normally, his detective's mind would have taken in the details of any building he entered, but for the moment the only thing that interested him was the man standing in the foyer.

"I didn't look in the pocket," Guillaume said.

"Ah." Émile appeared embarrassed. "I thought that was why you'd come yourself. I wasn't certain whether the error had truly been a mistake, or..." Émile shrugged, and took the bundle from him. Their hands brushed and Guillaume felt a little shock of lust.

"Thank you." Émile looked up at Guillaume, and his expression indicated he was grateful for more than the return of his coat.

"What did the message say?"

Émile merely looked up at him, a small smile curving his lips.

"Lock the door," Guillaume said quietly, holding his gaze. "And draw the curtains."

They'd made it to the bedroom...but only barely. A path of discarded clothing created a trail from the foyer to the small room in the back of the flat.

As Guillaume lay there, his body sated, damp, and warm—sticking pleasantly to the salty, lightly haired skin of his lover—he closed his eyes and savored.

A bed.

By God, he hadn't fucked in a bed since Étienne, and that was... thirteen years ago.

Since then, he hadn't taken his time with an assignation, hadn't been able to lie there and bask in the moment afterward. He always had, in the back of his mind, the fear that someone would see, that someone would interrupt, that he'd be discovered...

He smoothed his hand over Émile's firm, pale arse, enjoying the sensation of the light layer of fur over its bottom half...and down. Émile turned over and pulled him down into a kiss, his hand sliding between their bodies.

The bed creaked with their efforts, the pillows and coverlet were on the floor by the time they finished, he didn't have to hold back the sounds he needed to make...

It was ten o'clock when he became aware again—awakened by a clock somewhere in the house striking the hour.

Guillaume rose, delightfully tender on parts of his body he'd nearly forgotten existed, and padded off, naked, from the room.

He passed through the foyer on his way back from the lavatory, stepping over piles of clothing, which included the infamous coat that had brought him here tonight.

Something reminded him about his gloves—for they were still in the pocket from last night—and, smiling to himself, he picked up the fine wool garment. Foolishly sniffing it for Émile's scent, he dug in the pocket for his gloves. When he pulled them out, something bright fluttered to the floor.

Guillaume bent to pick it up, then went cold, staring at it as he plucked it from the rug.

It was a purplish-pink rose petal.

NINETEEN

G uillaume stared at the rose petal, crushed and velvety, and very damning.

No.

Oh, no. *No.*

But in an instant, it all made sense.

All of it—including how much of a fool he was.

A doctor. Of course...a doctor would know all of it. Everything. The poison, the contraceptive process; he'd be familiar with all of Château Lisette's gardens, nooks, crannies, rooms. He'd have access everywhere...

Cold, ever so cold, Guillaume realized he still held his gloves in one hand and the crumpled rose petal in the other. He crouched, scrabbling for his trousers and boxers.

"Guillaume?"

He was half dressed in shirt and bottoms when Émile appeared in the door of his bedchamber. The man's caramel curls were in charming disarray, and he was still naked—showing off his body, all slender and lean, fair, with hardly any extraneous hair, smooth muscles in his shoulders and upper arms.

"Are you leaving?" he asked in a tone that implied a silent "again?" at the end.

Guillaume had already thrust away every vestige of pleasure and diversion from his body and mind, and had thoroughly become Inspector Devré once more. An empty, imbecilic man, but the detective nonetheless.

"I found this. In your coat pocket, just now." He held up the offending rose petal. "You were with Paul Bacard the night he died." He wasn't quite able to keep the bitterness from his voice.

Émile sighed and nodded. "Yes. We were together." He bent, snatching up his trousers. "I should have told you, but—"

"It was you—all along. I knew he'd been doing something amiss. There was a point in time Bacard wasn't accounted for that night at Château Lisette. Did you meet in the greenhouse? Is that where you had your *tête-à-tête*? Where you fucked him? And was that how you got this?" Guillaume resisted the urge to throw the flimsy petal at the man.

Émile had begun to draw on his trousers, one leg at a time. He seemed slightly bewildered by the onslaught of questions. "Guillaume, we've only just met. And Paul was before you and I—"

"You murdered him," Guillaume said, out of patience—with himself and Émile. "But you meant to kill Hélène Brosette, didn't you? You wanted her out of the way because she was going to marry the man you loved."

"*What?*" Émile jolted as if he'd been slapped. "What are you talking about? Of course I didn't murder Paul—I didn't murder anyone, and certainly not Hélène."

"No, it all makes sense to me now. Perhaps Paul was the one who wanted her out of the way—and you agreed to help him. He was trapped—she was pregnant with his child, and she was blackmailing him into marrying her." Guillaume nodded. "And you told him you'd take care of things. After all, you're her doctor. You know about the way these women prevent pregnancy—what a brilliant way to do it. No one would ever know. And then you had to find a scapegoat, so you arranged Pierre Lansac to—"

"Guillaume, stop. Stop and listen to me. I was— Yes, Paul and I were lovers, on occasion, but that was all. It was little more than an occasional *cinq-à-sept*, so to speak. I didn't try to poison Hélène.

I didn't poison *anyone*. I only knew they were going to be married because she told me—and I can tell you unequivocally that Hélène Brosette is *not* pregnant.

"And if she was pregnant, and I knew about it from Paul Bacard's confidences, why in the bloody hell would I poison her contraceptive sponge?" His eyes were flashing with fury and insult, and he'd begun to finish dressing with sharp, angry movements. He yanked his shirt over his head.

Guillaume stared at him. "You're saying Hélène Brosette isn't pregnant?"

Émile shoved his hands into the sleeves of his shirt and his face reappeared. "Among other things, *yes*. She isn't pregnant—unless she became so within the last two weeks. And she wouldn't know that soon anyway."

"How do you know this?"

His elbows were akimbo behind him as he contorted in order to button his shirt. "Jesus Christ, Guillaume, I'm a damned *doctor*. If Hélène told you she's pregnant, she lied. Ask her maid, for Christ's sake—she knows when her mistress bleeds."

They looked at each other, both a little out of breath from their argument.

Guillaume wanted to believe him. "Where were you yesterday—where were you coming from when we met? The first time," he added quickly.

Émile looked at him with flat eyes. "I had been seeing patients from the time I left Château Lisette until the time you and I met. I'll get you a list. Why? What are you accusing me of doing during that time?"

"Pierre Lansac was found hanging in his hotel room. Time of death is between three and five o'clock. It wasn't suicide. A woman—or someone dressed as a woman—was seen visiting him."

"I'll get you a list," Émile said again.

Guillaume drew in a breath. "Thank you." He wanted to say something else—knew he should say something else—but words failed him.

He picked up his waistcoat and looked around for his stockings. "I have to leave. If you're right and Hélène lied about being pregnant, there might be other things she lied about. But why would she lie to you? She would know you'd know the truth." That ugly sense of distrust reared inside him...and then he remembered.

Hélène Brosette hadn't told him she was pregnant. *Lucie-Geneviève* had told him—in confidence. And neither Rose-Marie nor Camille had known about the pregnancy either. No one else had mentioned it during his interviews or Houssaye's.

Lucie-Geneviève was lying.

Or...perhaps she wasn't. Guillaume's movements slowed as his brain shot along at full speed. Someone had steeped the leaves and flowers of the lily of the valley to make the poison. *In a teapot.*

"I must go," he said breathlessly as everything crystallized in a small mental explosion. "I need to—" Guillaume didn't even finish the sentence; he jammed his bare feet into his shoes and reached for the doorknob. "I need to get to Château Lisette."

"*Adieu*, Guillaume," said Émile as he shut the door.

Rather more forcefully than necessary.

"Lucie-*san*, I am very sorry to bother you."

Lucie looked up to see Piquette standing in the doorway of the study. She blinked hard, for her eyes were tired and dry, and her head was pounding. After canceling her engagements for the evening, she'd cloistered herself in her private rooms. She had no interest in food—only God knew whether it would be poisoned or not—and she knew there was no chance for sleep. She wasn't too proud and stubborn to admit her distress was from a cold, insidious disquietude.

A disquietude related to the murders of Paul Bacard and Pierre Lansac, along with the attempted murders of herself and Hélène—and now, too, there was the newspaperwoman who'd somehow discovered Lucie's connection to Virginia Stoddard. *How could that be?*

Lucie couldn't remember the last time she'd been so afraid, when fear had simmered deep inside her like this in an ugly sort of bubbling stew that didn't boil over, but never quite settled.

A murderer. *Here. In my home.*

It wasn't Aloysius, she kept telling herself. *It can't be.*

But he wasn't at the chateau when she returned from the morgue, and no one knew where he was. No one knew where he'd been. And he'd been so distracted lately, so...not himself.

She shivered, feeling terribly ill and shaky, and even looked toward the rosewood box and her bottle of relief.

But no. Not tonight. She must keep her thoughts clear, her mind open.

So she'd turned to making a list of all the information she knew about Paul Bacard's murder—and now Pierre Lansac's murder as well. A list of suspects, of facts, of clues, and a timeline of events from the night Bacard had died through yesterday's death of Lansac.

She wasn't waiting for Inspector Devré to pretend to do his job. She was going to do it herself. She'd call in Christophe if she needed to, in order to have the Sûreté chief listen to her if she found something. Much as she would hate to do it, she might need to resort to asking him for help.

"Yes, Piquette?" she said now, rubbing her eyes after setting down her ink pen.

"There's been a bit of an episode with one of the maids. I know you normally leave it to Mme Frousand to manage those sorts of things, but it's her evening off and...well, there seems to be no resolution at hand. Estelle insists upon speaking with you. Perhaps you could intervene?"

"Yes, of course. Send her in." Lucie glanced at the clock. It was nearly eleven. Very early for someone who normally stayed out until dawn, but she was so utterly exhausted and heartsick that she felt as if it were three in the morning. "And ask Stanton to send word the minute Aloysius returns."

Moments later, there was a soft knock.

"Yes, come in, Estelle."

This was the same maid who'd unintentionally allowed Christophe access to Lucie's *suite privée* earlier today while Piquette was helping in Hélène's wing, and Lucie had a pang of remorse for the sharp way she'd spoken to her. Even Christophe had reprimanded her for her uncharacteristic reaction.

"Mademoiselle." Estelle's face was so drawn and white it matched her pristine cap and apron. "I apologize for disturbing you. I know I shouldn't have done, and Mme Frousand told me not to bother you..." Despite her nervousness, the young maid was speaking with surprising confidence. "But—but I thought it was important. Given... given what's going on here."

"Please tell me, Estelle." Lucie gestured to a chair, but the maid shook her head in horror.

"Oh, no. No. I'll stand, mademoiselle."

"Very well. Now, what is it you wanted to tell me?"

"It's about Mlle Brosette. She dismissed her chambermaid today—Christine-Léonie. Without a reference. She just dismissed her out of hand."

Lucie was taken aback. This was not the sort of thing a servant would ever dare complain about. It was simply none of their business, and in this case, it was none of *Lucie's* business what Hélène did with her staff. "It's within Mlle Brosette's right to dismiss any of her servants at any time, Estelle. Why are you bothering me with this?" She heard the impatience in her sharp tone, but this time knew it was warranted.

"Mademoiselle, please," replied the little maid. Now her fingers were twisting in her apron. "You might dismiss me, but please let me tell you all of it before you do. Christine-Léonie was a particular friend of mine, and she told me...she told me she cleaned under Mlle Brosette's bed yesterday. And—and when she came in to clean Mlle Brosette's chamber this morning, Mlle Brosette dismissed her immediately, saying she'd done a bad job with her cleaning and she didn't want such a poor chambermaid any longer."

Estelle had Lucie's full attention now. "Are you saying that Christine-Léonie would have seen the glass under Hélène's bed yesterday—if it had been there? The glass from which Paul Bacard drank? Or is this simply the maid's excuse for completing her task poorly and attempting to alleviate her responsibility? What does she want me to do—give her a reference?" She had intended to speak with whoever cleaned Hélène's private bedchamber, but apparently Hélène had taken matters into her own hands.

"No, mademoiselle, please understand...Christine and I often worked together in the upper chambers. She is an excellent maid— even better than I." Estelle straightened proudly, as if to emphasize what a compliment that statement was. "She never would have made a mistake like that. She says the glass *wasn't* there when she cleaned the morning after M. Bacard died."

Unease prickled over Lucie's shoulders. Something was wrong here. "Is there anything else, Estelle?"

The young woman's face turned even paler. "Yes," she whispered. "If I dare tell you." She glanced behind her as if to ensure no one was listening. "Christine told me that when Mlle Brosette was retired to her chamber yesterday afternoon, while you and M. Aloysius were gone, she—she wasn't there."

"Mlle Brosette wasn't there?"

"No, mademoiselle. She wasn't there, in her chamber. Christine saw her leaving."

"I see." Lucie was beginning to feel a little nauseated.

"And there is one more thing, mademoiselle." Estelle's eyes were so wide now that Lucie could see the whites all around her pale blue irises. Her breath was coming in short, audible puffs. "Mlle Brosette was in here last night. I saw her."

"What do you mean?"

"Sh-she was—"

"I was looking for something."

Lucie looked up to see Hélène standing in the doorway wearing a strange expression. Estelle gasped and swayed, her face draining to gray, but she managed to stay upright. Her breathing seemed to have stopped completely.

"Thank you, Estelle," Lucie said, standing. "You may go now." She didn't take her eyes from Hélène. "But understand this: Mlle Brosette's decision about Christine-Léonie is her decision. I can and will do nothing about it. Now, please do not bother me with such nonsense in the future, Estelle, or I will dismiss *you* without a reference."

The startled maid scuttled from the room as fast as her legs could carry her.

Lucie breathed more easily once the girl was gone and Hélène had come into the room.

That was, until she saw the gun in Hélène's hand.

TWENTY

H ave a seat, Hélène," Lucie said, eyeing the small weapon pointed at her. It was a delicate, feminine-sized derringer, but it was just as deadly as its larger counterparts—especially at this close range.

"I didn't expect it to come to this," Hélène said, ignoring the offer to sit. She did, however, come into the room and close the door behind her. With the gun still trained on Lucie, she turned the key in the lock.

"You were here in my private room," Lucie said. She'd remained standing as well, and her knees were surprisingly steady. It was as if her veil of fear had been whisked away the moment she realized the truth. The knowledge gave her strength and clarity of thought. "Putting the digitalis in my bottle. You tried to poison me."

Hélène grimaced. "I didn't think anyone had seen me."

She didn't appear the least bit remorseful, which stunned Lucie. "You tried to *kill* me." Then she realized with renewed shock that if she had invited Christophe here last night, she would most likely have used the sponge. And then she would have been poisoned too. The realization of how close she'd come to dying—and at the hands of a woman she'd called friend—turned her cold.

"I didn't put very much in," Hélène said. "I just wanted to make sure I wasn't the only one who had a poisoned bottle. To throw suspicion off me. That inspector was here too often, and he was asking too many questions. I thought Paul would be home before he got sick."

"So you killed Paul. Why did you do that? I thought you were happy together. You were going to be married. You're carrying his child." Lucie shook her head. "Why, Hélène?"

"I'm not pregnant. But I fooled you—and Tillé too. It's not hard to make oneself vomit, and to look ill—and everything else just falls into place."

"But why?"

"He never stopped loving you," Hélène spat. "He couldn't take his eyes off you when you were around, even when I was there. I did everything I could to make him love me, and it didn't work."

"But you convinced him to marry you."

"I wanted him to marry me, yes. I wanted to live a life as a *wife* in the fancy houses—not as a whore, like you. I wanted to be accepted in all of the best homes. I wanted a family. I wanted to be *better* than my mother. Better than *you*, the famed whore La Balise." Her eyes glittered with hatred and perhaps a little bit of madness.

"It wasn't until I saw Paul with Émile that I knew I could force him to marry me. He wouldn't want that information made public, and I told him so."

"Paul and Émile Huvet?" Lucie wasn't surprised about Émile.

"Yes. They used to rendezvous in the greenhouse at night, and sometimes outside on the side of the house. No one would see them there...except for me. I caught Paul once as he was coming back. That was his routine: he would arrive early to see me, and Émile would still be here. Paul would go to the kitchen while I got dressed, and then he'd leave to meet Émile. Once I caught on to them, I followed him a few times. The house is so big, it's easy to do."

"But Paul agreed to marry you. Why would you kill him?"

"Because he changed his mind. Because his father was going to disinherit him, and cut off his allowance if he didn't make a match. And I, apparently, am not a good enough match for the 'golden bourbon boy.'" Her eyes narrowed and she jiggled the gun at Lucie. "But you were. Did you know that? Even Paul's father would have approved of La Balise as his wife."

"I had no intention of marrying Paul Bacard," Lucie said.

"It didn't matter, Lucie. Don't you see? He changed his mind about marrying *me*, and even though I threatened to tell everyone what I'd seen with him and Émile, he didn't care. Even when I told him I was pregnant with his baby, he didn't care. He broke off our engagement, but he still wanted to see me. He said we could still have an arrangement even though he was getting married. Imagine *that*. He deserved to die for that alone."

Apparently Paul Bacard was not one of those men who couldn't stomach touching a woman. He seemed to be more versatile in his sexual preferences than men like Guillaume Devré, who clearly had no erotic interest in the female gender.

"So you decided to poison him."

Hélène's hand wasn't quite as steady as it had been, and Lucie watched her carefully without appearing to do so.

"Yes. Of course. What else was I going to do? Everyone was talking about the Labor Day holiday, and when I was in the garden with him one day, Lelo mentioned that lily of the valley was poisonous when made into a very strong tea."

"I wondered why you had a teapot in your room," Lucie said. "You only drink coffee."

"Yes. And so did that nosy maid Christine-Léonie. If I had known she was such a snoop, I would never have hired her."

"You cut down the lily of the valley and made a poison." Lucie knew she had to keep Hélène talking, for eventually, that hand pointing the pistol was going to waver or get tired. And since everyone else in Château Lisette had been told not to bother Lucie, there was no other chance of interference. "How did you have time to make it so quickly?"

"Paul ended our engagement several days earlier, and that was when I knew I had one last chance. I either needed to convince him to change his mind, or I was going to get rid of him. I couldn't take the chance that he'd warn anyone else about me—because I would find someone else. There are always more men, slathering and drooling and *begging*." Her face was horrible and twisted. "If I had to have the panting and gasping, I wanted the *husband*—and the status to go with it.

"So I invited Paul over, and then pretended I was sick. He would be alone in the room while I was gone, and I knew he was upset. I told him if he wanted something to drink, he could have what was in the bottle. I even poured him a glass of it. He didn't know what it was, of course," she said with a derisive laugh. "And the heavy sweetness of the mead helped to mask the taste of the digitalis."

"So he did drink it—just as we thought. But you must have planted the glass under the bed later, because the chambermaid would have seen it when she cleaned the next morning."

"Yes. You see, I didn't expect the poison to work so quickly, and I didn't think it would be traced back here. I thought it would be at least until morning before he got sick, and I knew when Paul left here he would go somewhere else—which would throw suspicion off me. But he didn't. He died too quickly, and then la Sûreté began to ask questions, and I had to do something to throw suspicion away from me, so I put the glass under the bed."

"And you visited Pierre Lansac."

Hélène gave a triumphant smile. "Yes. I would have married *him* if he'd had any money to speak of. But he was broke. Still, I knew he was desperate to learn how to be with a woman—he wasn't like Paul. He hated women. He despised the very thought of being with one. He particularly hated *you*. I think he was in love with Paul too, and that's why he hated you."

"Were Paul and Pierre lovers as well?"

"No. Pierre hid his secret very well, and he never approached Paul that I know of. I think he was afraid of what Paul would say. He didn't realize Paul was...well, accommodating to anyone." Her smile was ironic. "If Pierre was rich, I would have married him and everything would have been perfect. I wouldn't have cared if he touched me or not, and he would have had a wife."

"But you killed him instead."

Hélène shrugged again. "I couldn't let suspicion fall on me—Inspector Devré was right; I did have a motive. Not as much as you do, Lucie, *chérie*, but a motive. I could tell he didn't believe much of what I was saying, so I had to throw him off. It was actually quite easy to get to Pierre, and to make it look like suicide. He was so damned desperate to get it up and to be with a woman, he was willing to try anything. And so I offered to help him."

"By slinging a noose around his neck."

"He even helped me string the curtain cords over the light fixture because I told him I would climb it and use it to do an erotic dance like they do in Siam. He actually believed it. He let me do whatever I wanted." She laughed loudly and a little wildly. "But even with the blue dragon—you know about that, I presume?—he couldn't get it up. Of course, it might have been the vast amount of whisky I helped him to drink." Then she sobered. "But how did you know it wasn't suicide? I planned it very well."

"Devré figured it out."

"How?"

"It was the footprints on the bureau. They were too perfect. There were only two of them, and there should have been more if someone actually climbed up on there to jump. How did you make them, anyway?"

"*Damn.*" Hélène looked furious. "I thought I was being so clever! After he was done choking and clawing at himself"—she gave a little shudder—"I just pushed the bureau over a little and pressed his feet down onto it in the right position. Then I moved it back—and I wiped off *my* finger marks in the polish so no one would notice."

"That was your mistake. If you'd left them, maybe Devré wouldn't have figured it out."

"Well, he doesn't know it was me. In fact, I think he believes it's you who's been behind all of this. Especially since there was such a small trace of poison in your bottle. You're the lover scorned—the older woman, left behind for the younger woman." Hélène stepped closer.

"So now you're going to add a third murder to your list of crimes?" Lucie asked, tensing slightly.

"It'll be self-defense, my dear. You tried to shoot me—I'll take care of that part after you're dead—but I managed to get the gun away from you and shoot you dead. It's really quite simple."

"That will never work," Lucie said, curling her fingers around the chair next to her.

"Oh?" Hélène lifted the gun a little higher. It was very steady, and the dark circle of the barrel opening was very ominous. "I beg to dif—"

Lucie flung the chair at her and dove to the floor. Hélène shrieked with rage, but did not, as Lucie had hoped, fire one of her two bullets.

But Lucie, uncorseted and quite flexible due to her escape-artist abilities, had rolled under the tea table and, with a great shove, used her feet to thrust the table up and toward her assailant. This time, Hélène pulled the trigger, and Lucie felt the bullet streak past her and lodge into the floor. Heart pounding, she scrambled to her feet, nearly tripping on the skirt that wrapped around her legs.

She heard shouts from the distance along with the sounds of pounding feet. But Hélène still had the gun, and there would be one more bullet in a second chamber.

Panting from her exertions, Lucie looked at her former friend. "They're coming. You've got one bullet left, Hélène."

"I don't care. I might be visiting the guillotine, but you'll already be there in hell when I arrive." The gun was remarkably steady as she pointed it at Lucie once more.

Hélène stood much closer this time, and Lucie knew there was no chance of her missing if she fired. Unless she could distract her once more.

Someone knocked frantically. "Miss Lucie!" Stanton's voice came through the door.

Then, "Mademoiselle!" It was Inspector Devré. "Are you in there?"

Hélène nodded for Lucie to respond.

"Yes, inspector. I hope by now you've realized you were most certainly wrong in your suspicions of me and my brother," Lucie called, still watching the finger on the trigger in front of her.

"Yes, indeed, and I believe I owe you an apology, mademoiselle. Which I will be pleased to deliver in person once you open this door."

"Don't listen to her," cried Hélène suddenly. "She tried to kill me, monsieur!" As she flung her accusation at Lucie, Hélène unconsciously shifted toward the door, moving the gun away from her just a bit.

Lucie went into action, launching herself backward and to the side. Her opponent fired and the bullet whizzed past her ear...but it was the last one.

"Mademoiselle!"

"Lucie!"

More shouts, more urgent ones, came from the other side of the door, and all at once there was a loud thump against it. But Lucie couldn't take the time to respond or hardly to notice, for, with eyes wild and feral, Hélène had thrown herself at her.

The two fell to the floor in a wild battle of twisted skirts and loosened hair. The door shuddered under another onslaught, and Lucie heard the sound of wood splintering just as Hélène laid her hand sharply across her cheek.

That infuriated her, and Lucie grabbed her by the hair and slammed her head to the ground. The door crashed open as Hélène lay there, dazed and gasping.

"Miss Lucie!" Stanton was there, helping her to her feet as she turned to see Devré, out of breath and rumpled, rubbing the side of his arm.

"Apologies, mademoiselle," he said, looking at the mess of the chamber. "For more than one reason."

"Get her out of here," Lucie said, extricating herself from the butler to lean against the table. "She's a murderer...two times over... and meant for three."

"Hélène Brosette, I place you under arrest for the murder of Paul Bacard and Pierre Lansac, and the attempted murder of Lucie-Geneviève Madeleine."

"Don't forget Émile Huvet," Hélène said, tossing her head as he dragged her to her feet. "If I'm going to the guillotine, you must get it all right."

"Émile Huvet?" Devré stilled, looking at her as he pulled her arms behind her back.

Hélène laughed, the sound strident and mad. "If he's not dead yet, he will be very soon."

TWENTY-ONE

⬥

Less than ninety minutes after he'd left the place—now, nearly midnight—Guillaume pounded on Huvet's front door. This time, he wasn't alone, and this time he was even more agitated.

"If he doesn't answer, we must break the door down," Guillaume said needlessly to Houssaye and Damaris. In anticipation of what he might find, he'd urged Mlle Lucie to telephone Jackson as he left Chateau-Lisette.

"Huvet!" he shouted, pounding some more. "Huvet!"

He waited another two minutes, his insides churning even as he hoped his companions didn't realize his desperation was related to anything other than the possible murder of a random person.

"Break it down," he said, slamming against the door with his already-sore arm. "Break it down."

With the three of them, it still took far too long—and it attracted the notice of the neighbors as well. But finally, after several minutes of ramming the solid door (an exterior door being far sturdier than the door to Lucie-Geneviève's study), the doorjamb splintered and gave way.

Guillaume stumbled into the foyer where, only a short time ago, he'd made a most disturbing discovery. He prayed he wouldn't be about to make an even worse one.

"Huvet!" he called, moving toward the bedchamber. "Huvet! It's la Sûreté! It's the police! Are you here?"

"Inspector, in here! We need the doctor!"

Guillaume's heart plummeted as he ran toward the voice. When he burst into the study, the scene told its tale immediately.

Émile Huvet was on the floor, curled up in a position of agony. The evidence of his illness was in damp pools around him.

"Is he alive?" Guillaume knelt next to the man. His vision swam, and he fought to keep his mind clear. "Officer Damaris! See if there is another doctor on the block." But he thought, *Hurry, Jackson. Hurry.*

He answered his question when he touched Émile, who looked up with blank eyes. He was still breathing, gasping for breath, but his skin was pale and clammy and his face was speckled with flecks of saliva, blood, and vomit.

Someone pushed Guillaume aside, and he realized with a start it was Jackson. *Praise God.*

"Move the hell away." The pathologist lunged to his knees next to his unusually alive patient.

"Inspector."

With nothing left to do, Guillaume looked over at Houssaye, who was standing at the desk where Huvet had been sitting.

The scene there told its tale as well. A bottle of fine brandy, a glass containing the dregs of brandy, and, among the business papers spread out with it on the table, the beginning of a note.

Hélène Brosette sent me this as a gift. To G.D., I'm s

The note was barely legible, as if the doctor had tried to write it while fighting off his illness...and it ended with the ink trailing off the edge of the paper.

The pen lay on the floor next to Émile Huvet.

TWENTY-TWO

———◆———

Lucie sat at the small circular table in the courtyard the morning after Hélène was arrested.

She'd just received a telephone call that Émile Huvet was in hospital. It appeared he would live, though he'd ingested digitalis in a bottle of brandy that had been sent to him by Hélène. He seemed to have made himself vomit once he realized he was drinking poison. Fortunately, Dr. Jackson had arrived in time and was able to help save him.

Lucie reflected on the terror that had flashed across Devré's face when he realized what Hélène's taunt had meant. And how quickly and desperately he'd ordered her to telephone Jackson's home. She had a sense that Devré's concern for Émile Huvet went slightly further than mere worry for another victim.

Lucie's heart hurt, and she felt a wave of her own desperate need for the small bottle locked in the rosewood box in her bedchamber. The laudanum would help ease her erratic pulse; it would help smooth out her irregular breath. It would help, as it always did, to turn ugly and frightening memories into soft, murky pools.

For if Émile had died, that would've made three murders—with an attempted fourth—carried out by a woman Lucie had trusted, lived with, and for whom she'd even had affection.

How could she have been so easily fooled? Was it that Hélène reminded her so much of herself a decade ago—or, more precisely, what she could have been at that young age: untainted by the violence, betrayal, and abandonment that had colored her life before she met Onni, before she came to Paris?

"Loy," she said, firmly turning her thoughts from those morbid thoughts. She curled her trembling fingers tightly so he wouldn't see the telltale sign of her need. "I was so worried when Devré accused you of being involved in all of this, because I didn't know where you'd been. You've been gone so much, disappearing without a word, and you've seemed so distracted lately. Please, what's happening? What's going on?"

He looked down as he squeezed her hand. "Ginny, you have to trust me. It's nothing—nothing bad."

"Why won't you tell me? What are you hiding from me?" she asked, fear seizing her heart once more. What could it be? "Please tell me. You know all of my secrets...allow me to keep yours. Whatever it is."

Aloysius gave a long, deep sigh, and sunlight reflected off the side of his bald head. "Very well, my sweet. If you must know." To her surprise, he gave her a bashful look from beneath his curly lashes. "I've...I've fallen in love." The confession was followed by a shy but giddy smile.

Lucie was so shocked that she gasped. His words were so far from what she'd expected that she couldn't control herself. "In love? With whom? How did you meet her? Who is she?"

His smile faded. "That's the problem, Lucie-sweet. There is no chance for us at all. I'm a black-skinned man, a Moor...and she..." He shook his head miserably. "Trust me when I say there is no chance for us at all, for she is a sweet Jewish girl."

Lucie wanted to smile at the fact that her beloved brother had found love, but the truth of his words stung her. He was right. There was no chance in this world for a black man and a Jewish woman to be together.

She patted his hand. "If there is a way, Aloysius, you will find it. After all, did you not find and rescue me from Kyoto? Have you not forged through impossibilities, and at great personal risk, to shield me for years?"

"And I would do it again without hesitation. You're my sister. My only family. And you've changed my life so as well." His eyes, always so dark and liquid, seemed to glisten even more. "I would still be a miserable man in Morocco if it weren't for you. And as for the woman I love...well, I pray you are right. Now, how are you, my sweet?" he asked, swiftly changing the subject. "You aren't hurt?"

"Nothing more than a few bruises and cuts. I've had far worse."

He nodded soberly. "Indeed you have."

Lucie sighed, staring down at the filigree iron design of the table top beneath its glass covering. "I don't know how I could have been so easily fooled about Hélène. How could I not have seen that she was so evil? I opened my house to her."

He shook his head. "Sometimes the evil, she doesn't show herself right away. She is often swathed in beauty and light...and then she becomes something entirely different, revealing a dark, violent heart."

Lucie looked away. She'd been told she was beautiful since the age of ten, incomparable and exquisite since the age of fourteen. She'd had men falling at her feet, taking and violating her, manipulating her, imprisoning her, worshiping and wooing her since the age of sixteen.

And she was not entirely innocent herself.

Did the power wrought by beauty always breed evil?

"Ginny," Aloysius said quietly. "What you did was entirely different than Hélène's actions." This time, he covered her hand with his massive one. It completely enveloped her pale fingers. "You know that."

"But that doesn't make it any different in the eyes of the law," she replied, staring into the distance. Her heart swelled, threatening to choke off her breath.

She had come to realize it was only a matter of time until Lucie-Geneviève Madeleine was irrefutably connected to Virginia Stoddard.

She shrugged herself out of the melancholy. It had been thirteen years since she was known as Virginia Stoddard. Since then, she'd scrabbled through more than a decade of her own personal horrors, triumphs, and adventures, and she'd built a life now that was sweeter, safer, and more happy than she'd ever dreamt.

There was no reason to watch and wait for what might come. She could die in a heartbeat tomorrow—she had nearly died last night.

Instead, she would live her life as happily as she could, protecting herself and the ones she loved, and paying her own private penances as often as possible.

If the worst happened someday, she would receive it bravely. Until then...she would put it from her mind and carry on.

That was all she could do.

AUTHOR'S NOTE

Although the sensation-hungry press might seem to be a modern phenomenon, the manner in which I've depicted the French journalists here, including their fascination for and stalking of Lucie-Geneviève, is quite historically accurate. Today, the press feeds on drama and gossip, and turn-of-the-century Paris was no exception.

Also, for the curious, yes: the Paris Morgue, and the portrayal of its access to the public is also quite true. People really did line up for any excuse to look at dead bodies fished from the Seine or anywhere else. A rather morbid thought, to be sure, but then again...today we tend to watch crime shows and pore over gruesome newspaper articles, so apparently, the desire is buried deep in our humanity.

Regarding the poisoning of a woman with digitalis via her contraceptive sponge: whether that's possible I don't precisely know, but after having conferred with four different physicians (one of whom is a respected gynecologist), we all came to the conclusion it could very likely happen. Of course, we'll never know for certain, as no one died in that manner, but I'm sticking with my experts' opinions in this case.

Finally, while Lucie's arrangement with her boarders is a figment of my imagination, the way the courtesans as a whole were revered and admired in Paris is not. The *grandes horizontales* were the celebrities of their time—the Princess Dianas, the Marilyn Monroes, and the Angelina Jolies. Many of them were astute businesswomen who lived what we would consider a normal, modern day life: choosing their own lovers, declining to marry, and managing their vast wealth. Although the upper crust women of the *tout-Paris* might give Lucie and her peers a side-eye, they were nevertheless fascinated by these powerful and their life choices—even if in public, they had to give them the cut direct.

—Alex Mandon
September 2016

ACKNOWLEDGMENTS

The story of Inspector Devré and Lucie-Geneviève has been perking in my mind for almost ten years, and it was with great joy and humility that I now release it to the world, hopeful that readers will enjoy it with even a fraction of my own pleasure.

Because this was a project that required deep research and much patience, and considering the fact that my French is not at all serviceable, I have many people to thank for assisting me through the process of this project.

First of all, David Doherty-Jebb was not only instrumental in encouraging me to finish this project, but also he offered me so much in the way of feedback that I literally could not have done it without his thoughtful, expert direction. I am permanently indebted to you, David, for not only being a long-time reader and supporter of my other works, but also your critiques, guidance, and suggestions both early on and when the project was finished. And, yes, a definite fist-bump to you for helping me realize the story needed a better twist.

Trevor Krayer—your French expertise was also invaluable, and I cannot thank you enough for the times you spent reviewing and correcting my usage—and any lingering errors remain my own.

Timothy Sandusky—thank you very much for using not only your personal experience but also librarian skills to assist me with research, and a close read of the finished project. Again, I couldn't have done it without your feedback.

I am also grateful to Dr. Gary March, as always, for his medical expertise in all aspects for this book. Additionally, Dr. Diana Curran, Dr. Laris Galejs, and Dr. Kenda Murray weighed in with their opinions on the matter of poisoning a woman via her birth control method, and I appreciate their time and efforts on my behalf as well—especially since we all agreed it was possible.

Thanks also to Diane Knapp Davidson for being my research assistant and transcribing all of my crazy notes, as well as MaryAlice Galloway, Erin Wolfe, and Kathryn Lynn Davis for beta-reading the project and helping me to improve it on many fronts.

I've written more than forty books over the years, and I must admit, this is the book of my heart—the one I'm the most proud of, the one that feels the most accomplished. I hope you've enjoyed the read, and that you'll join me for the next Devré & Lucie mystery, coming in 2018.

—**Alex Mandon**
September 2016

ALEX MANDON is the pen name for an award-winning New York Times and USA Today bestselling author.

Alex has written more than forty books in a variety of genres, and is currently working on the next Lucie & Devré novel.

Find Alex online at:
AlexMandon.com
Facebook: Alex.Mandon.Books

To be notified of new releases, sign up for Alex's newsletter:
cgbks.com/Alex